**Two brand-new stories in every volume...
twice a month!**

Duets Vol. #35

Featured authors are Liz Ireland, who creates
"sassy characters, snappy dialogue and rip-roaring
adventures..." says *Romantic Times*,
and popular historical writer Cheryl Anne Porter, who
always delivers "a funny ride—a roller coaster of fun
and adventure."—*Romance Communications*

Duets Vol. #36

Voted Storyteller of the Year twice by *Romantic
Times*, Silhouette writer Carol Finch "presents her fans
with rollicking, wild adventures...and fun from
beginning to end." Also making their Duets debut
is the writing team of Selina Sinclair, who writes
"a fast-paced, funny and spicy...novel."
—*Women's Fiction Exchange*

Be sure to pick up both Duets volumes today!

Fit To Be Tied

"Are you trying to spy on me?" Jessica shrieked

"Uh, calm down a minute, blondie," Devlin called out from the balcony. "I'm only trying to be neighborly. Let me come in so we can—"

"No!"

"I'm not leaving till we talk, Porter."

"Then I'm calling the cops, Peeping Tom!"

When he saw her lunge for the phone, Devlin tried to open the door. Unfortunately his foot went through the rotted board on the balcony. Staggering backward, he howled in alarm when the rickety railing gave way behind him.

Devlin cartwheeled across the sloped roof and took a header downward. He landed spread-eagled in a myrtle bush.

"Are you all right?"

Devlin looked up to see Jessica standing on the broken balcony, staring down at him with a mixture of amusement and concern. He lay there, dazzled by the effect of her smile, wishing something besides his clumsiness was the cause of it....

For more, turn to page 9

Miss Hammond without her dull suit was...very nice

Lyon momentarily lost his train of thought and his eyes widened slightly as he took in her tiny waist, the flare of her spendidly curved hips.

She stopped and stared down at herself. "What's wrong?"

"Nothing," he managed to croak out. He watched as one small foot encased in sheer black hose emerged from beneath the long skirt and slid into a high-heeled pump. Perhaps the baby had pulled his tie too hard at some point during the day, because it suddenly seemed too tight.

He closed his eyes and yanked on the silken noose around his neck, wondering how things could change so much so quickly.

Last week, Miss Hammond had been nothing more than his personal assistant; this week, she was his "wife."

Last week, he'd thought of her as a machine; this week, in his mind she was very warm-blooded indeed.

It was madness. *Utter madness.*

For more, turn to page 197

HARLEQUIN DUETS

ISBN 0-373-44102-9

FIT TO BE TIED
Copyright © 2000 by Connie Feddersen

THE LYON'S DEN
Copyright © 2000 by Lenore Timm Providence & Salimah Kassam

Visit us at www.eHarlequin.com

Printed in U.S.A.

Fit To Be Tied
CAROL FINCH

HARLEQUIN®

TORONTO • NEW YORK • LONDON
AMSTERDAM • PARIS • SYDNEY • HAMBURG
STOCKHOLM • ATHENS • TOKYO • MILAN • MADRID
PRAGUE • WARSAW • BUDAPEST • AUCKLAND

Dear Reader,

I'm delighted to make my debut in Duets! There is nothing I enjoy more than writing romantic comedy, because I firmly believe love and laughter go hand in hand.

Unfortunately, it takes Devlin and Jessica, the hero and heroine of *Fit To Be Tied*, a while to realize what they're missing. Devlin is too busy fuming over the fact that his kooky female neighbor has established an exotic animal sanctuary across the fence from his ranch and his cattle are stampeding. He wants Jessica's squawking, roaring animals gone, pronto. And Jessica along with them! But nobody tells headstrong Jessica what to do—especially not her blustery, domineering neighbor.

The feud festers, but something more complicated and compelling than temper flares between these two spirited individuals. And what could be more confounding than falling in love with someone from the wrong side of the fence, and the opposing side of the feud? Devlin and Jessica are about to find out that love flagrantly disregards boundaries.

I hope *Fit To Be Tied* brings you a smile and a few hours of reading pleasure.

Enjoy!

Carol Finch

This book is dedicated to my husband Ed
and our children—Christie, Jill, Kurt, Jeff and Jon—
with much love. And to our grandchildren,
Brooklynn, Kennedy and Blake.
Hugs and kisses!

1

THIS IS THE LAST STRAW! Devlin Callahan fumed as he buried the needle of the speedometer on his pickup and barreled down the gravel road, leaving a cloud of dust in his wake. He did not have to put up with this nonsense! And he wasn't going to, either. He intended to confront this problem the same way he handled every other problem—head-on—even if he had to deal with that female kook who bought the forty acres bordering the west fence of the Rocking C Ranch.

The zoo—as Devlin referred to the menagerie of exotic animals housed next to his cattle and sheep—was a constant disturbance. The zookeeper was about to get an earful, because Devlin had had it up to his eyeballs! He and his brother had spent the whole cursed day on horseback, rounding up frightened cattle and repairing broken fences. Damn it, there was enough to do on the Rocking C without unscheduled roundups.

Devlin hadn't met his new neighbor, but he disliked her, and her zoo, sight unseen. The frustrated old biddy probably filled the emptiness in her meaningless life by surrounding herself with exotic animals that had no business whatsoever being housed in cattle country.

Slamming on the brake, Devlin skidded sideways

in the loose gravel, hung a left, then smirked when
the zookeeper's antiquated two-story farmhouse
came into view. The house was screaming for a coat
of paint. The yard begged to be spiffed up. Devlin
grudgingly admitted that the colorful flowers surrounding the foundation and gushing from the plastic pots on the porch perked up the place, but the
old house definitely needed some cosmetic repairs
to restore it to its former grandeur.

Of course, the female fruitcake who owned the
place probably couldn't spare the time because she
was too busy talking to all those wild animals caged
behind her house.

Devlin mentally kicked himself—and not for the
first time—because he hadn't purchased this property when it came up for sale eight months earlier.
At the time, Devlin and his brother thought the price
of the land was too steep. But Miz Jessica Porter—
who was obviously clueless about property value in
Oklahoma cattle country—had forked over the
dough for her homestead. Now Devlin had a nutty
neighbor he didn't want and a bunch of exotic animals who roared and howled and squawked and
drove his livestock through the fences.

He bounded from his pickup and stalked toward
the porch. He spied the puddle-jumper sports car
that was parked in the driveway. Typical city slicker,
he thought. That low-slung car wouldn't last a year
on these rough country roads. Anybody with half a
brain knew that. All except Miz Jessica Porter,
keeper of the zoo, that is.

Devlin pounded his fist against the door, waited
until he ran out of patience—which took all of two
seconds—then beat on the door with both fists.

"Porter! Open up! I know you're in there!" he shouted. "We have to talk! *Now!*"

His booming voice triggered the high-pitched cry of a peacock. A moose bellowed in the near distance, and a goose honked in chorus. Devlin rolled his eyes in frustration and swore inventively.

A few more seconds passed while unidentified screeches and roars erupted in the near distance. Devlin raised both fists to pound on the door again…and accidentally whacked Miz Jessica on the forehead when she whipped open the door unexpectedly.

His image of a frustrated, middle-aged spinster sporting a hooked nose, beady eyes and pointed chin dissolved when Devlin encountered a woman so astonishingly attractive he wondered if he was staring at some kind of optical illusion.

Eyes the color of a tropical rain forest zeroed in on him. Hair the color of sunbeams glistened around her enchanting face. His gaze dropped to survey an alluring figure that Hugh Hefner would kill to photograph.

Encountering Jessica Porter in the flesh was equivalent to being shot with a stun gun. *This* was his kooky neighbor? *This* was the zookeeper? No, couldn't be. Must be some mistake.

"Porter?" he asked doubtfully.

"Yes. You bellowed, sir?"

Her snippy tone and angry glare assured Devlin that this drop-dead-gorgeous female was no pushover. She met his gaze directly and took a combative stance in the doorway. She assessed his grimy T-shirt, dusty jeans and scuffed boots and frowned in blatant disapproval.

Devlin couldn't say why she so thoroughly disapproved of him. Could've been the fact that he'd pounded on her door, yelled at her, then accidentally konked her on the noggin. Or could've been that she didn't like the looks of a sweaty cowboy who'd spent the day riding the range and shared his horse's fragrance.

Sophisticated snob, Devlin concluded as he surveyed Jessica's crimson red silk power suit that shouted *expensive.* He suspected she had taken one look at his faded work clothes and decided she was entirely too good for him. Well, fine. She didn't like hardworking cowboys, and he didn't like prissy debutantes. So they were even.

"I'm Devlin Callahan, your nearest neighbor," he said abruptly.

"You're my closest neighbor? How unfortunate for me." Her voice dripped sarcasm.

"That goes double for me, Blondie," he countered, then glared at her.

Not to be outdone, she glared right back.

"I'm here because your zoo animals spooked my sheep and cattle for the fourth time in two months. You're gonna have to load up those animals and haul them to a wildlife refuge. As you can plainly see, this is ranch country."

Her chin shot up and, although the woman was a good eight inches shorter than Devlin, who stood six feet three inches in his riding boots, she still managed to look down her nose at him. How'd she do that?

"For your information, Culligan—"

"Callahan," he corrected tersely.

"Whatever," she said, dismissing him as if she

had the same regard for him as for a clump of Brussels sprouts. "For your information, I have a license to house and care for my exotic animals. Each animal has its own unique personality and special need. I can communicate with them. I understand them."

"You talk to your animals?" he asked, then scoffed. "Now why doesn't that surprise me?"

She glared meat cleavers at him. "I'm sure that if you toured my wildlife sanctuary even a man like you would realize that my animals are safely and securely housed and pose no threat whatsoever."

A man like him? Devlin wasn't sure what she implied, but her tone of voice alerted him that he had been insulted. "Lady, I don't care if your animals have rings through their noses and bells on their toes. They are upsetting my livestock, and I want them gone. And you along with them!"

That really must have ticked her off, because she braced her fists on those curvaceous hips, planted her well-shod feet shoulder-width apart, stuck her face in his and stated, "If you don't approve of living next door to my wildlife sanctuary, then *you* can pack up and move. I have no intention of budging from this spot, because I like it here, and so do my animals. Furthermore, if you have future complaints, then take them up with the sheriff in Buzzard's Grove, not that it will do you any good."

"Look, lady—"

"Jessica Porter. *Miss* Porter to you, Culligan," she said in that snippy tone that made Devlin grind his teeth in irritation.

"Here's the deal, *lady*. My brother and I run a large cattle and farming operation—"

"And I'm supposed to be impressed?" She gave

him another one of those condescending looks. "Sorry to disappoint you, Culligan. Cowboys are a nickel a dozen in this neck of the woods."

"I don't give a rip whether or not you're impressed," Devlin retorted. Damn—the woman knew exactly which buttons to push! "The point is that this zoo may be fun and games to you, may fill up the endless hours in your lonely, miserable life, but our livestock is our livelihood. Your exotic animals snarl, hoot, howl and growl all hours of the day and night and cause cattle stampedes. I spent the whole livelong day gathering cattle because of *your* zoo. The problem can be alleviated if you'll get rid of those menaces."

She glowered at him good and hard. "Can I help it if your wimpy cattle and timid sheep bolt and run because of an unfamiliar noise? You don't see my animals leaping fences just because dumb cows moo or sheep baa. My fences and pens are holding up just fine. Obviously your ability to build solid restraining fences is lacking."

Devlin was getting nowhere fast. Miss Hoity-Toity didn't want to see his side of the situation, didn't care that he'd busted his butt on roundup and fence repair.

"Fine," he muttered in exasperation. "Then *you* can pay for my time and the expenses, and I won't complain—as much."

She scoffed and looked down her nose at him again.

"*Your* livestock is on the rampage and you want *me* to pay for the fence repairs? My animals are housed in sturdy pens and cages, surrounded by twelve-feet-tall chain-link fences. It seems to me that I'm not the one with the problem here, Culligan. You are.''

"No, *you* are the problem!" Devlin snapped, at the end of his patience. He skewered her with a glower. "Snippy, dim-witted city slicker. Go back where you belong and take your zoo with you!"

Her chin went airborne as she squared her shoulders and clenched her fists by her sides. "This is where I belong, the *only* place I belong. I'm here to stay, so you better get used to the idea!" she said, puffing like a blowfish.

They exchanged significant glares, and Devlin was gearing up for a really terrific rejoinder when she slammed the door in his face.

A goose waddled around the corner of the house, honking in objection to Devlin's presence. A bear growled in the distance, accompanied by several sounds that Devlin couldn't identify—none of which sounded friendly. Hell, he wouldn't be surprised if there was an alligator living in that oversize pond, waiting to bite off his feet if he dared to stalk around to the back of the house.

Pond, he thought. That was another thing that really irritated him, come to think of it. That fire-breathing female had dammed up the spring-fed stream to form a gigantic pond in her pasture. The dam cut off the flow of water to Rocking C's stream. During the arid summer months Devlin and his brother had been forced to haul water to cattle in the west pasture and fill stock tanks.

Another major inconvenience he failed to mention to the dragon lady.

Devlin had half a mind to reverse his direction, pound on the front door again and insist that she dig a trench in the pond dam. No, on second thought, he'd take the matter up with Sheriff Osborn. Maybe the dragon lady had a legitimate license to shelter exotic animals, but she certainly didn't have the right to alter the flow of the stream and deprive Rocking C cattle of water.

Wheeling around, Devlin stalked away. The pesky goose lowered its head and charged after him, nipping and honking at his heels. Devlin ignored the feathered pest, piled into his pickup and revved the engine. He sprayed gravel on the low-slung car as he sped away—and he wouldn't be the least bit sorry if he accidentally cracked the dragon lady's windshield with flying rock. It would serve her right for being so stubborn.

Devlin muttered to himself as he roared toward home. His brother had recommended using diplomacy when confronting the neighbor lady. Devlin was pretty sure that wouldn't have worked any better than his direct, confrontational approach. He had noticed the look of disapproval when Jessica Porter gave him the once-over. Hell, he'd have to have been blind in both eyes not to realize she had no use for him. That woman would not have compromised under any circumstances.

What really baffled Devlin was that, despite his irritation, he found her physically attractive. He'd caught himself staring at her body with male appreciation a couple of times during their heated argument and had to jerk his attention to her face. Which didn't help a whole lot, because she had a bewitching face, to boot. It was humiliating for a man who usually had to fight off women with a stick to know that he liked what he saw and that Miss High and

Mighty Porter behaved as if he didn't measure up to her lofty standards.

What difference did that make? his smarting pride asked. No way would he be interested in dating Porter, not with their conflict over her exotic animals standing between them. And not that he was the teensiest bit interested, Devlin assured himself. The thought hadn't even crossed his mind. Well, okay, maybe for a nanosecond—until she'd opened her sassy mouth and let the wisecracks and zingers fly.

Glancing at his watch, Devlin made tracks toward home. It was his brother's night to cook, and Derrick got bent out of shape when Devlin was late. The Wednesday night menu at Rocking C was always the same: hamburger patties smothered in cream of mushroom soup, fried potatoes and okra. Devlin would have preferred cooked goose—specifically, the one that had appointed itself as Jessica Porter's guard dog.

Devlin glanced at the cattle herd grazing in the pasture, wondering if he'd wake up in the morning to another stampede. Jessica Porter's coyotes would probably be howling at the moon, causing the rest of the zoo to join in chorus. The cattle would be to hell and gone by sunrise, Devlin predicted.

He sighed heavily. Tomorrow would undoubtedly test his patience once again.

"STUBBORN, PIGHEADED COWBOY," Jessica muttered as she doffed her business suit, then snatched up her jeans and T-shirt.

The very last thing she'd needed, after dealing with an unreasonable, demanding client at her accounting office, was to confront her annoying neigh-

bor. She had lived in this community for almost six
months, and not once had Devlin Callahan dropped
by to welcome her. Oh, no, the jerk hadn't bothered
to set foot on the place until he came to complain
and shout ultimatums at her.

It hadn't helped that Jessica encountered Devlin
immediately after opening her credit card statement
to discover that her two-timing ex-fiancé had
charged a Caribbean cruise, for two, to her account.
Damn the man! No, damn all men in general, she
corrected bitterly. Why not? Every frustration she'd
dealt with during the course of the day had come at
the hands of the male of the species.

"Hell of a day, Jess," she said to herself as she
exited her bedroom and trotted down the staircase.
There was one surefire way to lighten her black
mood, and that was to wander among the exotic animals that had become her charges.

Jessica smiled fondly when her guard goose
greeted her on the back porch and performed its
usual head-dipping ritual. The goose followed her
across the lawn to retrieve feed from the barn. With
each step Jessica took toward the pens and cages in
the distance, the day's tension drained away. Despite
what Devlin Callahan presumed, these animals
could not be returned to the wilds because of their
handicaps and special needs. They needed her, she
reminded herself, and that cowboy with the attitude
wasn't going to force her to relocate them.

Jessica's lifelong love of animals and her tendency to pick up strays had become a crusade during
her post-college years in Tulsa, where she had
learned the ropes of the accounting business. Her
high-dollar salary had allowed her to purchase acre-

age to house her exotic animals, but the generous
offer from an industrial corporation convinced her
to sell the property and relocate. Jessica had quadru-
pled her investment and decided to move to the laid-
back hamlet of Buzzard's Grove to establish her
own accounting office.

The decision hadn't been difficult because there
were no close family ties to consider, only a few
friends from the office who had their own families
and personal lives.

Then, of course, there was her ex-fiancé—the hot-
shot Triple-A baseball star whose idea of a road trip
included notching his bedpost with different women
from different cities. It was only by accident that
Jessica discovered Rex's womanizing tendencies
and promptly canceled their engagement. Humiliated, outraged, Jessica had packed up her animals
and moved to the country. Unfortunately, Rex the
ex had the last laugh when he billed charges to her
credit card.

First thing in the morning, Jessica intended to
cancel her MasterCard and contact American Express. She was not paying for Rex's getaways again.

Jessica inhaled a breath of fresh country air, ex-
haled slowly and told herself to get a grip. Rex was
history. She'd played the naive fool once, but never
again. She vowed to avoid those macho, chauvinistic
jock types—like her disagreeable neighbor. Just because she found Devlin Callahan physically appealing, what with his shock of raven hair, midnight-
black eyes, broad shoulders, rock-hard muscles and
horseman's thighs, didn't mean she was the slightest
bit interested in getting involved with him. Besides,
she needed to channel her time and energy into mak-

ing a success of her business venture, refurbishing the house and providing care for her animals.

Jessica had known the moment she laid eyes on this forty-acre plot, with its rolling hills and thick groves of cottonwoods, elms and redbud trees, that she had finally found a place that felt like home. She had spent most of her life leaving behind what took forever to become comfortable and familiar. But she had known instinctively that she could happily put down roots here.

A sense of peace stole over her as she strode from one pen to the next, greeting and feeding her many charges. The brown bear she called Teddy performed his swaying ritual, then hobbled forward on his gimpy leg to devour the food Jessica placed in his pen. Each animal had its own way of greeting her, its special traits, that made her feel as if she was visiting with a dear friend.

Thoughts of her fussy client, Edgar Stokes, her aggravating neighbor and her traitorous ex skittered off in the evening breeze. Ah, yes, country life was the life for her. These maimed animals depended on her. Like Jessica, they were outcasts that didn't quite fit into society. That was okay, Jessica consoled herself. She had accepted the fact that she was an outsider, a misfit. But she and her unusual pets had settled into these wide-open spaces, and life was good.

Mother Goose honked, jolting Jessica from her pensive musings. "Not to worry, Mother, I haven't forgotten about you."

With the plump white goose waddling at her heels, Jessica ambled into the barn to scatter grain for her feathered friend. By the time Jessica returned to the house to pop a frozen dinner into the microwave her mood had brightened considerably. She wondered if her grouchy neighbor's mood had eased after their heated encounter. Not that she cared if he left mad and stayed that way. All she cared was that he left and never came back.

Fact was that Devlin Callahan's appearance triggered bitter memories of the time when she had fallen for a handsome face and muscled body. She wouldn't make that mistake twice. Until she met a man who was willing to give as much as he took, someone who wasn't interested in the tidy sum of money she'd made when she sold her property on the outskirts of Tulsa, she planned to avoid men, especially the ones who looked as if they stepped off a poster for Tall, Dark and Handsome. No, sirree, she wasn't going to fall for some hunk of a cowboy who had the disposition of a wounded rhinoceros.

Lord, she still couldn't believe that idiotic man tried to blame his problem with his flighty cattle on *her,* expected her to pay for his time and expenses. What unmitigated gall he had!

Refusing to give Devil Devlin another thought, Jessica shoved her frozen dinner in the microwave, then pivoted to pour herself a tall glass of iced tea.

DERRICK CALLAHAN slopped three hamburger patties, swimming in cream soup, on his plate, then glanced over his shoulder when he heard the footsteps that heralded his brother's arrival. "'Bout time. I decided not to wait any longer. I have a date tonight and I have no intention of showing up late just because you can't get your sorry butt back here on time."

"Date? In the middle of the week?" Devlin inquired as he plucked up his plate for the buffet-style meal sitting on the counter.

"Yeah? So?" Derrick challenged. "What's the matter with that? People do date on weekdays, you know."

"Only if they're getting serious." Devlin scooped up a large helping of fried okra, then moved on to the bowl of fried potatoes. "You and that new restaurant owner getting serious, are you?"

"Maybe," Derrick mumbled noncommittally, then pivoted toward the oblong oak table that sat in the middle of the spacious dining area. He used his free hand to scrape scattered mail out of his way, then plopped down on a chair. "So, how did your encounter go with the neighbor lady?"

Devlin might not have been the sharpest knife in the drawer, but he knew a diversion tactic when he heard one. His brother didn't want to discuss his feelings for Cassie Dixon, the vivacious brunette whose new café was the talk of the town. The fact that Derrick wanted to keep his relationship with Cassie a secret from his own brother, his only living relative, suggested that Derrick was already in over his head and sinking fast. Not that Devlin blamed his brother. Cassie Dixon had class, style and personality—unlike the female fruitcake with the attitude who lived down the road.

"Well?" Derrick prompted.

Devlin glanced up from his heaped plate. "Well, what?"

"Did you convince our neighbor to relocate her zoo so it won't disturb our livestock?"

"No, she slammed the door in my face after lambasting me with insults,'' Devlin grumbled as he grabbed his fork. ''The woman has a chip the size of Mount Rushmore on her shoulder, and her brain is obviously solid rock. There's no getting through to her, not without a jackhammer and dynamite.''

Derrick rolled his eyes, then stared at his brother. ''In other words, you used your standard, give-'em-hell approach and butted heads with her. I distinctly remember telling you to use diplomacy.''

''Diplomacy wouldn't have done any good,'' Devlin said.

Derrick shook his head and sighed audibly. ''It is totally beyond me why you didn't use your lady-killer smile and charm on her. There isn't an eligible female in Buzzard County who can resist you when you turn on the charm. You shouldn't have gone over to the neighbor's house while you were hot under the collar. I tried to tell you to wait until you'd cooled off. But no, you climbed off your horse after roundup and blazed off. I know how you operate, Dev. When in doubt you start yelling, as if that ever solves problems. It almost never works with women. Next time, try being tactful.''

The last thing he needed was a lecture from his brother, who had a history of leaving the difficult situations for Devlin to solve. Diplomacy? Hell!

''There won't be a next time,'' Devlin muttered crankily. ''If you think the charming, chivalrous approach will work—and I'll bet money that it won't—then you can march your candy butt over there and try to reason with her. After all, you've got the identical smile and more charm than I do.''

Derrick threw up his hand like a traffic cop. ''Me? No way. Just because we're identical twins doesn't mean I'm going over there after you screwed up. She'll take one look at me and think I'm you. I'll get nowhere.''

"Well, she started it with her snide remarks," Devlin said self-righteously. "But I'll admit that it didn't help when I accidentally smacked her right between the eyes when she abruptly opened the door."

Derrick groaned in dismay. "Well, there you go. What do you expect? If it had been me—" he tapped himself proudly on the chest "—I would have politely rung the doorbell, not hammered on the door. The accident would never have happened."

Devlin bared his teeth and glared at his twin. The thing about being an identical twin was that you never felt as if you had your own individuality, especially when you had to sit across the table every night and work side by side every day. Especially when Derrick was forever handing out free advice, just because he was all of three minutes older and considered himself twice as smart.

"I swear, Dev, you turned cantankerous after you went ape over that prissy redhead a few years back."

"Don't remind me," Devlin grumbled. "I got my heart trampled while you glided merrily from one woman to the next...until Cassie Dixon showed up in town and turned your brain into Malt-O-Meal."

Derrick scowled at the insult.

Devlin scowled back.

"Okay, so I didn't get my heart broken at the tender age of twenty-five."

"Exactly my point, Derr. You aren't jaded and

cynical. You're better prepared for dealing with Jessica Porter and the zoo. The woman is easy on the eye, which I'm sure you'll appreciate. You need to get over there and talk some sense into her before those squalling, bellowing zoo animals scatter our livestock to kingdom come.''

"Our neighbor lady is attractive?" Derrick asked.

"A regular knockout," Devlin confirmed, then munched on potatoes. "You probably won't open your mouth and say the wrong thing. You can sweet-talk her into being reasonable, even if she thinks you're me. In fact, you two might even hit it off—''

"Oh, no," Derrick loudly objected. "That's the last thing I need right now. I've got a good thing going with Cassie and I'm not about to screw it up. I'm not getting within a mile of the neighbor's house, for fear that Cassie might get the wrong idea.''

"Tell Cassie it was me," Devlin suggested. "It's not like she'll know the difference.''

"Absolutely, positively not," Derrick refused. "You made a mess of the negotiations with the Porter lady and you're going to straighten this out!''

Derrick swallowed the last bite of hamburger patty, then vaulted to his feet. "While you're cleaning up the kitchen I'm going to shower, then I'm out of here. Cassie and I are going to watch a movie at her place. You can spend the evening practicing being charming, polite and diplomatic. Tomorrow night you can waltz over to the neighbor's, bearing gifts of flowers and candy, and make amends.''

"You want me to court trouble with a capital T?" Devlin crowed. "No way in hell!''

"This is your feud, bro. You started it and you can end it. I'm staying completely out of it." Derrick frowned darkly. "Fix the problem, hear me?"

Devlin glared laser beams at his brother's departing back. Fix the problem? Yeah, right. The only way to resolve the situation was to lock Jessica Porter in a cage with her exotic animals, then ship her off to a wildlife refuge that was far, far away from the Rocking C Ranch.

An hour later, while Devlin was relaxing on the porch swing, reading the biweekly newspaper, he heard an unearthly scream that made the hair on the back of his neck stand on end. Cougar, he thought, then gnashed his teeth when a bobcat growled in the distance.

Damn it to hell, about the same time every night Porter's zoo orchestra struck up a racket that spoiled the serenity of the evening. Come morning, Devlin knew what he and his brother would be doing—chasing down spooked livestock.

"Charm the dragon lady?" he asked himself. "Pretend I actually like her? Not on your life."

An unnerving roar exploded in the twilight. Devlin slammed down the newspaper, then stormed into the house. His neighbor's zoo was disturbing his peace. Surely there was a law against that, wasn't there? Devlin vowed to drag Sheriff Osborn out here to listen to this racket. Then maybe Devlin would get some results!

2

"Good morning, boss," Teresa Harper greeted enthusiastically as Jessica walked into her office in Buzzard's Grove.

"Morning." Jessica set her briefcase on her desk and smiled at her red-haired secretary. Jessica still had trouble believing Teresa was the same desperate, withdrawn woman who had scurried into the office three months ago, begging for a job, vowing to do whatever necessary to earn money.

Teresa had lacked spirit and self-esteem and could barely make eye contact without ducking her head and wringing her hands. The poor, distraught woman had burst into tears and spilled her hard-luck story—in between sobs and shuddering gulps. Teresa had escaped an abusive husband, filed for divorce and moved to Buzzard's Grove to put distance between her ex and herself.

The woman desperately needed to make a new start, and Jessica felt compelled to help, because she knew what it was like to be alone and frightened and unsure where the next meal would come from, unsure if she was wanted or accepted. Jessica had hired the woman on the spot, though Teresa lacked certain secretarial skills.

Determined to see that Teresa had a new life, a positive self-image, Jessica had located an efficiency apartment in town, paid the deposit from her own pocket, offered Teresa a few garments from her own wardrobe and won an instant and devoted friend and employee.

To repay the kindness, Teresa had worked extra hours at the office to hone her skills and made every effort to be courteous and professional while dealing with clients. Once Teresa familiarized herself with business procedures, she fielded calls so Jessica could immerse herself in tallying and balancing accounts. Being the only certified accountant in town brought Jessica more business than she wanted—which was why she was so slow in making repairs around her grand old farm home.

"Whew, yesterday was a killer, wasn't it?" Teresa remarked as she handed Jessica a cup of steaming coffee and a homemade cinnamon roll. "I almost lost my cool when that grumpy old coot barreled in here to chew you up one side and down the other because you wouldn't fudge on his income tax form. For a minute there, I had flashbacks of dealing with my ex. If you hadn't come charging forward to take on Edgar Stokes I would have been cowering in the corner, reduced to tears." Teresa smiled. "I truly admire the way you stand up to men and refuse to let them intimidate you. If I keep watching those self-help videos you gave me, maybe I'll be a force to be reckoned with, too."

Jessica bit into the warm cinnamon roll. Her taste buds went into full-scale riot. Not only was Teresa turning into a dream employee, but she really could cook. She brought deli sandwiches for lunch, coffee cakes for breakfast, and Jessica's mouth watered like Pavlov's dogs at first sniff.

"Thanks for the compliment, Teresa. I've had lots of practice holding my own against the pushy men of the world. Edgar Stokes was just a warm-up for the annoying character who showed up on my doorstep when I got home last night."

Alarm registered in Teresa's wide hazel eyes. "Oh, my gosh! The man didn't try to assault you, did he? Do I need to notify Sheriff Osborn? Can you identify your assailant?"

"Yes, he is my nearest neighbor, who stopped by to voice his displeasure with my exotic animals. No need to call the sheriff."

"He didn't like your animals?" Teresa harrumphed as she walked around her desk to grab her cup of coffee. "I hope you let him have it—in spades."

"We pretty much let each other have it—in spades," Jessica reported, then took another bite of the delicious roll. "The cowboy with the attitude claimed my exotics were disturbing his livestock and he demanded that I pay him for the time and money required to round up his cattle and repair his fences."

"Who is this character?" Teresa questioned curiously.

"Devlin Callahan."

"Never heard of him, but then, I've only been in town a few months. The man obviously isn't one of your clients, otherwise I'd recognize his name from your files."

That much was true, Jessica mused as she polished off the cinnamon roll, then reached for another. Teresa made it a point to familiarize herself with every client on file. Devlin Callahan was not, and never would be, on file. Jessica would refuse to handle Rocking C Ranch accounts, even if Devil Devlin asked her nicely—and she seriously doubted he was capable of that. The less she had to deal with Callahan the better she'd like it.

"Oh, look! There's that nice Sheriff Osborn now," Teresa said. She pointed a red-tipped finger toward the window. "He's in the parking lot at Good Grub Diner. Want me to hustle over there and register a complaint for you? I wouldn't mind a bit, you know."

Jessica pivoted, her mouth wrapped around the scrumptious cinnamon roll, then choked for breath. Devlin Callahan stepped from his four-wheel-drive, fire-engine-red pickup truck and approached the sheriff. No doubt that black-eyed monster was following up her suggestion of taking complaints to the sheriff. Jessica couldn't say she was surprised to see Callahan bending the sheriff's ear. He certainly had bent hers during their shouting match last night, and she had let that arrogant cowboy have it with both barrels blazing.

Unwillingly, Jessica's assessing gaze drifted over Devlin's striking profile. The man was just too darn good-looking, she mused. If life was fair and just, Devlin's appearance would be as offensive as his personality. Jessica couldn't say exactly why she had reacted so unfavorably to Callahan at first glance. There was something about him that brought her feminine defenses to code-red alert. She supposed she found herself unwillingly attracted to the big galoot and went to extremes to offend and repel him.

Okay, so maybe she had gone overboard in an

attempt to prove to him, and to herself, that she didn't like the looks of him. After her fiasco with Rex the ex she resolved never to be taken in by a handsome face and magnificent male body. Rex, as it turned out, had all the emotional depth of a bar of soap. She suspected Devlin was the shining example of same-song-second-verse.

It didn't help the situation one iota when she suffered a knee-jerk reaction to Devlin's explosive temper. He irritated her, so naturally, she made a supreme effort to return the favor.

"Wow, who is that guy talking to the sheriff?" Teresa asked, her nose pressed to the windowpane. "He looks like a movie star or something. Is he handsome or what, boss?"

"That's Callahan," Jessica reported. "Don't be fooled by his good looks. He can be a fire-breathing dragon when the mood strikes. He's probably tattling to the sheriff as we speak, trying to convince Osborn to pressure me into relocating my exotic animals, because God-Almighty Callahan doesn't want me infringing on his cattle kingdom."

DEVLIN WAS INDEED airing his grievances to Sheriff Osborn at that very moment—for all the good it did him, just as Jessica prophesied.

"I realize you're tired and cranky, since you were up before five this morning chasing down your scattered cattle," Sheriff Reed Osborn commiserated. "But Miss Porter's land is zoned for a refuge and she has a license issued by the National Coordinator of the Association of Sanctuaries. The association deals with about twenty accredited sanctuaries nationwide. Porter's sanctuary is very reputable, and the association placed two large cats in her care a couple of months ago.''

"Two jungle cats?" Devlin hooted. "As in lions and tigers? No wonder my livestock bolts and runs! Criminey, Reed, I have wheat to plant for forage. Derrick and I need to service our tractors and machinery, not spend valuable time thundering across pastures and through ditches in an attempt to retrieve runaway cattle and sheep. This has got to stop! I'm getting no rest whatsoever, and repair bills for new barbed wire and steel fence posts are mounting up.''

Reed shrugged and sighed. "I hear ya, Dev, don't think I don't. But there really isn't much I can do about the situation. None of the exotics have escaped to terrorize the countryside or put humans or livestock at direct risk. Why don't you move your cattle to another pasture and put more distance between them and the exotics?''

"You expect me to sacrifice eighty acres of much-needed summer grass when I have hungry cattle? Sure, I can change the pasture rotation next year, but if I move those cattle to another pasture that has been grubbed to the ground because of the drought, Derrick and I will have to pay the extra expense of feeding cattle cubes. And another thing," Dev added hastily, "that woman dammed up the stream when she built her pond at the first of the summer. Her exotics are frolicking in the pond while my livestock are going thirsty. I've been transporting water to them for over a month. Porter shouldn't be allowed to block the water supply like that.''

Reed Osborn nodded his sandy blond head. "You've got her there, Dev. I don't think the Association of Sanctuaries would support her on that one. Want me to talk to her about reopening the water flow to your pasture?"

"Nothing would make me happier," Devlin replied in supreme satisfaction. "I'd rather not talk to that woman again if I don't have to. I swear she's placed some kind of curse on me. We haven't had many decent rains since she moved in six months ago and dammed up the creek. The pasture grass is fizzling out, and fence repairs are cutting into profit. When she moved in things started going wrong."

Reed chuckled in amusement. "You're holding her personally responsible for this two-month drought and record-setting heat wave?"

"Wouldn't surprise me a bit if she had something to do with it," Devlin said, then snorted. "I'd call her a witch, but she would probably sue me for slander, then take over the Rocking C and turn the whole blessed ranch into a sanctuary for killer cats, mauling bears and only God knows what else."

"Jessica Porter a witch?" Reed's eyebrows shot up like exclamation marks. "Are we talking about the same sweet, charming woman? The Jessica I know is a model citizen. You wouldn't believe all the charities and organizations she's donated money to since her arrival. She contributes to anything that benefits youth groups and underprivileged children in our community."

Devlin blinked, stunned by the glowing accolades heaped on the dragon lady. "Sweet and charming?" His arm shot out to indicate the building across the street from Good Grub Diner. "Are we talking about the Jessica Porter whose office is right over there? The woman who has the sharpest tongue in the county, even though she's built like Miss September?''

Reed burst out laughing at the shocked expression on Devlin's face. ''Yup, that's her. She also hired a woman who was on the run from an abusive ex-husband. Jessica marched herself over to my office to request a restraining order, in case the jerk showed up to terrorize Teresa. You should see the positive changes Teresa has undergone since Jessica took her under her wing.''

''Yeah? Turned the poor woman into a witch?'' Devlin asked sarcastically.

''Hell, no!'' Reed countered. ''I tell you the woman is a saint. Why, Jessica even went so far as to pay Teresa's deposit and first month's rent, outfit her with stylish clothes and buy some secondhand furniture at the sheriff's sale to furnish the apartment.''

Devlin blinked like a traffic caution light. Reed thought the dragon lady was a saint? Maybe it was Devlin who brought out the worst in Miss Model Citizen of the Year. From all indications, Porter only had a problem getting along with her nearest neighbor—him.

''I suggest you and the rest of the Jessica Porter fan club camp out at Rocking C and see how you like it,'' Devlin grumbled. ''After one night of listening to the zoo orchestra serenade you and rounding up frightened cattle, I guarantee that you'll change your tune. That woman and her zoo are a nuisance that is testing the limits of my temper.''

''I'll talk to Jessica about unleashing the water, but I'm telling you flat-out, Dev, you and Jess are going to have to come to some kind of reconciliation

and understanding. That's an order." He stared
meaningfully at Devlin. "I've got enough situations
to resolve around here without dealing with feuding
neighbors. Use a little of that Callahan charm instead of that short-fused temper."

Devlin gnashed his teeth until he practically wore
off the enamel. This was the second time in less than
twenty-four hours that he had been instructed to rely
on his charm—what there was left of it after his
embarrassing heartbreak seven years earlier. He
wasn't sure he had ever possessed enough charm
and patience to deal with the dragon lady.

"I mean it, Dev." The sheriff put on his cop face
and stared at Devlin. "You be especially nice to that
woman, hear me? She's done lots of good deeds
here in Buzzard's Grove. Everybody around here re-
spects her. It wouldn't be good for her professional
reputation, or yours, if you both decided to square
off at twenty paces for a showdown. I'd have to toss
you both in the slammer for disturbing the peace—"

"What about the fact that her zoo is disturbing
my peace?" Devlin broke in indignantly.

"Oh, for Pete's sake, Dev, we've had sightings
of bobcats and mountain lions over the years. We
have packs of coyotes running around all over the
place. Jessica's animals are penned up and cause
less threat. What are you gonna do? Try to sue the
Association of Sanctuaries? Of course not. It'd be a
waste of time. Now make an effort to mend your
fences."

"I've done enough of that already," Devlin said
sourly.

"That was a figure of speech," the sheriff remarked, then flashed a smile. "Just because you got

your heart broke a few years back doesn't mean you should take out your frustration on every woman you encounter, especially not Miss Porter.''

Exasperated, Devlin threw up his hands. "Is my personal life front-page news around here? Hell, it's like living in a fishbowl!"

Reed Osborn shrugged nonchalantly. "Typical small town stuff. Besides, you and your brother have always been the subject of gossip. You're good-looking, successful and eligible. Deal with it, Callahan. I wish I had your problems."

Devlin spun toward his truck. "Just talk to Porter about her blasted pond," he ordered.

"Okay, but polish up your smile and spray on a coat of charm," the sheriff demanded. "Work out your differences with Jessica, or you'll both answer to me. Got it?"

Oh, he had it, all right—a pain in the lower region of his anatomy that went by the name of Jessica Porter.

Swearing under his breath, Devlin piled into his pickup and aimed himself toward the ranch. He glanced over his shoulder toward the bed of the truck, which was heaped with new steel fence posts and rolls of shiny barbed wire. Damn, if only he could figure out a way to drown those alarming noises he wouldn't be building new stretches of fence....

An idea hatched in his head and Devlin smiled for the first time all day—one that began before five o'clock, thanks to the racket at Porter's zoo. Devlin made a U-turn and went to the farm supply store to purchase extension cords. Maybe piped music would muffle the howls, growls and screeches.

Grinning devilishly, Devlin made the extra purchases, then headed toward home. He'd see how Porter liked listening to blaring music all night. She might have grown accustomed to being serenaded by her zoo, but lively, fast-tempo honky-tonk music would bring her straight out of bed. Once she got a taste of her own medicine, she'd know how Devlin reacted to those roars and shrieks.

JESSICA WIPED the sweat from her brow and surveyed the trench she'd dug in the pond dam. Thanks to her cantankerous, tattletale neighbor, the sheriff insisted she allow water to flow from her pond to the stream that meandered across Devlin's pasture. Jessica was ashamed to say it hadn't occurred to her that she had unintentionally stifled Devlin's water supply and he'd been forced to haul water. That was inconsiderate and unneighborly of her.

Maybe she had been entirely too hard on the man, she thought as she shoveled more dirt. It wasn't Devlin's fault that his good looks and muscular physique reminded her of her ex-fiancé and that she had transferred her frustration to the cowboy.

That was not the mature approach, she told herself. How many times had Jessica advised Teresa not to compare her abusive ex-husband to the men she met in Buzzard's Grove? More times than she cared to count, Jessica realized. Teresa had begun to put her painful past behind her and had developed a crush on Sheriff Osborn. Teresa was getting on with her life. Eight months after her humiliating relationship with Rex, Jessica was still afraid to trust a man.

"You aren't being fair," Jessica said to herself.

Mother Goose honked as if in agreement, then fluttered into the pond to take an evening swim.

While water trickled through the V Jessica dug in the dam, she carted rocks up the steep incline to insure future rains didn't erode her waterway and empty her pond. Smiling, Jessica watched the pair of coyotes and their pups, the red foxes and a trio of horses drink from the pond. It was gratifying to see that the animals had learned to coexist in this sanctuary.

So why couldn't she get along with Devlin Callahan?

Recalling the sheriff's request to resolve her differences with Devlin, Jessica vowed to make an effort to be civil.

While she made her rounds to feed the exotics housed in covered pens and cages, she reminded herself that she needed to mow and clean up around the sanctuary this weekend. The local grade school students would be arriving for their field trip. Since Jessica's sanctuary was listed on the association's register, she had received several calls to schedule field trips. The money would help to defray costs for more pens and feed. Her exotic family would continue to grow as long as she had space.

Weary from digging the trench in the parched earth, Jessica trudged to the house to bathe. Partially revived, she opened the freezer to select a microwave dinner.

She had considered swinging by the new restaurant at the end of Main Street to pick up a carry-out meal, but she had been late getting away from the office, and she had to feed her animals before dark.

Ah well, Jessica didn't consider herself Suzie

Homemaker, and she wasn't one of those people who lived to eat; she simply ate to live. But every once in a while she craved a thick, juicy steak, home-cooked vegetables and dessert. It wasn't that she couldn't cook, it was just that she didn't have much time, what with getting her business off the ground, tending the exotics and doing minor refurbishing projects inside the house.

A faint smile twitched her lips as she recalled her shaky start in life, her difficult teens and her struggle to acquire a college education. The kid no one wanted—least of all her irresponsible, pleasure-seeking parents—had made something of herself. In fact, she could be living off the interest on the money she made when she sold the hot property in Tulsa. But Jessica didn't want to be a recluse on her sanctuary. She secretly longed to fit in, to feel a connection, to be accepted and respected in Buzzard's Grove.

So far so good—except for her feud with Devlin Callahan. He was the thorn in her paw, and Sheriff Osborn had all but ordered her to make nice to that hot-tempered rancher.

Okay, fine, she would apologize for biting off Devlin's head and insulting him. She could be nice to the man if she really tried. She could also move the big cats' and bears' cages farther west to the clump of cottonwood trees, so the overhanging limbs would trap the sounds. Yeah, she could do that this weekend, if she put in double days. The pens were built on skids so she could hook a chain to her car bumper and pull them to different locations.

Jessica sighed drowsily as she lay sprawled on the

sofa. Man, it had been a long week, and it wasn't over yet. She could use some shut-eye so she would have the energy to tackle the list of weekend chores.

She nodded off, only to bolt straight up on the sofa when blaring country music rattled the window-panes. Garth Brooks was singing "Ain't Goin' Down Till the Sun Comes Up," and the coyotes and wolves were howling to beat the band.

"What in blue blazes?" Jessica staggered to her feet and wobbled unsteadily to the window. Darkness had settled over the rolling Oklahoma hills. She could barely make out the glow of miniature red lights just beyond the barbed wire fence that separated her property from Rocking C Ranch.

It only took a moment to realize Devlin had rigged up his stereo system to counter the sounds of her exotic animals. Swearing, Jessica made a beeline for the back door to determine how her animals were reacting to the earsplitting music. Sure enough, the animals were pacing in their cages. Toucans and cockatoos were flinging themselves against the wire pens in an attempt to escape. The horses were thundering across the pasture to seek refuge in the trees.

Muttering, Jessica snatched up the phone book, then quickly dialed the number for Rocking C Ranch. Impatiently, she waited for Devil Devlin to answer.

"Hello," came a thick, velvety voice that oozed sensuality. Jessica refused to be affected by that seductive voice, because she knew what a jackass the man was.

"Devlin Callahan, I—"

"Hold on a sec."

A moment later the same voice was back, but Jessica ignored the unwilling tingle that slid through her body. She was mad as a wet hen and she wasn't about to let this man bedevil her with his sexy bedroom voice. Plus, there was no telling who was in the bedroom with him when she interrupted and was forced to wait for him to finish whatever it was he was doing.

"Callahan, this is Porter," she snapped. "Get your fanny over here and pull the plug on the blaring music. Now!"

"Sorry, darlin'," he drawled, "but I'm just too tired to get out of bed. I was up at the crack of dawn rounding up cattle."

"Tough," she spluttered angrily. "Your loud music is terrifying my animals!"

"Now they know how my cattle and sheep feel," he said unsympathetically.

"Look, Callahan, I'll have you know I spent the evening digging a trench so your cattle would have water. Now I'm exhausted and I need sleep."

"Thanks, that's mighty neighborly of you, Porter. Wish you'd done that a couple of months ago so I didn't have to haul water to my thirsty livestock."

"I would have if you had said something," she replied. "I wasn't aware that I was causing a problem."

"Gee, and I suppose it also escaped your notice that your zoo has been terrifying my livestock, that the cattle you saw grazing the ditches on your way to work this morning were supposed to be in the pasture. Do you know what happens when a motorist slams into a cow, Blondie? Not only does said cow wind up in the deep freeze, but I lose the cow, and her calf dies of starvation. Then I have to shell out money to replenish my herd, not to mention the potential threat of a lawsuit over personal injury.''

"Well, I—" Jessica couldn't get another word in edgewise, because Devlin was still running off at the mouth.

"But I suppose you're so wrapped up in yourself and your wildlife preservation crusade that you never stopped to think how it affects your nearest neighbor. Did you think of that? Hmm? No? I didn't think so.

"As for the honky-tonk music, Porter, my cattle like it dandy fine. It drowns out the racket at your place. If some of your exotics break loose and run scared, be sure to call me. I'll bring my stun gun and zap them for you.''

"Yeah, but I wouldn't put it past you to use live ammo. You're a world-class jerk, Callahan, know that? And here I had convinced myself that I had been too hard on you. I even planned to take pity—"

"Hey, lady, the last thing I want from you is pity," he said huffily.

"Take what you can get."

"If I could get you to pack up and leave I'd be the happiest man on the face of the planet. This was a peaceful place to work and live until you and your jungle animals showed up.''

"That's it, Callahan! Now you've really infuriated me!" Jessica exploded in bad temper.

"So, what are you gonna do about it, sugar? Come over here and beat the tar out of me?" he goaded her unmercifully.

"No, I'm calling the sheriff, and he can fine you for disturbing the peace!" she yelled at him.

"The sheriff refuses to get involved. I know because I asked him to fine you for disturbing my peace. We'll have to work this out by ourselves. But not to worry, Blondie. Give the country music a week, and I'm sure you and your exotics will be as fond of it as my cattle and sheep are."

Before Jessica could give him an earful of her frustration he hung up on her. She stared at the receiver in outrage. She hated for that devilish cowboy to have the last word. But she supposed he thought it was fitting, since she had shut the door in his face the previous night.

Jessica slammed down the phone, stormed upstairs to her bedroom, undressed, then buried herself beneath the quilts and clamped pillows over her ears. It didn't help. She could hear Allan Jackson belting out the words to "Don't Rock the Jukebox." The drumbeat thumped the windowpanes until Jessica was ready to scream in frustration.

"Damn the man!" she shouted to the world at large.

"YOU DID WHAT?" Derrick hooted in disbelief.

"You heard me," Devlin said over his breakfast of cold cereal and orange juice. "I hooked up the stereo and drowned out the uproar caused by those exotic animals."

Derrick tossed him a withering glance. "This is your idea of a compromise?"

"I didn't get anywhere with the sheriff," Devlin grumbled. "Porter charmed him to such extremes that Reed thinks she's God's gift to humanity. But Reed did convince Porter to cut her pond dam so we don't have to haul water. She dug the trench last night."

"So, to repay her, you hooked up a boom box and blew out her eardrums."

Devlin shifted uncomfortably in his chair. "Well, how was I to know she was going to dig the trench until after the fact?"

Derrick slammed his fist on the table. Silverware and bowls bounced like Mexican jumping beans. "This is juvenile, Dev. You're going to turn this into a grudge contest if you aren't careful. I insist that you go over there tonight and do your damnedest to make amends. If Jessica is as community-minded and financially generous as the sheriff says, then you're the one who is going to come off looking like a jerk…which reflects on me, because folks might think I'm a party to this nonsense, which I'm sure as hell not."

Devlin glowered at his identical twin. "Are you going to sit here and tell me that you don't mind chasing down cattle every other day?"

"Of course not, but I'll fix fences if that's what it takes to keep peace. I prefer to focus my free time on Cassie Dixon. She, being a woman and all, is sure to side with Jessica in this feud." Derrick stared placatingly at his brother. "Please, Dev, bury the hatchet. Ask the woman out and get to know her before you pass judgment. Find out why she is caught up in this crusade, make her understand that the cattle and sheep are our livelihood and that ranchers are facing tough times. Try to become the great guy you were before Sandi Saxon screwed you over for that high-rolling lawyer and moved to

Oklahoma City. Stop being so cautious and defensive when it comes to women.''

Having said his piece, Derrick rose to set his bowl and glass in the sink. "I'm going to change the oil and replace the hydraulic hoses on both tractors this morning while you clean out the drills and auger seed wheat into the trucks.'' Derrick glanced out the window. "There are a few clouds piling up on the horizon, so maybe we'll finally get some rain before we plant wheat.''

"It'd be nice if something went right,'' Devlin muttered.

"Oh, before I forget, I won't be here to cook supper tonight. Cassie invited me to her restaurant to eat with her. You're on your own, bro.''

When Derrick strode off, Devlin hunched over the table, mulling over his brother's criticism of the neighbor situation. Truth be known, Devlin enjoyed sparring with his feisty neighbor. She was quick-witted and sassy, and she amused him in a frustrated sort of way. Furthermore, he kind of liked the fact that she stood up to him.

As for setting up the boom box, it had seemed the perfect solution to muffle the unnerving noises. The tactic had made Jessica realize what Devlin and his cattle herd had been tolerating. But as it turned out, Porter had worn herself out trenching her pond dam—to be neighborly—and Devlin had kept her up most of the night with loud music. Damn, everything he tried to do in his dealings with Jessica kept backfiring on him.

Okay, so maybe it was time to try a different tack, bury the hatchet somewhere besides in Porter's back. Devlin could do nice and gentlemanly if the mood suited him. And okay, so he did have a tendency to project Sandi Saxon's failings on other women after she'd trampled his male pride into the ground. The experience had disillusioned and soured him on women, and he remained on guard to prevent getting hurt again.

One thing about playing nice with Jessica Porter, though, it would just be an act, a performance to form a truce. He already knew what Jessica was like when the thermometer attached to her temper shot through the roof. The woman was prickly, defensive and high-strung, which made it tough for Devlin, who was a little prickly, defensive and high-strung himself.

Well, he would consider this a test of his temper, patience and disposition, he told himself. This was a challenge. If he could deal with the dragon lady and get her to eat out of his hand, then he should be able to handle any woman.

Derrick was right, he mused. Devlin had allowed his disillusionment with Sandi to destroy potential relationships. But past was past. Sandi was a closed chapter in his life.

Resolved to negotiating a truce, Devlin crammed his bowl and glass in the dishwasher, then strode outside to tackle the chores that awaited him. After supper he'd get spruced up and drive over to the dragon...er, Miz Porter's place. He'd dust off the manners he hadn't used in a few years and do a little damage control.

The woman wouldn't stand a chance when he turned on the charm, he tried to convince himself. He'd be so suave, debonair, gallant and courteous that the dragon...er, Miz Porter would forget why she was upset with him.

3

JESSICA WAS SO TIRED by the time she returned home from work that she had trouble putting one foot in front of the other. Thanks to Devil Devlin's prank that caused sleep deprivation she had dozed off at her office and awakened to find a debit and expenditure form stuck to her face. If her secretary hadn't volunteered to stay late to type up the tax sheets and drop them in the mail, Jessica couldn't have gotten the federal forms and payroll checks completed on time. Teresa, devoted employee that she was, shooed Jessica from the office, insisting that she go home and get some rest.

That was precisely what Jessica planned to do—after tending her animals and mowing a few rounds on the riding mower. One glance at the ominous sky indicated a soggy weekend ahead. The TV meteorologists were forecasting a break in the drought that would undoubtedly test the strength of the trench Jessica dug in her pond dam.

Halfheartedly, Jessica made the rounds to feed her animals. As usual, Mother Goose followed like a shadow. After fueling the mower, Jessica shoved the machine into high gear. It was nearly dark before she found time to sit down, prop up her feet and nibble on the dinner she had nuked in the microwave oven.

A firm rap resounded at the door. Frowning curiously, Jessica set aside her plastic plate. She opened the door to see Devlin Callahan decked out in a starched and pressed Western shirt, trim-fitting blue jeans and polished boots. Her jaw dropped to her chest, and she stood there gaping at him like a tongue-tied idiot.

Good gracious, no man—especially not this man—had a right to look so devastatingly attractive. When he flashed her a knock-you-to-your-knees smile that generated enough wattage to see her through a blizzard, an unwilling jolt of attraction zapped her. In one tanned hand, which was devoid of jewelry, Devlin held a bouquet of roses.

Roses for her? Couldn't be. The man hated her, she was sure of it.

Jessica was not mentally, physically or emotionally prepared to confront this handsome rascal. She was too exhausted to go another round with him, most especially when he looked like every woman's secret dream standing there on her front porch. This man redefined the words *dangerous* and *tempting*, but Jessica had made a pact to play it safe. She wanted no part of him.

"I brought the roses for—" he began.

Jessica did the only thing she could possibly do to prevent being overwhelmed by the devil's own temptation, who had caught her off guard while she looked and felt her absolute worst.

She shut the door in his face.

The roses he had extended to her got caught inside the doorjamb, and the door snipped off their delicate heads in one vicious whack. Jessica glanced at the decapitated flowers that lay on her grungy barnyard boots, then took quick inventory of her attire. Gawd, she looked like an abandoned orphan in her jungle-print T-shirt and holey jeans that were tucked in the tops of her boots. Her off-center ponytail dangled in tangles on one side of her head. The long strands were snagged with twigs and coated with grass clippings. There wasn't a speck of makeup on her face to conceal the circles under her eyes. In short, she was a pitiful mess, and he, damn him, looked scrumptious enough to eat.

Well, she had blown any chance of reconciliation, even if now was the time for one—which it wasn't, not when she didn't look presentable or feel mentally alert.

Frustrated, exasperated by her purely feminine reaction to a man she wanted very much to dislike, Jessica marched across the room to plop down on the sofa, hoping Devlin would give up and go away.

DEVLIN STARED at the stems in his hand and willed himself not to lose his temper. He managed a grin, recalling Jessica's disheveled appearance and stunned expression. She didn't remotely resemble the sophisticated professional woman he had encountered earlier in the week. He approved of Jessica's looks when she was all mussed up like a hard-working farmhand. She appeared more approachable.

With that image firmly etched in his mind, Devlin rapped on the door. "Porter, I came by to ask you out to dinner," he called politely.

"I already ate," she called back.

"Well, then, how about tomorrow night?"

"Not interested," she hollered.

Hoo-kay, this wasn't going well, thought Devlin. Now what?

Tired of talking to the door, Devlin stepped carefully into the flower bed and tapped on the living room window. He could see Jessica sitting rigidly on her leather sofa, staring at the far wall.

"So how about going to the ice cream social with me Sunday evening?" he asked politely.

She turned briefly to glance in his direction, then faced forward again. "I'd rather eat gravel, but thanks so much for asking. Just go away."

When she bounded to her feet and headed toward the kitchen holding what looked to be a plastic food container, Devlin scurried around the house…and came face to beak with the guard goose, which quacked an objection to his presence.

"Well, tough," Devlin muttered as he veered around the feathered obstacle.

Devlin leaned close to the kitchen window to gain Jessica's attention. He had girded himself to be nice to this woman and, by damned, he wasn't leaving until she agreed to speak to him in a civil, rational, mature manner.

When Jessica saw him standing there, she gasped in surprise and clutched her chest as if her heart was about to pop out.

Before she could yell at him, he turned up the voltage on his smile and asked, "Okay, so how about if we take in a movie Saturday night?"

She glared at him even as she backed away from the window. "I'd have more fun dating a corpse," she said before she pivoted and stalked off.

Struggling for hard-won composure, resolved not to drop the reins on his temper, Devlin watched Jessica veer toward the staircase. He glanced at the rickety lattice and second-story balcony and decided to go for it. Never let his brother say that Devlin hadn't done all within his power to make amends with the dragon lady.

Tossing aside the rose stems, Dev stepped upon the supporting beam of the trellis, then hauled himself to the roof. He grabbed the base of the balcony railing to hoist himself upright, stepped over to the warped door, then rapped lightly on it.

Jessica shrieked in alarm. "Are you trying to spy on me while I'm undressing to take a bath, you pervert?" she asked huffily. "Be warned. Sheriff Osborn is definitely going to hear about this!"

"Calm down a minute, Blondie," he called before she made a grab for the phone. "I'm only trying to be neighborly and make amends for my prank. Only it wasn't exactly a prank, because I was trying to muffle the jungle sounds so my cattle wouldn't bolt and run again. And thank you for trenching your pond dam. My brother and I sincerely appreciate it." He tried out another charming smile. "If you'll only let me come in so we can sit down and work out our differences—"

"No," she interrupted.

Devlin noted Jessica was a decisive kind of person. She didn't take time to consider his offer, just cut him off with an unequivocal no. He, however, wasn't leaving until they negotiated some kind of truce.

"I want to talk to you, Porter. You might as well accept the fact that you aren't getting rid of me easily."

"Then I'm calling the cops, Peeping Tom!" she threatened loudly.

When he saw her lunge for the phone, Devlin tried to open the door. Unfortunately, his foot went through a rotted board on the balcony, and he staggered to regain his balance. He howled in alarm when the rickety railing gave way behind him.

Devlin cartwheeled across the sloped roof, clawing desperately for a handhold—and found none. When he took a header off the roof, he attempted to twist in midair so he could draw his legs beneath him.

Waste of time. The crape myrtle shrub that shaded the back porch came at him at alarming speed.

"Argh!" He landed spread-eagle in the bush, ripping a hole in the elbow of his brand-spanking-new shirt. Swearing and thrashing, he tried to dislodge himself from the shrub.

"Are you all right?"

Devlin twisted sideways to see Jessica standing on the broken balcony, staring at him with a mixture of amusement and concern. When she broke into a full-fledged smile, the frustration seeped right out of him. Damn, she had an engaging smile that affected every feature on her bewitching face.

He lay there, dazzled by the effect of her smile, wishing something besides his clumsiness was the cause of it. Despite his embarrassing position in the shrub, he grinned at her, hoping to assure her that he was capable of laughing at his own foolishness.

For a few moments their gazes locked and they smiled easily at each other.

Then, to his complete bemusement, her expression closed, her back stiffened and she stepped away from the broken railing.

"I'd like you to leave, Callahan. I want to take a bath without being spied on. I want to go to bed so I can get some rest."

Devlin suddenly wanted to go to bed himself, but getting some rest was far down on his list—after seeing his neighbor in a totally different light. Damn, he couldn't believe how quickly desire had hit him. Came right out of nowhere and nailed him the instant her face lit up in a dazzling smile. His perception of her changed in a heartbeat.

"I hope I can count on you not to serenade me and my exotic animals with that hillbilly music tonight. I don't think I can go another night without sleep."

Having said that, she wheeled like a soldier on parade and marched into the house. He heard the door slam shut behind her. Whatever ground Devlin thought he'd gained for that split second out of time was lost forever.

Cursing the temperamental woman and his attraction—which was apparently one-sided and a total waste of time—Devlin squirmed out of the shrubbery, dusted himself off, then panned the area to see that dozens of pens and cages, shaded by groves of trees, sat a hundred yards from the house. When the goose honked at him, the caged animals struck up their usual racket.

"To hell with this," Devlin grumbled as he limped around the house to return to his truck. "The ball is in her court now. I tried my best to call a truce."

Propelled by self-righteous irritation, Devlin

hopped in his truck and sped off, then remembered that he hadn't unplugged the extension cord. He stamped on the brake, whipped around and backed into the driveway beside the pasture gate. Within five minutes he had disconnected the extension cord from the outdoor outlet on the electric pole, packed up the stereo and headed home.

He had tried the direct, confrontational approach, then the charming, tactful approach with Porter. The only option left was to beg forgiveness. But Devlin had vowed seven years ago that he wouldn't beg a woman for anything, not after Sandi had hurt and embarrassed him and left him to deal with small-town gossip while she sauntered off to the big city on the arm of her new lover. As for Jessica Porter, she could sit on her forty acres and rot, for all he cared—as long as she did it quietly!

JESSICA SCRUBBED her hands over her face and cursed herself soundly for freezing up the moment Callahan had flashed her an honest-to-goodness smile. It had made her protective armor crack wide open and her heart slam against her ribs—and stick there. Even worse, her reaction to him inspired dangerously reckless and tempting feelings. Being hurt and humiliated in the past, Jessica was wary of men, and she had a tendency to back off the instant her hardened resolve began to soften up.

Reluctantly, Jessica smiled at the image of Devlin sprawled in the shrubs. She had to admit that his smile hadn't seemed predatory, manipulative or cajoling. He'd seemed natural, willing to admit that he'd looked pretty silly. It was at that precise moment, when Devlin had looked his most vulnerable and human, that he became devastatingly attractive to her. In that instant she had liked him, liked the looks of him, reacted to his boyish grin.

That was also the precise moment when Jessica felt most vulnerable, feared that a disaster was waiting to happen. Given her history with Rex, she knew she had a weakness for rugged, athletic men. She thought she had known Rex well enough to trust him, but she had been wrong. Humiliatingly, mortifyingly wrong. She knew even less about Callahan, except that he was persistent, that he could laugh at himself, that he didn't always take himself so seriously.

Yet Jessica suspected that Devlin had come by to kiss up to her, making an effort to mend fences. The fact that he probably had to put forth an effort made her leery—and yes, a little disappointed that it was such a chore for him to be nice to her. She couldn't afford to feel anything, especially not fierce sexual attraction to a man who wasn't totally honest and sincere.

Jessica inhaled a steadying breath and discarded all thoughts of the handsome cowboy. She had a weekend jam-packed with strenuous work and she desperately needed rest.

Jessica peeled off her clothes on the way to the bath and sank into the steamy water, letting her mind drift where it would. Her eyes popped open when Devlin's smiling face materialized out of nowhere. She banished his image and scrubbed herself squeaky clean.

Wrapped in an oversize towel, Jess padded to her bedroom and plunked on the bed. She fell asleep while mentally listing the chores that needed her attention this weekend...and she was too far gone to banish that cowboy's smiling image when he followed her into forbidden dreams.

THUNDER RUMBLED overhead as Jessica sped down the gravel road toward home. After mowing five acres of weeds and brush, she had changed into her business suit and made a hurried trip into town to restock microwavable meals. She had yet to hook the chain to her car and move the big cat cages farther west. If she didn't complete the task quickly, she predicted she'd be mired in mud and forced to ask her nearest neighbor to pull her out.

As if he'd lift a hand to help, she mused as she watched lightning spike from the low-hanging clouds. Last night had pretty much nixed her chances of a civilized friendship with Devlin. In spite of that, Jess detoured by his ranch to apologize for dismissing him so rudely and to insure Devlin hadn't suffered serious injury in his fall into the shrubbery. He hadn't been home to hear the polite apology she had rehearsed.

Thunder rumbled again, and huge raindrops pelted the windshield. Jessica increased her speed, hoping to outrun the storm so she could feed her animals before the sky opened up.

A half mile from home the rear tire blew out. Jessica gripped the wheel to steer toward the side of the road. "Great, just great," she muttered, then glanced at her royal blue silk suit, matching pumps and panty hose. "What are the chances of changing the tire without ruining this suit?"

Scowling at her damnable luck, Jess climbed from the car, then opened the trunk. Fat raindrops splattered on her back and hips as she bent to rummage in the trunk for the jack and doughnut tire. By the time she wrestled the tire from the trunk she had grime stuck to her jacket and skirt.

Hunkering down, Jess groaned and strained to work the lug nuts loose with the tire tool, but the darn things wouldn't budge. Bracing her feet, she tried to apply more muscle, but the tire tool slipped sideways, causing her to trip over large chunks of gravel.

"Ouch! Damn!" Jessica hissed in pain when her ankle landed at an unnatural angle. She stared at her skinned knees and shredded panty hose, then glowered at the offensive tire tool.

Pushing upright, Jessica tested her injured ankle. Minor damage, she diagnosed as she hobbled over to retrieve the tire tool and try again. Rain came down in torrents as she squatted to battle the lug nuts.

It was a waste of time.

Hope rose within her when she heard a vehicle approaching, but Jessica cursed colorfully when she recognized Devlin Callahan's pickup. He rolled down the window to give her the once-over, taking in her soggy silk suit, muddy blue pumps and wet blond hair that drooped around her face like a stringy mop.

"Having trouble, Blondie?" he asked around the wry smile that twitched his lips.

"No, I'm doing this for practice," she snapped, certain he was silently laughing—at her expense.

NOTHING was more gratifying for Devlin, after last night's fiasco in the shrubbery, than seeing Jessica doused with rain and mud, struggling in vain to change her tire. It was second nature for Devlin to lend a hand to a neighbor in times of need, but this wasn't the usual, garden-variety neighbor. This was the infuriating female who refused to negotiate the terms of a truce over a peace-treaty dinner.

Fact was, Devlin wasn't accustomed to being turned down flat, and his male pride was still smarting. If Porter wanted his assistance, then she could swallow her pride and ask for it.

"This is the drought buster I've been waiting for. Sure is wet out there, isn't it, Blondie?" he commented conversationally.

"Brilliant, Einstein." She threw the words over her shoulder as she stabbed the end of the tire tool at the lug nut. Devlin could have—should have—offered assistance, but he sat in his truck, watching her fumble with a task that she didn't have the physical strength to accomplish. He kept waiting for her to ask for his help, but after she had rudely rejected his attempt at a truce he figured she had too much pride to request assistance, for fear Devlin would tell her to fix her own flat.

Teeth gritted, Jessica pushed up her sleeves, then grabbed the tire tool once more. She braced herself, favoring her tender ankle, then strained to loosen the lug nuts.

While Jessica battled the lug nuts, Devlin sat there, grudgingly admiring her determination. Few women of his acquaintance would tackle such a task. But Jessica was as independent as the American flag and fully capable of teaching stubborn to a mule. She also had a jalapeño-flavored temper—not unlike his own, which was why he and Jessica clashed at every turn.

Devlin chuckled to himself when Jessica, her patience worn threadbare, threw down the tire tool, then kicked the flat tire in frustration.

"That'll help," he called over the sound of pounding rain.

She lurched, steam practically rising from her soggy collar. "Oh, you...you—"

"Yes?" he prompted, grinning devilishly.

Jessica was so frustrated and furious that she couldn't think of a suitably nasty name to hurl at him. Not that he could have heard her, because thunder boomed overhead.

Defeated, she whirled, deciding to hike home and return later to tackle the tire. She stalked off with more speed than dignity, then instantly regretted her tantrum. Her tender ankle gave way when the heel of her muddy pump spiked against an oversize chunk of gravel.

She skidded across the road, bumping her knees, hips and elbows, then wailed when hellish pain shot from her ankle. Jessica lay facedown on the road as rain hammered at her back. Near tears, she gritted her teeth against the pulsating throb that shot up her left leg to duel with the burning sensations in her kneecaps.

Despite all the trials and tribulations she had encountered and conquered, the triumph of rising above her lowly birth, she was reduced to wailing sobs. This was her reward, Jessica thought broodingly. She lay sprawled on a gravel road in the middle of the boondocks, pelted by rain. To compound her humiliation, the man whose opinion shouldn't have mattered in the least—but did, damn it—had witnessed her defeat. He had every right to taunt and ridicule her, because she had gone out of her way to irritate him every chance she got.

So when Devlin pulled his pickup beside her, she expected him to tease her unmercifully, then go his merry way. To her surprise, he bounded from the truck and dashed through the pouring rain.

DEVLIN CURSED HIMSELF soundly as he swooped to scoop up Jessica. The moment he saw her ankle give way on the uneven gravel, saw her skid on her knees and elbows, he knew that he was personally responsible for her injuries. Damnation, why hadn't he ignored his battered pride and replaced her blown-out tire before she lost patience and hiked off in the rain? If he hadn't wasted time harassing her, Jessica's ankle wouldn't be swelling up like a balloon and she'd still have skin left on her knees and elbows.

Yep, no doubt about it, everything backfired in his dealings with Jessica Porter.

"I won't waste time asking if you're all right, because I can plainly see that you aren't," he said as he carried her to the passenger side of his truck. Carefully, he situated her on the seat. He grimaced when he saw watered-down blood dripping from her shins. "I'm sorry, Jess."

She stared owlishly at him. "Why? I thought you'd enjoy this. I thought you hated me."

"We obviously have our differences, Blondie, and your temper and obstinacy are an equal match for mine, but I swear that I never wanted to see you hurt."

When he shut the door, then trotted around the truck to slide beneath the steering wheel, Jessica stared at him in amazement. She had seen concern glowing in the depths of those eyes that were as dark as a moonless night. He cared that her ankle hurt like hell blazing? He was sorry he hadn't intervened before she injured herself?

Pain, frustration, temper and exhaustion combined to put tears in her eyes. Lordy, she hadn't cried since she was a frightened kid who had been uprooted from one set of foster parents and passed along to another. She'd become tough, resilient...and she was on the verge of blubbering like a damn baby!

"Hurts, huh?" Devlin murmured as he shifted into drive, then started off. Involuntarily, he reached over to squeeze her fist, which was clenched in her soggy skirt. "Just hang on for a couple of minutes and I'll have you inside your house. We'll scrub the dirt from the skinned spots and ice down your ankle."

"Th-thanks," she said on a hitched breath.

Devlin flashed a cheery smile. "Hey, no problem. What are neighbors for? I'll have you know I was selected as Good Samaritan of the Year twice. Got plaques to prove it, too."

"Really?" Her voice crackled in attempt to bite back a shuddering sob.

"No, but if Buzzard's Grove handed out such an award I'm pretty sure I would've won, being the swell guy I am and all."

His attempt to cheer her up worked. Jessica smiled past the pain. "I should have asked for your help instead of trying to do the job myself," she murmured awkwardly. "I guess I'm just accustomed to taking care of myself. After the way I treated you last night…" She drew a shaky breath, then met his warm, sympathetic gaze. "I'm sorry I decapitated the roses. That was a thoughtful gesture on your part, and I was inexcusably rude."

"Don't worry about it," he said dismissively. "I deserved to have the door slammed in my face a couple of times. I'm the one who holds the title for rude and obnoxious."

"No, I do," she contradicted, then sniffled.

"Since we both made lousy first impressions, how 'bout we start over?" Devlin suggested as he came to a stop in her driveway.

Jessica nodded and extended a skinned hand. "Deal. Hi, I'm Jessica Porter."

He squeezed her fingertips gently and offered her a smile. "Devlin Callahan. My friends call me Dev. It's a pleasure to meet you."

Jessica wiped her eyes on her grimy sleeve, then waited for Devlin to climb down and stride around to her side of the truck. When he slid his arm beneath her knees and around her waist, Jessica objected to being carried inside. "I think I can manage on my own. The last thing I want is for you to hurt your back."

"I've lifted hay bales heavier than you," he insisted as he hoisted her easily into his arms. "I'm sure you can manage on your own, but why risk aggravating the injury?"

When he unintentionally bumped her ankle on the edge of the door, she shrieked abruptly and coiled against his chest. "Sorry," he apologized. "I…"

His breath clogged in his throat when she cuddled against him and he saw a fresh batch of tears welling in those rain-forest eyes. Devlin swallowed uncomfortably, then cursed his all-male reaction to the feel of her supple body in his arms, the feel of her head pressed to his shoulder. The whisper of her breath stirred against his neck like a lover's caress....

Whoa, boy, don't go there, Devlin cautioned himself. *The lady is injured, and it's all your fault. This isn't the time for an inflammation of testosterone.*

"House key?" he squeaked, cursing the effect her nearness had on his voice—among other things.

Jessica reached into the purse slung over her shoulder and handed him the key. The symbolism of the gesture didn't escape her, and she was a little uneasy about letting this man slip inside her defensive walls. "The door sticks when it rains, which hasn't been very often," she informed him. "You may have to nudge the door with your shoulder."

Balancing Jessica against his thigh, he freed one hand to shove the key into the lock. The door didn't budge when he turned the knob, so he rammed it with his boot heel. Once inside, he gently laid Jessica on the couch and elevated her foot on the armrest. He glanced around the expensively furnished room, noting all the landscape paintings that featured animals as the main subjects. The lady obviously had a soft spot for God's four-legged creatures, he decided. He also noticed the modernized wall texture and fresh coat of paint. Although the old farmhouse looked battered on the outside, it was obvious that Jessica had been busy refurbishing the inside.

When he saw the complete set of how-to books and videos for home remodeling on the shelves, he glanced at her. New admiration for Jessica dawned when he realized that she had made the remodeling improvements herself. The lady wasn't exaggerating when she said she was accustomed to taking care of things herself.

When he ambled into the kitchen to locate an improvised ice pack for Jessica's swollen ankle, he noticed the shiny new oak cabinets and Formica counter. Yup, Jessica was surrounding herself with modern conveniences and luxuries. He was impressed by her good taste and her willingness to work. This old house was coming back to life, thanks to her improvements.

Devlin rummaged through the drawer to locate a plastic bag, then filled it with ice. "Here we go," he said as he sailed into the living room. "I really like what you've done with the place."

"Thanks." Jessica grimaced when he placed the ice pack on her aching ankle. "I haven't had time to refurbish the upstairs yet, because it's taking a lot of time to get my accounting business established. I'm hoping to strip that atrocious wallpaper, then texture the walls in the bedrooms. I'm not too confident of my plumbing skills, so I'll probably hire someone to redo the two bathrooms."

"If you need help, my brother and I take on construction and carpentry projects when farming and ranching chores slow down in the winter."

"You do?" Jessica peered at Devlin, startled by the various facets she had learned about the man in the course of an hour. She'd discovered that he had a dry sense of humor, that he could be gentle and compassionate and that he obviously didn't hold a grudge, even if he was quick to temper.

"Yes, we do," Devlin affirmed. "We remodeled

those apartments on First Street two winters ago and replaced all the appliances."

"That's where my secretary lives," Jessica said, shifting to a more comfortable position. "I've seen Teresa's apartment. You do good work."

"Thanks." Devlin glanced over his shoulder. "If you'll point me toward the bathroom I'll get some antiseptic and bandages for your hands and knees. You might want to remove those shredded panty hose while I'm gone."

Jessica looked at the mutilated stockings and smudged skirt. Lord, she looked like road kill. "Um…would you bring my robe from the upstairs bathroom? I'd like to get out of these wet clothes."

"Coming right up." Devlin climbed the stairs and entered the bathroom, noting the organized array of feminine upkeep. The room had yet to be remodeled. Jessica was going to have one hell of a time getting into the old cast-iron bathtub without putting pressure on her ankle. She needed a modernized shower.

In the medicine cabinet Devlin found the antiseptic and bandages. He glanced around to see the flimsy nylon robe that definitely wouldn't be thick enough to conceal what he was sure was a curvaceous feminine figure.

Devlin clutched the robe and swallowed uneasily, then reminded himself that he was here in the capacity of a caregiver. That's where his attentions were supposed to stop—and he better not forget that.

4

ON HIS RETURN TRIP down the hall Devlin spotted a handmade quilt at the end of the twin bed in a small bedroom. He scooped it up, then made his way downstairs to the living room.

"Okay, Jess, let's doctor those knees...." Devlin stumbled to a halt and stared at about a mile of long, shapely bare legs.

Quickly, he shifted his attention to the alluring face that was surrounded by spring-loaded blond curls. Suddenly Jessica looked about fifteen years old—which made his lusty thoughts seem all the more inappropriate. He should not be feeling what he was feeling right now, shouldn't be wanting what he was beginning to want quite desperately. Hell! He'd found Jess all too attractive when he *didn't* like her. Now that he was warming to her, he couldn't seem to keep his eyes off her.

"Dev? Is something wrong?" she asked when he stood there staring at her.

"Yeah, you could say that." Devlin sank down on the edge of the couch, then opened the bottle of antiseptic. "You're too damned attractive for me not to notice." Before she got huffy, he rushed on. "Now don't get mad at me the way you usually do, because there are some things in life that can't be changed. A man's instinctive reaction to a beautiful woman is one of them.''

When she lay there gaping at him as if he'd sprouted antlers, Devlin muttered under his breath. ''Come on, Blondie, don't look at me like you don't know what a bombshell you are.'' To conceal his discomfort about blurting out the comment—something he had a bad habit of doing Devlin dabbed antiseptic on her knee.

''Geez!'' Jessica wailed when the stinging sensations blazed across her kneecap. Her breath evaporated when Devlin bent forward to blow on the sting and inadvertently blew his warm breath on her thigh. She could feel the blush working its way up her chest and neck to stain her cheeks. When she glanced up to meet those onyx-colored eyes, her heart stalled out. She watched a rakish grin glide across his sensuous lips as he blew on her knees again. Chills of carnal delight rippled to her very core.

''Better?'' he asked in a husky voice.

She frowned darkly. ''Hardly, and you damn well know it.''

Devlin chuckled as he peeled open the wrapper on the bandages. ''Okay, so that was a cheap trick to find out if you are half as aware of me as I am of you.''

''I'm aware, all right,'' she admitted grudgingly. ''I'm just lousy at being as direct as you are.''

''Yeah, well, my brother is all the time nagging me to be more tactful. We may bear a strong resemblance, but he's the one with the charming diplomacy. At least he *says* he is. He's never been all that diplomatic and charming around me.''

"I like direct," she said softly. "At least I know where I stand."

"Spoken like a woman who had a love affair that went south in a hurry," he remarked.

Jessica jerked up her head. "And she doesn't want to talk about it, so don't ask."

He shrugged those impossibly broad shoulders. His wet shirt accentuated rock-solid muscles and a washboard belly. Jessica tried exceptionally hard not to notice.

"That's fine by me. I don't want to talk about Sandi Saxon, the two-timing vamp who dumped me on her way up the social ladder so she could kick the dust of Buzzard's Grove off her heels and land a sophisticated lawyer, either. It's tough being left behind in a small town, hurt and humiliated, knowing your friends and acquaintances are discussing your personal disaster behind your back."

"The woman must've been an absolute idiot."

Devlin did a double take. "You don't like me, yet you're siding with me?"

It took a lot of gumption for Jessica to admit her feelings for him, since she had kept her emotions locked away most of her life. It was like sliding onto an operating table, prepped for open-heart surgery. Furthermore, she had learned not to let her affection show for fear it would be used against her.

"I like you fine, Callahan," she said awkwardly. "That's the problem. You happen to be devastatingly attractive, as if you don't know. So was the ten-timing Don Juan who used my heart as a doormat. If I've been hard on you, don't take it personally. It was unfair of me to transfer my disgust with Rex Cranfill to you."

Devlin braced his arms on either side of her shoulders and leaned down to press his lips to hers in a light, butterfly kiss. But it wasn't enough. Before he realized what he was doing he had deepened the kiss, plundered her mouth, as if he were starving to death for a taste of her—which he guessed he was and just refused to admit it to himself.

Sensations spiraled through him, giving him one hell of a head rush. He felt his arms contracting, pulling her closer. Devlin forced himself to back off and sit upright before he did something stupid, like running his hand down the column of her throat to cup the clinging fabric that covered her full breasts. Damn, this woman had an amazing, spontaneous effect on him. He'd gone from zero to hard-on in two seconds flat.

"All I have to say is that the guy you fell for must have been the world's biggest idiot." He made himself stand up and turn away before she noticed the bulge in the lower regions of his anatomy. "Peel off your wet clothes while I fix your flat tire. When I get back I'll rustle up something for supper."

"You don't have to do that."

Devlin was pleased to note that her voice was as unsteady as his. Made him feel ten times better. "You're right, Blondie, I don't have to, but I want to. If I'd jumped out to fix your tire you wouldn't have twisted your ankle."

"That wasn't your fault," she insisted.

"No? Try telling that to my conscience," he said before he walked into the rain, hoping it would cool him down.

THAT KISS was definitely a mistake of gigantic proportions, Devlin scolded himself as he shoved the pickup into reverse and backed from the driveway. Yup, that kiss was going to be right there between them when he returned. He probably should apologize, but he wasn't sorry to discover that she tasted sweet and passionate and was so damn responsive that desire hit him between the eyes when she kissed him back.

Devlin shook his head and sighed, knowing he had become too direct, blunt and straightforward for his own good these past few years. The lessons he'd learned with Sandi Saxon were still controlling his life to some extent.

After that humiliating episode, he had made his intentions perfectly clear to the women who came and went from his life. Not that there had been many of them. He'd been chased on a regular basis, but he refused to get caught just because he was considered good marriage material. Truth was, it had been a long dry spell for Devlin, which was probably why he'd gone off like a ticking time bomb when he leaned down to kiss Jessica.

Nowadays, if he was attracted to a woman he said so. He also set limitations, because he'd had no intention of getting serious again. He wanted that understood up front.

His mind wandering in a dozen different directions, Devlin stepped into the rain to make short shrift of the tire that had given Jessica fits. Then he hooked up her car to a sturdy chain and towed it to her house.

Devlin glanced at his watch. Thirty minutes had passed, and he still wasn't certain if he was ready to face Jessica again. But there was no postponing the inevitable, he told himself. He'd just play it cool. If she wanted to discuss that explosive, lip-sizzling kiss that rocked his world, then she could bring it up.

Devlin dashed through the downpour, then shouldered through the front door to see Jessica's ruined business suit piled on the coffee table. Thank goodness she had covered herself up with the handcrafted quilt. He didn't need to see her in that skimpy pink robe, because his imagination was already doing a number on him.

"Your flat is fixed, but you'll need a new tire," he said, striving for a nonchalant tone. "Anything else I can do for you before I fix supper?"

"Well, yes, but I doubt you'll want to do it," she murmured, then glanced quickly away.

Yup, she was definitely uncomfortable about that impulsive kiss he'd laid on her without warning. "Your wish is my command, Blondie." *Yeah, that's it, Callahan. Keep things light and impersonal, and maybe you both can relax.*

"My animals haven't been fed," she announced.

Devlin smacked himself on the forehead with the heel of his hand. "Damn, did I ever walk right into that. Now I have to feed the nuisances that started this feud between us."

Jessica grinned, but she couldn't maintain eye contact for more than a couple of seconds. He figured she felt as awkward as he did after that impulsive, electrifying kiss.

"Don'tcha just love the irony of this, Callahan?" she asked.

Good girl, Blondie, keep it light and we'll get past this awkward moment, he mused. "Yeah, and when

I get eaten by a bear you can tend my wimpy cattle herd. I'd probably appreciate the irony of that even more.''

"I'm really sorry about the extra work and all the trouble my animals caused," Jessica apologized. She stared at the air over his left shoulder. "I realize we have a problem, and I tried to solve it by moving some of the cages farther west. But since it's raining, and I can't walk, it will be a while before I can move the loud-mouth animals away from your fence."

"I appreciate your effort. Now where's the feed and who gets how much of what?"

Jessica grabbed a pen and notepad off the coffee table, then made a list of the rations for her exotic animals.

"Criminey, your feed bill must be staggering," Devlin said when she kept writing and writing.

"The association picks up part of the tab, but the rest comes out of my pocket. Not that I mind. The animals are my hobby, and they have become like family to me."

"A husband might be cheaper," he retorted.

Jessica picked up her credit-card bill and thrust the invoice at him. "Think so? My ex-fiancé sneaked a peek in my wallet and jotted down the account number and charged a cruise for two to my tab. He was clever about spending my money more often than his after we started dating." She gave herself a self-deprecating smirk. "Being a number cruncher by profession, you'd have thought I'd notice. Go figure."

"A fine pair we make," Devlin said, then snorted. "Your ex-fiancé wanted to get his hands on your money and my ex-fiancée didn't think I could make enough of the green stuff to keep her in the manner to which she aspired. If I ever find myself on the verge of what feels like love, money sure as hell isn't going to enter into the equation. If the lady doesn't love me for who and what I am, doesn't approve of the same things I stand for, and against, doesn't return my loyalty, then I want no part of it.''

"Same goes for me," Jessica quickly affirmed. "I hated playing the fool."

"There, you see? Despite our conflicts we have something in common. We both got tripped up once in our search for the real thing. And, Jessica, about that—" Devlin slammed his mouth shut and nearly clipped off his tongue. He had promised himself that he wasn't going to bring up that kiss, which had an impact equivalent to the detonation of a heat-seeking missile. "About that list of which animals get what," he finished.

She handed the list to him, and he breathed a thankful sigh that he hadn't crammed both feet in his mouth.

"If you want an umbrella, there's one on the back porch," Jessica informed him.

"Naw, I can't imagine how I could get wetter than I already am," he said as he made a beeline for the back door.

JESSICA SCRUNCHED sideways on the couch, then winced when agonizing pain shot up her leg. This twisted ankle was going to be a major inconvenience.

And speaking of inconvenience, that kiss had hit her with the force of a nuclear bomb—which was very untimely, because she had vowed not to let herself become interested in a man for at least half a decade. Time enough to learn to control her defensive mechanisms, which locked into place when she found herself the slightest bit attracted to a man. Plus, she didn't have time to devote to a meaningful relationship or to get to know a man. The accounting business was hectic several months of the year. And there were always chores and repairs that needed her attention on the farm. When could she possibly fit in time for a man?

Better yet, Porter, answer this question. Despite all your excuses, how are you going to ignore the effects that impromptu kiss had on you? Hmm? Devlin Callahan may be quick-tempered, stubborn and opinionated, but he blew your mind with that searing kiss. Wanna deny it? Go ahead, turn yourself into a pathological liar. Then try to tell yourself that you haven't learned more about Devlin Callahan in a week than you knew about that devious, underhanded baseball jock after six months.

"Okay, so Dev is nothing like Rex," she admitted to herself. "Yes, he's drop-dead handsome, but he also has substance."

Indeed he did, Jessica acknowledged. Although Devlin could be mischievous, he was honest, sincere and hardworking, and he had dealt with humiliation and rejection and survived a broken heart. He was also reliable. Why, at this moment he was outside feeding the animals he wanted packed up and gone. He was willing to do the chores Jessica was physically unable to do. That said something about his personality and character, something Jessica couldn't ignore and greatly admired.

Yet there was still a niggling little voice inside

her that warned her to be cautious. Despite what Devlin said, he might very well be charming her into relocating her sanctuary. At present, she suspected he was operating on guilt because he held himself personally accountable for her twisted ankle.

Did she dare let her guard down completely and retest her reaction to his mind-boggling kiss?

After several minutes of concentrated deliberation Jessica decided to give Devlin the benefit of the doubt. She wouldn't purposely antagonize him to protect herself. She'd stick her neck out a bit, test the waters, let him get to know the real Jessica Porter.

Yeah, she could do that, ease from her protective shell an inch at a time. Besides, she kinda liked the way he fussed over her, tended to her while she was injured. It had been a long time—as in never—since Jessica had felt protected, cared about. Though it might feel awkward and unnatural for her, she would allow Devlin to help her in her time of need. She would be gracious and appreciative—without constantly probing for hidden motives.

Smiling, Jessica snuggled beneath the quilt and closed her eyes to catch a few z's. Devlin was here, and he was taking care of things. She could relax for a few minutes and catch up on lost sleep.

WITH A BUCKET of feed in each hand, Devlin hiked toward the first of dozens of pens and cages that sat a hundred yards from the house. The rain had let up, but lightning still flickered in the distance, indicating the drought-breaking storm approaching from the northwest had yet to vent its full fury.

Devlin drew in a deep breath of rain-scented air

and sent a prayer heavenward, thanking the man upstairs for the relief needed to bring life back to the
pasture grasses and provide the needed moisture for
planting crops. Mother Nature hadn't been kind to
farmers and ranchers the past two years. It had been
a struggle to provide forage for his livestock....

His thoughts trailed off and he halted abruptly
when a growl erupted from the shadowy cage in
front of him. Devlin stared uneasily at the brown
bear that paced its narrow confines. Then Devlin noticed the animal was missing the bottom half of a
front leg. The crippled bear sniffed the air, testing
Devlin's scent, then growled threateningly.

"Okay, buddy, so I don't smell like Jess, but I'm
bringing the grub tonight, so don't bite the hand that
feeds you." Cautiously, Devlin opened the trap door
to fill the food tray. The bear, which Jess had named
Winnie the Pooh, stared him down for a full minute
before hobbling over to sample the vittles.

Devlin repeated the process at the second bear
cage, noting that the animal called Teddy had a
handicap like Winnie's. On and on he went, making
the rounds, feeding the lame and declawed animals
Jessica had taken in. There were four battered cou-
gars, three hobbling wolves, two foxes, a couple of
bobcats, two jungle cats that stared at Devlin as if
he was their meal of choice, three unusual-looking
raccoons, an assortment of peacocks, a boar and a
couple of species Devlin didn't recognize. That
wasn't counting the aviary cage, which was built
around dwarf apple trees and housed a slew of exotic birds.

As he made the rounds with Mother Goose at his
heels, Devlin wondered what compelled Jessica to

care for these animals. He understood why they couldn't be returned to the wilds. Each animal had an imperfection that made it difficult to protect itself from predators or hunt for its own food.

Devlin was thoroughly annoyed with himself for not gathering all the facts about this unusual zoo before he'd gone off half-cocked and confronted Jessica. Maybe this zoo wasn't his thing, but he respected Jessica's efforts to care for and protect these animals.

Devlin was feeling exceptionally sympathetic toward the exotics until a llama strode past him, halted, then spit in his face. "Ungrateful jerk," he muttered as he wiped his cheek on his shirtsleeve. "Expect to have your kibble poisoned tomorrow, pal."

When thunder clamored and raindrops pattered against the leaves of the overhanging trees, Devlin sprinted to the barn to drop off the feed buckets, scattered seed for Mother Goose, then hightailed it to the house. Lightning popped and crackled as he leaped onto the back porch.

Devlin had spent enough years on horseback and on tractors, studying the weather, to know when a full-fledged thunderstorm was about to break loose. This, he predicted, was going to be a real toad strangler. His ranch was likely to go from drought to flood in the course of one night.

The instant he stepped into the kitchen his stomach growled, reminding him that it was long past suppertime. He veered toward the refrigerator to see what he could scrape together. To his amusement and distaste, he discovered the freezing unit was jam-packed with frozen dinners.

Devlin remembered those years when he and Derrick had burned out on packaged meals. They had made a pact several years ago to take turns cooking Monday through Thursday so they didn't have to eat out constantly.

Devlin poked his head in the fridge to find a dozen eggs, bread, cheese and milk. While he was fixing breakfast for supper, he predicted his brother would be dining on a gourmet meal at Cassie's restaurant. Maybe Dev should have made a play for the pretty restaurateur instead of granting his twin exclusive rights.

That was the thing about being a twin, Dev reminded himself. You had to check with your look-alike before showing any interest whatsoever in a female. That kind of sibling rivalry could get real tricky. Thus far, Devlin and Derrick had avoided potentially uncomfortable situations, but they had worked at it. Of course, that wasn't counting that first-and-only fistfight over a cute little babe with pigtails when they were in the fifth grade.

With ingredients in hand, Devlin strode to the counter, then rummaged to find a skillet. Yeah, at this moment he could be sprawled in a padded booth, being fussed over by a wonderful cook and restaurant owner. But for some reason Devlin found himself more interested in the zookeeper who had come up lame herself.

That feisty blonde stirred something in Devlin that he couldn't name. Although she was tough, prickly and defensive at times, he admired and respected independence in a woman. Heaven knew he'd been chased by enough clingy types to realize they couldn't hold his interest.

Now that Devlin could step back and review his first two confrontations with Jessica, he could chuckle about the incidents where zinging insults flew like bullets. They set off fiery reactions in each other from the get-go. If that kiss was any indication, they could ignite explosive sparks of an entirely different nature—if they could put the bitterness from past relationships gone sour behind them.

Humming a country and western song, Devlin set to work on supper. The electricity flickered momentarily, but he managed to cook the eggs and toast before the storm came crashing down like gangbusters.

"Dinner is served," he called as he carried two plates into the living room. When he saw Jessica stir beneath the quilt, her hair a mass of curlicues, his heart fluttered oddly. "Hey, sleepyhead, if I'm gonna wait on you foot and hand the least you can do is wake up and appreciate my efforts."

Jessica blinked like a subterranean creature emerging from a tunnel. When she spied the food she tossed aside the quilt and reached eagerly for a plate. "You cooked?" she said drowsily. "This looks wonderful!"

Devlin inwardly groaned when the quilt fell away and he got an appetizing view of satiny cleavage exposed by that flimsy robe. The damn thing could be the death of him if he wasn't careful where he looked.

"Lordy, real food," she said after the first bite, then sighed in appreciation. "I haven't had any in months."

He hadn't had any in months, either, but he didn't figure Jessica was referring to the same thing.

Devlin forced himself to look the other way when Jessica propped herself on her elbow to balance the plate. The cursed robe gaped, partially exposing the creamy mounds of her breasts.

The lusty side of his nature silently begged her to lean a teensy-weensy bit to the left so he could admire all the appealing scenery.

The gentlemanly half of him strenuously objected. Hell!

"Oh, God, this is fabulous," Jessica complimented after taking a second bite of the omelette.

"Thanks. My brother and I alternate shifts in the kitchen. I've been at this cooking business for several years now. It was a real struggle after we lost our parents in a small plane crash. It's a wonder we didn't burn down the kitchen that first year."

Jessica studied him pensively. "You took care of yourselves? How old were you?"

"Eighteen," Devlin reported, then munched on his toast.

"No family or grandparents to take you in?"

Devlin shook his dark head. "There was a bachelor uncle in the armed forces who stopped in during furloughs, but Derrick and I were determined to keep the ranch going. We already had the necessary skills, but it took time to learn the financial end of the operation. We approached older, knowledgeable ranchers in the area for advice and managed to come through the crisis without losing the ranch. Then we took turns attending college every other semester so we could complete our education, just as our parents would have wanted. It took seven years, but we earned our agricultural degrees."

He glanced quickly at Jessica, trying very hard

not to dwell on the tempting swells nestled beneath that flimsy pink fabric.

Jessica shifted uneasily. She wasn't in the habit of discussing her past with anyone, but she acknowledged that she felt more comfortable with Devlin than she had with anyone—ever. In fact, she had never confided much of anything to Rex, because the time never felt right and she never got the impression that he was all that interested in her past. Turned out his main interest in her was the money she made on her property.

"I don't even know who my parents are," she confessed. "I spent my childhood in one foster home or another. Then I ran away from an undesirable situation because the man who was supposed to be my substitute father began to take a slightly different interest in his role."

Obviously, Devlin understood what she implied, because he muttered a foul oath that voiced her sentiments exactly. "If he laid a hand on you, I'll look him up and tear the son of a bitch apart, limb from limb."

The fact that he cared enough to defend her honor gave Jessica a warm, fuzzy feeling. "I appreciate the offer, but I saw it coming and skipped out. When I graduated high school I took a job as a waitress, then figured that if I wanted to get anywhere in this world I needed more education."

Jessica relaxed when Devlin nodded and smiled. He wasn't the least bit judgmental, thank goodness. Of course, she hadn't gone into detail about living a hand-to-mouth existence, hadn't mentioned the near misses with men who waited like vultures to take advantage of a vulnerable woman living on her own.

"Tough way to grow up, I expect," he commented as he reached out to brush corkscrew curls behind her ear.

"You don't know the half of it."

"Any time you feel like getting it off your chest, I'm willing to listen, Jess. I want you to know that."

Head downcast, she fiddled with her robe. "Thanks."

Having seen Jessica's zoo of outcasts and hearing the boiled-down version of her life story, Devlin figured she was accustomed to keeping her own counsel. He knew she felt a close attachment to the stray animals who lived on her forty acres. He also suspected that she considered herself like them.

Feelings of tenderness and compassion for this woman overcame him. He understood why she thought it was necessary to put up that tough, keep-your-distance front. No doubt, that defensive attitude was essential in getting her through the unsung ordeals in her life. She had admitted that she was unaccustomed to being cared for. He also remembered what Reed Osborn said about Jessica taking in a young woman on the run from an abusive ex-husband, about the generous donations to youth groups and charities benefiting needy children.

Yup, there was definitely more to Jessica's story, he realized. Incidents that made deep, lasting impressions structured her life and made her wary. His protective instincts stirred. He wished he could have been there to make her life easier, though his had been no fairy tale. But a young woman alone? No doubt, there had been dozens of pitfalls awaiting her, dozens of harrowing experiences that made her mistrusting and cautious.

"Where did you collect all your animals?" he asked as he reached for his glass of iced tea.

"Some were placed by the association," she informed him. "Some were brought to me out of desperation. You wouldn't believe how many people purchase exotic animals, thinking they can be domesticated. The jungle cats are especially cute kittens...until they grow up. Then people find a full-size African lion on their hands and don't know what to do with it. It takes special training to care for those animals, and without intensive seminars, the average person is totally at a loss."

"You've had training, I take it."

Jessica nodded. Tangled curls bobbed around her face. "Yes. I've also been taught to look for signs of illness. The local vet stops by once a month to check the condition of my animals."

"I'm impressed."

Startled, she glanced up. "I thought you disapproved of my exotic misfits."

Devlin shrugged. "I didn't say I was all that crazy about ranching next door to your zoo, but I admire your dedication, especially after I saw, firsthand, the handicaps of your charges. I guess a declawed cougar with a crippled hind quarter wouldn't fare well in the wilderness. Kinda like a young kid fighting her way through the jungle on the streets, I suspect. Interesting similarity, I'd say."

Jessica shifted uncomfortably. "Okay, Freud, so you figured out that I see myself in some of those animals, feel a strong kinship toward them."

"How can I not? As I recall, you came at me

with teeth bared the first time we met.'' He chuckled good-naturedly, then winked in amusement. ''Not that I wasn't spoiling for a fight, mind you, because I definitely was.''

''You reminded me of a roaring lion. It was a learned response to fight fire with fire,'' she replied.

Devlin set his empty plate aside, then came down on his knees in front of her. ''How about if we get past our lousy start? I'm willing to admit you are nothing like my gold-digging ex-girlfriend. I sure as hell hope I'm nothing like your ex-fiancé.''

''I'll concede that you aren't,'' she murmured.

He noticed that Jessica swallowed nervously when he got up close and personal. The room shrank to the space she occupied, stealing much-needed air and making it impossible for him to breathe normally. The woman was so darn appealing. Even when she didn't look her best, she was still the embodiment of every man's wildest fantasy. Devlin felt the impossible lure and wondered if he needed a refresher course in willpower to withstand the kind of temptation Jessica Porter represented. If Devlin hadn't known it before, he knew it now. He was wading in over his head.

5

DEVLIN COCKED his head and studied her. "Am I making you nervous, Jess?" he asked in a husky voice.

"Uh-huh," she wheezed.

"Want me to back off?"

"Uh-uh," she said honestly, spontaneously.

"Smart woman like you has probably figured out that I really want to kiss you again. Is that a problem?" he whispered, his coal-black eyes locked on hers.

"Definitely could be the start of one," she murmured, her gaze dropping helplessly to his full lips that were mere inches from her suddenly dry mouth. "You aren't going to take advantage while I'm injured and vulnerable, are you?"

"Funny, I thought I was the vulnerable one at the moment." His gaze dropped, then returned to her face. "Do you have the slightest idea what effect that skimpy robe is having on me? You don't happen to have something in a floor-length terry cloth, do you?"

Jessica glanced down to see that her breasts were dangerously close to spilling from the gaping robe. She made a grab for the fabric. "I wasn't doing that on purpose."

"I know. That's what makes you all the more appealing to me," he admitted hoarsely.

"Yeah?" Her breath hitched when he inched nearer.

"Yeah, and I'm going to kiss you now."

Having made his intentions known, and giving her a second to object—which she didn't, thank goodness—Devlin tasted her rosebud lips and experienced the same dizzying head rush that had assailed him earlier. He wasn't sure if the sound he heard was pounding rain or his heart thrumming in his ears. Didn't matter, really. The effect was the same—it drowned out everything except the hot, mushy sensations that spread through every nerve and muscle in his body. Even his wet clothes couldn't cool him down when Jessica looped her arms around his neck and kissed him back. He was burning alive in the time it took to draw breath—one so thick with her unique scent that every sensible thought launched into orbit around Pluto.

When Jessica drew him closer, the peaks of her breasts teasing his chest, Devlin deepened the kiss. He eased her back on the sofa and heard the forgotten plate thunk on the carpet. His knee slid between her legs, ever mindful of her elevated left ankle. He knew she felt the throbbing length of his arousal against her thigh, but she made no protest when he pulled her flush against him and made a feast of her lips.

Suddenly, everything went dark and silent—except for the hot and heavy breathing that echoed in Devlin's ears. He fell into the depths of a blazing kiss that spoke of passion threatening to burst from its dormant confines.

This kiss was even more chemically charged than the first, he realized. He couldn't even remember the last time he'd felt so involved, so hungry that he trembled with wanting. Sandi Saxon had never kissed him like this, left him feeling as if he was feeding her desire and she couldn't get enough of him.

The feelings were mutual. Devlin couldn't get enough of the taste of Jessica, either. The need to touch and explore her shapely contours was overwhelming. He slid his hand downward to trail his fingertips over one taut nipple.

She gasped, and he groaned. When he teased the turgid peak with thumb and forefinger he heard a wobbly moan escape her, felt the ripple of her desire echo through him. Heady from the feeling of male power he wielded, he bent his head to flick his tongue over the other nipple. She arched toward his caressing hand and seeking lips, and another jolt of desire sizzled through him.

There was something incredibly satisfying about arousing Jessica. He yearned to hear more of those breathless sounds he could summon from her. Devlin ached to get his greedy hands—and lips—on every inch of her lush body. He longed to know her by touch and scent and follow this unexpected interlude to its natural conclusion.

How'd he get so lost in a woman so fast? He'd spent years avoiding encounters that put his heart at risk and left his male pride in shambles. And then, wham! He was down on his knees—figuratively and literally—willing to take another chance with this woman who appealed to him on so many different levels.

The muffled ring of a phone finally registered in Devlin's windmilling brain. Cursing the interruption, he lifted his head to note that every light in the house was off, along with the television. There was utter darkness and silence—except for the heavy breathing still going on.

"My purse." Jessica croaked like a waterlogged bullfrog.

"Huh?" he said, dazed.

"Cell phone in my purse. Can you reach it?"

"I can't see a damn thing." Struck blind by desire, he groped for her purse.

"Far end of the coffee table."

Devlin fumbled with the leather purse, then fished for the phone. With shaky hands, he clicked the button, then handed the phone to Jessica. He would have given just about anything he owned to get a glimpse of her face, to see if she looked half as tormented and disoriented as he felt.

"Hello?" Jessica chirped as she pulled her gaping robe together and stared into the darkness, frantically willing her accelerated pulse to a normal pace. She still couldn't believe how quickly her inhibitions had fled in the face of the sensual wildfire that exploded between them. The moment Devlin kissed her, caressed her, she forgot everything she knew. What he did to her emotional equilibrium didn't bear thinking about!

"Boss? Teresa here. The sheriff said he got a call informing him that a transformer had been lightning struck west of town. Do you have a power outage?"

Jessica glanced at the inky profile of the man who had sat down cross-legged beside the couch. Power outage? Nope, definitely a mega surge, she mused.

Nothing wrong with her transformer, but then she presumed Teresa was referring to the lack of electricity.

"Yes, the lights went off...recently." Jessica hadn't the slightest idea when, because her senses had been under sensual siege and her world had exploded in Technicolor.

"You're more than welcome to spend the night at my place," Teresa offered generously.

"Thanks, but I can manage." Jessica frowned curiously when her befuddled brain began to function normally again. "How did you hear about the lightning damage from the sheriff so quickly?"

There was a noticeable pause. Jessica smiled wryly while Teresa hemmed and hawed.

"Er, well, um..."

"Reed Osborn is there with you, isn't he?" Jessica guessed.

"Yes."

"Making a feast of those to-die-for cinnamon rolls you brought to the office last week?"

"As a matter of fact."

"Enjoy your weekend, Teresa," Jessica murmured. "See you Monday."

"I always enjoy my time off," Teresa replied. "But if you need anything, boss, anything at all, don't hesitate to call. I'm indebted to you and I'm anxious to repay you any way I can."

Jessica knew better than to mention her sprained ankle to her devoted secretary. Teresa would have braved the storm and been here in a flash. Her loyalty, though greatly appreciated, could interfere with her budding relationship with Sheriff Osborn. Jessica wanted Teresa to enjoy the attentions of a good and decent man for once in her life. This could be the start of something very promising for Teresa.

When Jessica clicked off the phone she could feel Devlin's intense gaze on her. Of course, she had known he was intense and dynamic at first meeting. It was a wonder she hadn't caved in days ago, considering the astonishing effect he had on her. If tonight was any indication, they would be dynamite together. If Jessica dared to take the plunge—and she wasn't about to commit to anything when she felt as rattled as she did right now.

"May I use your cell phone?" Devlin asked, rousing her from her pensive reverie. "I presume the cordless phones in your house don't function without electricity, and my cell phone is in the truck."

"Sure." Jessica fumbled in the darkness to hand him the phone.

"I'm spending the night here with you," he announced abruptly.

"I don't think that's a good idea," she said. "We've barely known each other a week. And yes, I'll admit the, um, sexual energy flowing around here could generate enough voltage to provide power for the house, but—"

"It's not what you're thinking." He cut in, a smile in his voice. "It's because of the storm and your sprained ankle. The last thing you need is to bang up your ankle in the darkness. Besides, you already told me not to take advantage while you're laid up and feeling vulnerable. Remember?"

"Oh." She wasn't sure if she was disappointed or relieved.

"Which is another reason you don't have to

worry about us ending up in bed together so soon,''
he murmured as he reached out to trace her lips—
and accidentally poked her in the eye. "Sorry about
that."

"That's okay. It doesn't hurt as much as my ankle."

"That's why I'm being so damn noble," he informed her. "I'd probably end up hurting you and
I feel bad enough about your injury already."

"I keep telling you that isn't your fault. And if
this is all about guilt—"

This time he found her lips with unerring accu-
racy. His mouth came down on hers with an urgency
she understood all too well. It was a long moment
before they found the urge to come up for air.

"Does this feel like guilt to you, darlin'?" he
asked. "You make me hot all over. You've managed
to dry my clothing from inside out."

"Devlin—"

"I know. Too blunt and candid again. My brother
swears it's one of my worst faults."

"I think it's one of your most admirable traits,"
she insisted. "I like your honesty, even if I don't
always agree with everything you say."

"You don't agree that we could burn down both
ends of the night if we went to bed together?" he
asked after a moment.

Jessica wasn't accustomed to straightforward
men. Rex was anything but. She felt self-conscious,
and it required courage for her to come right out and
confide what she was feeling. "I don't question the
fact that we're both pyromaniacs," she said, striving
for a light tone. "I'm just not in the habit of jumping

into bed with a man. There is a reason Rex wasn't loyal to me. The truth is—''

He pressed his fingertips to her lips to shush her. ''I don't care about your past relationships. I care about how you make me feel, how I make you feel.''

''I agree, but there is something—''

When his lips settled gently on hers, Jessica felt herself melt into the sofa. All too soon Devlin lifted his head, sighed audibly, then withdrew.

''I'll never get that phone call made if I start kissing you. Damn, Blondie, I'm having a hell of a time keeping my hands off you.''

Jessica listened to him punch in numbers. She wondered what happened to the staunch defenses she'd relied on for years. They had dissolved at first touch, and she felt unbelievably vulnerable and positively reckless with Devlin.

''Derrick? It's me,'' Devlin said when his brother picked up the phone.

''Anybody ever tell you that you have miserable timing?''

Devlin grinned. He'd obviously interrupted Romeo Callahan while he was doing his best work. Good. Served Mr. I'm-Older-and-Smarter-and-I-Always-Do-Everything-Right right. ''I assume you're in town, waiting out the storm.''

''So?'' Derrick asked defensively.

''Is this an example of your enviable tact, bro?'' Devlin taunted.

''Go to hell. What do you want?''

''Just called to let you know that the electricity is off. Jessica sprained her ankle and I'm staying here to play nursemaid.''

''The feud must be easing up,'' Derrick surmised.

"Yeah, we can now have a conversation without yelling at each other," Devlin reported. He wasn't about to confide to his brother that their kisses were as explosive and devastating as their arguments.

"That's progress for you. Glad to hear it. Is that all that's going on over there in the dark? I'm beginning to get some very intense vibrations."

There were times, like now, when Devlin wished the telepathic communication he and Derrick had developed over the years wasn't so acute. Well, except for the time when Derrick had been bucked off a cantankerous horse and suffered a concussion. Devlin had instinctively known his brother was in trouble and raced off to find him.

"I'll be back at the house in the morning," Devlin informed him. "Don't forget we volunteered to set up the tables and chairs for the ice cream social at church."

"Right. Um…I'll meet you there after lunch."

Devlin disconnected, then rose to his feet. "I recommend that you sleep in your downstairs guest room. Do you need to make a pit stop in the bathroom before I tuck you in bed?"

The darkness didn't entirely conceal her embarrassment, but she didn't object when Devlin scooped her up and carried her down the hall. "Watch where you're going," she cautioned. "My ankle is throbbing something fierce. If I bang it against the wall, I refuse to be responsible for blowing out your eardrums when I scream bloody murder."

"Maybe I should have asked where to find a lantern or flashlight first," he said as he inched cautiously down the hall.

"In the drawer of the nightstand in my upstairs bedroom," she directed. "First door on the right."

"Which side of the bed?"

"West."

Devlin navigated into the downstairs bathroom without slamming Jessica's ankle against the wall, then set her on her feet. "I'll be back in a jiffy."

Feeling his way down the hall, Devlin waited for a flash of lightning before tackling the mountain of steps. Rain hammered incessantly at the windows as he climbed the stairs to locate Jessica's room.

Man, this storm sounds like hell breaking loose, he mused as he moved blindly across the room to retrieve the flashlight.

Once he could see his surroundings he took a moment to survey Jessica's bedroom. Nothing had been done in the way of renovation, but the room was spacious. It was decorated with a colorful patriotic comforter and pillow shams. He noticed that Jessica carried out the patriotic theme with knickknacks and photographs hanging on the wall. There wasn't a family photo anywhere in the room. It saddened him to think that she had grown up on the move, never feeling as if she had anyone to count on when the chips were down.

Devlin had a treasure trove of fond memories of his parents from childhood, and Jessica had virtually nothing.

He also agreed that the wallpaper in this room was hideous.

Devlin hurried downstairs to put Jess to bed. "Here I come, ready or not," he announced before he entered the bathroom.

Jessica steadied herself against the sink, her left

leg upraised. Her face was white as cornstarch. It only took one glance to realize her ankle was killing her.

"Did you take something for the pain?" he questioned.

She nodded. Corkscrew curls jiggled around her ashen face. "Yes, but it hasn't had time to take effect."

"I'll get another ice pack after I get you situated." He lifted her carefully into his arms, then strode into the guest room. "Tomorrow, while I'm in town, I'll pick up some crutches. Make a list of anything else you might need."

Say, a supply of contraceptives?

Don't think about that, Callahan!

Okay, but it never hurts to be prepared, just in case.

She grasped his hand as he tucked the quilt around her. "Devlin?"

He cleared his throat and discarded his lusty thoughts. "Yeah?"

"I really appreciate your kindness and your help. I'm...well, I don't have much practice at being grateful, so if I don't say thank-you often enough, it's only because I haven't had a chance to get good at it."

He bent to graze her lips, then forced himself to withdraw. "You're welcome."

When Devlin returned with a fresh ice pack, then dropped another kiss to her lips, he felt the pleasurable sensations chip away at his heart.

"I'll be upstairs in your bed if you need anything. Just holler and I'll be here in a flash," Devlin murmured huskily.

"Thank you." Her voice crackled like static on a phone line.

"'Night, Blondie," he murmured before he turned and walked away.

JESSICA FOUND HERSELF pampered the following week. She had only to look as if she was in need and Devlin saw that her every whim was met. Although he complained that the llama spit at him every chance it got, he dutifully fed the animals, cleaned the pens and hooked several cages to his four-wheel-drive pickup to relocate them near the west border of her property.

Devlin watched over her like a guardian angel each time she hobbled around on the crutches he provided—at his expense, because he insisted he was responsible for her injury. If Jessica wanted to go outdoors for fresh air and a visit with her exotic charges, Devlin carried her down the steps to the cages and allowed her all the privacy she wanted.

When he didn't have time to cook in between tending his ranch chores and hers, he showed up at the door with foam boxes heaped with delicious food he'd picked up at the new café, called Cassie's Place. The man saw to her every need with such cheerful efficiency that it was impossible for Jessica not to admire and respect his willingness to lend a helping hand.

Since Teresa had delivered several files from the office, Jessica didn't have to worry about getting behind on her work. Between Teresa bending over backward to make Jessica's recuperation easier and Devlin becoming Johnny-on-the-spot, she wanted for nothing. She grew accustomed to being fussed over—to some extent, anyway.

The only disappointment Jessica suffered was Devlin's gentlemanly behavior—and who would've thought any woman would complain about something like that! Since the night he promised to keep his hands off her, he had been the perfect gentleman. Too perfect. Now that Jessica had accepted the fact that she was wildly attracted to the ruggedly handsome cowboy, she wouldn't object to his brand of TLC. Yet long-held inhibitions prevented her from initiating romantic contact.

And so, for a week, Devlin came and went from her house without offering a single kiss and only incidental touches. It made her wonder if he'd grown tired of her while her fascination for him multiplied by leaps and bounds. It wasn't very flattering to be all puckered up and waiting for tantalizing kisses that never came her way.

By far, the most exhausting day Jessica endured was the day of the field trip. She hobbled around on her crutches, spouting off information about the natural habitats and habits of the exotic animals in her care. By the time the students loaded up on the bus and waved farewell, Jessica's ankle was throbbing in rhythm with her pulse. She banged her tender leg climbing in and out of the bathtub, and she was tired and cranky by the time Devlin arrived, bearing trays of steaming food from the café.

"Told you that you should have rescheduled that field trip," he said as he placed roast beef, mashed potatoes, gravy and corn on the cob on the coffee table. "You look wrung out, Jess." He inspected her ankle, then frowned. "You definitely spent too much time on your feet. Told you—"

"Finish that sentence and you'll be wearing this roast beef, buster," she threatened. "I screwed up, okay? Deal with it. I am."

"And so cheerfully, too," he observed, his sensuous lips twitching.

"Don't you have some place you need to be?"

"Are you sick of me?"

"I'm sick of—" Jessica shut her trap before she blurted that she was starving to death for a kiss and he didn't act the least bit interested in taking up where they left off the previous week.

"Sick of what?" he prompted, studying her speculatively.

She shrugged as nonchalantly as she could manage. "Nothing. I'm just in a foul mood."

"Really? I hadn't noticed," he said with a wry smile.

They ate in companionable silence while watching the news broadcast, then Devlin tidied up the kitchen, as had become his habit.

"I have some catching up to do around the ranch, then I'll be gone a couple of days," he announced. "If you need anything, call your secretary. As devoted as she is, she'll probably move heaven and earth to insure that you have whatever you want."

When Devlin turned to leave, disappointment crashed down on Jessica. That was it? He was leaving? Not a goodbye kiss, not, I'll call you while I'm gone? Not even, I'll see you when I get back? Zilch, zip, nada?

"Stay off your feet as much as possible," he ordered as he opened the front door. "Take care of yourself, Blondie."

Then he was gone. Just like that. Poof!

Jessica stared at the door, felt silence descend. Funny, she'd never minded being alone before. Now, loneliness closed in around her like a suffocating cloud of smoke.

What had gone wrong? Was it something she'd said? Something she'd done? Something she hadn't done? Damn, maybe she'd been right all along. Maybe Devlin had been operating on guilt since her injury. Now, he figured he'd repaid her satisfactorily and was anxious to go his own way. If that was true, then why hadn't he tried to sweet-talk her into giving up her sanctuary so his livestock would have some peace and quiet? That's what she would have expected.

Her leg throbbing, her heart aching, Jessica plunked against the leather sofa and listened to the sound of silence crowd in on her. Devlin—that devil—had made his presence felt in every room of her home. He'd left, but the memory of the kind, caring, conscientious man she'd spent the past week with was still here, tormenting her.

The longer Jessica sat there the more she wondered if the reason her engagement with Rex failed miserably, the reason this…well, whatever this thing with Devlin was, failed, was because of her. Maybe she didn't have what it took to create a strong, lasting relationship with a man. Maybe her dominant personality worked like insect repellent. Maybe she needed to express her feelings openly on occasion. Maybe she needed to initiate physical contact.

Maybe she needed to purchase a self-help video

that provided step-by-step instructions on how to inform a man who was getting to her on every level imaginable that she was extremely attracted and growing unbelievably attached to him.

Muttering in frustration, Jessica propped up her foot, which had turned fascinating shades of blue and purple, and endured the numbing sensation of the ice pack Devlin had provided.

Too bad ice packs were ineffective when it came to numbing injured emotions of the heart, she thought glumly.

6

"I DON'T KNOW why in hell I need to accompany you on this trip," Devlin grumbled as he flounced on the seat of his brother's pickup. "What happened? You start dating Cassie and your mind turns to Jell-O and you can't remember the way to Tulsa and back?"

Derrick scowled sourly. "Damn it, I ask a simple favor, ask for a little brotherly companionship during the long drive, and you whine."

"I'm not whining. I'm bitching," Devlin clarified.

Hell! He didn't want to leave Jessica on her farm all alone for the weekend. He wanted to be there for her, with her...even if he suffered another dozen kinds of frustration by politely keeping his distance and not rushing her into the heated affair he wanted. Badly.

This trip, which Derrick adamantly insisted Devlin take, was screwing up his plan of negotiation for more than a truce with Jessica.

And why all the secrecy from Derrick? he wondered. Derrick refused to divulge the reason for the trip. Furthermore, Derrick had been quiet and distracted all week, and his work at the ranch had suffered.

Two miles later, Devlin couldn't stand another

moment of suspense. "What gives, Derr? If I have to make this damn trip I'd like to know why and I want to know now."

Derrick drummed his fingers on the steering wheel and stared straight ahead. "It's sort of personal," he mumbled uneasily.

"Then what the hell am I doing riding shotgun?" An alarming thought skittered through Devlin's mind. "Geez, you aren't ill, are you?" The thought hit him like a freight train. He and Derr might grouse and razz each other unmercifully, but the prospect of Derr suffering made him queasy.

"No, I'm not sick," Derrick informed him, then darted a quick glance in Devlin's general direction before focusing his attention on the highway.

Devlin slumped in relief. "Glad to hear that, bro. So what's this secretive, personal matter we have to tend to?"

"There's something I need to talk to you about...privately."

"We have to drive all the way to Tulsa for a private chitchat? C'mon, spill it, Derr. I'm not a patient man."

"Now there's a news flash," Derrick muttered sarcastically.

"Damn it, Derrick!"

"Okay, okay, here's the deal," Derrick said, still staring at the highway, his long, lean body rigid as a fence post. "I'm, uh, thinking...of asking...Cassie to marry me. I want you to help me pick out an engagement ring in some other town besides Buzzard's Grove, where gossip flies fast and furiously. I don't want the news to reach Cassie beforehand. Plus, I don't want anyone else to know why we're taking this trip...you know...just in case things don't work out."

A gust of wind could have knocked Devlin flat. He stared goggle-eyed at his look-alike. After a moment of stunned silence, he burst out laughing.

"It's not funny," Derrick growled.

"Yeah, it is," he said between snickers. "You've been acting like a man suffering terminal illness all week. You've been so distracted that you hooked up the hydraulic hoses on the tractors assbackward, and you forgot to replace vital parts after making mechanical repairs." Devlin shook his head and chuckled again. "The lovebug bit you, did it? Well, isn't that something."

Derrick rolled his eyes when Devlin cackled again. "I don't know why the hell I expected compassion and moral support from a bozo like you."

"Hey, I can do compassionate and supportive." And he could, thank you very much. He'd been the perfect neighbor, the model caregiver, the epitome of kindness and caring all week—for Jessica. Of course, his male body had suffered mightily, but that was beside the point.

"Right," Derrick snapped. "I'm nervous and uncertain as hell, wondering if I'm going to get shot down when I pop the big question, and you're harassing me. I was wondering how you'd feel about this. It affects you, too, ya know. Cass will be moving in with us. Some changes will have to be made around the ranch."

"Yeah, I suppose you won't want me strolling around in my underwear whenever I want," Devlin commented, grinning. "But then again, Cass probably won't be able to tell the difference."

Derrick glared pitchforks at him. "That isn't funny."

"No?" Devlin asked devilishly.

"No." Derrick's dark eyes narrowed threateningly. "We have a long-standing policy about that sort of thing, as you well know."

"Okay, so you and Cassie can take up residence in Mom and Dad's room with its private bath. I won't prance around in my skivvies. Problem solved."

Bemused, Devlin watched his brother fidget on the seat, as if he had termites in his breeches.

"There's another potential problem," Derrick said apprehensively.

Devlin frowned, trying to remember the last time he'd seen his self-confident brother look so edgy and insecure. No incidents came readily to mind. "Well, what's the catastrophic problem?" he asked impatiently.

Derrick's breath came out in a gushing sigh. "What if she says no?"

Aha, so that explained it, thought Devlin. His brother was twitching at the prospect of rejection. The idea petrified Derrick. Devlin supposed Derrick had watched him suffer through the various phases of rejection when Sandi Saxon dumped on him and figured out there was nothing pleasant about the situation. Well, Derrick certainly had that right!

"Is there some reason to suspect Cassie won't say yes?" Devlin asked, then shot out his arm. "Hey, don't miss the turn, bro. Unless you want to end up in Oklahoma City, you better slow down."

He braced himself when Derrick hit the brake,

then hung a sharp left to cruise up the ramp to the interstate.

"You're turning into a space cadet," Devlin muttered.

"Well, hell!" Derrick erupted defensively. "I haven't been in love before. Lust, yes. Several times. But love? I'm nuts about this woman. Wondering if I should take the next step is turning me wrong side out. Cass says she loves me, too, but what if she isn't in as deep as I am? What if she just wants to stay on this same path of dating for the next fifty years? I want a commitment.... At least I think I do. Does a guy ever truly know for certain? I know I get possessive and frustrated when other men come on to her at the restaurant, on the street, in the grocery store. I don't want to be with anyone else and I don't want her to, either. But what if marriage doesn't work between us? What if—"

Devlin flung up his hand to halt the barrage of doubts flying from his brother's lips at supersonic speed. "Whoa, bro, get a grip. Are you planning to marry this woman just to hold the pack of panting men in Buzzard's Grove at bay?"

"Well, no, but—"

"Because she's incredibly attractive?"

"Partially, I guess. Is that a bad thing?" Derrick questioned earnestly.

"No, that may have captured your interest initially, but if you're in it just for the sex, then you have no business buying diamonds. If you can't get her off your mind, want to spend every spare minute with her, have the same ideals and beliefs, then you're talking a sound commitment and a strong desire to make things work."

Derrick set the cruise control, then glanced pensively at his brother. "Since when did you get so smart?"

Devlin smiled. "I've always been the smart one. Oh, yeah, and I also got my heart broke into about a zillion pieces once, so I've had time to analyze where the relationship went wrong. Problem was I was nuts about Sandi, but I was only the time she was killing while waiting to land the big fish." He glanced intently at Derrick. "Are you Cassie's big fish or her baited minnow?"

Derrick was silent for a long moment, his face set in profound deliberation. "Neither."

"Ding! Right answer," Devlin said, congratulating him. "That indicates you aren't being used. As difficult as it is for me to believe, I think Cassie might actually want you just for yourself, though I can't for the life of me imagine what she could possibly see in a cocky, dim-witted cowboy like you."

The teasing remark served to drain Derrick's tension. He smiled good-naturedly—which was an improvement over sitting behind the wheel like a glassy-eyed robot.

"I happen to have lots of redeeming qualities," Derrick declared.

"Yeah? Name three," Devlin challenged playfully.

"I'm honest, hardworking, reliable, morally sound. That's four. I could go on—"

"And on, ad nauseam," Devlin broke in. "So you are worthy of Cassie's affection, and she is worthy of yours. So go for it, bro. Take the plunge. Buy the ring and put your heart on the line."

The tension returned. Derrick's mouth thinned into a flat line. "But what if she says no?"

"Then she's an idiot, and you'll deal with the rejection. I'll admit it's no picnic, but I survived. You will, too."

"Yeah, I saw how well you endured," Derrick grumbled. "You bit my head off once a day for the first two months, then you sulked for about a year. After that, you never gave yourself a chance with another woman for fear of getting hammered again. If that's what I have to look forward to, count me out. I don't want to play that game."

"I've fully recovered," Devlin announced, forcing a cheery smile.

"Gee, that's encouraging. It only took you seven years to cure the rash that caused the itch."

True, but then a certain feisty, independent neighbor who wasn't afraid to stand up to him, who got his blood pumping for various reasons, hadn't come along until now. For the first time in years—seven, to be exact—Devlin could see a light at the end of the tunnel, feel the sparks of attraction, and he had the urge to go wading in the dating pool again. Problem was, his brother had dragged him off to buy an engagement ring just when Devlin was making himself indispensable to a wary female who aroused his interest and put his sex drive in overdrive.

"This isn't about me," Devlin said, discarding his meandering thoughts. "This is all about you and Cassie. She doesn't strike me as a socialite with dollar signs in her eyes. In addition, she isn't high maintenance like Sandi. But since you constantly claim that you're older, smarter and wiser than I am, I'm sure you already figured out for yourself that

Cassie is nothing like Sandi. What woman in her right mind wouldn't want you?'' Devlin encouraged. ''You're housebroken. You can cook, clean, do laundry and you've made a success at ranching, even during these hard times. Hey, if you want to be a candidate for Best Potential Husband of the Year, I'll vote for you.''

Derrick's broad shoulders sagged, and he nodded. ''Thanks, Dev. So, if I do find the nerve to go through with this, are you really okay with the idea of sharing your space with Cassie and me? You won't harangue me unmercifully if we spend considerable time in the privacy of our bedroom?''

''Well, I wouldn't go so far as to agree to that last part, but yeah, I like Cassie—a whole lot.'' When Derrick frowned darkly, Devlin smiled. ''As in potential sister-in-law,'' he qualified. ''I intend to honor the pact we made in the fifth grade not to compete for the affection of the same woman. I can deal with your wife living in our house. If you want me to move out—''

''Hell, no, never even considered that. Wouldn't, either. It's our home. I suppose we could move into Cassie's apartment in town and I could commute to the ranch. Maybe she would prefer that since she has to spend a lot of time getting her café up and running.''

''You think she would prefer a cracker-box apartment when we have our spacious house paid for? You think she wants to spend all her time in town when she has to deal with customers six days a week? That's a no-brainer. Who wouldn't want a country getaway?''

''Well, I can't just make all the decisions without

asking her opinion,'' Derrick replied. ''I don't want to come off sounding dictatorial or something. Modern women don't go for that stuff.''

''You don't have to remind me,'' Devlin murmured. ''Today's women don't go for the domineering, commanding types. They want a man willing to do his share of the housework, take a hand in child-raising instead of swaggering off to pursue his masculine whims. We're supposed to be getting in touch with our feminine side these days. Whatever the hell that means.''

Derrick chuckled. ''If that means getting to touch the feminine body you want by your side for the rest of your life, then I'm all for it. I'll vacuum, attack dust bunnies, tidy up the kitchen if it means I'll have more time to spend with Cassie.''

When Derrick got that super-duper-deluxe serious look on his face, Devlin braced himself. He knew what was coming, could sense it.

''I'm crazy in love with her, Dev. I can't think of one thing I don't love about her. Except maybe that she razzes me about switching TV channels with the remote control. I love the way she looks at me, the way she makes me feel inside. I love her laughter, her optimism, her smiles, her work ethics. I...love... her.''

Man, Derrick had it bad, Devlin diagnosed as he studied the sappy, lovesick expression that dripped from his brother's tanned features. ''Okay, then, let's go pick out a ring. Hey! There's our exit ramp, you big doofus. Slow this thing down!''

While Derrick swerved into the right lane to exit the interstate, Devlin shook his head in dismay. Any road trip with Derrick was going to be nerve-racking until the man had a ring on Cassie's finger. Devlin vowed to himself, right there and then, not to climb into the pickup with his brother again until he was married. Besides, Devlin had other places he'd rather be. He'd grown accustomed to having Jessica underfoot, learning her habits and her moods, wanting her like crazy and forcing himself to keep a proper, respectable distance so she wouldn't think he was coming on too strong too fast.

Devlin wasn't sure how long he could portray the gentleman when his gorgeous neighbor appealed to everything male in him. He'd vowed to give her time and space, but every time he saw her he wanted her like hell blazing.

Would she miss him while he was gone? he wondered. He sure hoped so, because if he didn't kiss her, hold her, inhale that alluring scent that fogged his senses pretty damn quick, he'd probably reduce himself to a pile of frustrated ashes.

The burning question was: Did she want him anywhere near as much as he wanted her? Devlin wished he knew the answer. Jessica was always cautious around him. If Devlin knew where he stood with Jessica, knew if this neighborly friendship had sensual possibilities, it would make this secretive trip with his sappy brother much easier to handle.

"Boss...boss? Yoohoo, anybody in there?"

Dazed, Jessica glanced up to see Teresa, in a colorful yellow dress that emphasized her trim figure, staring quizzically at her. "Yes?"

"Are you okay?" Teresa questioned. "Every time I come in your office you're staring at the painting on the far wall. Something wrong?"

Jessica snapped to attention, put on her best smile and said, "Everything is fine."

"Then how come you aren't finished with that tax file I've been waiting two hours to type up? You're usually finished with these things in a half hour. Complications?"

Definitely complications, Jessica mused as she stared at the empty Schedule E and F tax forms. For two days—and nights, which were the absolute pits—Jessica had been mulling over Devlin's stand-offish manner and his unexplained trip from every possible angle. The man had taken up permanent residence in her mind, and she wasn't getting a thing done at the office or at home.

This wasn't like her. Nothing had interfered with her work before. She prided herself on being efficiency personified. She was the woman who had it together and depended on no one to supply her happiness and contentment in life.

Jessica had gone so far as to eat dinner at the new café, called Cassie's Place, the previous night so she wouldn't have to dine alone and deal with the insufferable silence in her home. She had met the bubbly, vivacious restaurateur and liked her immediately.

Jessica felt an instant kinship for the attractive brunette who'd gone into business for herself and put in the long hours required to make her venture a success. And it was successful, Jessica knew, because the tables and booths were filled to capacity and the food was marvelous. Cassie had asked Jessica to handle her accounts so she could spend more time with hands-on duties in the kitchen and the restaurant.

Jessica had acquired another client, made a new friend and dined with a crowd. But it hadn't stopped her from missing Devlin, damn it. She felt confused and lonely, and it was all Devlin's fault, curse him. He'd come barging into her life like a steamroller, filling up the empty spaces, the empty hours, making her totally aware of him. Then he skipped out without a word of explanation.

Men. Couldn't live with 'em, or without 'em. Wasn't that the curse of a woman's life?

"Boss?" Teresa prompted again. "Is your ankle bothering you? Maybe you should go home early and I'll hold the fort."

"I'm fine." *Not!* She was confused, frustrated and miserable.

"Okay." Teresa backed from the door, smiling wryly. "Just so you know, you're the only one around here who thinks you're fine."

Jessica slumped in her chair, forearms draped on her desk, and glared at Miss Cheerful's departing back. Teresa's life was on the upswing, while Jessica's was mired in confusion. Teresa was gushing enthusiasm about her budding romance with Sheriff Osborn. They'd hit it off immediately and they were going great guns. Jessica was stuck in neutral and couldn't figure out why. She had allowed Devlin to see the real Jessica Porter, confided her past to him—something she wasn't in the habit of doing with anybody.

Heavens, one evening last week she'd even gone into detail about the difficulties of battling her way through life without a penny to her name. She'd confided the incident that could have turned into rape if she hadn't fought like a wildcat and left a few claw marks on her assailant who'd pounced on her after she completed her graveyard shift at the diner where she worked to pay her way through college.

Devlin had listened intently when she took him into her confidence about Rex Cranfill and his road trips, about the long string of women he'd been seeing, about her feelings of humiliation and outrage. In return, Devlin had explained his romance with Sandi Saxon. He'd told her that he'd been in it for the love and she'd been after money. More money than he had, apparently, because Sandi latched onto an upstart attorney who arrived in town to glean information for a case that made him oodles of money.

Jessica's heart had gone out to Devlin, because she had experienced those same feelings of betrayal and dejection and that deep sense of hurt. She thought they had bonded tightly that evening. Then, out of the blue, he'd taken off on this mysterious trip and hadn't been seen or heard from since. Jessica had hobbled around on foot, and in her car, gathering his stray cattle one evening when the herd had been startled by her shrieking peacocks and roaring lions.

She had understood his frustration with rounding up those spooked cattle. They milled around in circles, staring at the pasture gate she had opened wide. Those beefsteaks on the hoof had turned tail and run in the opposite direction. It took two hours to get those brainless bovines in the pasture where they belonged.

She knew her exotic animals were giving Devlin fits, but she didn't have the heart to ship them off. The animals needed her care. Placing them somewhere else, when sanctuaries were filled to capacity, wasn't easy. It was an unsolvable problem, though she and Devlin had avoided the subject the past week.

Where is he? Jessica asked herself for the umpteenth time. *Why hadn't he called? What did she do to put him off? Why did she attract men who were trouble in her youth and why did she have difficulty settling into mutually satisfying relationships as an adult? She was twenty-nine years old, for Pete's sake. Would she ever get this man-woman thing right?*

"I'm going home," Jessica announced in a voice loud enough to carry to the outer office.

"Glad to hear it. Have a nice weekend, boss," Teresa called.

With the incomplete tax form crammed in her briefcase, Jessica sailed from her office. Yes, sailed, she thought. She could walk with only a slight limp. Her ankle had regained partial flexibility, and pain no longer shot up her leg with each step.

Refusing to face the silence on an empty stomach, Jessica swung by Cassie's Place for supper. Cassie was scurrying around, taking care of last-minute details before the evening crowd descended in droves.

"Hi, Jess. What'll you have tonight?" Cassie asked on her way down the aisle, carrying a tray of steaming fajitas.

Jessica gestured toward the heaping tray in Cassie's hands. "I'll have what they're having plus a diet Coke."

While Cassie greeted every customer with a smile, Jessica observed. She wished she was as outgoing as Cassie. She noticed how the male patrons' gazes followed her around the restaurant without Cassie reacting one way or the other. Jessica envied her new friend's ease with men. Maybe if Jessica was more outgoing and teasingly playful she could have held Devlin's interest.

"Here's your diet cola," Cassie said as she set a glass on the table.

Jessica picked it up, then offered it to the harried brunette. "Here, you look like you need this worse than I do."

Cassie accepted the drink gratefully. "Thanks. Friday nights are hell around here. I've got more customers than I know what to do with. One of my waitresses didn't show up. Claimed she was sick, but my money is on the Friday flu. I had hoped to take a couple of days for R and R, but if waitresses decide not to show up I'll be chained to this place."

"Problem solved," Jessica said, rising to her feet. "I waitressed my way through college, so I know the drill."

Cassie gaped at her. "You'd volunteer for Friday night's rowdy crowd?"

"Been there, done that, survived it." She glanced around the café, which was filling up fast. "Which tables are mine?"

Cassie gestured to the west side of the diner. "Thanks, Jess. You're a lifesaver. I owe you, big-time. I'll pay you——"

"Dinner," Jessica negotiated.

"But——" Cassie tried to object.

"Don't push it, lady, or you'll lose your new accountant."

Cassie smiled gratefully. "Thank you."

In the next two hours Jessica slid into the routine she'd memorized years earlier. She enjoyed waitress duty. She visited with some of her clients and made several new acquaintances. She emulated Cassie's cheerful enthusiasm and ignored a few suggestive glances and comments dished out by male patrons.

The highlight of the evening was when Teresa and Reed Osborn showed up, then gaped at her as if she had ivy sprouting from her ears.

"What are you doing?" Teresa asked.

"Waiting tables. Have a seat. What can I get you to drink?"

Teresa squirmed in her chair. "I don't know, boss. Having you wait on me feels peculiar."

"Deal with it," Jessica said breezily. "I'm helping Cassie out in a pinch, so don't give me any grief or I'll poison your food."

"This is really nice of you, boss. But then, I already know you're an angel ready to lend a hand to a friend in need."

"Born to serve," Jessica agreed, smiling. "So what'll it be, folks? I hear the chicken fajita special is to die for."

Reed Osborn glanced at Teresa, who nodded agreeably. "Fajita special for two," he requested.

"Coming right up."

AFTER WORKING LATE at the office for the second night in a row, Jessica arrived home to face the empty house and maddening silence—again. It was long past dark. She quickly changed her clothes, then grabbed a flashlight so she could see to feed and water her charges. The animals were especially noisy, as if punishing her for being late with their meals. Mother Goose ignored her and swam in the pond for a good thirty minutes. However, her feathered friend eventually forgave Jessica's tardiness and followed her on the last of her rounds.

"I do have to work late occasionally," Jessica muttered at the goose. She panned the cages and pens and frowned warningly. "And the rest of you better put a lid on it, or our neighbor might decide to muzzle you. If his cattle break loose again, he is not going to be a happy camper."

Her lecture fell on deaf ears. The animals were in rare voice, and nothing Jessica said or did could shut them up. Coyotes and wolves bayed at the Indian moon that hung in the sky like a gigantic neon orange ball. The still night air carried the sounds across the pasture, and Jessica cursed when she heard thundering hooves in the distance.

If her attempts to repair broken wires on Devlin's fence didn't hold, the cattle would be grazing the ditches. She remembered what Devlin said about traffic accidents involving his cattle and passing motorists. She was going to feel personally responsible if his livestock collided with a pickup.

Having completed her evening chores, Jessica breezed through the back door, intent on checking the fences and the flighty cattle. She grabbed a quick glass of water, then snatched up her car keys, wondering if she was dreaming up an excuse to flee from this all-too-quiet house. Plus, she didn't want Devlin to return from his mysterious trip to find his livestock scattered, then storm over here to complain about her animals.

Jessica whipped open the front door, then staggered back when Devlin rapped his knuckles on her forehead. He looked as surprised and stricken as she felt. An uneasy feeling of déjà vu settled over her. Devlin was back. He was probably here to complain.

Oh, hell, thought Jessica. *Here we go again!*

7

DEVLIN GRIMACED when he accidentally smacked Jessica on the forehead. "Sorry. Are you okay?"

"Sure, I'm getting used to being whacked on the head."

Devlin frowned warily at her tone of voice, her rigid stance. The No Trespassing signs had gone up while he was away. Damn it, he'd been afraid his untimely absence would work to his disadvantage. Jessica must've decided she was happier without him underfoot, and she was ready to resume her previous life-style—one that didn't include him.

"I was just on my way over to check your cattle," she said. "My animals have been especially noisy tonight."

"I already stopped a potential stampede," he reported. "That's why I'm late getting here."

"Oh." Jessica glanced this way and that. "Well, then…" She trailed off, unsure what to say next. Certainly not what she wanted to say, which was: *Where the hell have you been and why didn't you call? Are you tired of me already, though I'm nowhere near tired of you? Plus, the silence you left behind is driving me crazy, damn it!*

Devlin shifted from one booted foot to the other, then stared at the air over her lopsided ponytail. "So…is your ankle feeling better?"

"Swell...I mean, it's not quite so swollen."
Where the hell have you been? I missed you!

"Glad to hear it." Devlin raked his fingers
through his wind-tossed hair and sighed audibly.
"Has it been long enough yet?"

Jessica blinked, befuddled. "Has what been long
enough?"

"My absence. Too long or not long enough?" he
asked. "Are you still feeling rushed and vulnerable?"

Jessica frowned. He left her head pinwheeling
with his rapid-fire questions. "What the blazes are
you talking about?"

"You. Me. Us," he replied hurriedly. "You said
you didn't want things to get complicated between
us, because we haven't known each other very long.
You said you didn't want me to take advantage
while you were lame and vulnerable. So I backed
off, kept my distance, didn't get close enough to
touch, even though it practically killed me.

"I'm sorry, Jess, I tried to do that Platonic pal
thing while you were recuperating, but I'm going to
explode if I can't kiss you pretty damn quick!"

Jessica gaped at him, amazed at his blunt honesty,
wishing she was capable of speaking so freely. All
the insecurities and feelings of rejection that had
hounded her the past several days scattered like a
covey of quail. The dear, sweet, wonderful man! He
had been doing exactly as she requested, and she
hadn't been sure enough of herself as a woman to
realize it.

"You really want to kiss me?" she asked.

"For starters." A smile softened the tense lines

bracketing his mouth. "But that's nowhere near where I want to finish."

She smiled back. "So you didn't come over here to jump down my throat because my exotics frightened your cattle again?"

"No, not this time," he informed her.

"I see. So this is strictly a kissing type visit, you say?"

"Yes," he said in feigned seriousness. "Very personal and private. Absolutely nothing whatsoever to do with business. If this is a bad time I could come back." He glanced at his watch, then smiled seductively at her. "If you need time I'll come around in, oh, say, two minutes."

"No, now is fine," she assured him.

When she grinned at him, Devlin felt his knees wobble. *Okay, Callahan, she looks as if she is glad to see you. Lay it on the line right now.* "I've missed you, Jess—"

To his surprise and delight, she launched herself at him. Her arms wound around his neck and she pulled his head to hers, then she practically kissed off his lips. Well, hell, if he hadn't been paddling his way across uncertain waters and had simply met her at the door with "I missed you," he could have been kissing her for a good five minutes.

His thoughts skittered away, and Devlin forgot to breathe when wildly arousing sensations pelted him. He drowned in her welcoming kiss. She came alive in his arms, and he clasped her so tightly to him that he wondered if he was dangerously close to cracking her ribs. But hell! He couldn't seem to ease off. He wanted her exactly where she was and he wouldn't consider letting go.

The feel of her lush body meshed to his caused need to clench inside him. He was hard and aching in the blink of an eye—which had to be some sort of record, because no woman had ever had such an immediate, spontaneous, intense effect on him. Her tantalizing scent clogged his senses, short-circuited his brain. He tasted her, devoured her, came up for a quick breath, then drowned in the sweet nectar of her kiss again and again. His pulse thundered like a racehorse. His legs turned to rubber. His water-logged brain swam in dizzying circles. He would have begged for mercy, except he didn't want mercy. He wanted Jessica Porter so badly he couldn't see straight, think straight.

When Devlin heard a pickup whiz by, heard the rattle of flying gravel, he remembered he was still standing on the front porch. Although it was dark, the lights inside the house silhouetted them. Devlin wasn't taking any chances of a passerby seeing him practically giving Jess a tonsillectomy and squeezing the stuffing out of her on the porch. They definitely needed to take this inside.

He set her abruptly on her feet. When she swayed unsteadily, he snaked out a hand to support her. "May I come in?" he asked in ragged breaths.

"Depends," she said, her voice crackling.

"Depends on what?" he wheezed, devouring her with his eyes.

"Depends on what you plan to do when you get in here."

He grinned, then lifted his brows suggestively. "I thought I'd made myself crystal clear about what I wanted. I'm not a patient man, Jess. Never have been. I spent several tormenting nights sleeping alone in your bed, surrounded by your lingering scent, tossing and turning on your silk sheets. It was sheer torture, because my imagination kept running away with itself.

"Then I had to leave town, and I couldn't wait to get back. So you better decide real quick if you want us to be more than neighbors, confidants and friends. I think you know I want more than that. I don't know how many other ways there are to diplomatically explain that I want you, want to be with you every chance I get."

I want you, want to be with you every chance I get....

Ah, that was what Jessica loved about this man. Devlin Callahan had the courage to say what was on his mind.... *Loved?* Good God, where had that come from? When had that happened? During his absence?

No, be honest with yourself, Jess. It was long before that. Like maybe the instant he scooped you up from the mud, took you home and looked after you as if you deserved to be looked after, deserved to be treated with kindness and respect, because you mattered. Maybe it was all those moments when he didn't kiss you, didn't touch you, because you were exceptionally vulnerable, though you secretly wanted him to make a pass so you would have an excuse for being wild and reckless.

"Jess? Is your silence a no?" he asked, watching her astutely. "Am I coming on too strong, too soon again?"

She peered at him, noting his hair was ruffled because she had raked her fingers through those thick raven strands about half a dozen times. His pupils were dilated, which, according to the experts, indicated interest and sexual arousal. Her gaze dipped to the fly of his blue jeans. Yep, definitely aroused. She had aroused him. The knowledge that she had the power to affect him dramatically gave her the courage to reach out and grab him by the collar of his Western shirt. Slowly, steadily, she drew him into the house.

"You're absolutely sure about this?" he murmured, staring deeply into her eyes. "You better be sure because if I come in I want us to get naked together."

"Do you come with a guarantee not to break my heart?" she asked, unable to take her eyes off him.

"Are you going to guarantee that you won't break mine?" He questioned her question. "I'll still be here in the morning. Will you want me to be, Jess?"

Jessica made her decision the instant she saw the sincerity glistening in those fathomless eyes. Yes, he could be Mr. Right, even if he lived on the wrong side of the fence and he didn't much care for her noisy zoo. They could work something out, she tried to assure herself. This was the man she had spent her whole life waiting for.

"I don't think I want you to leave in the morning," she whispered. "The silence you left behind has been driving me crazy."

His mouth came down on hers with an urgency that left her mind whirring like the spin cycle of a washing machine. He picked her up and carried her toward the staircase without breaking the sizzling kiss that seared her from inside out. She clung to him in breathless desperation, marveling at the indescribable feelings of reckless wanting that assailed her.

For a fleeting moment Jessica remembered she had something important to tell him, something he would probably want to know before they ended up in bed together. But for the life of her she couldn't get the words past her lips.

He set her on her feet beside her bed, and his hands began to roam everywhere at once. Her heart pounded like a crazed jackhammer and her body blazed each place he touched, causing her to arch into his intimate caresses with wild abandon.

Being seduced by Devlin Callahan was equivalent to being swept into the eye of a cyclone and tossed in four different directions at once. Erotic sensations buffeted her as he caressed her, teased her, pleasured her, kissed her senseless.

Jessica offered no objection when he peeled away her T-shirt, then bent to flick his tongue against her beaded nipple.

"You're beautiful," he breathed against her quivering skin. "Touching you burns me up inside."

Jessica presumed, knowing how impatient he was by nature, that he would overwhelm her with urgency. But in this aspect of their relationship he was too patient for her tastes...and he was driving her right out of her mind with those slow, deliberate caresses that ignited fires from the base of her throat, around the peaks of her breasts and down to the flat plane of her belly. Sweet mercy! How did he know where to touch, how to touch, to drive her wild?

His gentleness, his attentiveness to her responses and her needs blew her away. Modesty fled when he glided her jeans and panties over her hips and left them in a pool at her feet. He devoured her with his gaze, and though she blushed profusely, she let him look his fill.

"Definitely Miss September and every other month of the year," Devlin murmured, smiling in male appreciation.

He made her feel like a goddess who had mesmerized him. He touched her with amazing tenderness, and she longed to return the pleasure radiating from every cell of her body.

"One of us is overdressed," she rasped as he urged her down to the bed.

"One of us got sidetracked by the gorgeous scenery. Namely me."

Devlin still hadn't taken his eyes off her, couldn't. He fumbled with the pearl snaps on his shirt, got impatient and ripped the garment open. The sight of Jess in the flesh, an endearing blush on her cheeks, took hold of his heart and squeezed tightly. He wanted to make this good for her so she wouldn't boot him out first thing in the morning. But damn, his patience was stretched to its limits—and so were his jeans. She made him ache, and the anticipation of sliding into her, being surrounded by her, had him near to bursting.

Slow and easy, Callahan. Don't blow it now, he cautioned himself. He was going to be there for her as much as for himself, even if it killed him. Death by explosive lovemaking wouldn't be a bad way to go. Not if Jessica was the woman in his arms, he decided.

Devlin finally got loose from his shirt and tossed it aside. He watched her watch him as he unzipped his jeans, then heeled and toed out of his boots. Her cheeks turned ferocious pink when he shoved down his jeans and briefs. Her gaze leaped from his throbbing arousal to his face, then back again. Her rainforest eyes widened when he stretched out beside her. She started to say something, but when he nipped gently at her nipple, then suckled her, her breath evaporated, and a ragged moan bubbled in her throat.

He was pretty sure that she approved of what she saw of him, though she didn't say anything. He wanted to think that the sight of him, the feel of his caresses, robbed her of breath. Now that they'd gotten past that initial awkwardness of getting naked together, Devlin set out to make double damn certain that she didn't regret letting him through the front door and into her bed. He wanted her breathless, panting, aching and needy when he glided over her and drove home.

To that dedicated end, he spread moist kisses over her nipples, over each hypnotic curve and swell of her body. He memorized the feel of her silky skin and decided it was fitting that she favored suits made of silk, because that's what she was—soft and luxurious to the sight, to the touch, to the taste.

When his questing hand glided over her belly to skim the sensitive flesh of her inner thighs he heard her soft moan, felt her quiver beneath his fingertips. So incredibly responsive, so amazingly passionate. Jess was everything Sandi Saxon hadn't been. Making love to Jess taught him the difference in one hell of a hurry. She made him feel like the world's greatest lover, and he repaid the silent compliment by displaying all the tender affection he could offer.

And when he dipped his finger inside her, felt her

burning him with liquid fire, he nearly lost it. She shimmered around his fingertip in the wildest, sweetest kind of caress. He knew, right there and then, that he wanted and needed more. He bent his head and tasted the scented fire of her desire. He heard her muffled shriek, felt her body clench, then tremble in helpless release.

"Devlin!" she gasped, clawing at him, urging him closer. "Oh!"

He moved like a house afire to locate the condom he'd tossed on the nightstand. He'd never moved so fast in his life in an effort to be there when he was wanted and needed so desperately. But then, he didn't recall being wanted and needed quite this desperately by anyone but Jess.

He came to her in one eager, urgent thrust, then stopped dead still when he encountered unexpected resistance. His eyes popped open as he held himself braced above her on both hands. His jaw dropped on its hinges, and he gaped at her in stunned disbelief.

"I swear I was going to tell you," she pleaded, shifting uneasily beneath him. "I never dreamed you were going to make me forget everything I ever knew when you... Well, you know what you did. Drove me out of my mind."

An incredible feeling of tenderness washed over Devlin as he stared into her crimson-red face. This tough, feisty, independent woman was full of delightful surprises. But this wasn't the time to ask a whole lot of distracting questions. This was the time to experience the pleasure they created when they made love together.

Devlin withdrew slightly, felt her untried body respond, then he surged gently forward again.

"Are you mad?" she murmured. "It's not like I'm trying to trap—"

"Shh," he whispered, smiling tenderly. He eased away, and her responsive body arched toward him, as if calling him back. Over and over, he caressed her, aroused her, until she was clutching frantically at him, sinking her nails into his back to hold him to her. He moved inside her, feeling the crescendo of pleasure building. And then suddenly she let go, melted into the mattress and took him with her over the edge into oblivion.

Devlin felt as if he was free-falling through space, bombarded by such intense pleasure that he nearly blacked out. He shuddered in release, then half collapsed to catch his breath. He lay there for what seemed like a couple of centuries, marveling at the utter satisfaction rippling through him. Somewhere outside, a peacock yelped in a shrill voice that resembled the sound of a woman crying for help.

Devlin could have used a little help himself. He couldn't muster the energy to move away before he smothered Jessica. She lay still beneath him, her uneven breath whispering against the hammering pulse in his chest.

"Dev?" she said sometime later.

"Hmm?"

"I really did have every intention of telling you that I hadn't—" Her voice evaporated.

He levered onto his elbows to peer at her. "Why me, Jess? Why now?"

Leave it to this man to ask the most direct and difficult question, Jessica thought. She wasn't sure he was prepared to hear the answer. It was too soon to say, *I fell in love with you and I instinctively knew that the time was right. I know because it never felt this right before.*

"This better not have anything to do with Mr. Baseball and proving to him that he blew it with you."

That he thought she would do something that foolish to get back at Rex, that she still felt something for her ex-fiancé, irritated her. She swatted him on his meaty shoulder to show her displeasure, then glared laser beams at him. "Don't be an idiot, Callahan. I'm a bit old-fashioned and I wanted to wait until I was married. I thought the reason Rex agreed was because he cared, which he obviously didn't if he could cheat on me, repeatedly."

He grinned mischievously. "Just checking," he said, then chuckled when she swatted him again. "So why me, Jess? Why now?"

"Because I like you, damn it!" she sputtered, temper rising. Then she blurted, "Because for the first time in my life this feels right!"

"Yeah?" He grinned again, apparently pleased by the compliment. He refused to let her up when she squirmed and blushed in Technicolor. "How much do you like me?"

"Go away," she muttered, refusing to meet that ornery, smug — He moved sensuously above her, distracting her with tingling sensations. Now where was she? Oh, yeah. Conceited, conquering-male grin.

"I'm not going away. We're both going to be here until morning," he reminded her. "Because I like you, too. A lot."

She peeked at him from beneath a fringe of thick lashes. "You do? Really? Or is that just something guys say after—"

He silenced her with a whispery kiss that caused fluttery feelings to riot, like butterflies, in her stomach. Then he did that thing he did so expertly with his hips. He aroused her, and she forgot the awkwardness of the moment after lovemaking for that very first time. She responded to his erotic, gliding motion, trailed her hand over the corded muscles of his back and gave herself up to the indescribable sensations spiraling through her.

Later, she would find a way to pleasure him as completely as he had pleasured her, she promised herself. She wanted the chance to explore him, to know him by touch and by heart, to learn how and where he liked to be touched, make him burn with the kind of hungry need he instilled in her.

But not now. Now, she could only respond and marvel at the intrinsic sense of right, the unconditional trust she had placed in him—and hope he wouldn't betray her, because she wanted him to be a part of her life. Wanted him to fill up the emptiness he'd left behind when he left her lonely for so many days…and nights.

Now that Jessica knew exactly what she'd been missing, she regretted those empty nights even more than before.

YOU REALLY DO need to get up, Devlin lectured himself sternly. He had chores to do at home—not the least of which was checking to see that his cattle hadn't plowed through fences to escape the loud sound effects coming from the zoo.

Devlin pried one eye open, then squinted at the clock. Damn, it was eight o'clock. Couldn't be, could it? He never slept this late. Then again, maybe it could, considering he hadn't gotten much sleep last night. Sometime after midnight Jessica had overcome her modesty, announced that she wanted to get to know him better—as if they didn't already know each other backward, forward and sideways after hours of mind-boggling, body-tingling, knock-your-socks-off lovemaking.

It was a wonder either of them had gotten out alive.

Whatever inhibitions she'd brought to bed soared off after midnight, because she had turned him every which way but loose in her crusade to please and arouse him—which she had about a million times. Jessica Porter, as it turned out, was a quick and eager student of the art of intimacy. She also got that mighty-pleased-with-herself look on her face when she had him down to begging for her to end the sweet torment of having her hands and lips all over him....

The very thought aroused him, but Devlin knew he had to rise and shine or nothing would get done at Rocking C.

Easing onto his elbow, he stared at the tangle of curly blond hair that spilled across the pillow. His body clenched, remembering the feel of those silky tendrils gliding over his chest, his belly, his thighs. Lord, the things she'd done to him in the middle of the night!

And he'd loved every breathtaking minute of it.

Get up and get moving, Callahan, he told himself again. *You'll be back here tonight, and the night*

*after, because this is for real, and Jessica will have
plenty of time to figure out that you're loyal and
committed to this incredible thing that is going on
between you.*

He reached over to pull the corkscrew curls from
her cheek, then bent to kiss her. "I gotta go, darlin'."

"Is it morning yet?" she mumbled, without opening her eyes.

She smiled a sleepy smile, and his heart flip-
flopped in his chest. Yeah, he could get used to wak-
ing up beside her, kissing her to consciousness after
making love to her until they were both uncon-
scious, sated and depleted.

"Definitely morning," he reported. "You're going to be late for work if you don't get up."

Her head popped off the pillow. She looked
around, as if trying to orient herself. "Good God,
Callahan, I don't think I have the strength to move."

"Sore?" he asked.

Her face turned fuchsia.

"Want me to run a bath before I go? Or would
you rather wait until tonight...when I come back."

How was that for tact? Not bad, he congratulated
himself.

She glanced sideways at him. "Since when did
you turn diplomatic?"

"Just thought I'd give it my best shot. See how
it worked." He trailed his forefinger over her lush
lips. "I want to come back, if that's okay with you.
But if you want to catch a flick in town, or dine out,
we can do that. You know, like that whole dating
extravaganza scene that people do when they're involved. But, as for me, I'd rather come over here. I

don't want to share you with anyone yet. I want it to be just us for a while.... And before you start thinking I want to keep this a secret, like it's sordid or cheap, don't even think it. I'm just being selfish and possessive," he told her hurriedly.

She shifted to her side, then reached up to trail her hand over his bare chest. His pulse leapfrogged, and desire sucker punched him. Lord, he was amazingly responsive to this woman's touch.

"Are we involved?" she asked, not quite meeting his gaze.

"I'd say so. What do you say, Blondie?"

She nodded her curly head, then flashed an impish smile that made his heart cave in. "I was kinda looking forward to doing the things we were doing last night. You know, just to polish up on my new-found skills and techniques. I kinda got a late start in life and all—"

He kissed her soundly, wondering what he had done to deserve the trust and affection of a woman like Jessica. She made him feel hot and hungry and wanted, and he wanted to shout his pleasure to high heaven.

Before he got carried away again—and that was a constant threat when he was around Jess—he forcefully pried himself from bed. "I've really gotta go before the ranch falls down around my ears. I got behind because I was gone longer than originally planned. I'll be back tonight, with supper."

"No, I'll cook," she volunteered. "Where did you go while you were gone?"

Devlin inwardly grimaced at the question he couldn't answer, not without betraying Derrick, who swore him to secrecy. "It doesn't really matter where I went or what I did. All that matters is that I'm back to stay."

She studied him for a long moment, as if contemplating and analyzing his evasive reply, then nodded. "See you at six then."

"I'll be here with bells on."

"And nothing else? That I'd like to see," she said, smiling elfishly.

Devlin forced himself to exit and tried to wrap his mind around the idea of putting in a day's work. But it wasn't easy. Jessica looked so tempting and sweet lying there that he wanted to climb back in bed and forget everything except the fantastic enjoyment he experienced when he was with her.

This wasn't just about sex, he assured himself on his way off the porch. He'd been around the block enough times to know that, even if Jessica hadn't. They definitely had a great thing going, and Devlin wasn't going to screw it up. She had given him the gift of her innocence, her trust, and he wasn't going to mess this up.

THE MOMENT Devlin exited the room, Jessica's smile evaporated. Although she still felt the innate sense of right with Devlin, the fact that he refused to disclose where he'd gone, with whom and why disturbed her greatly. She had seen him wince when she posed the direct question—as if there was something he couldn't tell her. What was that something? Had he gone off to check on relocating her exotics? Or had he been with another woman?

Having dealt with dozens of Rex's convenient excuses and outright lies, Jessica had learned not to be so naive and trusting. Until she was absolutely certain she could trust Devlin not to deceive her, not to hurt her, she had to be cautious with her heart.

Jessica flicked a glance at the alarm clock, then forced herself to get up and get moving. She was meeting a potential client at nine-thirty. This wasn't a good day to arrive late.

During the drive to work, Jessica contemplated possible scenarios to explain Devlin's mysterious trip—one that turned out to be lengthier than planned. None of the scenarios comforted her. Had he been with another woman? Had he planned the secluded getaway before he and Jessica became involved?

Muttering, Jessica pulled into the parking lot at her office. Stewing about what Devlin had done— and to whom—gave her a headache that registered about twenty on a scale of ten. She reached into her purse to retrieve a small bottle of aspirin, then told herself to focus on her job and put her involvement with Devlin on the back burner until after office hours.

But, she added as she whizzed through the door, if that man had betrayed her, lied to her, she was going to strangle him, because she was well and truly in love for the first time in her life. She knew it, felt it. This was so much more fulfilling and intense than her relationship with Rex. Her feelings for Devlin, her need for him, were beyond anything she'd ever imagined or tried to control. She didn't know how to fight it.

Jessica sincerely hoped Devlin was feeling everything she was feeling. Otherwise, she had given him the power to inflict the worst kind of pain, to shatter her heart and to demolish what was left of her feminine pride.

8

WHEN DEVLIN showed up on Jessica's doorstep a few days later carrying a picnic basket, wearing his usual appealing attire of boots, jeans and Western shirt, Jessica frowned curiously. "We aren't dining in tonight, I gather."

"Nope. It's such a nice evening I thought we might take a horseback ride. Are you game?"

"I've never ridden before," she informed him. "There wasn't room in the compact neighborhoods where I lived as a kid for anything larger than a Chihuahua."

A wry smile pursed his lips as he reached out to tuck an errant, spring-loaded curl behind her left ear. "I was kinda hoping you hadn't ridden before. I had visions of riding double so I could teach you."

Jessica surveyed his roguish grin. "Are you having erotic fantasies, Callahan?"

"Very erotic, Blondie," he said, almost purring. His gaze darkened sensuously, sending a warm tingle down her spine. "And they're about you and me all alone in an isolated corner of the pasture, doing all sorts of interesting things to each other." He grabbed her hand, tugging her hurriedly after him. "The horse is saddled and waiting beside my pasture gate."

Jessica went without hesitation. The past week,

with Devlin arriving at dusk and staying until dawn, had flown by at supersonic speed. These days she looked forward to coming home at night because he was there. Jessica couldn't imagine falling deeper in love with this man, but it happened, kept happening. It had reached the point that she couldn't remember when Devlin hadn't been a vital part of her life. He gave her a reason to go to work, to come home. He filled her home with laughter, teasing humor and incredible lovemaking.

Jessica couldn't name a time when she'd been so happy, carefree or content, and she had resolved to take each day as it came and make the most of her time with Devlin. She didn't ask him for commitment, because she'd been there with Rex and nothing good had come of it.

"Earth to Jess. Come in," Devlin murmured, jostling her from her pensive musings. "Where are you, woman?"

Jessica glanced up to see Devlin leaning negligently against a saddled strawberry roan gelding. Her heart lurched at the breathtaking image of this man in his natural element—his sturdy mount behind him, rolling green hills tumbling toward the cloudless blue sky. Lord, how she loved the sight of this man, loved *him*.

Impulsively, Jess flung her arms around his waist, pushed up on tiptoe and pressed her lips to his. "I'm right here with you, pa'dner. It's the place I like best of all."

He groaned deep in his throat, then his mouth came down on hers with lightning-quick urgency. She could feel the hard length of his arousal pressing against her abdomen and marveled at her ability to excite him as quickly as he excited her.

After several sizzling kisses, Devlin sighed shakily, then set her away from him. "Damn, woman, you're turning me into a walking hormone. If we don't get going, I'll change my mind about this picnic and make a feast of you right here, right now."

"You don't hear me objecting, do you?"

Devlin groaned aloud. "You're not helping, Blondie. Get on this blasted horse and be quick about it."

Jessica eyed the strawberry roan warily, then patted its soft muzzle. "Be gentle, it's my first time, you know."

Devlin helped her onto the saddle, then swung up behind her. Sure enough, having Jessica's curvaceous rump nestled between his legs was everything he'd anticipated. Another surge of desire hit him like a doubled fist south of his belt buckle. Torment and pleasure in one, he thought as he looped his arms around her hips to take the reins, then handed them to Jess. "We're all yours, darlin'. You lead the way."

Jessica tried to concentrate on guiding the gelding downhill. It wasn't easy when her mind and body were focused on the feel of Devlin's sinewy strength surrounding her, his breath caressing that extra-sensitive spot he'd discovered beneath her ear. The horse's gait didn't help her concentrate on her riding skills, either. She and Devlin rocked together, then apart, and she had difficulty breathing normally. His fresh, clean scent wrapped itself around her, lulling her into indescribable contentment.

Yup, she could most definitely get used to leisurely rides into the sunset, followed by hot, breath-less nights of passion.

Her thoughts scattered when Devlin reached into the picnic basket that sat on her lap. To her surprise, he withdrew a velvet case. "What's that?" she asked.

"A gift," he whispered against the side of her neck, sending a skein of goose bumps flying down her arms. "It occurred to me that since you don't have family you probably got stiffed when it came to birthdays and Christmas. I wanted to get you something."

Jessica blinked rapidly when tears misted her eyes. She hadn't cried in years, had refused to dis-play weakness in front of anyone. But Devlin's thoughtfulness hit her right where she lived.

"Open it," Devlin prompted.

Hands trembling, she opened the case, then stared, through a swimming blur, at the emerald teardrop pendant that dangled from a gold chain. "Oh, Dev, it's so beautiful, but I don't deserve..." Her breath broke, and she swallowed hard. "I don't have any-thing to give you in return—"

Her voice faded when he shifted her to face him, her legs draped over his thighs. His intense gaze zeroed in on her. She hadn't seen him look this se-rious all week.

"Don't deserve?" He challenged her careless slip of tongue. "What's that all about, Jess? Insecurity left over from a childhood of being dumped in one place, then uprooted and transplanted somewhere else?" He snorted at her perception of herself. "That was the result of irresponsible parents and a fallible system where kids slip through the cracks and come out thinking they're nothing but extra people in the world. That's a lot of bull, darlin'. Just look at you. You're intelligent, witty, successful and attractive. What you've become you owe to your own self-discipline and determination. As for that business about not getting me anything, you're wrong. You've given me happiness, the likes of which I haven't experienced in years, decades maybe. That's all I need from you. Got that?''

Tears bled down her cheeks unchecked. Jessica desperately wanted to believe this expensive gift was an expression of his affection, that she really and truly mattered to him. When she stared into those midnight-black eyes, noted the solemn expression on his face, she did believe. Or maybe she allowed herself to believe him, to believe in him wholeheartedly.

Despite lingering doubts that he was too good to be true, Jessica felt the last corner of her heart crumble. ''I love—'' She caught herself before she spoke straight from the heart. Quickly, she continued. ''This necklace. Thank you, Dev.''

''It's as close a match to your sparkling green eyes as I could find,'' he said as he brushed away her tears. ''Your eyes were the first things I noticed about you.'' He grinned, then added, ''Well, aside from your fantastic body, your spunk and your sass. I admire a woman who stands up to me. Fact is, I've been chased around town, catered to and fawned over by women who see me as low-maintenance marriage material. You are a welcome change.''

''Yeah?'' Jessica sniffed, then looped her arms around his shoulders.

''Definitely a change for the better,'' he affirmed.

He reached around to retrieve the velvet case in her hand. "Let's put this on, shall we?"

While the strawberry roan moseyed downhill, the reins draped over the pommel of the saddle, Devlin fastened the necklace in place. A devilish grin quirked his lips as he stared at her.

"Now what?" Jessica asked.

"Another of those X-rated fantasies suddenly occurred to me. I'd like to see you wearing nothing but that emerald…and me…."

His lips slanted over hers in a kiss that spoke of burning hunger and urgent need. Jessica could feel her body responding instantaneously, and she wormed closer to his solid warmth. His arms contracted, pressing her against his aroused flesh. Jessica decided there was nothing more erotic than being draped over Devlin's lap while the gliding motion of the horse brought them together, then apart. She melted against him in helpless surrender, feeling, once again, that deep, unmistakable sense of right.

This was definitely the man she'd been waiting for. He was the reason she had never recklessly tossed away her innocence for a fleeting moment of sexual experimentation. Devlin made her glad she'd had the good sense to wait for someone special.

Distracted and deeply immersed in a white-hot kiss, Devlin didn't realize they had reached their destination until the roan came to a halt. Devlin withdrew from Jessica's kiss to survey his surroundings, then smiled approvingly at his horse. He wondered if the roan could read his mind. Considering how much time they'd spent joined at the saddle, chasing down spooked cattle, he wouldn't be surprised. Whatever the case, the roan had halted near the isolated pond that sat at the bottom of a grassy draw, surrounded by towering cottonwoods.

Devlin suddenly realized that he wasn't nearly as hungry for the picnic supper as he was starved for this woman in his arms. He wanted to make love to her in these wide open spaces, feel her respond as wildly and passionately as she always did. He wanted to lose himself in her completely, as he always did.

"We're here," he rasped as he grabbed the picnic basket, then dismounted. Never taking his eyes off Jess, he lifted her down, letting her lush body slide sensuously against him until she was standing on her feet.

Her gaze locked with his. "Where are we, exactly?"

Devlin may not have been a rocket scientist, but he was sharp enough to know that Jessica wasn't referring to a topographical location. He smiled tenderly as he traced her rosebud lips with the pad of his thumb.

"Feels like heaven to me."

When she kissed him so sweetly, so tenderly, Devlin forgot about the folded blanket tucked in the picnic basket. He was peeling away clothes—his and hers—using them as an improvised quilt. Jessica suddenly seemed as impatient as he felt, thank goodness. Her hands were roaming everywhere at once, while he caressed her in return.

Devlin couldn't remember how and when they became tangled together on the discarded clothes. Didn't really care. Desire, like a phoenix rising, soared and exploded inside him. His need for Jess had become such a tangible, spontaneous thing that he felt trembly and desperate.

He had mistakenly presumed, after a week of hot and heavy passion that often lasted from dusk until dawn, that he could learn to control this fierce need she instilled in him. Control? Hell! When she touched him, and vice versa, he pretty much lost the ability to reason. He simply responded to the urgency that bombarded him from all directions at once.

He heard Jessica gasp when his bold caresses and intimate kisses swept her. He felt need ripple through her body. She reached for him, urging him to ease the ache he'd created. He had made her want him desperately.

"Please!" she panted as he slid up and over her writhing body.

"I thought I was," he murmured, smiling.

"Damn you, Dev," she moaned when he held himself above her—so intimately close, so maddeningly far away.

When he came to her, driving hard and fast and deep, he felt the wondrous sensations roll through her and vibrate through him. She clung to him while the world wobbled on its axis and the ground shifted beneath him. His pulse roared in his ears as passion took him higher, then higher still.

Devlin pinwheeled over the edge of oblivion like a comet racing to its fiery destruction. Aftershocks of flaming sensations sizzled through him as he shuddered, then collapsed heavily upon her. He clung to her, fearing he would scatter if he didn't.

"Is this normal, do you think?" she whispered.

Devlin braced himself on his forearms and chuckled at her bewildered expression. "I don't think so. What we have here is an astounding ability to express and communicate. You wipe me out, darlin'."

"How long do you think this is going to go on?" she asked.

"You mean if you don't kill me with passion by tomorrow?"

She nodded and grinned impishly.

"I'd say about a hundred years, give or take."

Damn, he was getting better at this tact business, even if he did say so himself. But then, maybe it'd be better if he just came right out and told Jess that he wanted to spend the next century with her, that he was absolutely crazy about her and he didn't want to let go. Ever.

Yet Devlin refused to rush her or scare her off. He wanted her to be certain of him, of herself. How much time would she need to realize this thing they had going was for real, that he would never betray her the way that ten-timing Triple-A slugger had?

Before Devlin allowed himself to become frustrated by thoughts of Jessica's humiliating ordeal with Rex, he eased away to stare appreciatively at her. Definitely a fantasy come true, he mused. Her silky skin glowed in the glorious, angled rays of sunset. The glistening emerald at her throat matched the lingering effect of passion in her eyes. God, she was so lovely that she took his breath away.

Devlin leaned over to drop a feathery kiss to her lips, then stifled the urge to express his affection for her. Too soon, he cautioned himself. She wasn't ready to hear the words he'd refused to speak in seven years. He'd said them, and they hadn't mattered to Sandi. Would they matter to Jess? Or had she simply gotten caught up in the incredible passion that exploded between them and she couldn't see past it, didn't want to see past it after Rex had disappointed and betrayed her?

Okay, so maybe he'd wait a while longer to tell her how he felt. Maybe he'd wait until Derrick quit dragging his size-twelve feet and popped the question to Cassie. Then Devlin could lay it all on the line, explain where he'd gone on that mysterious trip and why. He knew Jessica wondered about that, and he felt guilty because he couldn't confide in her.

Damn it, if Derrick didn't stop pussyfooting around and give Cassie that ring, Devlin might be forced to exchange places with his numskull brother and do the proposing himself!

"Hungry?" he questioned as he eased to his side. "I picked up fried chicken, potato salad and hot rolls at Cassie's Place."

"Mm, sounds wonderful."

When Devlin reached for his briefs and jeans, Jessica playfully snatched them from his hand. "Oh, no, you don't, pa'dner. I have my own X-rated fantasy to fulfill here."

Devlin chuckled as he rolled to his feet. "And what might that be? A naked love slave feeding you supper?"

He loved the sound of her bright, ringing laughter, the sight of her infectious smile. She struck a pose Cleopatra would envy, then flicked her wrist at him.

"Dinner, slave," she said loftily.

"As you wish," he murmured, bowing devotedly.

Buck naked, with Jess whistling at him in feminine appreciation, he ambled over to retrieve the picnic basket. Each time he glanced at Jess she was watching him intently—devouring him with her eyes, was more like it. If nothing else, she enjoyed and appreciated the looks of him, his ability to pleasure her. He hoped her feelings for him would eventually turn to love, because he was sure that's what he felt for her. He just couldn't figure out what to do about those noisy creatures that were, at this moment, serenading them from a distance. Muzzling the whole bunch of them had tremendous appeal. Damn, why couldn't she have settled for a dog or cat for a pet instead of the whole cursed zoo?

Thus far, cattle, sheep and wild animals living in close proximity had been a disaster. Devlin had bit his tongue and kept silent a number of times after rounding up livestock and repairing fence. He'd been trying to keep the peace with Jess so they could concentrate on getting to know each other completely, so they could enjoy stolen moments like this one. But damn it, something needed to be done about the zoo. Soon, Devlin and Derrick would have to channel their time into sowing wheat. Unscheduled roundups and fence repairs would be impossible.

Forcing the troubling thoughts aside, Devlin sauntered to Jess, picnic basket in hand. "Dinner is served, m'lady," he announced.

Jessica took the basket, set it aside, then reached up to caress him. His body responded immediately, as always.

"Dinner," she murmured as she came to her knees in front of him, "can wait…"

When her moist lips glided over his throbbing length and she flicked at him with her tongue, Devlin forgot to breathe, couldn't remember why he needed to. A soundless purr of desire rumbled through his body. As dusk surrendered to darkness, Devlin surrendered to the indescribable pleasure surging, pulsating, then bursting through him like a thermonuclear blast.

He was, he realized, a devoted slave to the love he felt for this unique woman. She could do anything she wanted with him—and she did—and he reveled in the breathless sensations that whirled around him like a devastating monsoon.

And then, one by one, Jessica satisfied each aching need she'd created. They came together beneath a dome of stars to skyrocket into a galaxy of wild, sweet ecstasy.

DERRICK GLANCED UP from reading the newspaper. He critically appraised his brother's disheveled appearance. "Where the hell have you been? I fixed supper, and you never showed up. You could have called, you know. We do have cell phones for that express purpose."

"I forgot," Devlin said as he plunked down in his recliner.

"You *forgot*," Derrick mocked sarcastically. "We might as well forget about our cooking arrangements on odd and even days. You've forgotten just about everything you ever knew this past week."

"Nag, nag." Devlin had an ax to grind with his brother and he wasn't inclined to listen to a lecture about cooking when there were important issues to discuss. "When are you going to give the ring to Cassie?" He wanted to know that very second.

Derrick glanced away, then fidgeted in his chair. "I, uh, haven't decided yet."

"I see. I assume you're waiting until you're at the top of the spine donor list."

Derrick braced his hands on the armrest and jerked upright. "I'll do it in my own time," he growled defensively.

"Well, if your own time doesn't arrive pretty damn quick, I'll take the situation in hand, coward."

"Hey!" Derrick shouted, affronted. "I am not a coward. I am trying not to rush hastily into things."

Devlin couldn't argue that point, because he'd tried to move slowly with Jessica so he wouldn't overwhelm her. But hell! Derrick had been seeing Cassie for four months, and the big clown was nuts about the woman. If Derrick wanted to be engaged for a couple of years, fine and dandy, but it was high time he made his move.

Because Devlin wouldn't feel comfortable making his move until his brother was settled.

Call it superstitious, call it silly, but this twin thing had always been tricky, and they had worked hard at avoiding complications—and failed occasionally. Hell, there had been a few times, when Devlin had gone into the restaurant to grab a take-out, that Cassie had confused him with Derrick. Once, she'd approached from his blind side, slipped around in front of him and plastered a kiss on his lips before he could tell her she'd made a mistake. He'd felt uncomfortable, and she'd been embarrassed.

Devlin and Cassie had made a pact, there and then, not to mention the incident to Derrick, just in case he decided to get bent out of shape about it.

Devlin had never come right out and told Jessica that he was a twin. Likewise, Derrick hadn't mentioned being a twin until he and Cassie had dated for over a month. That had become standard procedure. Until Devlin knew exactly where he stood with Jess, he wasn't taking chances by introducing her to Derrick. Not until the big, stubborn ox popped the question.

No way was Devlin going to risk having Jessica become interested in his look-alike, because despite what Derrick said about being wiser, less impatient and more tactful, the plain and simple fact was that they were two identical peas in a pod who shared similar characteristics and personality traits. Sibling rivalry, compounded with brotherhood, plus the complication of being an identical twin led to unpleasant situations involving competition and hard feelings that Devlin and Derrick wanted to avoid.

Derrick didn't want to screw up the good thing he had going with Cassie. Ditto for Devlin. But Derrick needed to get his rear in gear. Devlin had to find a way to light a fire under his brother and nudge him into giving Cassie that ring that was burning a hole in his pocket!

"So," Devlin said, "just when do you expect the celestial stars will be perfectly aligned and the barometric pressure will be stable enough for you to ask Cass to marry you, hmm?"

"I don't know, damn it. I haven't consulted the astrological charts!" Derrick said, blustering. "What's it to you anyway?"

Only everything, you meathead, Devlin thought. Instead he said, "I'd like to introduce you to Jessica, but you and I have our policy of waiting until after the other one has things squared away in the romance department.''

Derrick smiled, slumped in his chair, then nodded in complete understanding. Devlin didn't have to go into detail. Derrick knew exactly where his twin was coming from.

Funny how that fifth-grade incident over a pug-nosed little girl had left such a lasting impression on twins who now established their unique identity with the women in their lives before agreeing to things like introductions and double dates.

"So, things with you and Jessica are getting serious," Derrick concluded, grinning wryly. "If you can't beat the exotic animals, then join them, huh?"

"We're skirting that issue in an effort to get to know each other," Devlin replied, then gnashed his teeth when Derrick—the ornery rascal—snickered.

"Judging by the fact that your hair and clothes are covered with grass, I'd say you're getting to know each other exceptionally well. What'd you do? Take her to our favorite fishing hole in that out-of-the-way corner of the south pasture?"

"So? How many times have you been there with Cassie?" Devlin retorted.

"None of your damn business," Derrick snapped.

"Same goes for you, bro. There are certain things we never discuss, as you well know. So, are you going to give that ring to Cass or do I have to do it for you? Same as I usually have to tackle the difficult situations around here. I attack a problem while you yammer and yackety-yack about how tact and diplomacy work best. You never take the initiative and apply your theory, Mr. All Talk and No Action.''

"Hey!" Derrick objected. "Just because I don't go off half-cocked doesn't mean I can't solve problems!"

"No? Then what the hell are you waiting for? Still afraid she'll shoot you down?"

"No," Derrick muttered. "She's crazy about me."

"So you keep saying, but you aren't doing anything about it," Devlin went on relentlessly. "So, when are you going to do something? Next week? Next month? Next decade? What time frame are we looking at here?"

"After we plant wheat, after Cass settles into her routine at the restaurant and finds reliable help so we can spend more time together," he blurted.

Devlin flung his brother an exasperated glance. "That's this week's excuse. What'll it be next week?"

Derrick vaulted to his feet, made a big production of tossing aside the newspaper, then stamped toward his bedroom. "Get off my case!" he bellowed.

"Fine, I will," Devlin hollered. "We'll bust our butts planting wheat, starting first thing in the morning. Soon as we're finished you are going to propose or I'll drag your yellow-bellied carcass to town and do it for you!"

"You will not!" Derrick roared.

"Don't bet on it unless you want to lose, big-time!"

Derrick slammed the door. Devlin scowled. He supposed he was to blame—indirectly, at least—for Derrick's hesitation and wavering nerve. It was true that Devlin had been hell to live with after Sandi used and betrayed him. Derrick had watched, listened and learned from Devlin's disastrous romance with that devious socialite. Now Derrick had slowed to a crawl, making certain every step he took was planted on solid ground.

Two weeks, Devlin decided. He'd give his brother some time, with a little nudging and prodding along the way for good measure. If Derrick didn't make his move, Devlin was going to break a few long-standing rules between them and force that doofus into action.

On that determined thought, Devlin stalked to his bedroom to call Jess and tell her that he was going to be tied up sowing wheat. He was going to keep Derrick so busy he couldn't spend a spare minute with Cassie. Then he'd realize he didn't like living without seeing her. Devlin would add a few jabs about the male patrons at the café ogling Cass, and Derrick would turn an unattractive shade of green. That should get the coward all steamed up.

Great plan, thought Devlin. But then, if he kept Derrick busy night and day, Devlin wouldn't have time to see Jess....

"Hello?"

Frustration gnawed at him the instant he heard her sultry voice. He wanted to be with Jess, needed his recommended daily dose of her. But his brother needed to be quarantined for the sake of love—which meant Devlin got quarantined, too, damn it.

"How ya doing, darlin'?" Devlin murmured.

"It's lonely here without you."

His body clenched. He gritted his teeth and silently cursed his reluctant twin. "It's lonely over here, too. It's gonna get lonelier, because Derrick and I are going to start planting wheat in the morning. It'll take us more than a week, barring the complications of machinery breakdowns. We'll be putting in double days, in hopes of sowing before the next rain. What spare time we have will be occupied with servicing tractors, trucks and drills.''

"In other words, you won't be around at all.''

He swore he heard disappointment in her voice. Or was that wishful thinking on his part?

"'Fraid not. Next to harvest, this is one of the busiest, most hectic times of the year.''

"Sort of like tax season,'' she concluded.

"Exactly. No rest for the weary and all that.''

"Anything I can do to help?''

"No, but thanks for the offer. Derrick and I can get short-tempered and testy. I'd rather you didn't see us at our worst.''

"I'll remind you about short-tempered and testy when tax season rolls around.''

"You do that, Jess. In the meantime, I'll call you every night, but it might be pretty late.''

"Okay, Dev. 'Night. I...I'll be thinking about you.''

Devlin swore ripely as he replaced the receiver. Jessica was beginning to open up to him, to shed her reserve and inhibitions. She could say things like I miss you, I'm thinking of you, I need you, without feeling self-conscious and vulnerable. And wham! He was taking more than a week of absence from her life, and he didn't want her to adjust to not having him around. Damn!

Devlin stripped naked, then plopped on his bed to stare at the darkness. Twelve days, two weeks at the most, he consoled himself. If Derrick didn't give

Cassie that ring, then Devlin might just haul off and offer it to Jessica.

The impulsive thought had him squirming uneasily. What if she said no? He gulped. What if she wasn't ready for permanence and lifetime commitment because she'd gotten burned once? Did she want children? He hadn't asked. They hadn't discussed the possibility—though they should have, because tonight, Jess had made him so hot and hungry and desperate that he'd totally forgotten about using protection. He had behaved recklessly and irresponsibly.

Calm down, Callahan, he lectured himself. If Jessica became pregnant with his child he'd be pleased about it. He wanted kids…. Did she, considering the way she was jostled around during her youth?

Devlin closed his eyes and told himself that he'd have endless hours to think about all this stuff. He'd be riding on the tractor, drilling wheat. Yeah, he'd have oodles of time to imagine what it would be like to be married with children—if Jess would have him. That was the big if.

Suddenly, Devlin understood Derrick's lack of confidence, his hesitation. He sympathized with his twin. The big step might be a doozy if the woman a man loved didn't share the depth of his feelings, didn't have the same visions for the future. Devlin had been there and done that once upon a time, and he'd been shot down without an emotional parachute to make his landing softer. He'd crashed—and burned.

Well, hell, thought Devlin.

It was a couple of hours before he quit tossing, turning and counting a few hundred sheep. Finally, he drifted into a fitful sleep.

9

JESSICA SWORE her animals were trying to cause conflict between Devlin and her the whole livelong week. The exotics had been roaring, bellowing and squawking every night since Devlin began drilling wheat. Twice, she'd climbed out of bed after midnight to insure the cattle hadn't broken loose. They had once, and it had taken two hours to herd them to the pasture.

Devlin had called every night, sounding exhausted. Jessica lived for those brief conversations. Yes, the wheat planting was going well, except for a few minor breakdowns that cost him more time than he planned, he'd reported. Yes, he missed her like crazy, he'd said.

It was becoming easier for Jessica to come right out and admit she missed him, too, wanted to be with him. This past week was worse than those few days Devlin had been gone on his mysterious trip. The loneliness Jess experienced was almost unbearable, and it mushroomed, intensified with each long day—and even longer night.

"You've got it bad, Jess," she told herself as she wandered aimlessly around the kitchen. When she realized she resembled a hamster on a treadmill she made herself stop pacing. She definitely needed something to occupy herself.

Jess decided to bake Devlin a cake. That should surprise him, give her something to do. She could leave the cake on his front porch so he would find it when he dragged himself home after another tedious workday.

Jessica rummaged through the cabinet to find a cake mix. Chocolate to match his eyes, she mused with a smile. Industriously, she whipped up the cake, stuck it in the oven, set the timer, then strode outside to feed her animals.

The vet had swung by the previous evening, and she was pleased that all her charges had received clean bills of health. Jess had jokingly requested nightly sedatives to put the animals out like lights, so they would cause less uproar. The vet, a stern, no-nonsense individual with a balding head and protruding paunch, hadn't been amused.

The encounter with the vet served to remind her that she had taken herself too seriously before she became involved with Devlin. He'd been a positive influence on her, made her laugh, made her immensely happy.

Which was why she was positively miserable while Devlin was working day and night to plant his crop.

Jessica checked her watch, then quickened her pace so she could finish her rounds before the cake burned up in the oven. She hoofed it to the house to hear the timer buzzing. Grabbing an oven mitt, she retrieved the cake, set it aside to cool, then mixed the icing.

An hour and a half later, with cake in hand, Jessica strode up the brick walkway to the modernized, spacious ranch house. She admired Devlin's well-kept home, yet she wondered why he had never invited her to his place. Maybe he figured things might get complicated and embarrassing if his brother arrived unexpectedly to find them in a clinch. Yes, it was definitely better for Devlin to come to her house, she decided. There were times when living alone had its advantages.

Jessica glanced around and saw a wrought-iron table that held a potted plant. She retrieved the table, set it directly in front of the door, then exchanged the cake for the plant. She smiled at the boldly printed words she had written in yellow icing: Miss You. And she did miss that man like nobody's business. When he finished sowing wheat she was going to take a day off work and spend her time proving to him just how much she cared. She was also going to put her heart on the line and tell him, flat-out, that she loved him.

It was going to be a perfect evening, Jessica envisioned. A candlelight dinner, a candlelit bedroom with rose petals strewn across the bed.

Dreamily, Jessica ambled away, then noticed the headlights from two tractors working in the field to the south. Poor Devlin. Considering all the hours he'd spent sitting behind a steering wheel, bouncing over rough terrain, he could have driven from L.A. to New York and back. She imagined the jarring, jostling ride on a tractor would be enough to wear Devlin out, not to mention the tedious hours of sitting in one place from dawn until long past midnight.

When Jessica returned home, the answering machine was blinking. She punched Play to hear Devlin's rich, baritone voice crackling with static.

"Hey, darlin', where are you? Sorry about the bad connection. I'm on the cell phone." More static crackled, then faded. "I decided to work extra late tonight so I can finish this last field. I have a few errands to run in town tomorrow afternoon, but I'll be at your place—" crackle, crackle "—tomorrow night about—"

The line went dead, indicating the cell phone had clicked off while Devlin was on the downside of the hill. But it didn't matter what time he arrived tomorrow evening, because Jessica would be ready and waiting.

When the phone rang, Jessica lunged for it, hoping it was Devlin. "Hello?"

"Hi, boss," Teresa said weakly.

"Are you okay?"

"Not very okay." Teresa groaned miserably. "I caught a nasty, evil flu bug. I can't stand up without getting light-headed and nauseous. I'm really sorry, but I don't think I can make it to work tomorrow."

Well, so much for taking a day off in preparation for Devlin's arrival. "Don't worry about it, Teresa. I've got it covered at the office. Just stay home and take it easy until you feel better."

"Thanks for understanding, boss. I want you to know that I'm not faking it like that waitress you filled in for at Cassie's Place."

"I know you well enough to know you wouldn't do something like that. You are too dedicated to your job."

"You've got that right. I'd never intentionally let you down…uh-oh, I gotta go. The nausea is back in full force—"

Jessica heard a clatter at the other end of the line.

It sounded as if her secretary was in bad shape. Jess made a mental note to stop by Cassie's Place to pick up a bowl of soup and crackers tomorrow for Teresa's lunch.

When the zoo struck up a noisy racket, Jessica stamped to the back door and flung it wide open. "Enough already!" she yelled. "You guys tone it down. Hear me? I don't want to chase cattle again tonight."

The demand was met with another loud commotion. Jessica glanced southeast, seeing the headlights of the tractors, hearing the distant growl of the engines. Apparently, the sights and sounds alarmed her animals. No wonder they had been jittery all week.

Sighing in exasperation, Jessica closed the door and locked up for the night. It was late, and she needed her sleep, because she would be serving double duty at the office tomorrow.

Jessica ascended the stairs, then quickly undressed. When she lay down on her bed she automatically reached for the empty pillow, wishing Devlin was beside her.

He will be tomorrow, and the day after, she assured herself. And when he was, she was going to tell him how much she cared, tell him that her life was empty without the sound of his laughter, the feel of his brawny arms around her. She only hoped he felt some of the intense affection she felt for him. Otherwise, she was going to get her heart twisted inside out tomorrow.

BLEARY-EYED, STIFF AND SORE from long hours on the tractor, Devlin trudged onto the porch. God, in his younger days he'd had hangovers that couldn't compare to this. He glanced at his watch. It was three-thirty in the morning, and he'd been keeping vampire hours for more days than he cared to count.

Devlin opened the front door, then stumbled to a halt when he saw his brother camped out on the couch, a half-eaten chocolate cake in front of him. Derrick was beaming like a lighthouse.

"See this?" He pointed at what was left of the cake. "Cassie must have dropped it by while we were in the field."

Devlin stared at the letters *ss, ou,* then frowned curiously.

"Miss you," Derrick translated. "I already ate the *m, i* and *y.* She misses me. Do you know what that means, Dev?"

"Yeah, exactly what it sounds like, I suspect."

Derrick smirked at Dev's obvious stupidity. "No, dumb ass, it's a sign that my absence has made her heart grow fonder. I think it's time to pop the question."

"Well, duh, I've been telling you that all week."

"No kidding. You've been nagging at me over the CB radio in the tractor until hell wouldn't have it," Derrick grumbled sourly.

"So, when's the big event?" Devlin plunked down to gobble up the chocolate cake—he hadn't taken time to eat since lunch, and he was ravenous.

"Tomorrow afternoon," Derrick announced, then took a bite of cake. "I'll have time to help you clean out the drills and trucks and service them for the winter so we can park them in the barn. Then I can catch Cassie during the lull after the noon rush at the café."

Devlin devoured another bite of melt-in-your-mouth cake, then shook his head in disbelief. If he'd known this cake was the sign of encouragement Derr needed Dev would have baked it himself. Finally, after crawdadding around for over three weeks, Derrick had decided to make his move. Which allowed Dev to make his—or to introduce Jess to his brother and fiancée, at least.

After scarfing down what was left of the cake, Devlin staggered toward the bedroom. He was sore and achy from twisting this way and that on the tractor seat, constantly checking to insure the drill hadn't clogged up, that he hadn't blown a tire, that the tractor wasn't functioning improperly.

He plopped limply on the bed...and fell asleep the moment his head hit the pillow.

JESSICA fully appreciated her secretary after manning the office alone. Since Teresa wasn't around to answer the phone, Jessica couldn't get anything done. Halfway through expenditure tallies the blasted phone rang, and she had to mark her place with her index finger, confer with a long-winded client, then resume her tallies. It was a hectic morning, and Jessica barely had time to breathe until two in the afternoon.

Two o'clock? Jessica double-checked her watch. Where had the morning gone? Damn, she had intended to take lunch to Teresa and see how she was feeling, see if she needed anything.

When the phone rang for the umpteenth time, Jessica tried to glare it into silence. When it continued to shrill at her, she ignored it. She was not going to take the call. She was going to grab a take-out for Teresa and herself, visit her ailing secretary, then rush back to work. She'd also have to leave the office early if she wanted to make time to prepare a meal for Devlin. Lord, could this day get any busier, more complicated?

Grabbing her purse, Jessica fled the ringing phone, then hopped in her car. Groceries! She needed to pick up a few ingredients to make lasagna.

Jess hung a left and whipped into the parking lot, then hotfooted it into the supermarket. In record time, she gathered supplies for supper, hurried through the express line, then jogged to her car. When she backed from her parking space she heard the crunch of metal, felt the jarring thud of a collision.

"Well, damn!" Jessica piled from her car to see the bumper of Dorothy Pike's car crammed into Jessica's fender panel. The dear, sweet lady with steel wool hair rolled down the window of her ancient tank of a Cadillac.

"Oh, dear, hon," Dorothy said as she assessed the damage. "I didn't see you when I backed out. But not to worry, my insurance will take care of it."

Jessica appraised the dent, which was the size of Rhode Island, then noted the smear of champagne-colored paint that had been scraped off the Caddy and left on the sports car. How was she going to get back and forth to work while her car was in the body shop being repaired?

"Do you think there is too much damage for you to drive that little ol' thing, hon?" Dorothy asked. "I'll be glad to give you a lift to your office."

"Thanks, but this looks to be only cosmetic damage," Jessica replied. "If you can drive back into your parking slot, I think I can pull away. I'll call you tomorrow to exchange insurance information.''

When Dorothy's car lumbered forward, metal creaked, and the fender on Jessica's car dangled at an unnatural angle, but it didn't fall to the pavement. Jessica pulled away, then glanced every direction—twice—before cruising past the stop sign.

This was not turning out to be a good day, she thought as she headed to Cassie's Place for a take-out. What else could possibly go wrong?

Jessica veered into the parking lot, then noticed Cassie standing outside the door with... Her heart nose-dived to her empty stomach when she realized Cassie was talking to Devlin, who was decked out in his Western finery. To her utter disbelief and dismay, she saw Cassie fling her arms around Devlin's neck and hug the stuffing out of him. Then Devlin—the two-timing, dirty, rotten creep—clutched Cassie to him and kissed her right smack-dab on the lips, right smack-dab on Main Street!

Jessica sat there, stunned. Hurt, anger and humiliation roiled inside her. She felt as if her heart had been ripped from her chest without the luxury of anesthetic. Damn that man to hell, she fumed as she watched Devlin give Cassie a mouth-to-mouth resuscitation kind of kiss. They clung together, lip-locked, for what had to be a good five minutes without coming up for air.

All those horrible feelings of betrayal and rejection that she'd experienced when she discovered Rex had been fooling around on the side returned to torment her. Devlin had acted as if he cared about her, cared what she thought, how she felt, what she had to say. Knowing he had betrayed her trust and her affection hurt a zillion times worse because she intrinsically knew, felt, that Devlin Callahan—the deceitful, lying devil!—was the one true love of her life. She had given a part of herself to him that could never belong to anyone else. Problem was, Devlin had been carrying on with Cassie, a woman Jessica valued as a friend as well as a client.

Of course, none of this was Cassie's fault. Jessica steamed as she watched the sizzling kiss and crushing embrace go on forever. Ten to one, Cassie didn't know Devlin had been seeing Jessica on the sly.

Jessica spouted several unladylike obscenities when she remembered Devlin telling her that he wanted to keep their relationship private, just so the two of them could get to know each other, because he wanted her all to himself, yadda, yadda. Why, that sneaky weasel had even rushed to assure her that he didn't consider their involvement a cheap, sordid affair. No wonder he'd been so intent and determined to make that point, because he didn't want Jess to see their trysts for exactly what they were!

Jessica sat there smoldering, raining dozens of curses on Devlin's raven head. He was going to pay dearly for this betrayal. She had confided her past to him, and to him alone. She had given him the gift of her innocence, and she had only been another notch on his bedpost. She had taken the leap of faith and put her trust in him, shared her feelings with him…and he had used her.

First thing in the morning she would sick the IRS on him, demand an audit of his ranching accounts. If Devlin Callahan's expenditures and profits weren't perfectly documented he'd pay a hefty fine. Then, after the IRS had their way with him, fined him big-time, she was going to strangle him for hurting her in ways no one had been able to do before, not even Rex with his half-baked excuses and twisted lies.

Jessica clutched the necklace that burned against her throat, then jerked it off. The gift was nothing more than a payment for sex, she realized. Damn him! Fool that she was, she had been so appreciative of his gift that she had gone mushy and teary-eyed. Plus, she had baked him a cake that declared she missed him. Jess had never baked for a man before, and had she known what a jerk Devlin was she would have smeared that chocolate cake all over his face!

Swiping at the tears bleeding down her cheeks, Jessica shoved her wrecked car into reverse, then drove off before Devlin noticed her. And to think she had worked up the nerve to tell Devil Devlin she loved him. Thank goodness she hadn't made that disastrous mistake before she learned the truth about him.

Hard as she tried, Jessica couldn't halt the flowing tears that boiled down her cheeks. For sure and certain, she couldn't walk into Good Grub Diner to order a take-out for Teresa, not without drawing curious stares. Rummaging through her purse, Jess grabbed her cell phone, inhaled a deep, fortifying breath, then dialed the sheriff's office.

"County sheriff's department," the female dispatcher said.

Jess cleared her throat. "This is Jessica Porter. I'd like to speak with Reed, please."

"I'm sorry, the sheriff drove over to Teresa Harper's apartment to take her some lunch. I guess you know she's sick, since she works for you.''

''That's why I called Reed. I was hoping he could check on her.'' She managed to speak without her voice cracking.

''Not to worry on that count.'' The dispatcher chuckled wryly. ''The sheriff has been stopping by Teresa's every hour on the hour. I think it's hilarious the way he's fussing over her. I've never seen him act like this before. He's got it bad.''

Jessica hung up, feeling even sorrier for herself. Teresa had captured the sheriff's attention, and they were dating. She, however, couldn't capture a man's interest without relying on sex or money.

What was wrong with her, anyway? She had tried to be a good and decent person, even as a kid. But she'd always been dispensable, cast off, as if her feelings counted for nothing.

Self-pity took such a fierce and mighty hold on her emotions that she didn't trust herself to drive. She'd already been involved in one wreck, and she didn't want to be the cause of another. She veered into the city park, switched off the ignition, then sat there and bawled like an abandoned baby. This was positively, absolutely the last time she wasted her emotion and wore her heart out on a man, she vowed. Furthermore, she wasn't going to fret if her animals spooked Callahan's cattle and sheep. She didn't give a damn if Devlin had to spend his evenings on horseback, rounding up livestock and repairing fences. She didn't care about him, period! She didn't love him, didn't need him in her life— ever. And if that two-timing jerk showed up on her doorstep he was going to discover the full meaning of the word *feud!* That fiasco between the Hatfields and McCoys would be mere child's play compared to this!

DEVLIN WAITED impatiently while the phone rang a dozen times at Jessica's office. Where the hell was she? She hadn't been home when he called last night, and she wasn't at her office this afternoon. That wasn't like her. And where the blazes was Jess's secretary? Someone should have answered that phone.

Worried, Devlin disconnected, then dialed Jessica's home number. After three rings the answering machine picked up.

"Jess? What's going on? I called your office and received no answer. I'll be there this evening to pick you up. I have a surprise for you. I thought we'd go out tonight. Just dress casually, okay?"

Devlin stared pensively through the living room window, wondering if something might have happened to Jess. Considering the wild, man-eating animals caged at her farm, she might have gotten hurt.

Hell, why didn't he think of that earlier? She could be sprawled beside a cage, injured and bleeding, unable to call for assistance.

The frantic thought put Devlin in motion. He grabbed his wallet and keys and raced to his pickup. Gravel pinged against the underside of the truck as he roared down the road to check on Jessica.

He breathed a gusty sigh of relief when he noticed her car wasn't in the driveway. He was reasonably assured the lions and tigers hadn't made a meal of her, but that still didn't explain her absence from home and office. Where the hell could she be in the middle of the afternoon on a workday?

Just to be on the safe side, Devlin parked the truck, then strode around the house to check the animal pens. Mother Goose waddled out to greet him, doing her usual honk-and-dance number before paddling along at his heels. Devlin saw neither hide nor hair of Jessica, but he decided to feed her menagerie of animals while he was here. That would save Jess time this evening before they went out to paint the town red.

An hour later—and after two annoying spits from that pesky llama—Devlin had fed, watered and cleaned the cages. When he returned to his truck, he grabbed his cell phone to call Jessica's office. Still no answer.

A smile pursed his lips, and the tension eased from his shoulders. Maybe he was stewing for nothing. Maybe Jess was at the beauty shop getting a haircut or makeover so she'd look her best this evening. Women were into that sort of thing, he reminded himself. Of course, Jess didn't need cosmetic enhancement because she possessed a natural, wholesome beauty.

Devlin frowned ponderously. Even if Jess was at the beauty salon, that didn't explain her secretary's absence. Devlin punched in the number to his brother's cell phone. Since Derr was in town, maybe he could provide a few answers.

"Hello?"

Devlin grinned. His brother sounded as if he was floating on cloud nine. "It's me. How'd it go with Cass?"

"Great! She said yes!"

Devlin jerked the phone away before his enthusiastic brother blasted an eardrum. "Well, there you go. You simmered in your own juice for over three weeks, and it was all for nothing."

"Thanks for calling to rub it in, bro," Derrick said. "But since I'm sitting on top of the world, I'll forgive you. Hey, why don't you and Jessica meet Cassie and me at the café this evening? We can celebrate the engagement and make the introductions."

"Sounds fine. We'll do that," Devlin affirmed. "In the meantime I'd like you to do me a favor. If you can tear yourself away from Cassie for a few minutes, that is. I can't get hold of Jessica or her secretary. Could you drive by the accounting office and check things out?"

"I'll swing by to see if her car's there, but Cassie told me that Teresa Harper has the flu and the sheriff came by to pick up some food for lunch."

Well, that explained why Teresa hadn't answered the office phone, but Jessica was still missing.

"You want me to call you if Jessica's car is at the office? She could be taking a late lunch with a client, you know."

"At Good Grub Diner? I doubt it. She obviously isn't at Cassie's Place or you would have said so."

"Hell, Dev, I don't even know what Jessica looks like," Derrick reminded him. "I'll swing by the accounting office to see if there's a car in the parking lot. I'll call you back if there is."

Devlin hung up and drove home, but he didn't receive a return call from his brother—which meant Jessica was still nowhere to be found.

Along the road toward home he noticed the sagging strands of wire that indicated a few cattle had decided to make a break for it. Grumbling, he arrived home and saddled a horse. Looked as if he would be spending a couple of hours playing hide-and-seek with the livestock. Apparently, Jessica wasn't the only one who'd turned up missing.

JESSICA DROVE HOME, barely remembering how she'd gotten there. Her eyes were red and puffy from crying her heart out at the park. She'd passed through the first phase of angry humiliation and betrayal and was feeling positively vicious by the time she slammed the door of her dented car. She stalked onto the front porch, then glanced around, noting dozens of odd jobs that needed tending on the farm.

That's what she'd do, she decided. She'd put on her work clothes and attack a few chores, vent her anger and frustration. Then, when she simmered down, she'd take a sturdy shovel—her weapon of choice—drive over to Devlin's place, pound him over the head until he was as flat as an envelope, then mail him to Borneo.

"Damn that man!" she muttered as she stalked upstairs. What an idiot she'd been to trust that handsome Don Juan. And what about Cassie Dixon? Should Jessica tell the poor woman that Devlin was two-timing her, too?

Jessica contemplated that while she changed clothes. Ten minutes later, whacking weeds along the fencerow, she still hadn't decided whether to inform Cassie of her disastrous mistake. Maybe in a couple of days she'd approach Cassie. Once Jess had a strong grasp on her emotions, once she'd worked up a good, solid hatred for Devlin, she would expose him for the bastard he was.

Yeah, a couple of days of reminding herself how many times, how many ways, Devlin had played her for a fool, and she'd be ready for some good, old-fashioned revenge.

Maybe in two days she would overcome the hurt of loving him, believing he was the man she'd been waiting for.

Two days? Yeah, right. More like two decades!

When fresh tears clouded her eyes, Jessica worked all the harder at her chore. She pretended every weed she decapitated was Devlin's head rolling in the grass. She'd kill every memory associated with him. She'd forget how she'd once admired his straightforward approach, his honesty—which turned out to be nothing more than clever, manipulative lies devised to crumble her defenses and get her into bed. What hurt worse, Jessica realized as she attacked the weed patch with a fiendish vengeance, was that she had trusted him enough to spill her life story, to admit her feelings of being unwanted, unloved and rejected.

Devlin had put on a spectacular act of sympathy and compassion and fooled her completely. Then he fed her that malarkey about how he'd gotten her a gift because he realized no one had been there to help her, to reassure her, to share birthdays and holidays with her. And she, world-class imbecile that she was, had swallowed that baloney, had been touched by his supposed sensitivity and had fallen deeper in love with him.

What sensitivity? she asked herself derisively, then hatcheted a few more weeds. Devlin Callahan

had the sensitivity of a toothpick. Truth be known—
and it was now—Devlin was probably punishing her
and Cassie by transferring his anger that resulted
from his soured romance with Sandi Saxon. Furthermore, Devlin had undoubtedly been kissing up
to Jessica, hoping she'd relocate her exotics when
he asked her to.

Her body buzzing with frustration and outrage,
Jessica climbed on the riding lawn mower. With
every round she made she cursed Devlin Callahan
and his tormenting image. Damn it, she couldn't
even walk through her house without remembering
that he'd been in every room, filling it with once-
cherished memories that she had to come to despise.

She'd rearrange all the furniture to give the place
a different look, that's what she'd do. Maybe that
would exorcise thoughts of that devil. She'd fumi-
gate the house with air freshener to smother any
lingering scent that reminded her of him. Then she'd
take a vacation. Maybe a cruise. Fill up every hour
with activities like scuba diving, sight-seeing, hang
gliding, mountain climbing—whatever. She'd outrun the hurt and anger. She'd grow accustomed to
not seeing him, not wanting him, not loving him....

The thought fractured her wobbling emotions, and
Jessica dropped her head to the steering wheel and
blubbered in tears. She had loved Devlin. She had
given her heart and soul to him, and he had betrayed
her with a newfound friend. How cruel was that?

Damn it, she couldn't hate Cassie for falling for
that devil's charm, since Jessica had done the very
same thing herself. And worse, Jessica could understand why Devlin had taken an interest in Cassie.

She was bubbly, vivacious and outgoing. She was everything Jess aspired to be.

"Damn you, Devlin," she whispered between gulping sobs. "Damn you for making me fall in love with you!"

10

DEVLIN CHECKED his appearance in the mirror one last time. If Jess had gone to the beauty shop for a makeover—which she didn't need, because he loved her just the way she was—then he intended to look his best this evening. He'd starched and pressed his blue jeans and cream-colored Western shirt and polished his Sunday-go-to-meeting boots. Devlin turned from the mirror, tucked the ticket voucher in the vest pocket of his jacket, then strode out the door.

This was his big night, he reminded himself. He was going to tell Jessica how he felt about her, lay it all on the line, then take her to meet the man who looked and acted like him. Derrick was safely tied to another woman, and Jessica could adjust to the fact that Dev wasn't particularly special because he didn't have his own unique identity—had to share his body and face and several personality traits with his clone.

Maybe the belief Derrick and Devlin shared seemed silly to outsiders, but it was serious business to identical twins who didn't want the women they adored to see them as interchangeable.

On the way to the truck Devlin experienced an uneasy feeling of hesitation. What if he bared his heart and Jess didn't share his deep, all-consuming feelings? He'd been down that one-way street before and had nothing but seven years of bitterness to show for it.

Did he have the gumption to take the advice he'd been dishing out to his brother for three weeks? Damn the torpedoes and full steam ahead? What if Jess wasn't ready for commitment or the prospect of marriage and children? What if she'd gotten caught up in the newness of sexual gratification and that was all she felt or wanted from him?

"Hell, Dev, you keep playing that what if game and you're going to sound like your brother," Devlin muttered to himself. "Take heart, pal, things turned out dandy-fine for Derrick, didn't they? Why not you, too?"

On that optimistic thought, Devlin piled into his truck and marshaled his self-confidence and determination. Jessica cared about him, he knew she did. She had opened up to him, shared her unpleasant past, her vulnerabilities. He could tell she didn't do that with just anybody. She'd developed enough trust in him to let him know where she was coming from, hadn't she? Did that mean something? It meant something to him when he confided his past to her.

"Okay, pa'dner, so just hightail it over there and tell her how you feel," Devlin told himself. "Everything will work out fine."

He pulled into the driveway and immediately noticed the gigantic dent in Jessica's sports car. Holy hell! Had she been injured and in need of help? Why hadn't she called? He would have dropped what he was doing to be there for her. Didn't she know that?

Concerned about Jess, Dev dashed up the steps

and pounded on the door. Seconds passed. Impatient, he rapped his knuckles on the warped wood again.

"Jess! Open up," he yelled. "Are you okay?"

The door whipped open, and Devlin gaped at puffy, red-streaked eyes, an off-center ponytail, smudged cheeks and grimy garments that belonged in a rag bag.

"You go straight to hell!" she bellowed at him, then gave him the Queen Mother of all glares.

Devlin stood there, totally bewildered by the unexpected reception. Her hostile expression perfectly matched her words—ones that wished him to the hottest climate imaginable, doing things to himself that were anatomically impossible.

"What'd I do?" he implored.

"Like you don't know," she sputtered, then hissed venomously. "But of course, you didn't expect me to find out, did you, Casanova Callahan?"

Casanova? "What the hell are you talking about?"

"And to think I almost fell for your devious lies." She spat the words hatefully. "Does it bolster your male pride to do unto others what was done to you? Was that what this secretive little affair of ours was all about?"

"Secret affair?" he repeated stupidly.

"At least you have the guts to admit it," she snarled, glaring holes through him. "Rex didn't. He lied right up to the bitter end." Tears floated in Jessica's eyes, but she ranted on, intent on having her say before she slammed the door in this good-for-nothing cowboy's handsome face once and for all. "I *trusted* you, damn you. I *confided* in you, double damn you! I even baked a blasted cake and put it in *icing* that I missed you!''

Devlin's jaw sagged to his chest. "*You* baked that cake?"

"Who'd you think did it? Santa Claus?" She lashed out sarcastically. "Well, let me tell you something, Don Juan, you don't get to have your cake and eat it, too. If you *ever* set foot on my property again, I'll call the sheriff and have you evicted. Now, get out of here and never come back!"

When she tried to slam the door in his face, Devlin rammed his booted foot against the doorjamb. "Hold it, wildcat. I've got something to say."

"Tough. I'm through listening to your manipulative lies. I saw you with Cassie this afternoon!"

Suddenly, her livid tirade, her glares that left third-degree burns, her absence from her office made sense to him. Jessica had baked the cake that solidified Derrick's courage and sent him racing into town to pop the question to Cassie. Jessica must have seen them together and presumed it was Devlin.

Something else occurred to Devlin that made him grin broadly—which incited Jessica to spit a foul curse at him. The woman was jealous, furious and hurt, he diagnosed. That, Devlin decided, was an exceptionally good sign, because it indicated that she cared enough to be angry, cared enough to wish him in hell for what she perceived as an unforgivable betrayal. Well, that was a gigantic relief to him. It made it easier for him to express his feelings for her, knowing she cared enough to be upset—to the extreme.

"I love you, Jess," he said.

"No, you don't, you devious, two-timing jerk!" she shrieked at him.

"Jess, I want to take you out to supper," he insisted, playing tug-of-war with the door.

"Only if I get to eat your fried heart, Callahan," she snarled as she shoved her shoulder against the inside of the door. "And another thing, you better have your business expenses and profits listed in precise order, because I'm calling the IRS tomorrow. If they don't tax you to death, then I'll come after you with a shotgun, soon as I buy one. Get your foot out of my door, damn it!"

"No, not until you listen to what I have to say."

"Never!" she shouted angrily. "Go the hell away!"

Enough of this, Devlin decided. He shouldered his way inside to watch Jessica huff and puff with indignation. Her eyes blazed like green flames. The necklace he'd given her was not around her neck. She was fit to be roped and tied, and Devlin was never so pleased by a woman's fury in his entire life. The woman was crazy about him, thank goodness. All he had to do was find a way to remind her of it.

"I'm taking you out tonight, and that's that," he declared in no uncertain terms. "You can go as you are or clean up. Doesn't matter to me, but you are going, even if I have to drag you."

"Where are we going? To the Betrayal Ball to dance the Cheater's Waltz? No, thanks," she sassed him. "The only place I'd agree to go with you is to hell, just to make sure you got there, before I turned around and came home. I hate you, Callahan. Get the picture? Or do I need to spell it out for you? H-A-T-E!''

"Fine, you hate my guts. Point noted. Now go change your clothes, Blondie. If nothing else, you'll get a free meal out of me.''

Jessica couldn't believe Devlin's audacity. He was standing there grinning while she breathed fire and brimstone at him. The man was insane. Did he think he could sweet-talk her back into his arms?

"Not cooperating?'' He snagged her arm and towed her onto the porch. "Fine. Go as you are.''

Jessica put on the brakes, but his strength and forward momentum sent her skidding across the porch. When she launched herself backward, he dragged her forward. It was obvious that she couldn't out-muscle him.

"Okay, you bastard, I'll change,'' she muttered, admitting defeat—temporarily. "You're right. The very least I deserve from you is a meal, but don't expect conversation after I order the most expensive dinner on the menu, plus dessert!''

"Okay, so give me the silent treatment,'' he said, negotiating, trying to bite back a grin—and failing miserably.

She wanted to clobber him, but she figured the big brute would block her attack. So why waste the energy? Besides, she'd let the IRS do her dirty work for her.

Jess jerked her arm from his grasp, then wheeled around and marched toward the staircase.

"Ten minutes,'' he called after her. "If you're not down here by then, I'm coming to get you.''

She glared nuclear warheads at him, stuck her nose in the air and stalked up the steps.

Devlin chuckled in amusement, recalling the fiery tirade that met him at the door. Ah, he did love that feisty, hot-tempered female. She was a dozen kinds of passion waiting to explode.

So, she had seen Derrick and Cassie slobbering all over each other, had she? Any other woman would have put on that wounded, betrayed expression and sent a man on the Guilt-Trip Express. Not this firebrand. She came out of her corner throwing punches and verbal right crosses. She had threatened him with death and taxes because she believed he had betrayed her trust and her affection. Well, if that wasn't true love, then Devlin didn't know what was—unless it was just wounded pride roaring.

Devlin frowned, not quite as sure of himself as he'd been a moment earlier. Considering Jessica's volatile temper—and he had seen the evidence of it during their first and second encounters—she just might be plain furious and feeling used.

He checked his watch, then waited another five minutes.

Jessica appeared at the head of the staircase thirty seconds before he was ready to do as he'd threatened. A shallow coat of makeup glazed her brittle features. Head held high, she stared down her nose at him.

Devlin stifled another amused grin.

IN HER ROOM, Jessica had vowed to contain and bury the turbulent emotions that were churning inside her. She was not going to break down, simper and snivel. Neither was she going to waver when Devlin tried to talk himself out of the grave he'd dug for himself. He was not—repeat, not, with great emphasis—going to convince her that the kiss he'd plastered on Cassie's lips meant nothing, that Jessica was the one he really cared about. Jess had heard that same song and dance from Rex, and she hadn't bought it.

It occurred to her, halfway down the steps, that her tantrum had been premature and inappropriate. What right did she have to expect fidelity when Devlin hadn't made a verbal commitment to her, nor she to him? They were having an affair. End of story. She was the one who'd fallen in love and expected things she had no right to expect from him.

God, she was an idiot, she realized. Since time immemorial, men had taken sexual advantage of women, making no promises. She was the one who didn't know the score here, didn't know how to play the game.

Okay, fine. So she was out of her league. She'd made another humiliating mistake by trying to strike up a dead-end relationship. Yes, she was hurt, angry, embarrassed and mortified, but she'd get over it—in about a hundred years. She wouldn't give Devlin the satisfaction of witnessing another outburst. She'd be cool, remote even. She'd let him think she'd gotten her act together after her tirade. She'd let him think she didn't care, even if her heart had broken wide open and was bleeding in her chest.

DEVLIN FELT DESIRE slam into him like a speeding locomotive while he watched Jessica saunter down the steps. She probably thought she was punishing him by looking drop-dead gorgeous in that form-fitting red silk dress that emphasized every voluptuous curve and swell. He'd give her high marks for the effective tactic, because he was definitely affected by her alluring appearance. However, he could read the invisible sign—Eat your heart out, cowboy, but touch and die. She was making it obvious that he'd blown it with her.

He swallowed a snicker when she came down the last five steps one hip at a time, tormenting him, spiting him for what she considered betrayal in the first degree.

He bowed chivalrously, then indicated that she should precede him through the door. She hitched her chin to an aloof angle, looked down her nose at him again, then sashayed outside, giving her best impersonation of Mae West.

"I noticed that you wrecked your car," he commented on his way off the porch. "How did that happen?"

She didn't reply, just stared at him. When Devlin tried to open the passenger door for her, she beat him to it. Miss Independent wanted it known that she didn't need his assistance.

Devlin climbed into the cab of the pickup, backed from the driveway, then headed toward town. "I hear your secretary has the flu. Hope she's feeling better."

Dead silence.

Hoo-kay. So she was sticking to the effective frostbit-shoulder routine, he mused. He was surprised the windows didn't ice over. He'd give her ten minutes of frigid peace and quiet, then he'd start digging, just to see where he stood with her.

Precisely ten minutes later, Devlin said, "I'd like to break the silence for just a couple of minutes. I have a hypothetical question for you."

She sliced him a glance sharp enough to cut glass, then stared at the gravel road.

Hoo-boy, talk about uncooperative. Devlin tried very hard not to let it bother him.

"Okay, Blondie, let's assume for a moment that you and I had made a commitment to each other. Oh, say, a wedding engagement. Something like that. Then let's say that you discovered that I had cheated on you after I'd told you I was in love with you and that I wanted us to be together forever and ever. What would you do?"

Jessica considered keeping the silence, then decided this was too good to pass up. "You and me?"

He nodded his raven head. "You and me. Not you and Rex. You and me, specifically."

Jessica thought it over for about a minute, then asked, "You told me outright that you loved me and then gave me a ring as proof of your undying loyalty and commitment?"

"Right. We're an official item and everybody in Buzzard's Grove knows it. The announcement has already come out in the newspaper. We've ordered the wedding invitations, the whole nine yards."

"Well, then, I'd drive you to a bridge, like the one spanning the Royal Gorge. Then I'd shove you off headfirst and curse you all the way down."

Devlin swallowed a snicker. The lady didn't mess around when it came to revenge, did she? If she expected loyalty and love and had a ring on her finger, then she'd make double damn certain he wouldn't be around to hurt her, or anybody else, ever again.

"Second question," he said.

"You said you only had one question. I answered

it,'' she snapped as she crossed her arms beneath her well-displayed bosom.

"Aw, c'mon, Blondie," Devlin prodded. "Technically, this is Part B of the first question."

"Fine, since I'm a generous person, I'll cut you some slack, but only because you're buying me the most expensive meal at Good Grub Diner. It's a cinch that you aren't taking me to Cassie's Place. *She* might discover what *I* know, which is that you are a lying, cheating creep."

Devlin ignored the insult. "What I want to know is, could you actually love me enough to throw me off a bridge?"

Jessica stiffened, wouldn't look at him. No way was she going to confess that she already loved him that much, that she wanted him to suffer all the torments of the damned for hurting her. He would not have the satisfaction of knowing how she felt.

"Well?" he prompted.

Jessica absolutely refused to answer. Instead, she posed her own question. "Okay, Callahan, let's reverse the question. Let's say that I—and this is still hypothetical, of course—said I loved you and I agreed to marry you. Then you found out that I fooled around behind your back. What would you do?"

Devlin didn't bother to conceal his smile, since Jessica refused to glance in his direction. "Same thing, actually. I'd haul you to the Royal Gorge and let you take the short way down."

"Why?" she asked.

"Because I wouldn't want to be lied to, cheated on, any more than you would," he replied.

Jessica snorted, then lapsed into silence. When

Devlin drove into the parking lot at Cassie's Place, Jessica's delicately arched brows shot up in surprise.

"My brother and his fiancée are meeting us here for dinner," he explained.

"You're either a glutton for punishment or an idiot," she said, then smirked.

"Yeah, I must enjoy living dangerously to be dating a woman who'd pitch me off a bridge if I stepped out of line."

"Which you already did," she pointed out brusquely. "And this is not a date," she added. "When I go out with someone I despise, it's only for the free meal. In fact, if you'd sit at another booth, I'd like it all the better."

Devlin climbed from the pickup to open Jessica's door, but she beat him to it—again. Chin held high, she approached the café, giving the impression that she wasn't actually *with* him, only that they had arrived at the same time.

Despite her rigid resistance, Devlin took her arm and guided her toward the corner booth. He knew the instant Jessica spotted Derrick and Cassie cozied up, smiling adoringly at each other, because she stopped in her tracks and her mouth dropped open. She swung around to stare incredulously at Devlin, then gaped at Derrick, who waved and summoned them forward.

"My identical twin," Devlin said while she was still struck speechless. "He proposed to Cassie this afternoon, although we made the trip to Tulsa three weeks ago in secrecy to pick out the ring. Derrick didn't want me to say anything to anyone until he worked up the nerve to ask Cassie to marry him. Ironically, the cake you delivered finally convinced him it was time to pop the question. He thought the cake was from Cass, that it was the sign he'd been waiting for. Turns out he didn't really need a sign, because Cassie is as crazy in love with him as he is with her.''

Jessica struggled to absorb his explanation. Finally, when she recovered her powers of speech, she asked, ''Why didn't you tell me you were a twin?''

Devlin shifted awkwardly. ''It's sort of complicated.''

''So simplify it,'' she demanded.

''Since you don't have siblings it might be difficult to understand that it's hard to share your identity, your life's profession, your home with somebody who looks exactly like you. I don't have my own individuality, and neither does Derrick,'' he continued. ''We adhere to this strict policy, see? When one or the other of us dates a woman, we don't go around announcing we're twins before we're certain that the relationship goes deeper than physical appearance. We're careful to insure that we don't become interested in the same woman, or that a woman is looking to rebound with the other twin for spite.'' He scratched his head and glanced at her. ''I told you this was sort of complicated.''

''In other words, you strive to avoid rivalry and competition with women so you'll know you're wanted just for yourself, even though you have a clone underfoot who also shares your traits and characteristics.''

Devlin nodded. ''During those years when we were struggling with the loss of our parents, all we had was each other. We didn't want anyone to come between us. Is that too hard to understand? Would you want to lose someone you cared about to your twin and feel that you didn't measure up, that you were interchangeable?''

All Jessica's anger and resentment fizzled out when she met Devlin's searching gaze. She realized the situation was a sensitive issue—for Devlin as well as Derrick.

''If it's any consolation, Derrick didn't introduce me to Cassie until they'd been dating for six weeks. He requested that I steer clear of the new café until... Well, like I said, until he felt secure.

''We dealt with girls trying to move from one twin to the next, then back again, during high school, but we refused to let it happen so nothing could come between us. Couldn't afford to, because we practically live in each other's pockets.''

The love Jessica had tried to bury beneath the hurt and anger bubbled up like a wellspring. ''The answer to Part B of your question is yes,'' she told him, her heart in her eyes. ''I love you enough to throw you off a bridge for cheating on me.''

There, she'd said it. She watched a wide grin make its way across his lips. She wanted to fly into his arms and kiss him senseless, but not in the middle of a busy restaurant.

''I love you that much, too,'' he whispered as he traced the elegant curve of her cheek. ''But nobody is going to take a header off a bridge, because I care too much to betray your trust and your love for me. I want what Derrick has found. I want an official commitment, but I don't want to rush you if you aren't ready for that step. I also want kids, that is, if you didn't get soured by your childhood ordeals. I swear I'll do my part raising our kids. I'm not afraid of commitment or the responsibility of fatherhood, because I grew up with loving parents who gave their children top priority. I'll be there for you, for our kids, every step of the way, Jess. But there is one thing I've gotta know.''

''What's that?'' she murmured, unable to take her eyes off the man she loved with every breath she took, with every beat of her heart.

''Do you love me enough to relocate your zoo if I asked you to? I don't want to play second fiddle to a quest for money or a bunch of exotics.''

Jessica hesitated for only a half second. She understood that Devlin's livelihood depended on his livestock. She also knew how frustrated he became when he was forced to make unscheduled roundups because of the uproar coming from her animal sanctuary. She had experienced that same exasperation when she gathered spooked cattle in his stead. As much as she loved those maimed and crippled animals, she would find them good homes at another reputable sanctuary if necessary.

''You don't have to play second fiddle to anyone,'' she assured him. ''If my exotics have to be relocated, then I'll relocate them.''

''Glad to hear that.'' He beamed with satisfaction. ''Of course, I wouldn't think of shipping off your feathered and furry friends, because I know what they mean to you. But I gotta tell ya, Blondie, I'm never gonna like that spitting llama of yours. No way, no how. But I will build a pipe-and-cable fence beside the road to insure the cattle don't escape.''

''I'll pay for it,'' she volunteered.

His brows jackknifed in response to her offer. ''It'll be expensive.''

"I have a nest egg I didn't mention, just in case you were after my money," she confided, green eyes sparkling.

Devlin grinned rakishly. "I'm after your sensational body—which is knocking me out in that hot red dress, by the way. And I'm after your love. I'm crazy about the whole appealing package, Blondie."

Even if this wasn't the place, it was the time, Jessica decided. Despite the attentive crowd, she flung her arms around Devlin's neck and kissed him in front of God and everybody. She loved this man and she didn't care who knew it. He was hers and she was his and that was all that mattered.

Devlin ignored the applause and laughter and returned the kiss that expressed everything he needed to know. Jessica loved him. She trusted him to honor her, respect her and remain faithful to her, just as she would honor, respect and remain faithful to him.

"A double ceremony with my double has a nice ring to it," Devlin murmured playfully. "You want to see what it's like to share your limelight with someone else? Like your attractive sister-in-law-to-be, for instance?"

She grinned impishly. "That's fine by me, but you boys don't have to do everything together, do you?"

"I draw the line at sharing a honeymoon," Devlin assured her. "Speaking of which..." He reached into the vest pocket of his jacket to retrieve the printed voucher. "While Derrick and I were in Tulsa picking out a ring and buying that emerald necklace, I looked up Rex Cranfill and got this back for you."

Jessica gaped at the voucher for a Caribbean cruise for two that Rex had charged to her credit card. "He actually let you have it?" she questioned, astonished.

Devlin chuckled. "Actually, I let *him* have it. Gave Mr. Baseball a taste of my wicked curve, right in the chops. Figured he deserved it after what he did to you."

"I'm surprised he didn't charge you with assault and battery," Jessica replied.

"Couldn't," Devlin insisted. "Had an eyewitness with me who claimed Rex tripped clumsily over the uneven sidewalk outside his apartment and slammed his jaw on the pavement."

Devlin cupped her chin, commanding her undivided attention while he looked deeply into her eyes. "I know I'm no one special." His gaze darted to his mirror image, who was sitting in the corner, then focused intently, earnestly, on Jessica. "But I love you, Jess, and I'll be true to you till the day I die. Marry me?"

She nodded eagerly, delightedly. "Name any day, but don't even think about scheduling anything during tax season."

"I hadn't planned on waiting that long. Neither did Derrick. I was thinking that a honeymoon in the Caribbean would be a great way to spend the Christmas holidays."

Amid another round of applause he took her arm and led her toward the corner booth. "Come meet my brother. But I warn you, don't fall for him, Blondie, or you'll be right back on that bridge, and I'll be the one giving you a shove."

Jessica walked—floated was nearer the mark—to the table to meet Derrick and to ooh and aah over Cassie's engagement ring. It really was a beaut, and

Cassie looked so enormously pleased and happy that she was about to burst.

TWO HOURS LATER, after Jessica had been well fed and loved tenderly, she nestled in Devlin's encircling arms. She had run the gamut of emotion during the course of the day. Tired though she was, she marveled at the sheer contentment rippling through her.

"Would you mind very much if we fixed up my bedroom and the bathrooms and made our home here?" she asked him.

"No, not all. In fact, I told Derr that he and Cass could have the master bedroom at Rocking C. I really like this place. It's where I fell in love with you," he whispered as he stroked the gentle curve of her bare hip. "Derrick and I can remodel this place now that the wheat has been planted. We'll move the cattle to another pasture next week, begin the stretch of pipe fence, then you and I can decide what changes we want to make here."

Jessica turned to face him, staring into those onyx eyes that mystified and entranced her. After years of battling life alone, trying to justify her worth and prove to herself that she wasn't an extra person in the world, Jessica had found her niche. She knew this forty-acre plot and her exotic animals weren't all she needed to make her happy. First and foremost, she needed Devlin's love. *He* was that special place she'd been looking for. *He* was the other half of her lonely heart.

"Do you have any idea how much I love you?" she asked.

"Even more than making me take a header off a bridge?" he said, grinning playfully.

"Much wider and deeper than the Royal Gorge itself," she whispered.

"Then show me, darlin'. Then I'll love away any doubt you might have left, because this is definitely about forever and ever. I'll always love you, Jess."

Together, serenaded by the howls, hoots and growls from the zoo, they burned down the night and fell in love all over again.

"You rock my world, Blondie," Devlin whispered a long while later.

Jessica smiled drowsily and cuddled in his arms. Life was good in Buzzard's Grove. She didn't want for anything...except perhaps a couple of babies who had their daddy's laughter, his smile and his limitless capacity to love.

PLAY THE
Lucky Key Game
and get

HOW TO PLAY:

1. With a coin, carefully scratch off gold area at the right. Then check the claim chart to see what we have for you — **2 FREE BOOKS** and a **FREE GIFT** — **ALL YOURS FREE!**

2. Send back the card and you'll receive two brand-new Harlequin Duets™ novels. These books have a cover price of $5.99 each in the U.S. and $6.99 each in Canada, but they are yours to keep absolutely free.

3. There's no catch. You're under no obligation to buy anything. We charge nothing —ZERO — for your first shipment. And you don't have to make any minimum number of purchases — not even one!

4. The fact is, thousands of readers enjoy receiving books by mail from the Harlequin Reader Service®. They enjoy the convenience of home delivery...they like getting the best new novels at discount prices, BEFORE they're available in stores...and they love their *Heart to Heart* subscriber newsletter featuring author news, horoscopes, recipes, book reviews and much more!

5. We hope that after receiving your free books you'll want to remain a subscriber. But the choice is yours — to continue or cancel, any time at all! So why not take us up on our invitation, with no risk of any kind. You'll be glad you did!

YOURS FREE!
A SURPRISE MYSTERY GIFT

We can't tell you what it is...but we're sure you'll like it! A
FREE GIFT—
just for playing the
LUCKY KEY game!

Visit us online at
www.eHarlequin.com

The Harlequin Reader Service® — Here's how it works:

Accepting your 2 free books and gift places you under no obligation to buy anything. You may keep the books and gift and return the shipping statement marked "cancel." If you do not cancel, about a month later we'll send you 2 additional novels and bill you just $5.14 each in the U.S., or $6.14 each in Canada, plus 50¢ delivery per book and applicable taxes if any.* That's the complete price and — compared to cover prices of $5.99 each in the U.S. and $6.99 each in Canada — it's quite a bargain! You may cancel at any time, but if you choose to continue, every month we'll send you 2 more books, which you may either purchase at the discount price or return to us and cancel your subscription.

*Terms and prices subject to change without notice. Sales tax applicable in N.Y. Canadian residents will be charged applicable provincial taxes and GST.

If offer card is missing write to: Harlequin Reader Service, 3010 Walden Ave., P.O. Box 1867, Buffalo NY 14240-1867

BUSINESS REPLY MAIL
FIRST-CLASS MAIL   PERMIT NO. 717   BUFFALO, NY

POSTAGE WILL BE PAID BY ADDRESSEE

HARLEQUIN READER SERVICE
3010 WALDEN AVE
PO BOX 1867
BUFFALO NY 14240-9952

NO POSTAGE
NECESSARY
IF MAILED
IN THE
UNITED STATES

The Lyon's Den

SELINA SINCLAIR

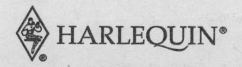

HARLEQUIN®

TORONTO • NEW YORK • LONDON
AMSTERDAM • PARIS • SYDNEY • HAMBURG
STOCKHOLM • ATHENS • TOKYO • MILAN • MADRID
PRAGUE • WARSAW • BUDAPEST • AUCKLAND

Dear Reader,

*It Happened One Night, Bringing Up Baby,
The Philadelphia Story...*

There's something magical about those old romantic
comedies. Maybe it's the larger-than-life characters
or the snappy repartee or all those crazy situations
the hero and heroine manage to get themselves into.
(Then again, maybe it's just Cary Grant. *Sigh.*)

It was one night after we'd just finished watching
Cary and Rosalind Russell in *His Girl Friday* that the
idea for *The Lyon's Den* was born.

When Lyon Mackenzie's personal assistant
resigns, Lyon is desperate to get her to stay. With
the biggest advertising account of his career—and
his dreams of success—at stake, he can't afford to
lose Miss Hammond. But Liv has a dream of her
own—one she has no intention of giving up for
the comfort of her boss. Can a bird, a baby, an old-
fashioned client, a bird-crazy mother-in-law-to-be
and an *outrageous* lie make both of their dreams
come true?

We invite you into *The Lyon's Den* to find out....

Happy reading,

Selina Sinclair

Books by Selina Sinclair

HARLEQUIN TEMPTATION®
688—DIAMOND IN THE ROUGH

To my sister, Shaffina,
who's always there when I need her. I love you.

To my best friend Salimah who, after eighteen years
of writing together, still manages to inspire
my creative side.

1

At precisely 7:50 a.m., Olivia Hammond stepped out of the calm peacefulness of the elevator and into the pandemonium of Monday morning at Mackensie Marketing. The usual medley of shrilling phones, squealing fax machines, assorted computer peripherals and raised voices assaulted her ears. She paused, deliberately cocking her ear toward the inner suite of offices, and listened carefully, until she was able to make out the familiar bellowing coming from the Den. Then she nodded to herself in satisfaction.

The Beast was in fine form this morning.

That was good.

In fact, the more decibels he could produce, the better. At least then it wouldn't be quite so difficult to appease her conscience for what she was about to do. Why was it, she wondered, that the stupid thing always had to kick in at the most inconvenient moments?

Because you're a sap, Liv. A chump who lets anything that roars loud enough walk all over you for a few measly bucks every week.

Well, okay. So the bucks weren't so measly. In fact, they were pretty phenomenal. Heck, for that much money, she'd let a herd of elephants walk all over her, never mind one human male whose only resemblance to Dumbo was in how loud he could roar on occasion.

Every occasion.

Luckily for her, as of this month, the ridiculous sum of money she received for allowing the Beast the privilege of using her as a human doormat-cum-personal assistant was no longer necessary. She'd put her sister through university and now that Jenny had received a full scholarship to do her graduate degree, Liv could afford to indulge her backbone.

Which basically meant that, conscience or no conscience, she was determined to ensure her colleague's future at Mackensie's before she resigned. If Lyon Mackensie was too stubborn to see the talent under his very nose, she would just have to grab him by the ears and force him to take a closer look.

And if her conscience decided to poke its nose in where it didn't belong, well, she'd just have to give it a mental kick in the pants.

So there.

She nodded to herself again, took a deep, fortifying breath and strode briskly forward, briefcase in hand. A moment later, Annie materialized beside her, looking distinctly harried.

"I thought I'd better warn you, Liv. The Beast is on the rampage again!"

Liv strode breezily by her secretary. "Not to worry, Annie. The head zookeeper has arrived."

"I hope you came prepared."

Before she had a chance to pull the earplugs out

of her briefcase and show Annie just how prepared she was, Liv was bombarded with a chorus of greetings.

"Morning, Liv!"

Without breaking her stride, she smiled at everyone before turning her attention back to Annie. "What's he bellowing about this time?"

"He can't find the Ellison file, marketing at TLI wants you to re-fax the copy for their new ad ASAP but no one can find it, and he wants the demographics report for the laundry detergent on his desk pronto." Annie took a deep breath and finished ominously, "And *then* there's the Tate file."

Her conscience niggled, but Liv forced herself to stomp on her fiendish nemesis with the biggest, baddest pair of boots she could conjure up. Then she turned to Annie and, with what she hoped was the perfect hint of innocent nonchalance, asked, "What about it?"

Annie rolled her eyes. "What do you think? He can't find it and, boy, is he in a rage."

"What did you tell him?"

Annie shot her an incredulous look. "Are you *crazy?* I'd have to get near him to tell him anything and I don't happen to have my whip and chair handy today." She shuddered delicately, her short strawberry-blond curls bouncing around her face. "Uhuh. I'm keeping out of this one. Not that I don't support the risk you guys are taking for Peter, but I'd rather show my support from a distance. *Long* distance."

"Somewhere where no one can reach out and touch you, huh?" said Liv dryly.

"Exactly."

It was too bad the Shuttle wasn't accepting passengers, thought Liv. She'd be willing to bet there were a whole lot of people at Mackensie's who'd much rather be anywhere else than here today. Preferably in another galaxy. The heavenly vision of cleaning out her desk and disappearing to the nether regions of the universe, somewhere Lyon Mackensie's howls of outrage couldn't penetrate, shimmered in front of Liv. She allowed herself to be momentarily seduced into the happy, blessedly *silent* fantasy before it broke up under the weight of reality.

And the reality was that she couldn't let Lyon Mackensie take out his mighty wrath on Peter or anyone else. Her conscience—the damnable nuisance—would only let her get away with so much before it decided to kick back.

Liv sighed inwardly, crossed her fingers behind her back and did the loyal employee thing. After all, she was still on Lyon Mackensie's dime. "C'mon, Annie, he's not that bad."

Annie snorted in disbelief. "Oh yeah? Wait until you hear what *else* he had to say."

Liv had a pretty good idea what else he had to say and she'd bet the last pair of earplugs in her possession that it wasn't in any way complimentary.

"Oh, gee, Annie, I don't know if I can stand to have any more illusions shattered today," she said with a grin. "Listen, I need to talk to Howard for a minute."

"If you're going to talk to him about you-know-what, I don't think I want to hear it. I figure the less I know, the less damage my eardrums will sustain in the long run."

"Coward."

"Absolutely."

Momentarily awed by the presence of a spinelessness greater than her own, Liv gave in. "Okay, why don't you go grab the demo report from Jack and the Ellison file from Leroy?"

Annie disappeared with admirable speed.

Liv made a detour past the cluster of drafting tables and computers, and stopped in front of a pale, tired-looking man in a rumpled suit.

"Morning, Howard. Is the Tate file where it's supposed to be?"

He nodded in the middle of a yawn. "Filed it under *M* for missing in action, just like you asked. Now let's just hope this plan doesn't backfire."

"Don't worry. This new ad concept is fantastic. Tate's people are going to love it."

"I hope so." Suddenly, Howard looked uncomfortable. "Uh, Liv? If it does backfire, you won't tell Mr. Mackensie that I—"

"That you what? Tried valiantly to talk me out of making the biggest mistake of my misbegotten career?" Liv smiled and patted his arm in reassurance. "Don't worry, Howard. It'll all turn out fine. You know how he is. He thinks very quickly on his feet. Remember the Fantastic Foods account? You told me yourself that he changed the ad concept in midsentence. And once he realizes what a great idea it really is, I know he'll thank us. Until then, just keep those earplugs handy.''

''You'll be happy to know,'' said Howard airily, leaning back in his chair and crossing his hands behind his head, ''that I won't be needing them. I've become immune to all varieties of bellowing, howling, screeching, wailing and whimpering.''

''The twins?''

Howard nodded. ''They're teething.''

Liv winced, remembering when her godson Sam had gone through that stage. The little stinker had yowled like a banshee nonstop for days, until Tina had been beside herself. ''Poor Howard. How's Kathy holding up?''

''She's doing okay. Tired though. She wants me to take some vacation time. I don't suppose you could...?''

She grinned at him. ''I'll see what I can do.''

Howard tossed her a grateful look just as Annie returned, breathless. ''You'd better hurry, Liv.''

Liv glanced at her watch as they rushed back to her office. ''Did you get the report and the file?''

Annie handed her the folders. ''Liv, he said if he doesn't get the Tate file in the next two minutes, heads are going to roll, starting with—and I quote—'that damned humorless, bespectacled Tartar of an assistant I had the misfortune to hire.'''

For the first time since she'd exited the elevator, Liv's stride faltered.

"Four thousand, nine hundred and ninety-nine," she muttered darkly.

Annie whistled softly. "He's fired you that many times already?"

Two-and-a-half times a day was the average, although there were days when the Beast truly outdid himself.

"Uh-huh."

"But you've only been here, what? Three years?"

"Five years, three months and twenty-two days."

Which, as far as Liv was concerned, was five years, three months and twenty-one days too many.

Annie shook her head in amazement. "I don't know how you do it, Liv. If I were his personal assistant, I'd probably either be in the funny farm or the state pen by now."

"Instead, you've managed to find the only place in the known universe that's like being in both at once," teased Liv.

"Tell me about it."

They were nearly at Annie's desk when a nervously earnest voice intercepted Liv. "Uh, Miss Hammond?" She turned to find Peter O'Brien trailing behind her like an eager puppy. "Did you get him to look at it yet?"

Annie groaned. "Here we go again. I don't think I want to be part of *this* conversation either."

"All right, you can re-fax the TLI copy. It's in the 'to be filed' tray on my desk."

"Okay, I'm outta here." Annie stopped and gave Liv a meaningful look. "Just remember, he's already threatened to fire you once today."

"Oh, dear. It's barely eight in the morning and he's already behind schedule."

"Liv, I mean it."

"Don't worry about me, Annie. I've got my best pair of butt-kicking boots on today."

Annie's glance flicked down to Liv's sensible black pumps and back up again. "Right," she said and, turning on her own three-inch spikes, shook her head and walked off.

Liv grinned after her, then turned back to Peter. "Just hang in there until this afternoon, okay, Peter? We've hit the point of no return and we'll know one way or the other when he gets back from his meeting."

He nodded and handed her the morning's mail. "You don't know how much I appreciate what you're doing for me, Miss Hammond, braving the Beast and all. I took this gofer job because I'd do anything to work with Mr. Mackensie, but it's just that I could be doing so much more and—"

"Hey, I'm already sold, remember?" she said gently. "And believe me, if anyone should be thankful around here, it's Mr. Mackensie. Pretty soon, he'll be getting a brilliant new addition to his Creative Team."

Peter tossed her an adoringly grateful look. "Thanks, Miss Hammond."

Liv sighed, wondering if she'd still be worthy of his adoration at the end of the day. "Sure thing, kid."

When Peter had gone, Liv riffled through the

stack of envelopes and flyers, tossing a handful into the trash can beside Annie's desk as she passed by.

Just as she entered her office, a roar sounded from the one next door.

"Where the hell is she anyway? I don't pay her good money to saunter in any damn time she feels like it!"

Liv calmly placed the mail and her briefcase on the desk before shedding her navy trench coat and hanging it up on the coatrack in the corner. Finally, she stepped in front of the small oval mirror mounted on the wall near the coatrack and grimaced. Five more days of dressing like Miss Ratchett, seventh-grade typing teacher extraordinaire, and then she would be free. No more granny buns, no more gray tweed suits and no more dinner plate-sized glasses perching on the end of her nose. Although the disguise had helped her project the image of emotional detachment and robotic efficiency Lyon Mackensie preferred, Liv sometimes wondered whether he'd notice if she appeared before him buck-naked, wearing nothing but a smear of red-hot lipstick and a smile. She suspected not, although the smile might puzzle him for all of ten seconds before he put it down to some strange trick of the light. Sighing, Liv smoothed a hand over her hair, straightened the jacket of her suit, and pushed the glasses farther up the bridge of her nose.

At precisely 7:59 a.m., she gathered together everything she needed and marched to the door joining her office with Lyon Mackensie's. She paused, marshaling the cloak of cool efficiency with which she always greeted him, then walked into the Lyon's Den.

For a moment, her composure slipped, her eyes widening in dismay as she glimpsed the disaster area that was his once immaculate office. The black filing cabinets lined up along one wall of the office stood open, their contents spilling out and covering every available surface. Files lay scattered haphazardly on the black leather sofa and on the glass-and-steel coffee table in front of it. The hardwood floor was littered with loose sheets of paper, all of which were probably hopelessly mixed up by now.

And in the middle of the chaos, behind a massive black desk, sat Lyon Mackensie, his bright blue eyes crackling with anger.

She was tempted to cross her eyes and stick out her tongue at him, just to see what he would do. Instead, she schooled her features into a suitably robotlike expression and stared back at him. "Good morning, Mr. Mackensie. You wanted to see me?"

"You're late," he growled.

She glanced at her watch. "Actually, sir, it is now precisely fifteen seconds after eight o'clock."

His glare turned into a ferocious scowl. "I don't care what time it is. I pay you to be here when I need you, not when you think it's convenient."

"Perhaps I can be of some assistance now, sir?"

"What did you do with the Tate file? I have to leave for a meeting with their people in a few minutes and I can't find it."

Wordlessly, Liv walked across the carpet of papers to the second filing cabinet, her fingers unerringly zeroing in on the decoy she'd purposely planted there on Friday afternoon. Of course, she'd had no fears that he'd actually find it by himself. Brilliant as he was, the man couldn't find a file even if she stuck it on his forehead and stood him in front of a mirror. Calmly, she lifted out the missing file, walked to his desk and handed it to him, all the while hoping like hell he wouldn't open it until it was too late.

"Will there be anything else, sir?"

"Where's the Ellison file?"

She set the file on the desk in front of him.

"And the demo report for Sunshine Suds?"

She placed the folder on top of the file.

"Re-fax the TLI copy and make sure they get it this time."

"Already taken care of, sir. Anything else?"

"Yeah," he grunted, getting up in one fluid motion, tossing everything into his briefcase and striding past her to the door leading out to the open work area. "Get someone to clean up this mess."

She watched his departing back with narrowed eyes, until it disappeared out the door. Then she slammed the door shut, turned around and stomped deliberately over the carpet of papers back to her office.

"Get someone to clean up this mess," she mimicked, heading straight for her computer.

Who did he think cleaned up after him? A battalion of vacuum-wielding fairies? She snorted inelegantly and began typing furiously. He'd be lucky if the fairies didn't turn him into a braying ass within two minutes of hearing all that barking and bellowing.

Luckily for him, she was no fairy. She didn't have the power to turn him into a toad or a donkey or the mother of tantrum-throwing twin two-year-olds in order to punish him. But, thanks to dear, sweet Ralph's proposal, she finally had the power to quit this job and pursue her own dreams. Dreams which had nothing whatsoever to do with beastly bosses and everything to do with a husband and children and nurturing her own perfect family.

She printed out her resignation, skimmed through its succinct message one last time and nodded to herself in satisfaction.

From now on, she was through cleaning up after Lyon Mackensie.

She was through putting up with his ranting and raving.

And, most of all, she was through playing robot to a thankless tyrant.

Provided, of course, she survived his wrath when he returned from his meeting.

Otherwise, she'd just be plain *through*.

AT PRECISELY 12:49 p.m., a door slammed in the adjacent office.

Liv knew exactly what time it was because she'd been glancing at her watch every two minutes for the past hour and, even though she'd been expecting it, she jumped at the sound.

The Beast was back.

Annie bounded from the chair where she'd been

taking notes and made rapidly for the door. "That's my cue. If you need anything, police, ambulance…tranquilizer gun, I'll be on the other side of the intercom." She stopped at the door and gave Liv a last, lingering look. "It's been nice knowing you, *bwana*," she said, closing the door behind her.

"Oh, for Pete's sake," muttered Liv. "You'd think I was being thrown to the lions."

She grimaced to herself at the terrible pun, then winced as a muffled thud sounded from next door. His briefcase hitting the floor, no doubt. There was a moment's silence, then the ominous sound of footsteps heading toward the door connecting their offices. Liv forced herself to take a deep, calming breath.

She knew precisely how she was going to handle this confrontation. She'd practiced all morning, and she knew she had good reasons for the unforgivable liberty she'd taken in switching the award-winning Mackensie Creative Team's ad concept for the one created by Peter O'Brien, Mackensie's resident gofer.

It was good for the company. Mackensie's needed bright, talented new employees if it was going to continue to grow. Peter was more talented than most and deserved a chance to prove his ability. Besides, Peter's concept was brilliant; Tate's people had probably loved it. Yes, she nodded to herself, a calm, rational approach would be best. Robotic efficiency at its finest to counter the Beast's earblisteringly unique brand of ranting and raving.

The doorknob turned.

Liv squeezed her eyes shut and offered up a fervent prayer that it would be over quickly.

The door swung open with a crash.

Liv opened her eyes and then wished she hadn't.

He resembled nothing so much as a black-haired avenging angel, his eyes shooting bright blue sparks at her as he stood silhouetted in the doorway.

Why was it, she wondered inanely, that she'd never before noticed just how *large* he was? He towered over her desk, his massive shoulders blocking out the light, his anger seeming to suck up all the air in the room.

You're hyperventilating, Liv. Breathe...breathe. That's it. Remain calm. Remember, robotic efficiency.

She forced herself to ask as expressionlessly as possible, "Did you want something, sir?"

"I want to know just what the *hell* you think you're playing at."

Liv swallowed.

He wasn't ranting. He wasn't raving. He hadn't even raised his voice.

In fact, his question had been asked with a cold, quiet menace that she'd never heard from him before.

And it scared the living bejeebers out of her.

Before she could help herself, she jumped out of her chair and blurted, "But it's brilliant! You have to admit, it's brilliant!"

"Brilliant!" he roared finally, waving a piece of paper in front of her nose. "You call these two bloody trite sentences brilliant?"

Liv opened her mouth, closed it, flopped down in her chair again and blinked as the truth hit her.

He wasn't angry over the Tate fiasco. He hadn't even mentioned it. He was, however, *livid* over her resignation.

An overpowering tide of relief poured through her and she had to suppress the insane urge to giggle.

"Answer me, damn it!"

"I believe, sir, that my intention is stated quite clearly on that piece of paper you're waving around. I'm resigning as your personal assistant, effective immediately."

His eyes narrowed as he studied her for a moment.

"How much?" he asked suddenly.

She stared at him in confusion. "How much what?"

"How much more money do you want?"

Liv nearly laughed out loud. He thought her resignation was a ploy to get a raise?

"You pay me quite enough, sir, thank you," she said demurely.

"If you don't want a raise, then what the hell is this all about?"

Liv almost felt sorry for him. For the first time in living memory, Lyon Mackensie was at a loss.

"As I said in the letter, I'm resigning for personal reasons."

"Personal reasons?" he barked. "What personal reasons?"

"I'm getting married, sir."

LYON MACKENSIE STARED at the woman sitting in front of him and tried to imagine her engaged to be married.

He could feel his mind boggling from the strain. In order to be engaged, she would have to go out on a date with a man, kiss him, make love to him.... Why, the entire notion was unthinkable!

This was Miss Hammond, for God's sake, his efficient, bespectacled personal assistant, the one who wore dull suits and bound her hair in a bun! A woman...a woman looked different. A woman acted differently. A woman was supposed to be shapely and sexy, soft and sweet-smelling, with big breasts, a tiny waist and long, long legs encased in black silk stockings....

''Of course, I'll work the one-week notice as stipulated in my contract.''

Her expressionless voice brought him back to earth with a crash.

''One week! Where's Smith? Why would he put a ridiculous clause like that in a contract? I don't pay him to—''

''He didn't, sir. You did.''

''Me? Why would I do an asinine thing like that?''

''I believe your reasoning was very simple. You said one personal assistant or secretary was as good—or as bad—as another and, therefore, quite dispensable.''

Lyon groaned inwardly. That sounded like something he'd say and, under normal circumstances, he'd probably have been right, too. But Miss Hammond was different. She'd been with him since the inception of Mackensie's. She was efficient. She had things done even before he knew he wanted them done. Sometimes, he was convinced that she could read his mind. But the best thing about her was that she never, *ever* acted like a woman; she never cried when he lost his temper, never looked at him with big, reproachful eyes that made him feel like a heel. She was...well, she was the next best thing to having a *real* robot as a P.A.

He couldn't lose her. Not now. Not when he was about to reel in the biggest account this company had ever landed. He needed her, at least until the Tate deal was settled.

But how could he convince her to stay?

He thought quickly, sifting through the possibilities until he hit on something.

She was supposed to be a woman, wasn't she? And women were invariably susceptible to anything that engaged their emotions. Maybe if he tried to appeal to her feminine side...

He tried to dig up a wounded expression and clasped his hands behind his back in what he hoped was a suitably humble stance. "In all the time you've been with us, I've never questioned your devotion to this company and I can't tell you how much it pains me to do so now. My dear Miss Hammond, where is your sense of loyalty?"

He deliberately paused a moment, until he saw her eyes widen in surprise at his unexpected attack. Just as she opened her mouth to say something, he launched into his diatribe with renewed vigor. "I must say, I'm disappointed. Very disappointed, indeed. That you should choose to leave us now, at this crucial moment in our history, just as Mackensie Marketing teeters on the brink of greatness." He shook his head gravely. "I didn't think you were the type of person who would abandon us all in our greatest hour of need, leaving us to tumble to ruin while you go gallivanting off with...with..."

"Ralph," she said flatly.

"Ralph?" He turned and scowled at her. "For God's sake, what kind of a name is Ralph?"

"I'm afraid, sir, we can't all be as blessed as you in the name department."

He glanced at her, narrowing his eyes in suspicion at the hint of sarcasm he thought he detected in her voice. But she continued to stare at him with the bland expression that was rapidly beginning to grate on his nerves.

"You were saying, sir?"

He shoved a hand through his hair. Damn it, what had he been blabbering about?

"I believe you were in the middle of tumbling to ruin," she prompted.

Ah, yes.

"How could you go off with Ralph and leave me here to fend for myself, helpless as a newborn babe? I—"

"The only resemblance between you and a baby is the amount of gibberish you can spout at any given moment," she said, cutting him off with the ruthless efficiency he'd come to expect from her. "Now why don't we skip the guilt trip and cut right to the chase. What do you want from me?"

He shot her a disgusted look. He should have known better than to think she had a feminine side. He shouldn't have let all this nonsense about marriage sidetrack him. She was simply Miss Hammond and he was going to approach this ridiculous whim of hers in the same way he would approach her about any other business matter. He was going to tell her what he wanted and she was going to do whatever was necessary in order to get it for him.

Satisfied that this was the right course of action to take, he held up her letter of resignation and, with a flourish, tore it into pieces.

''The bottom line, Miss Hammond, is that I'm not going to accept your resignation. I'm afraid I can't let you leave Mackensie's right now.''

Liv stared in mute horror as the white scraps of paper fluttered through the air, feeling irrationally as though they were her long-cherished dreams landing in the trash can by her desk.

''If you want to get married to this…Ralph character, you go right ahead, as long as your private life doesn't interfere with my comfort or the way I run my business. I expect—''

His comfort?

After putting up with this arrogant ass—who couldn't act his way out of a second-grade school play—for five years, she had finally found a man she could spend the rest of her life with, a man who could help her make all her dreams of the perfect family, the perfect life, come true, and he expected her to put all that aside for *his* comfort?

Liv felt her blood cells frothing and fizzing in her

veins like air bubbles in a champagne bottle before
surging to her brain in a dizzying rush. There they
exploded in a fountain of rage.

She marched around her desk, coming closer and
closer to her target, intent on one thing and one thing
only.

I'll show him comfort.

She stopped only when her nose was nearly
touching his chest, and found to her chagrin that she
still had to strain her neck to look at him. Recklessly, she grabbed his designer silk tie and wrapped
it around her hand, slowly pulling him down until
they were nose to nose and she was staring into his
stunned eyes.

"You listen to me, mister," she ground out, "and
you listen good because I'm going to tell you once
and for all exactly what I think of you and your
comfort. You—" she poked a finger into his chest
with her free hand "—are a bully. Nothing but a
loudmouthed—"

Poke.

"—obnoxious—"

Poke.

"—bully who thinks he can treat people like dirt
just because they work for him. I've put up with
your rude behavior and your tactless demands for
five years because I thought that somewhere under
those thousand-dollar suits and that thick skin you
actually had something remotely resembling a heart.
Hell, I even defended you to the others! I should
have known better." Abruptly, she released his tie
and stalked to the coatrack. "Even a robot is entitled

to a little respect and consideration, and since it's obvious that you have none to give " she snatched up her coat and flung it over her arm "—it's only fitting that I should reciprocate. So consider this all the *comfort* you're going to get from me." She marched to her desk and grabbed her briefcase. "I quit!"

"You can't quit," he roared, "because you're fired!"

Liv halted on her way to the door. With calm deliberation, she turned around and walked back to where he was standing.

And then she kicked him in the shin.

Hard.

"Five thousand," she counted with considerable satisfaction as she walked out the door.

2

AT PRECISELY 1:14 p.m., Liv walked into Jake's, a crowded restaurant-bar located a couple of blocks away from Mackensie Marketing. She'd gotten some very strange looks on the way here, but that was understandable. It wasn't every day people saw a well-dressed woman stomping down the street, muttering, cursing and occasionally waving her fist at an imaginary adversary. It wasn't something she did very often. In fact, she'd never done it before, but then again, she hadn't kicked anyone in the shin before, either, with the possible exception of Kenny Cradock, but she'd been five at the time and Kenny had been a royal pain in the butt, so that didn't count.

Of course, Lyon Mackensie was a royal pain in the butt, too, so maybe that didn't count, either. Except that she wasn't five anymore, she was thirty, and she should have learned how to control her temper better in the intervening twenty-five years.

But, damn it, the moment her foot had connected with his shin—not to mention his ensuing howl of pain—had been so… Well, perhaps orgasmic was too strong a word. Her lips curved into a smile as she took off her trench coat. Close though. Very, very close.

"Hi, can I help you?" The cute, perky-looking hostess greeted Liv with a megawatt smile.

Liv grinned at her in return. "Yes, I'm meeting a friend here. Tina Moretti."

She couldn't wait to tell Tina everything. Not only about this morning, but about Ralph and the proposal and her plans for the rest of her life. Even though she and Tina had drifted further apart in the last couple of years, ever since Tina had gotten married and had little Sam, Liv knew that Tina would understand.

Unlike *some* people.

Tina would be happy for her.

Unlike *some* people.

Tina would probably laugh and cry and congratulate her.

Unlike…well, actually, Tina would probably squeal louder than a stuck pig, hug her to death and then order two Bloody Marys to celebrate, but that was what best friends were supposed to do, wasn't it?

"Ms. Moretti is waiting for you at table eleven." The hostess pointed to a table for two near the back of the restaurant. Liv spotted Tina right away, flirting outrageously with a waiter. The man left with a smile that guaranteed outstanding service, and Liv made a mental note to invite Tina to lunch more often.

As Liv approached the table, Tina caught sight of

her, looked her up and down, and blinked. "Tell me it's Halloween."

Liv grinned and sat down opposite her friend. "'Fraid not. Last time I looked, it was still April."

Tina shuddered. "Then I don't think it's safe to sit near you. Whatever you have might be catching."

Liv eyed Tina's hot little pink suit, flawless makeup and wild black curls and snorted. "Don't worry, you've got a built-in antidote."

"And speaking of antidotes, what's with the get-up?"

"It's not a getup. It's what I wear to work."

"*Every day?* And your boss hasn't thrown you into the pokey for committing crimes against good taste?"

Liv snorted. "He wouldn't know good taste if it bit him on the nose."

Well, that wasn't precisely true. Lyon Mackensie dressed with immaculate style himself. It was just *her* bad taste he didn't notice.

"By the way, since you were a little late, I ordered for us. Hope you don't mind. Colin said it should be here any minute."

Puzzled, Liv asked, "Colin?"

"Our cute waiter with the outstanding buns."

Liv shook her head in mock reproof. "You know, sometimes I look at you and wonder how you ever produced a sweet little baby like Sam."

"It's no secret. He might have his father's good looks and personality, but he gets his superior drooling ability from his mama," said Tina smugly, bestowing a charming smile on the waiter as he arrived with their order.

"Okay, ladies, here we are. A fresh garden salad, dressing on the side, and mineral water with a twist of lime for you." He placed the order in front of Liv without so much as glancing at her and then turned to Tina with a blinding smile. "And a hamburger with a double order of fries and two Bloody Marys for the lovely lady here. Enjoy your meal."

"Thank you, Colin."

Liv picked up her fork, frowned at her salad, eyed Tina's basket of golden fries, shoved the salad away and speared a French fry. "Anyway, the outfit's not that bad, is it?"

"Trust me, you don't want me to answer that. Here, have a Bloody Mary instead."

Liv considered her options for a moment before grabbing the glass Tina slid her way and taking a big gulp. "Okay, I agree it's hideous, but you can soothe your offended fashion sense with the fact that I won't be needing it after today."

Tina put down the hamburger she'd been about to bite into and sighed in resignation. "All right, Liv, what have you done this time?"

"YOU DIDN'T." Tina shook her head in disbelief. "Tell me you didn't."

"You bet I did. And I'd do it again." Except next time, she'd remember to wear pointy-toed shoes.

"Let me get this straight. You switched the ad campaign that the pros came up with for something from a kid from the mailroom?"

"Yes, but—"

"Without telling your boss?"

"Yes, but—"

"Just before he went to a meeting with the client?"

"You don't have to make it sound so horrible! I wouldn't have done it if I hadn't known he could handle it," Liv replied defensively.

"But why didn't you just *tell* him about the kid's idea?"

"It's this Tate Birdseed account," said Liv irritably. "He's lost all objectivity about it. He's been trying to lure Mr. Tate, who happens to be ultraconservative, into signing with Mackensie's for the past six months and he's convinced the only way to do it is to play it safe. Peter's idea is brilliant, but it also involves two birds basking in a post-coital glow."

"Okay, so he plays it safe and he doesn't get the account. Big deal."

"You don't understand, Tina. If he doesn't get this account, he's going to be even more insufferable to work with than he is now. Besides, if Mackensie's gets the account, we get to play in the big leagues. It's good for all of us."

"So you decided to take the matter into your own hands?"

"Right. We figured the only way the client was going to hear Peter's concept was if Mr. Mackensie was forced to use it, and then once he'd seen how brilliantly it worked, he'd be so grateful, he'd *have* to promote Peter."

Tina arched a delicate black brow. "We? So it wasn't just your idea? Some other lunatic agreed to it, too?"

Liv nodded. Actually the idea had been Howard's, but they'd all agreed to take a chance on it, if only for the sake of their collective sanity.

"And what if—call me crazy for asking—this Tate guy didn't like the concept? Who was supposed to take the fall?"

Liv shifted in her seat. "Well, I guess I was."

"Uh-huh."

"Don't look at me like that! Howard has newborn twins and Jack and his wife just bought a house and Leroy's trying to finance his music career and Annie..." Well, Annie was just a coward.

"So you decided to be the sacrificial lamb."

"Please don't start with the 'you let everyone take advantage of you' speech again," pleaded Liv. "Anyway, it doesn't matter because I'd already planned to resign."

"Except that Mackensie didn't want you to resign, but you got carried away, called him a loud-mouthed, obnoxious bully and physically assaulted him. Have I got that right?"

"Pretty much." When Tina put it like that, it sounded...slightly irrational.

"Are you completely out of your mind?"

"Hey, whose side are you on, anyway?"

"Yours! I'm always on your side. Except when you temporarily lose your mind and do stupid, impulsive things. For Pete's sake, Liv, you're supposed to be the rational one here! What are you going to do now? I know Jenny's got a scholarship to grad school and everything, but you've still got yourself to look after. How are you going to pay the rent?''

''I've got enough money saved to get me through to June.''

''What then? What's going to happen in June?''

Liv took a deep breath and prepared to tell Tina the one thing she hadn't quite gotten around to mentioning yet. ''I'm getting married.''

Tina choked on her Bloody Mary. *''You're what?''*

Liv rolled her eyes and handed Tina a napkin. Why was it that everyone had such a hard time believing she was getting married? ''You heard me.''

Tina squeezed her eyes shut. ''Tell me it's April Fool's today.''

''It's *not* April Fool's.''

''Okay, okay, I'm sorry. It's just that, last time we talked you weren't even dating anyone remotely interested in marriage, except for that guy with the bird-happy mother. What was his name? Rover? Randolph?''

''Ralph,'' said Liv with gritted teeth. ''His name is Ralph!''

''That's right, Ralph, and if I recall correctly, he didn't exactly sound like the kind of guy to sweep you off your feet.''

''No, but he's kind and sweet and gentle. He doesn't roar and bellow and bark at me, not like *some* men I know. And he doesn't go out with a different blonde every month and get me to send her a kiss-off gift when he's tired of her. Honestly, I don't know what women see in him. He's rude and obnoxious and he thinks he can buy everyone with his money. He—''

"Uh, Liv?"

"Yeah?"

"We were talking about Ralph."

"Ralph?"

"Uh-huh. Ralph. The man you're going to marry?"

Liv flushed guiltily. "Sorry. It's just that that man makes my blood boil every time I think about him."

"And Ralph doesn't."

"Well, no—I mean yes—I mean no, not in that way, but— Oh, you know what I mean!"

"I'm beginning to," muttered Tina.

"Anyway, I happen to think he's perfect. I just know he's going to be a good husband and a great father."

"But what about love and excitement and *passion?* Don't you want that, too?"

"As far as I'm concerned, passion is overrated," said Liv.

Passion, after all, was what she felt for Lyon Mackensie.

A passionate dislike.

A passionate desire to bop him in the kisser.

Yeah, passion was a powerful emotion, all right. That and a quarter would get her a phone call to either a shrink or a lawyer, but not much else.

Liv swallowed a fry and took a big gulp of her Bloody Mary. "Besides, I've had enough excitement at Mackensie's to last me a lifetime. I'm tired of it. At this point in my life, I'll take security, affection and companionship over excitement any day.''

"Security, affection and companionship," repeated Tina in disgust. "Maybe the granny bun isn't such a bad look for you after all.''

"I'm trying to be realistic here!" said Liv in exasperation. "I'm thirty years old, Tina, and the men aren't exactly lined up at my doorstep, begging to give me children and a lifetime commitment.''

"So you're going to settle—"

"I'm not settling! I'm marrying a man who loves me. We're going to get married, raise a family and live happily ever after. I thought you'd be happy for me!"

Tina was instantly apologetic. "I'm sorry, Liv. I didn't mean to rain on your parade." She took one of Liv's hands and squeezed tightly. "And I *am* happy for you. It's just that…''

"It's just that what?''

"It's just that sometimes love and marriage and children aren't enough.''

Liv sat up ramrod straight. Aside from her parents, who had passed away in a car accident five years ago, Tina and Paul had the happiest marriage of anyone Liv knew. What could possibly be wrong? "What do you mean? Tina, what's wrong?''

Tina sighed. "Everything. Paul doesn't want me to go back to work after my maternity leave is over. When we were at his cousin's wedding on Saturday, he had his whole family on my case. His mother, his sisters, his uncles and aunts and cousins, all telling me how they think I should stay at home, at least until Sam starts school. I love Sam and I love Paul, but after staying home alone with the baby for nine months, I need to have a life of my own, Liv. Besides, my job's just as important to me as his is to him, and I can't risk losing my skills. But Paul says if I was home I'd be able to pay more attention to him and the baby. I just don't know what to do anymore!''

Liv kicked herself mentally. She should have known Tina wasn't acting normally, but she'd been so preoccupied with her own news, she hadn't even realized. ''Oh, Tina, I'm so sorry. Is there anything I can do?'' she asked gently.

''Thanks, honey, but I don't think so. I know Paul and I need to spend some time together and work out some of the things we should have decided on before we got married, but with the baby and everything, there just doesn't seem to be enough time.''

''Look, why don't you and Paul go away for a few days? Maybe just the weekend. Talk to Paul and see what he says, and if he's agreeable, I'll take care of Sam for you. Deal?''

Tina bit her lip uncertainly. ''I don't know.... Are you sure you wouldn't mind? Sam can be a handful and I—''

''Of course I won't mind! I've been dying to get my hands on that adorable little baby for ages! And it'll be good practice for me. Besides, I'm a free woman now, remember?''

Tina laughed, her relief evident. ''How could I

forget? Come on, let's have a toast.'' She raised her glass. ''To my best friend Liv. Here's to losing your job and finding a fiancé!''

''Hear, hear.''

They clinked glasses and downed the rest of their drinks in one go.

''Okay, Hammond, let's get to the good stuff. Tell me everything. How did he propose? Was it terribly romantic? I remember when Paul proposed. He brought me flowers and candy and champagne, and then when I said yes, he got down on his knees and—''

''He got down on his knees *after* you said yes?''

''How do you think we ended up with Sam nine months later?'' asked Tina with a grin. ''Well, was it romantic?''

''Uh, not quite as romantic as that. It happened on Thursday night. He was teaching me how to play bridge when—''

Tina waved a French fry in the air. ''Whoa, back up here. He was teaching you how to play *what?*''

''Bridge. His mother is a bridge fanatic and he thought he'd teach me so I'd have something in common with her. Isn't that sweet?''

''Yeah, peachy. Listen, Liv, you gotta get out more, you know?''

''Oh, be quiet! *I* thought it was sweet. Anyway, I finally got the hang of it and he was so excited, he just kind of blurted it out.''

After he'd proposed, she didn't know who had been more surprised, she or Ralph. They'd been going out for over six months and she really liked him. He treated her with respect and dignity, and he was kind and thoughtful and undemanding.

And, most important of all, he loved her.

All right, so his kisses didn't exactly inspire her to tear off his clothes and he was a little, well, *pre-occupied* with his mother, but what did that matter? Here was a man who loved her, who wanted to marry her, who wanted children, and who was old-fashioned enough to want her to stay home and look after her family. What more could she ask for?

Besides, Ralph *needed* her.

"I like being with you, Olivia," he'd confessed shyly after he'd blurted out his proposal. "I don't know what I would have done without you. When I moved here from Baltimore, away from Mother, I was at a loss, but since I've known you, my life's been so different. Better. You…you understand, don't you, Olivia?"

She understood perfectly. Ralph was just like her father. He needed someone to look after him, and when they were married, she was going to do her best to be a good wife to him. The first step toward doing that was forgetting about Lyon Mackensie and her job. From now on, she was going to concentrate on being Mrs. Ralph Fortescue V, and everything that entailed. Hey, maybe she'd even join his mother's bridge club and the Bird Society.

She ran the idea past Tina. "What do you think?"

"Bridge club? Bird society?" Tina sighed. "I think I need another drink."

AT PRECISELY 3:46 p.m. that afternoon, Lyon stopped pacing in front of his desk just long enough to glower at the red-faced kid cowering in front of him.

"Where is she?"

"But, sir, don't you remember? You fired her at noon!"

"So what?" said Lyon, resuming his pacing. "I fire her twice a day, every day, but the damn woman never leaves."

She was as stubborn as a cross between a mule and a billy goat. The first time he'd fired her, on her first day of work, she'd just given him that trademark who-do-you-think-you-are look of hers and carried on as though he wasn't even there.

"But, sir," stammered O'Brien, "she walked out at lunchtime."

"You mean to tell me she just left without a word?"

"Yes, sir. Well, no, not exactly, sir. She did say something, sir."

Lyon stopped in midstride, turned around and pinned the kid on the spot. "What did she say?"

"She…she called you a…a—" the kid swallowed before straightening manfully and blurting out "—a pigheaded horse's ass, sir."

"I see." At least, he was beginning to. "And she hasn't been seen since?"

"No, sir. And you know Miss Hammond." An admiring glint came into the kid's eyes. "She never leaves early."

Lyon frowned. He *thought* he knew Miss Hammond, but after their dust-up earlier in the day, he wasn't so sure. The shrew with the flashing brown eyes and angry flags of color in her cheeks hadn't been anything like the Miss Hammond *he* knew. The Miss Hammond *he* knew would never have shouted such blatantly ridiculous accusations at him, nor would she have kicked him in the shin with such zealous satisfaction.

No, this new Miss Hammond was different. She was a seething bundle of female hormones. And if that's what the prospect of marriage did to a reasonably sane woman, he'd hate to think of what it would do to a somewhat *in*sane woman. It was just as well that he never intended to find out.

As for this new Miss Hammond, perhaps he was well rid of her. The prospect of dealing with a bossy, overly emotional personal assistant didn't appeal to him. He was sad at losing her, but if that's what she wanted, Ralph was welcome to her.

And if she thought she was indispensable to Mackensie Marketing, she was mistaken! No one was indispensable, least of all that termagant of a personal assistant.

After all, how hard could it be to get along without her?

LESS THAN TWENTY-FOUR hours later, Lyon was holed up in his office, hiding from the conspiracy outside. He'd been driven to take cover by the yelling (his own), the crying (Annie's) and the *looks* (everybody's). He could have survived the rest—it would have been no different from any other day— but it was those accusing stares, the ones that made him feel like he'd just slaughtered a forest full of furry creatures, that made the difference.

The day had started out fine. He'd come in early, ready to begin just another day at the office.

By eight-thirty, he'd been hoarse.

By nine-thirty, he'd been frantically trying to stay one step ahead of the chaos that seemed to be swallowing up his life.

By ten-thirty, he'd been a life-sentence away from murdering Annie.

By eleven-thirty, he'd fired the entire staff at least twice.

By twelve-thirty, he'd been tempted to fire himself and get the hell out while he still had his sanity, except that he still had a Creative Team meeting to get through this afternoon.

He was planning on chewing out the entire team for switching the Tate ad concept on him yesterday. Luckily, Tate's people had seemed to like the new concept, and even he had to admit the idea was pretty good. But that wasn't the point. Whoever had masterminded the scheme deserved to be fired, although, if he wasn't mistaken, she already had been. Nevertheless, he was determined to make it absolutely clear that he never wanted a stunt like that to be pulled again.

So when Annie had burst into tears that last time—just because he'd reprimanded her for disconnecting an important phone call, for Pete's sake— instead of running for the elevator, he'd pivoted on his heel, marched back to his office, closed the door, locked it, picked up the phone and called the employment agency.

Apparently, they were in on the conspiracy, too, because they couldn't send a replacement for Miss Hammond until next Monday.

He wasn't sure he could survive that long.

Sighing, he prepared himself to leave his safe little hideaway and brave the outside world again.

Just then, the phone rang. He snatched up the receiver before Annie could get her disconnect-happy hands on it.

"Mackensie speaking."

"Lyon, my boy, how are you?"

At the sound of the bluff, hearty voice, a cold sweat broke out on his forehead. This was the phone call he'd been waiting for—and dreading—ever since yesterday. The entire future of Mackensie's rested on its outcome.

"Fine, Mr. Tate."

"Glad to hear it. I'm calling to congratulate you on the fine presentation yesterday. My marketing people were very impressed with your team's work."

Lyon felt light-headed with relief. "Thank you, sir."

"We're seriously thinking about giving Mackensie's the birdseed account..."

He sat up in his chair. Thinking about it? *Thinking about it?* What was there to think about? They'd done everything but turn cartwheels for Tate in the past six months, and they'd delivered a solid ad concept yesterday. What the hell was there to think about?

"...but we have a reputation to uphold, you know. Why, we've been selling birdseed for over forty years..."

Lyon forced himself to remain calm as Tate launched into a speech that had obviously been delivered many times before.

"...and we pride ourselves on only dealing with companies that share our values, the same values we started out with forty years ago: family, honesty and integrity. Those are the cornerstones of any good company, along with good management and organization. Now, some people think it's silly and old-fashioned—"

Lyon roused himself enough to say, "Not at all, sir!"

"I'm glad you agree with me, my boy. So you won't mind if I fly in on Monday to meet your people and see how you do things."

The cold fingers of dread crept up Lyon's spine.

"By the way, where's Olivia?"

"Olivia?"

"Yes, your assistant. A lovely, charming woman, your Olivia. Smart as a whip and very knowledgeable about birds. Reminds me of my Millie, God rest her soul. We had a very interesting little chat last week."

Lovely? Charming? *His* Olivia?

"She's, uh, she's not here at the moment."

Hell, the woman Tate was describing had *never* been here.

"Well you tell her I'm looking forward to meeting her in person and discussing her thoughts on the Purple-Bellied Polka-Dotted Cuckoo's mating habits on Monday."

The Purple-Bellied Polka-Dotted Cuckoo?

"I'll be sure to pass on the message, sir."

A moment later, he hung up the phone, put his head down on his desk and groaned.

The conspiracy, it seemed, was complete.

3

"OH MY GOD," whispered Liv as she stopped short in front of the elevator.

The carefully ordered office she had left on Monday afternoon had disappeared, buried, it seemed, under a blanket of utter chaos. Stacks of files, topped with coffee cups and stale sandwiches, were piled on every available surface, papers and sketches littered the floors, computer monitors flashed psychedelic screen savers and chairs had been left upturned. It seemed as though an emergency evacuation had taken place and Liv had a pretty good idea of the destructive force everyone had been running from.

"You should have seen them, Liv. They couldn't get out of here fast enough when four o'clock rolled around. Like rats abandoning a sinking ship," said Annie in disgust. "Not that I blame them. I told you, he's been impossible all day. If we weren't all such cowards, we would have mutinied by now."

Liv was afraid to go any farther for fear of what she would find. "Is the rest this bad?"

Annie grimaced. "Worse."

"And he managed to do this all by himself in one day?"

"Well, not exactly. You see, it's not so much that he turned the office upside down himself…"

"Then how did this happen?"

"It's his *attitude,* Liv. When you were here, he used to just yell and roar at you, and then you'd calmly tell us all what had to get done. You acted as a buffer, see? But with you gone, he comes out here and makes everybody so nervous and jittery with all his carrying on, it's hard to get anything done. This morning, he sneaked up on me while I was stuffing the courier packs and he made me so nervous I got them mixed up. This afternoon he got a call from the Sunshine Suds people wondering why they got a chicken wiener contract instead of the demographics report. And then I accidentally disconnected the call and that's when he yelled at me and told me I was incompetent and threatened to fire me and I couldn't take it anymore so I started to cry, and you know how he hates that, so he slammed back into the Den and that's when I called you."

"Breathe, Annie! That's it, love. Okay, look, why don't we start by cleaning up this mess? And then I'll give you a rundown of the Tate account. You start out here and I'll take care of the Den, okay?"

Annie nodded.

"All right, let's get to work."

Liv went into Lyon Mackensie's office, grimacing at what she found. An hour later, she found herself crawling under his massive desk in an attempt to finish tidying his office.

"Why is it that I always end up under here trolling for missing papers?" she asked herself.

There was no reply, just the echo of her own mutterings in the darkness under the desk. Not that she needed a reply. She already knew the answer: she was a pushover and she hadn't been able to resist Annie's pleas for help over the phone this afternoon. When Annie had told her that the Beast had bawled everyone out at the Creative Team meeting this afternoon and had seriously threatened to fire people if anything went wrong with the Tate account, she couldn't help but feel guilty. She'd agreed to come down and help Annie. Nevertheless, she'd been absolutely insistent on not seeing Lyon Mackensie again. She was still so mad at him, she could spit.

"What if you didn't have to see him?" Annie had asked, suddenly excited.

"What do you mean?"

"I mean, if you come down right now, you won't have to! He slammed out of the office at five muttering something about a conspiracy and he has a date with the blond dimbo tonight, so I don't think he'll be coming back."

Liv had smiled reluctantly at Annie's description of Lyon Mackensie's latest girlfriend, then made a quick decision. "All right, if you're sure he won't be there."

"He won't," said Annie with absolute conviction. "He'll be too busy staring at two of Melanie's biggest assets over the dinner table to even think about work."

And while he was staring at his girlfriend's "assets," she was cleaning under this mausoleum he called a desk.

Liv sighed and swept her arm over her face to try and dislodge the strand of hair that had slipped out of her ponytail.

A moment later, she thought she heard a door slam outside and she wondered how Annie was doing. She cocked her head and listened for a minute, but everything was quiet.

A little too quiet.

No phones ringing, no faxes squealing, no people scurrying to and fro and, most unusually of all, no Lyon Mackensie.

Liv frowned. She'd never actually been in the office alone before. Even when she worked late, Lyon Mackensie invariably worked later, and he had no qualms about expecting the rest of his staff to put in overtime. He paid them handsomely for their time and thought nothing of the fact that they might have families waiting for them at home.

"The inconsiderate swine," she muttered, reaching way back under his chair for the last sheet of paper.

Just then, she heard the door open behind her.

"Great timing, Annie. I'm just about done here," she said, crawling backwards from under the desk. "Just let me put this stuff away and then we'll talk about the Tate account."

She stood, put the sheaf of papers she'd collected into the open file on the desk, turned around...and screamed.

THE FIRST THING Lyon saw when he returned to his office was a deliciously curved female derriere encased in tight-fitting jeans mooning up at him. He was pleasantly surprised and properly appreciative. Then he heard the owner of said derriere speak and something in his brain recoiled at the sound.

It couldn't be.

But when she turned around, he knew without a doubt that it was. The large, round-framed glasses gave her away. Without them, he might have been appreciative a while longer. But that was impossible when her features began transforming themselves from a look of animated shock into the usual blank mask.

He frowned. Even with that familiar look on her face, there was something different about her. Something that made his heart beat faster in his chest and his tongue stick to the roof of his mouth. Maybe it was the shapeless gray sweatshirt, or the shiny nose, or the streak of dirt across her forehead, or the scraggly lopsided ponytail. Whatever it was, it made him uneasy because his cool, efficient Miss Hammond had never looked less like a robot.

Or more like a flesh-and-blood woman.

He stepped closer and reached out a hand to touch the soft, flushed skin of her cheek, to feel if she was real, but he stopped himself in the nick of time. Instead, he sent her a black scowl.

"So this is where you've been hiding! I've been looking all over town for you."

Liv let out the pent-up breath she'd been holding.

The silence had been too good to last. *This* was more like it. "You've been looking for me?"

"What are you doing here anyway? Spying on me?"

She stared at him in astonishment. Surely, even for him, this was taking ranting and raving too far.

"Don't look at me like that! We both know you're as guilty as sin. I talked to Mr. Tate this afternoon and it's finally become clear to me. You planned it all along, didn't you?" With his hands clasped behind him, he began prowling back and forth in front of her. "Getting married. Ha!" he muttered. Suddenly, he stopped and pinned her with his laser-beam blue gaze. "Why? Why would you do this to me?"

Liv picked up a stack of files from the desk and headed for the filing cabinets. "Why would I do what to you?"

"You know, sabotage me!"

"Sabotage you." She sighed inwardly and prayed for patience. "What exactly did Mr. Tate say to you?"

"Does the Purple-Bellied Polka-Dotted Cuckoo ring a bell?" he asked grimly.

Startled, she glanced up at him. "The Purple-Bellied Polka-Dotted Cuckoo? What does *that* have to do with anything?"

"Since you're the lovely, charming bird expert, why don't you tell me?"

"Look, all I know is that Mr. Tate has an unusual fondness for the little things," she said, opening the filing cabinet.

"And so, I take it, do you?"

"Me? Oh no, that would be Mrs. Fortescue."

"And who," he asked ominously, "is Mrs. Fortescue?"

"Ralph's mother. You see, last week she had an article published in the Bird Society magazine on the Purple-Bellied Polka-Dotted Cuckoo. It's her favorite bird, you know, and it's very rare. Ralph gave me the article and I was reading it when you asked me to get Mr. Tate on the phone for you. Remember?"

He nodded impatiently and she continued. "Well, he picked up his own phone because his secretary was out. I asked him a question about birdseed and one thing led to another and we got to talking about the Purple-Bellied Polka-Dotted Cuckoo. I just happened to mention that they migrate to this part of the country to mate once every five years and that this year is mating year. And then I suggested that if he was coming out here to see you on business, he should think about doing a little bird-watching. That's all."

"That's all," he repeated as he absentmindedly picked up some files and began slotting them haphazardly into the cabinet.

She watched him for a moment, noting the way his brows were knitted together in concentration. She knew for a fact that it wasn't the filing he was concentrating on, so... She waited for his Machiavellian mind to finish plotting his next move.

A moment later, he slid the drawer of the filing

cabinet closed. "Tate liked the ad concept," he said abruptly.

"He did? That's great news!"

"Don't get too excited. He's not giving us the account yet, not until he checks us out."

"What do you mean, 'checks us out'?"

"He's big on family values and organization. He's flying in on Monday to see if we meet his standards."

She shrugged. "So what's the problem? You've got nothing to hide. All you have to do is show him around the office a little, maybe do a short presentation on the way we work and take him to dinner. It's simple."

"The problem, Miss Hammond," he said softly, "is you."

Liv didn't like the way he was looking at her. She didn't trust him at the best of times, and the assessing, almost predatory blue gaze he was leveling at her now didn't bode well for her. *What can he do to you?* she asked herself. She didn't even work for him anymore. There was no reason to be intimidated. Liv stared right back at him.

"Is that so?" she asked.

He opened his mouth, closed it and then started pacing again. "Did I mention that he's looking forward to meeting you and discussing the mating habits of that damn dotty bird with you?"

"What difference does that make? Just tell him I resigned. He'll understand."

He stopped in midstride and turned accusing eyes

on her. "You're going to make me say it, aren't you?"

She threw up her hands in frustration. "Make you say what? For once, could you just get to the point?"

"All right, here's the point. I can't do it without you! There, are you satisfied?"

"What do you mean, you can't do it without me? Of course you can!"

"You don't understand! You're the only one here with any sense. Just look around you. This is what happened in one day. Can you imagine the state this place is going to be in by Monday? And do you honestly imagine that Tate's going to come in here and think we're a well-run company?"

"Annie's cleaning up out there—"

"Annie scurried out of here as soon as she heard me coming. And all the others are just as useless. If it isn't the crying it's all that endless stammering. Every time I come near someone, they either drop something or they have an uncontrollable urge to disappear."

"The employment agency—"

"Can't send anyone until Monday and, let's face it, I don't have time to train someone else while Mr. Tate is here."

Liv was overwhelmed. This was the closest he'd ever come to complimenting her and the closest, she suspected, he'd ever come to begging. But there was no way she could do what he was suggesting. She'd promised both Ralph and herself that she'd put this job behind her. She needed to get on with her life, with planning the wedding of her dreams. She didn't have time to play robot to Lyon Mackensie.

"I'm sorry about this predicament you're in, but I can't do it. Ralph—"

"Predicament? Is that what you call it? This company, the deal we've been working half a year on, the future of all my employees—it's all at your mercy!"

"Oh, for heaven's sake! Not getting the Tate account is hardly going to bankrupt Mackensie's."

"Do you know what's going to happen when word gets out that Tate was considering using us, then decided against it? Everyone's going to start wondering why and then we're going to lose the opportunity to capture any other large corporate accounts." He turned around and walked to his desk. "Well that's loyalty for you. The Tate deal is our chance to make it big and, instead of helping, you're going to run off to a life of eternal domestic bliss with some idiot chump named Ralph Fortescue and his bird-crazy mother!"

"Ralph might have an unusual name—" she was goaded into replying "—but at least he's civilized!"

He turned around to face her. "What's that supposed to mean?"

"It means that you wouldn't know civilized if it came up and bit you on the—"

He wagged a finger at her. "Tut, tut, Miss Hammond."

"—behind," she finished deliberately. "And furthermore, if this company's future is in jeopardy, it isn't because of me. It's because of you!"

"Me? I'll have you know—"

"Oh, spare me the company rhetoric. I've heard it all before. You might be brilliant at creating ad concepts and analyzing marketing trends, but you don't know diddly about dealing with people. You treat your employees like little machines who have no feelings and then you expect them to be loyal?"

"I pay them to be loyal."

"You pay them to do their jobs," she corrected. "Loyalty has to be earned through mutual respect."

"Who says I don't respect them?"

"I do. I've been watching you for five years, and I'm willing to bet you haven't even learned half their names."

"Of course I know their names!"

"All right. What's O'Brien's first name?"

"Why it's…it's…I know it starts with a *P*, so it must be…Paul!"

Liv sighed. "Wrong saint. It's Peter. And for some strange reason, he worships the ground you walk on. He's good enough to get a job with any other marketing firm in the city, but he's willing to run around here and be your gofer."

He had the grace to look ashamed. "I didn't know that."

"No, you didn't. And I bet you also don't know who came up with the new Tate concept."

He looked up at her in surprise. "I thought *you*—"

"I'm probably the best P.A. you'll ever have, but I don't know squat about creating ad concepts. It was Peter."

"*He* did that?"

"Uh-huh. If you're smart, you'll promote him to Creative before his hero-worship cracks under the strain of reality."

He made a note on his desk. "I'll talk to Jack first thing on Monday morning."

"Good. Now, while we're at it, let's talk about Howard."

He frowned. "Howard?"

"Howard Carmichael in Research."

"Oh, you mean the pale guy with the rumpled suits."

"Exactly. Six months ago, Howard's wife Kathy gave birth to twin boys, Kevin and Keith."

"And you're upset because I didn't send a card, right?"

"No, Howard's wife was upset because Howard wasn't there when she gave birth."

"What's that got to do with me?"

"Howard wasn't there because he was at work, and he was too afraid to ask you for the day off in case you fired him. He can't afford to lose his job right now."

"Oh, for Pete's sake!" he ejaculated. "I'm not that much of a monster!"

"Howard seems to think you are and, frankly, I don't think anyone around here would disagree. And in case you're interested, the twins are fine, but Kathy is exhausted and Howard would like some time off to be with her and the boys."

He looked at her in resignation. "Tell Howard to come see me on Monday morning."

Liv reached around him to pick up her purse from his desk and slung it over her shoulder. "Tell him yourself. I won't be here on Monday morning."

"What do you mean, you won't be here? You've got to be here! I told you, Mr. Tate is expecting you and if you're not here, Mackensie's will lose the biggest account in its history! Then what will happen to Peter and Howard and Kathy and the twins?"

She narrowed her eyes at him. "Don't even *think* about using your emotional blackmail on me. It's not going to work."

"All right. How much?"

So they were back to that again. "I told you before, I don't need your money."

"Everybody needs money. Just name your price."

Liv stared thoughtfully at him. It was obvious to her that Lyon Mackensie only thought in terms of money and price. He thought his cold, hard cash could buy everyone and everything, but he was wrong. He needed to be taught a lesson, and she was just the person to teach it to him.

She crossed her arms in front of her chest. "The price, Mr. Mackensie, is civility and a certain measure of peacefulness."

"What the hell does that mean?"

"It means that I will return to work for one week starting on Monday morning and I will even find you my replacement. In exchange, however, I want to be treated with respect and dignity. I'm a flesh-and-blood human being and I want to be treated like one. So do the rest of your staff."

And then maybe, just maybe, after she was gone he would continue treating them like human beings and they wouldn't need her to act as a buffer.

"So, as of Monday morning, there will be no more bellowing or growling or roaring."

"I do not roar!" he roared.

She pointedly ignored him. "You're going to be polite and approachable and civilized. You're going to show concern for your employees and, what's more, you're going to get to know each of them personally."

"You've got to be kidding, right?"

"Oh, but I have no sense of humor, remember?" she reminded him sweetly.

"Damn it, that's ridiculous! I'm not going to be blackmailed into mollycoddling my own employees."

"Those are my terms," said Liv, turning around and heading for the door. "Take them or leave them."

Her hand was on the doorknob when he said, "Wait!"

She stopped.

"All right, damn it. You win."

Liv turned back to face him with a gleeful smile.

"Just make sure you're here on time Monday morning," he growled, reaching for the phone. "I don't want to have to fire you."

Her smile faded and she opened her mouth to set him straight, but he had clearly dismissed her from his mind. Perched on the edge of his desk with the phone tucked in his ear, he was already apologizing to Melanie for being late for their date.

Liv gnashed her teeth and was about to turn around again when he put a hand over the mouth-piece and said in the most pleasant tone she'd ever heard him use, "Oh, and Miss Hammond?"

She stopped again and he leveled a smile at her.

It devastated her, that smile, through its sheer blinding novelty.

Liv stared at him, marveling that the mere up-turning of his lips could transform his normally harsh features into a bone-melting tapestry of warm blue eyes and coolly kissable lips, laughter-filled crinkles and—Liv nearly whimpered in pleasure—a beguiling set of dimples.

"Yes, Mr. Mackensie?" she breathed.

"Do something about your hair before Monday."

It was all Liv could do to slam out of his office without ripping the dimples off his face.

LYON LEANED BACK into the plush velvet upholstery of the chair at his favorite restaurant and studied the woman seated across the dinner table from him. The cherry-red dress she wore set off her sleek platinum-blond hair and stunning figure to perfection. The low V neckline allowed the candlelight to create a soft, enticing shadow between her magnificent breasts.

He took a small sip of cognac, his gaze lingering on her breasts, and reflected that Melanie Worth was a very beautiful woman.

Which was why it puzzled him that, every time he had looked at her through dinner, he hadn't felt the tug of attraction he usually felt when he was with her. Instead, he'd been plagued by visions of a lushly rounded bottom in tight-fitting denims, warm brown eyes and pink lips shaped into a gleefully self-satisfied smirk.

He tried to shake the image and attempted instead to concentrate on what Melanie was saying.

"…at the country club last night. I had to get Rafael to escort me and, although he's very charming, he isn't you. Really, darling, I'm getting tired of playing second fiddle to your work." She pouted prettily. "What's the point of having a relationship when all we ever do together is have sex?"

Lyon frowned. Melanie had never complained about their sex life before. None of his women had.

"What's wrong with having sex?"

"Nothing. But I like to go out and have fun and all you ever want to do is sit in your study and work on those dreadfully boring ads or reports or whatever they are."

He didn't tell her that those "dreadfully boring" ads, along with long hours and hard work, were what allowed him to shower her with all the expensive jewelry and presents she liked to receive.

"I'm not working now," he pointed out, although, now that he thought about it, perhaps he should have been. There were a lot of details he needed to take care of before Tate arrived.

"Only because I had to nag you into coming and even then, you were late," she accused. "Really, Lyon, I can't…"

Lyon watched her mouth move and, slowly, the

full, glossy red lips in front of him began to morph into pale pink lips pursed in a thin, disapproving line. Then Miss Hammond's mouth began to move, accusing him of all sorts of horrible transgressions against his employees.

He frowned again. Surely he wasn't the complete ogre she'd accused him of being? Okay, maybe he did have a temper and a nasty habit of threatening to fire people, but she of all people should know that he never really meant it. He paid his employees well—in fact, he had a reputation for paying outrageous salaries—and, in return, he expected hard work and a measure of loyalty from them. Surely that was fair? And now she expected him to pamper them, too, and cater to their fragile emotions.

Ridiculous.

He was running a business, not a summer camp. Miss Hammond, by her own modest admission, might be the best P.A. he'd ever had, but she didn't know beans about the real world.

In the real world, where he'd grown up, there was no room for sensitivity or fragility or the finer feelings. They were an unnecessary distraction, a weakness. The only way he'd survived, first in the orphanage and later in the streets, was to build an iron wall around himself and block out the distractions, that included the heart Miss Hammond had once accused him of lacking.

He'd had to be strong and self-reliant because there hadn't been anybody else to turn to for help. He'd been on his own and the only things that had value on the streets were a reputation for ruthlessness and cold, hard cash. A reputation bought you time and cash bought you survival: food, shelter and protection. A heart, on the other hand, was a worthless commodity. He'd learned that the hard way and, as a result, he'd managed to work his way off the streets, put himself through school and build a relatively successful company out of nothing.

Now, after all that, he was being blackmailed by his little tyrant of a personal assistant.

"Ridiculous," he muttered.

"You're not even listening to me, are you?" Melanie's outraged accusation suddenly snapped him out of his thoughts. "You don't care! All you ever think about is work, work, work!"

He looked across at her, noting her flashing green eyes and heaving bosom and decided it was time to placate her. "You know that's not true."

Her eyes suddenly narrowed into dangerous green slits. "You were thinking about *her* again, weren't you?"

"Who?" he asked blankly.

"Miss Hammond!" she shouted, and he started guiltily. "That's who! Well, I'm sick and tired of hearing about her." She threw her napkin down on the table and stood up. "It's always Miss Hammond this and Miss Hammond that. If she's such a paragon of virtue, why don't you just order her to take care of *all* your needs!"

He jumped to his feet. "Melanie! You know I don't think of her in that way!"

At least, he hadn't until today. But that was just

a temporary lapse in sanity. Come Monday morning, he would go back to thinking of her as a robot.

"I know exactly how you think of her. You think of her as a machine. Well, you might as well get used to the idea of making love to a machine because no warm-blooded woman in her right mind would put up with you. And that includes me. Good-bye!"

Before he could protest, she raised her chin to a haughty angle and stormed out of the restaurant.

Lyon sat back down and scowled into his drink. Women! What the hell was it with them anyway, suddenly ganging up on him and screaming at him like shrews? Must have something to do with the phase of the moon or female hormones run amok because it sure as hell didn't have anything to do with reason.

He shook his head and gulped down the rest of his cognac. Well, he'd just let Melanie stew for a while and then he'd buy her one of those little baubles she liked so much and everything would be fine again. He made a mental note to tell Miss Hammond to purchase it and send it, along with a note telling Melanie that they could spend next weekend together. By then, he'd have a new P.A. and the Tate deal would be complete and he'd be able to afford to take a couple of days off. In the meantime, he was looking forward to Monday morning.

Yes, sir, on Monday morning he was going to pull off the biggest deal of his career.

4

AT PRECISELY 8:22 a.m. on Monday morning, Liv stepped briskly out of the elevator at Mackensie Marketing, juggling her briefcase, a garment bag, a diaper bag and a baby.

A moment later, Annie materialized beside her. "He's waiting for you and, in case you haven't guessed by the amount of noise coming from back there, he's livid. I took the liberty of—hey, what's that?"

"A baby," replied Liv brusquely. "You took the liberty of what?"

"Of making a list of His Beastly Majesty's demands so far this morning." She handed Liv a quarter roll of adding machine tape and reached out to tickle the baby. "Say, he's cute. Look at all that yummy black hair and those big brown eyes. What's his name?"

"Sam. Is this all of it?"

"Hey there, Sammy," crooned Annie with a smile. Sam gurgled his pleasure. "Yup, that's it."

"Okay, this what I want you to do. Take my briefcase and garment bag and drop them in my office and then get the boardroom ready for the presentation. Check to make sure the coffee things are all ready and that the caterers have delivered the refreshments. Make a reservation for two at La Italia for twelve o'clock and get the limo service to pick up Mr. Tate at his hotel for nine-thirty. Oh, and instruct the driver to call me five minutes before he gets here. Got it?''

''Got it!'' Annie grabbed the briefcase and garment bag from Liv and hurried toward her office while Liv made a beeline for Leroy.

''Hey, Leroy, I need you to do me a favor.''

''Sure thing, Liv. Hey, what's that you've got there?''

''A baby. I need you to make sure all the equipment for the presentation is set up in the boardroom.''

''You got it. What's the little tyke's name?''

''Sam. Get Jack to show you exactly how he wants everything done, okay?''

''Gotcha,'' he said, crossing his eyes and waggling his fingers at Sam. Sam showed his approval by reaching for Leroy's nose. ''Sorry, kid, gotta go.''

The trip to her office, which usually took only about thirty seconds, took five minutes as Liv skirted the maze of desks while trying to hold on to a squirming baby and an unwieldy diaper bag, and stop repeatedly while everyone oohed and aahed over Sam.

Sam, being his mother's son, enjoyed every second of the attention, gurgling and cooing and grabbing anything his little fingers could reach.

"If one more person stops me to ask about you, I swear I'll scream," she said to Sam.

Fortunately, they made it to her office without any more questions, just as a bellow sounded from next door.

"Where the hell is she? She's late. O'Brien, did you call her apartment like I told you to?"

"Yes, sir. There's no answer."

"Well, don't just stand there! Go out and find her."

"Yes, sir, Mr. Mackensie. Right away, sir."

Peter rushed out of the Den to do Lyon Mackensie's bidding just as Liv walked in, her hair clenched tightly in Sam's little fists.

As usual, the Beast was seated behind his desk glaring at her when she walked in. "You're late!" he barked.

Liv tried to coax Sam into letting go of her hair. "Yes, I—"

"I thought I told you to do something about that hair."

"I did, but—"

His gaze slipped from her to Sam and his eyes narrowed. "What's that?"

"A baby!" she snapped. "Hasn't anybody around here seen a baby before?"

"Well, get rid of it. We have a lot of work to do this morning. I want you to make sure that the limo picks up Mr. Tate from his hotel at nine-thirty and that we have lunch reservations for twelve. Let's go with La Italia. Make sure the boardroom is ready for—"

Liv turned away in the middle of his instructions, walked through the connecting door to her office and slammed the door shut. Reaching into the diaper bag, she pulled out a colorful teething ring and offered it to Sam with a kiss on his soft, plump cheek, then slipped him out of his coat.

A moment later, the connecting door opened and Lyon Mackensie stormed through it.

"You're not listening to me!"

"That's right. I'm not."

He stared accusingly at Sam. "And I thought I told you to get rid of that thing."

Sam stared back at him for a microsecond before his adorable baby face began to crumple. Then he opened his little rosebud mouth and let out an offended howl.

Liv glared at Lyon. "He's not a 'thing.' He's a baby and his name is Sam. Now look what you've done. You've scared him." She cuddled Sam protectively closer, cooing softly, "It's all right, sweetheart. I'm here. I won't let the big, bad beast hurt you."

Sam howled louder.

She rocked him soothingly back and forth. "Shh, precious. I know he looks mean, but he's all bluster."

Sam's wails slowed to a series of soft hiccups and he stared at Lyon assessingly, as if trying to weigh the truth of her words.

"Miss Hammond, I'm ordering you to get rid of him and get back to work. Mr. Tate will be here in less than an hour and fifteen minutes and—"

"Oh, be quiet. You're going to scare him again. And while we're on the subject of scary, you promised you'd stop being such a beast and terrifying all your employees."

"Now look here," he said impatiently, "you're not going to start that nonsense again, are you?"

"You bet I am. If you want me to stay, you'd better shape up. Otherwise, I'm cleaning out my desk and Sam and I will be hitting the road for the nearest zoo. And then *you* can explain the mating habits of the Purple-Bellied Polka-Dotted Cuckoo to Mr. Tate."

Lyon opened his mouth, thought better of it, and snapped it shut.

"That's the best decision you've made all day. Here, hold him for a minute. I'll go downstairs and get Sam's portable playpen from the car."

Then, before he could protest, the demented woman plopped the squirming little bundle of humanity into his arms and walked out the door.

Instinctively, he thrust his arms out and looked down at the baby dangling from his hands.

Big brown eyes stared earnestly back at him.

Lyon panicked.

"Annie!"

Annie burst breathlessly through the door a moment later and stopped short when she saw him, her eyes widening in surprise.

He glared at her.

"You called, Your Hi—sir?"

"What are you doing right now?"

"Setting up the boardroom for the presentation."

He grunted.

"Did you want something, sir?"

"Yeah, tell O'Brien to get in here."

"He's gone down to help Miss Hammond."

"Annoying Tartar," he muttered.

"What was that, sir?"

"Nothing. Get back to work."

Annie left with gratifying speed and he was back to staring at the baby.

"What now, kid?" he asked.

Sam gurgled, the baby drool sliding down his chin, gave Lyon a toothless grin and reached for his colorful silk tie.

"WE CAN SET IT UP by my desk," said Liv, opening the door to her office and stepping back to allow Peter in first.

Struggling with the weight of the playpen, Peter walked across the threshold and halted.

"Oh gosh," he croaked.

Liv peeked over his shoulder, her eyes widening at the scene before her.

Lyon Mackensie stood just as she'd left him, his arms thrust out in front of him, Sam suspended in his outstretched hands.

However, it was obvious that, at some point, he and Sam had come into close contact with each other.

Very close contact.

Liv looked from Sam, who was smiling and babbling happily, to Lyon, who was staring down at the wet patches on his shirt and trousers with dawning horror.

Her lips began to twitch.

Peter took one look at her, another at Lyon, set down the playpen, mumbled a hasty excuse and hightailed it out of the office just before Liv burst into peals of laughter.

When she finally managed to get herself under control, she found Lyon watching her, his jaw clenched, his lips pursed and his blue eyes promising bloody murder.

"Do something," he rasped.

Wordlessly, Liv dug out a blanket and a clean diaper from the diaper bag and spread the blanket across her desk.

"Put him down here and I'll change him."

He set the baby gently down on the blanket and backed away.

Sam immediately started crying.

"Shh, baby. We'll have you cleaned up in no time," said Liv, expertly unbuttoning his sleeper and slipping it off his squirming body.

But Sam didn't seem to care. He stared piteously at Lyon and continued to cry.

Lyon frowned. "I think he likes my tie."

"Maybe you should let him play with it while I get this done."

She watched in amusement as Lyon reluctantly moved closer and leaned over Sam.

Sam immediately stopped crying. He ignored the tie Lyon dangled in front of him, reaching instead for Lyon's hand.

"I don't think it's the tie he wants. I think it's you."

"You don't have to sound so surprised. I'm not the monster everyone seems to think I am."

Liv decided silence was the better part of discretion.

"Who does he belong to?"

"My friend Tina and her husband Paul."

"So what's he doing with you?"

"He's my godson. I was looking after him over the weekend."

"How come you still have him? The weekend's over."

Liv exchanged Sam's dirty diaper for a fresh one. "His parents have been having some personal problems and they needed to get away for the weekend. I offered to look after Sam for them. Yesterday, Tina called me and said she and Paul needed a couple more days and could I take care of him for a little longer. I told her to take as long as she needed."

His blue eyes stared curiously at her. "You said yes, just like that?"

"She's my best friend and she needed me," said Liv simply. "Besides, Sam's a good baby, aren't you, love?"

"That," said Lyon, looking down at his ruined clothes, "is a matter of opinion."

Liv grinned as she buttoned Sam into another sleeper and lifted him up for a cuddle.

"Don't you dare start laughing again," he warned. "Tate's going to be here in an hour!"

"I have an idea," said Liv. "Why don't you take

off your clothes and I'll have Peter run them to the one-hour dry cleaners downstairs?''

''And what am I supposed to wear in the meantime? I'm not parading around the office in a jacket and my Skivvies.''

''The jacket will have to be cleaned, too.''

''Why? There's nothing wrong with it.''

''Not unless you consider baby spit on the shoulder a fashion statement,'' she said dryly.

He took a closer look and grimaced at the white blob drying on his shoulder.

''Don't you have an extra suit hanging around here somewhere for emergencies?''

''Sorry, I didn't anticipate your godson eliminating on me when I left the house this morning,'' he said sarcastically.

''Never mind. Go take your suit and shirt off. I have another idea.''

As soon as Lyon left the room, he heard Sam crying behind him.

''Traitor,'' he heard her mutter through the door.

Two minutes later, a knock sounded on the connecting door.

''Yeah?'' he growled, unzipping his pants.

''I have some clothes for you.''

The door opened a crack and a hanger with clothes on it was thrust through.

''I was going to wear these on my date with Ralph tonight. The blouse probably won't button up but that'll be okay and, luckily, the skirt is flared so you'll be able to roll up the waist and have it fit you.''

He stared in disbelief at the frilly white blouse and black skirt hanging in front of him.

"No way," he said, shoving the hanger back through the door. "Somebody in the office must go to the gym. Borrow some track pants for me."

"What should I say? 'Boss in briefs urgently needs covering. Preferably size large. Leave with Liv'?"

"I don't want everyone to know!"

"Well, what else were you planning to do?"

"Never mind that. Just give me a second and then come in and get the suit."

He barely had time to shuck off his pants, hightail it to his desk and jump behind his high-backed black leather chair before she opened the door, the skirt and blouse draped over her arm, and walked in. Usually, he wasn't anything approaching shy about his body with women, but there was something a little embarrassing about walking around in his underwear in the office and having his very proper—at least, she had been up until a week ago—personal assistant eye him up and down over the rims of her glasses. He glanced down to assure himself the chair was hiding all his crucial parts, then smiled up at her, pleased with his ingenuity.

"The clothes are on my desk," he told her.

She set the skirt and blouse down, picked up the suit and shirt and walked to the door, where she turned around and looked pointedly at the chair. "Very clever. Next time, just make sure you close the blinds first," she said, and walked out.

Lyon spun around.

The first thing he discovered was that his very proper personal assistant had probably seen a perfect reflection of his backside, covered only by a pair of black bikini briefs, on the glass behind him.

The second thing he discovered was that his window looked out on another office building where it was obvious that the employees were all female and that they had nothing better to do all day than stand around at the window, spying on him.

A moment later, in tandem, the women held up sheets of paper with numbers on them and, for the first time in his adult life, Lyon Mackensie blushed.

He and his black bikini briefs had just rated five perfect tens and an eleven.

"IT'S NOT FAIR, Sam. First the dimples, now black bikini briefs. How's a woman supposed to keep her mind on work with so much temptation around?" asked Liv, sitting behind her desk with Sam on her lap.

Sam babbled something incoherent and banged his teething ring on the desk.

"Easy for you to say," she muttered. "You don't have little estrogen hormones running around inside you. And what's more, you're not engaged to a very nice man who doesn't deserve to have his fiancée ogling her boss."

"Ba, ba, ba," shouted Sam.

"That's right. He's my boss. And until last Friday, he was a beast. Ranting and raving at all of us and just generally being obnoxious. Then, all of a sudden, he's showing his dimples and holding babies and wearing sexy underwear and I'm having hot flashes.''

''Uh?'' asked Sam.

''Never mind. You'll learn about them soon enough. Oh, Sam, I can't believe I'm having such…such *carnal* thoughts about *him*. It's not like I don't know what a rat fink he really is. He's a womanizer of the worst sort and he treats all his girlfriends like…like kept women. Thank God I only have to suffer through this for four more days. Then I can put him and his dimples behind me and begin my new life with Ralph. What do you think about that?''

Sam stuck out his tongue and let out a long, wet raspberry.

''You know, Sammy, sometimes you remind me more of your mother than I'd like.''

A few minutes later, the intercom on Liv's desk buzzed. She pressed the button and said, ''You called, sir?''

''I want to see you in my office.''

''Come on, Sam,'' said Liv, picking up a steno pad and pencil. ''The master beckons.''

She knocked perfunctorily on the door before walking in. He was sitting behind his desk, but his usual air of command was somewhat undermined by the frilly white blouse stretched across his powerful shoulders. The buttons were undone, the frills hung to one side, revealing a muscled chest covered with a light matting of dark hair, and the sleeves reached just below his elbows.

Liv opened her mouth, but before she could say

anything, he gritted out through clenched teeth, "Not a word. I don't want to hear a word from you. Just listen."

She bit her lip to keep from laughing and moved closer to his desk.

Suddenly, Sam started to squirm and whimper, reaching out his arms toward Lyon.

He looked at Sam and frowned. "What's wrong with him?"

Liv shrugged. "Maybe he thinks you're his mother."

"Shut up and sit down," he growled. "And for God's sake, give him to me before you drop him."

Liv was so astonished at his request, she did exactly as he ordered.

As soon as Sam was settled quietly on his lap and Liv's pencil was poised over the pad, he said tersely, "I need you to pick up something at the jeweller's for Melanie and have it delivered for Friday."

Liv stared at him with narrowed eyes for a moment before firing off the first in the usual round of questions. "Emeralds, sapphires or diamonds?"

"Diamonds."

She raised a brow. "Special occasion or argument?"

His jaw clenched and his expression became dogged. "Argument."

"Serious or mild?"

"Serious." He paused for a moment, then said uncertainly, "I think."

Liv glanced up at him in surprise. "You think?"

In five years, she'd never seen Lyon Mackensie

uncertain about anything, not business and certainly not his personal life. If anything, he was the most unemotional person she'd ever met when it came to relationships. At least in business he roared and growled and got upset. But in his relationships with women he was invariably blasé. She had to hand it to Melanie if the woman had him even a little rattled.

"How could you not know?" she asked, then thought better of the question. "Never mind. It's none of my business."

He turned accusing blue eyes to her. "If you must know, we argued about you."

"Me?" she asked incredulously.

"Yeah, you." He sounded disgusted and frustrated and angry, all at once. "She says I talk about you all the time and think about work too much, and that I don't pay enough attention to her."

A little dart of pleasure coursed through Liv at his words. To know that he talked about her to his girlfriends told her that she was an important and valued part of his company. It was a little like receiving a compliment, she thought with a tingle of delight, and she didn't get many of those from him. Not that his approval meant anything to her, she assured herself hastily, especially since she wasn't going to be working for him for much longer.

"Well, you can explain to her that I'll be out of your hair at the end of the week."

"I intend to. Which reminds me, put in a card telling her I'll make time for her this weekend, after the deal with Tate is settled."

Liv wondered how Melanie would feel, knowing that she ranked second in his affections after a sixty-five-year-old man and his birdseed. She found herself feeling sorry for the other woman and resolved to couch his order in a more tactful manner. Just one last question and then she could get on with other things.

"How do you want the card signed?" she asked.

He looked at her blankly.

She sighed. "Grovellingly mushy?"

He looked mortified.

"Affectionately offhand?"

He frowned.

"Interested yet noncommittal?"

He nodded curtly.

"Yeah, I thought that would be the one," she muttered to herself as she flipped her notebook closed and walked to the door.

"Hey, what about Sam?"

She looked at the baby sitting contentedly in Lyon's lap. "He's happy where he is. You can take care of him while I go see if everything's ready for Mr. Tate."

She marched out of his office and slammed the door behind her.

This, she thought savagely, was exactly what she'd been telling Sam about. The rat fink treated all his girlfriends like kept women. Instead of talking to them or trying to work out the problems in their relationship, he simply bought them a present. But what galled Liv no end was that, in most cases, his method worked. The women would accept his gifts with delight, or if it was a kiss-off gift, they would disappear gracefully from his life. Perhaps they realized the futility of asking for anything more, such as a long-term commitment, from him.

The only thing Lyon Mackensie was committed to was his company. He lived, ate and breathed work, becoming more successful, bringing in bigger and more lucrative accounts with every year that passed. And just as he paid his employees well, he paid his girlfriends well, too. Money was no object. He never stinted on his presents, nor did he ever balk at some of the exorbitant bills he was presented with. She knew just how exorbitant they could be, since she was usually the one who presented them.

And that was another thing. He never bothered picking out the presents himself. Granted, he didn't exactly have a flair for buying presents. Witness the disaster with Lonnie and the car mats and Cindy and the elaborate Swiss cuckoo clock. He didn't understand the concept that a gift should be something that the recipient should enjoy; rather, he had a tendency to pick out things that interested him. After watching the aftermath of his gift-giving disasters, Liv had taken pity, not so much on him as on the recipients of his bounty. She had started going shopping on her lunch hour, usually enjoying the errand because it gave her a vicarious thrill; she could never have afforded the luxurious items herself. In fact, that's how she'd met Ralph, at the jewelry counter where she'd helped him pick out a birthday gift for his mother.

But today, she just didn't feel in the mood. Maybe

she'd call Mr. Kohler, the jeweller, tomorrow or Wednesday instead of making the trip herself and ask him for a repeat order on that diamond bracelet she'd picked out for Tracy's birthday last year.

It was, she thought, not without a little vicious satisfaction, the most expensive item in the store.

THE PHONE CALL came at 9:53 a.m., just as Liv had assured herself that everything was all set for the presentation. Quickly, she put down the phone and sent Peter to get Mr. Mackensie's suit. She went into his office and found him in the skirt and blouse, crouched down on the floor beside Sam's playpen, picking up Sam's stuffed frog with the dumb resignation of someone who'd done it a hundred times before.

"He's on his way!" she announced.

He scrambled to his feet, nearly tripping over the hem of the skirt. "How far away is he?"

"About four minutes. I've sent Peter down to get your clothes."

"Thank God. I don't know how you women can do anything in these skirts," he grumbled. "Is everything ready?"

"Yes, sir."

"Here, you take Sam and send O'Brien in with my suit as soon as he gets back."

Three minutes later, Peter arrived in Liv's office, breathless, with the suit and shirt.

"He's here! I saw the limo pull up downstairs just as I was getting into the elevator."

"Thanks, Peter. I'll take these in to Mr. Mac-kensie. You go warn the others."

Peter left and Liv knocked on the connecting door. "The suit's here and Mr. Tate is on his way up."

A muffled curse came through the door.

"What's wrong?" she asked.

"It's this damn zipper on your skirt," he growled. "I can't get it undone."

"Be careful. It's my favorite skirt."

"The material's stuck inside the zip, I think, but I can't see anything."

She heard a series of grunts on the other side of the door and had visions of him ripping the skirt apart.

She barged into the office. He was standing by his desk, bare-chested, struggling to see behind him. Liv only hesitated for a moment to take a quick, lusty peek at his powerful chest before rushing to his desk, putting Sam down and saying breathlessly, "Here, let me try. It'll be a lot quicker."

He glanced up, his gaze falling on Sam. "Do you think that's wise?"

Liv turned around to see Sam reaching for the telephone. "Whatever it takes to keep him quiet and out of my hair. At the rate he's going, I'll be bald by the end of the day."

Just then, Sam reached out with both hands and pressed all the buttons on the phone. Liv winced.

"Here," Lyon reached out and picked up Sam. "I'll hold him while you work on the zip. And for God's sake, hurry!"

AT THE SAME MOMENT in the outer office, the elevator doors opened and a short, stout little man with a round, nearly bald head, plump cheeks and big blue eyes stepped out.

A flustered Annie greeted him with a nervous smile, took his coat and informed him politely that Mr. Mackensie would be with him momentarily. She offered him a seat at her desk and disappeared into Liv's office.

He was about to sit down when a woman's voice said, "The trouble with you men is that you think everything requires brawn."

He glanced around in puzzlement, but there was no one around. The employees sitting in the open area were too far away and, besides, they were all engrossed in their work. He shrugged and sat down.

A moment later, the same voice said, "You've got to be gentle, use a delicate touch."

Mr. Tate jumped at the sound and looked around again, but this time, he noticed that the voice had come from somewhere on the paper-strewn desk in front of him. Curious, he glanced around to make sure no one was watching, then moved the papers aside to reveal a speaker phone.

"My hands are too big to be delicate," said a gruff male voice.

"Nonsense. All it needs is a gentle back and forth motion, like this."

"What's taking so long? I thought you said this would be quick."

"Don't worry, it's coming."

"You sure?"

"Mmm."

"Does it help if I do this?"

"Oh, yes."

"Well, hurry up, Mr. Tate will be here any minute."

"You don't have to remind me."

"I just wouldn't want him to catch us in an awkward position."

"Don't worry, he won't because I—" the woman paused and let out one last breathy grunt, "—am done. How's that for quick?"

"Not bad, but I'll be quicker. Here, you take little Sammy in your hands while I get this on…"

The rest was drowned out by what sounded like the rustling of clothes, but by this time, Mr. Tate had heard enough.

He jumped up, his face a bright tomato-red, his hands clenched into fists, his expression one of shocked outrage, and stormed into Liv's office.

Annie, who was gathering up papers from Liv's desk, turned around in surprise. "Oh, Mr. Tate, Mr. Mackensie will be with you in a moment. He's just—"

"I know exactly what he's up to. Where is he?"

"In there," she said, nodding to the connecting door. "But you can't—"

Before Annie could stop him, Mr. Tate marched to the door and threw it open.

5

LYON HAD JUST FINISHED pulling up his pants when the door burst open. He looked up to see Mr. Tate framed in the doorway, his heavy jowls quivering with outrage, his face purple as he took in the little tableau in front of him.

"What's going on here? What's the meaning of this, Mackensie?"

Lyon groaned inwardly.

He could picture the scene as Mr. Tate saw it, and it didn't look good. Miss Hammond was standing there, staring at him with her bun askew, thanks to Sam's determined little fingers, her cheeks flushed from embarrassment, her eyes wide, her mouth open in a little *O* of astonishment. And as for him…his shirt was unbuttoned, his pants were unzipped, his hair was probably a mess, and his breaths were coming in harsh pants from hopping up and down in an effort to get his trousers on quickly.

No, it didn't look good at all.

"Well?" barked Mr. Tate.

Lyon thought hard. If he didn't come up with an extremely good cxcuse for this very odd state of affairs, he was going to lose the biggest account of his career.

The truth, of course, was out of the question. It was too nutty and would sound like an outrageous lie. What he needed to do was come up with an outrageous lie that would sound more like the truth.

Before he could think twice about it, Lyon plastered a hearty smile on his face and said, "Mr. Tate, I'd like to introduce you to Miss Hammond...my wife."

Annie gasped.

Miss Hammond stared at him as though he'd lost his mind.

Sam gurgled with helpless laughter, clenched his fists in Lyon's hair and pulled hard.

Lyon kept smiling fatuously.

"Eh, what's that you say? Your wife?" asked Mr. Tate.

"Yes, sir."

"But I thought she was your personal assistant."

"She's that, too, sir."

"Well, well, well." Slowly, Mr. Tate's expression became thoughtful and then he began to chuckle. "So you had the good sense to marry her, eh? Wonderful, wonderful. And this little fella here," he smiled at Sam, "must be your son. The family resemblance is uncanny."

Lyon's smile faltered.

Mr. Tate clutched the top of his vest in both hands and suddenly beamed at Lyon. "Well, Lyon, my boy, this is a real treat for me. I like a man who takes pride in his family. In this day and age, it's very rare to see a happy family like yours."

"No kidding," muttered Lyon's new wife.

LYON SETTLED into the black leather sofa in his office with an exhausted sigh. Carefully, he propped his feet up on the coffee table in front of him so as not to disturb the baby nestled in his arms.

Thank God this day was almost over.

For a brief moment in his office this morning, he'd been afraid that the fib he'd come up with might have been a little too outrageous to be entirely believable. But Tate had swallowed it whole and Miss Hammond hadn't given him any time to change his mind. With her usual brisk efficiency, she'd whisked both Sam and Mr. Tate out of the office, leaving Lyon to put on his clothes and regain his dignity in private. The presentation, thankfully, had gone without a hitch, with the exception of Sam, who had insisted on sitting in Lyon's lap through the entire thing, alternately pulling his hair and drooling on his best tie. Tate had been delighted at little Sam's antics and had left Mackensie's this afternoon happy and delusional.

Now, as soon as Miss Hammond finished dressing for her date with old what's-his-name and took a sleepy Sam out of Lyon's hands, he was going to go home and gulp down a nice, stiff drink to calm his shattered nerves. He closed his eyes, leaned his head back and contemplated the soothing properties of twelve-year-old scotch.

"What on earth made you come up with such an asinine story?" Miss Hammond's voice floated through the connecting door, which was slightly ajar.

"I didn't have much choice. You have to admit,

the situation must have looked pretty odd, and you saw the look on his face when he burst in, like he was going to have an apoplectic fit.''

He thought he heard a giggle on the other side of the door, but he knew he was mistaken. Miss Hammond did not giggle.

But there was definite laughter in her voice when she said, "You looked pretty strange yourself, hopping around with your pants unzipped and your shirt flapping around like that.''

"And whose fault was that?" he growled.

Sam stirred in his sleep at the sound and Lyon automatically patted his back to soothe him.

"Yours. You should always keep a spare suit in the office for emergencies.''

Lyon rolled his eyes at this demented piece of female logic.

"Anyway, now what? How are you going to keep Mr. Tate from finding out the truth?" she asked.

"All we have to do is keep up this charade for a couple of days, maybe through a dinner or two and that's it. He'll go back none the wiser and Mackensie's will have snared the biggest account in its history. Which reminds me, can you arrange a dinner for tomorrow night?''

"Do you want to make reservations at La Italia again or that new French place that just opened up?''

"Reservations? We're not going to need reservations. You can arrange it at my house."

"Your house?''

Lyon grinned. "I beg your pardon, Mrs. Mackensie. *Our* house."

"Oh, no! You can't expect me to—"

"Don't you remember how lonely he sounded over lunch? How much he said he missed his family now that his wife is gone and all his kids have grown up and moved away? What he needs is a nice, home-cooked meal with the Mackensie family to cheer him up."

"And where am I supposed to get a nice, home-cooked meal?"

"Have it catered. Do whatever you have to do, I don't care how much it costs. I'll give you an extra set of keys to my place tonight, and you can go straight there in the morning instead of coming in to work. I'll pick him up from his hotel and bring him round at six for cocktails."

"You really think we can pull this off?" she asked, emerging from her office.

"Trust me. It'll be a piece of..." he trailed off, his eyes widening at the sight that met them. "...cake."

The black skirt and white blouse that had seemed to be instruments of torture to him this morning had suddenly, magically transformed themselves into elegant pieces of couture on Miss Hammond's much smaller frame. The shiny, opaque fabric of the blouse revealed smooth, rounded shoulders and slender arms emerging from a lacy white camisole, and the skirt showed off a tiny waist that flared into splendidly curved hips and legs.

Miss Hammond without her dull suit was...very nice.

She stopped and stared down at herself. "What's wrong?"

"Nothing," he managed to croak out, even though his breath seemed to be stuck in his throat. "Those clothes look a lot better on you than they did on me."

"I should hope so," she muttered, stopping to lean on a filing cabinet and slip her shoes on.

He watched first one small, narrow foot, encased in sheer black hose, emerge from beneath the long, flared skirt and slide into a black-heeled pump, then the other. Perhaps Sam had pulled his tie too hard at some point during the day, because it suddenly seemed too tight. He closed his eyes and yanked on the silken noose around his neck, wondering how things could change so much so quickly.

Last week, Miss Hammond had been nothing more than his personal assistant; this week, she was his wife. Last week, he'd thought of her as a machine; this week, he was having trouble *not* thinking about her, and in the thoughts he *was* having, she was very warm-blooded indeed.

It was madness. Pure, utter madness.

Suddenly, he heard the soft swish and rustling of silky fabric and caught a delicate whiff of flowery perfume. He opened his eyes and found her directly in front of him. She leaned down, her expression soft and tender, and brushed her knuckles across Sam's flushed cheek.

"Poor little tyke," she whispered. "He must be exhausted after the day he's had."

"Yeah, peeing and pulling hair and drooling and throwing food…it can really tire a guy out."

She laughed softly and he hastily cleared his throat. "Uh, Miss Hammond, I—"

"I think that as my better half—" she smiled, her dark eyes twinkling with mischief "—you should call me Liv."

Liv. It seemed to suit the vibrant, laughing woman in front of him.

"I just wanted to, uh, thank you for going along with all of this."

For a moment, she looked like she was going to pass out. Then she grinned. "No need for thanks. Just remember, Mackensie, civility and peacefulness."

LIV WAS LATE for her date with Ralph. She arrived, breathless, at the posh new French restaurant that had just opened up in town. The maître d' glanced with barely concealed disdain at the baby in her arms and the diaper bag trailing behind her as he escorted her to the table.

Ralph, looking elegantly groomed in a navy suit and a conservatively muted tie, his fair hair glinting under the pot lights, stood to greet her with an enthusiastic smile. Then his gaze slid down to the baby in her arms and his smile disappeared.

"What's that?" he asked, staring wide-eyed at Sam.

Here we go again.

"A baby," she said.

"I know that, Olivia. *Whose* baby?"

"Tina and Paul's. You remember I told you about them?"

"Oh…yes. Then this must be little Samuel," said Ralph, smiling tentatively at the baby.

Liv beamed, pleased that he'd remembered. "That's right. Say hi, Sam."

Sam stuck his tongue out and let forth his trademark wet raspberry.

Ralph blinked in surprise.

"Oh, Sam, that's not nice," scolded Liv. "I'm sorry, Ralph. He just woke up, so he's a little cranky right now."

"Yes, well…" he trailed off, looking in bewildered fascination at Sam, who stared back at him with a mutinous expression on his face. "Here, let's sit down," he suggested, holding out her chair for her. "I, uh, I have a little surprise for you tonight."

Liv sat down with Sam in her lap, and that was when she noticed the table setting. There was a single red rose in an exquisite crystal vase standing in the middle of the table, flanked on both sides by tall red candles. The table setting was different from all the others in the restaurant, and it was obvious that Ralph had taken pains to make tonight special.

"Oh, Ralph, it's all so beautiful," she exclaimed.

A pleased flush touched his cheeks. "I'm glad you like it, Olivia. I wanted tonight to be special for you because I know that my proposal last week came out of the blue, and I wanted to make it up to you."

Liv was touched at his thoughtfulness. "You didn't have to do that, Ralph."

"I wanted to. And I have another surprise for you, too. I—"

He was cut off in the middle of his sentence when Sam reached for one of the lit candles.

"No, Sam!"

Liv quickly grabbed his fingers and Sam looked at her in hurt surprise before his big brown eyes started filling up with tears. He began to whimper and Liv looked around frantically for something to give him before he could let out the howl she knew was lurking somewhere inside that tiny body of his. She settled on a mini French-stick from the bread basket and held out the peace offering to him. He took it and, of course, it went immediately into his mouth, where he rubbed it against his gums and sucked on it happily, all thoughts of offense forgotten. Liv breathed a silent sigh of relief before turning her attention back to Ralph. "I'm sorry, Ralph. What was it you were saying?"

Ralph frowned. "Olivia, wouldn't it have been better to leave him with a baby-sitter?"

"I didn't have time today. Besides, I *am* the baby-sitter."

"What do you mean, you didn't have time today?"

Liv wanted to tell him about the deal she'd made with Lyon Mackensie and about going back to work. She didn't plan on keeping secrets from Ralph. A husband and wife had to share everything. Besides, Ralph was a reasonable man. Surely he'd see that this was something she had to do. After all, her friends needed her. So she opened her mouth and prepared to blurt it all out, but Sam had other ideas. He opened his mouth first and began to shout "Ma, ma, ma, ma!" and thump the table with the hand that was fisted tightly around the breadstick she'd given him.

Ralph looked around uncomfortably and whispered, "Olivia, for heaven's sake, do something!"

Liv reached down to wipe the mush and drool from Sam's mouth, dropped a kiss on the top of his baby-fine hair and hugged him close.

Sam kept thumping and shouting and sucking happily.

"That's not what I meant, Olivia. Can't you quiet him down?"

"He's a baby, Ralph. That's what babies do. Now, you said something about a surprise?"

"Oh, yes." He smiled excitedly at her, reached into the inner pocket of his jacket and brought out a red velvet ring box. "I wanted to give you a little something to make our engagement official."

He held the box in front of her and opened it. She gasped. Inside was a gold ring set with the biggest ruby she'd ever seen, surrounded by tiny diamonds. Liv swallowed, completely at a loss for words.

"It's my great-grandmother Bernice's ruby engagement ring," explained Ralph. "It's been passed down through the generations in my family. My mother wore it last."

"It's, uh, very unusual," murmured Liv as Ralph took it out of the box and slid it onto her finger. The ring felt heavy and looked a little too big for her hand, but she was thrilled that Ralph had managed to convince his mother to part with it.

It took her a few seconds before the impact of her last thought sank in. She looked up hopefully. "Ralph, does this mean what I think it means?"

He nodded, excitement lighting up his gray eyes behind the wire-rimmed glasses. "I told Mother that we're engaged."

"And? What did she say?"

"She's flying in from Baltimore to meet you."

"That's wonderful, Ralph!"

He nodded. "She suggested dinner on Wednesday."

"Great!" said Liv, beaming at him over Sam's head. "I'll make my special meat loaf. I know how much you enjoyed it last Thursday night."

Ralph started rubbing his stomach. "Uh, actually, I was thinking we'd go out for dinner."

"Oh." Liv was disappointed. She'd been looking forward to showing Ralph's mother just what a good wife she'd make him. She knew how nervous Ralph had been about telling his mother that he was going to marry someone she'd never met. She could understand that his mother doted on him and wanted the very best kind of wife for him, and Liv wanted to make sure that she did Ralph proud.

"I don't want you to go through any trouble, Olivia. Everything will go much better if you're relaxed and not worrying about cooking dinner. Mother is very particular about her food."

"That's very thoughtful of you, Ralph. Don't

worry, I'll do my best to pick a restaurant your mother will like.''

Ralph looked at her with earnest gray eyes. "I trust you, Olivia. And now that you don't have to worry about that job of yours, everything will go much more smoothly. Mother is very old-fashioned. I'm afraid she doesn't approve of wives who work outside the home," he said apologetically. "But we don't have to worry about that anymore, do we?"

Liv's conscience battled with her desire to reassure Ralph. He had a tendency to become anxious when it came to his mother. If she told him now about going back to work, he'd only worry until Wednesday. What he didn't know couldn't hurt him. Besides, it was only for four more days. After that, she would be the best stay-at-home wife any mother could ever want for her son. Surely there was nothing wrong with that?

Liv patted his hand in reassurance. "You don't have to worry about anything, Ralph. I promise that I'll get your mother to like me at dinner the day after tomorrow." *Even if it kills me.* "Now, what did you say her favorite meal was?"

"ROAST PARTRIDGE with spinach and date stuffing," said Liv to Sam the next morning as she unstrapped him from his car seat. "Where am I going to find a restaurant that serves *that?* Why couldn't she just like meat loaf?"

Sam babbled something in response.

She lifted him out of the seat, grabbed her purse and the diaper bag and nudged the car door shut with her hip. "I don't know, either. And on top of that, I've got to come up with a nice, home-cooked meal for tonight."

She turned around and stopped to look at the house and whistled softly. "Will you look at that, Sam?"

Liv had never been to Lyon Mackensie's house before. She knew he lived in one of the nicer neighborhoods in the city, but she'd never dreamed that he'd own something this...perfect.

It was an elegant little Georgian-style house, yellow brick with white trim, lots of gleaming windows and steps leading up to an entryway that was flanked by two white columns. The front lawn was huge, with big, sturdy trees that looked like they'd provide cool shade in the summer and protection from the elements in the winter. Beds of red tulips had been planted under the windows to give the house spring color and tendrils of ivy crept up the side walls.

Liv walked up the little pathway to the front door, put the diaper bag down and dug out the keys Lyon had given her yesterday from her purse. She opened the door, eager to see what the inside of the house looked like, and walked in.

"Oh. My. God."

He couldn't be serious. He couldn't do this. Not to this beautiful, perfect house. This house deserved antiques that had been lovingly maintained for generations. It deserved warm, buttery walls and cozy fireplaces and family pictures on the mantel. It deserved children and love and laughter and tradition.

But what it deserved and what Lyon Mackensie

had inflicted upon it were two different things. White carpeting covered every inch of floor, and the walls were painted a bright, sterile white, their painful monotony broken only by huge blocks of unintelligible art. The furniture consisted of black leather and weirdly shaped black-and-steel pieces that looked to Liv like medieval instruments of torture. The house was a lesson in modernity run amok.

Mr. Tate would never believe that the Mackensie family lived in this cold, lifeless mausoleum.

She sighed. "It's a good thing money is no object," she told Sam, then picked up the phone and dialed. "Hi, Annie. Listen, I need a favor...."

6

LYON WAS HUNGRY. He was also beginning to get a little nervous.

He hadn't had anything to eat since breakfast this morning, hence the hunger. And once again, his day at the office had been chaotic, not because people had been running around like chickens with their heads cut off, but because there had hardly been any people running around at all. Every time he'd asked for someone to come into his office, he'd been informed by a suspiciously nervous O'Brien that they were out on an errand.

He was rapidly developing an instinct for detecting impending disaster, and his instinct had been sending him smoke signals all day. He'd ignored the feeling until this moment, but now that he was in the car with Mr. Tate, pulling up to his house, the hairs at his nape began to stand on end, hence the nervousness.

He was sure that the feeling was somehow connected to Liv. He'd tried calling her this afternoon, just to see how the preparations for dinner were coming along, but some guy had answered the phone. The background noise on the other end had been loud, a strange mixture of what sounded like buzzing power tools, dragging furniture and raised voices, and had resulted in the man on the other end shouting at him that Liv wasn't around, call back later, click.

He really, really needed to start paying more attention to his instincts.

"Lyon, my boy, you don't know how much I'm looking forward to this dinner with you and Olivia and Sam. It's not something I have an opportunity to do very often on my business trips," said Mr. Tate as Lyon parked the car in the driveway.

"Liv and I are delighted that you could come, Mr. Tate," said Lyon absently as he got out of his car. He was too busy looking up at his house, at all the lights blazing out of the windows, to pay much attention to what he was saying.

Because this was the first time in his entire life that Lyon Mackensie had come home to somebody waiting for him.

And he *liked* it.

He liked the idea that Liv and Sam were inside waiting for him, and he especially liked this strange warmth that was radiating from his chest to all the cold, empty places inside him.

"This is a fine-looking house you have here," said Mr. Tate.

"Thank you, sir. It's, er, home," he said, and then frowned.

Until today, it hadn't felt like a home. It had felt like a house, just one in a long line of acquisitions to attest to his hard-won success. For the first time, he looked at his house and tried to see what Mr. Tate saw.

The lawn was well manicured, the bushes perfectly trimmed, and there was even an assortment of spring flowers under the bay windows. The house looked well taken care of, and it was.

By the landscaping company he hired to look after the outside.

The inside was a whole different story. It had been decorated by Lauren a few years ago, just before he'd broken up with her. At the time, she'd assured him that the minimalist look suited his personality and his life-style. But now that he thought about it, minimalist just sounded…well, clinical.

Mr. Tate wasn't going to believe clinical. Clinical didn't go well with babies and diapers and home-cooked meals.

With a feeling of trepidation, Lyon followed Mr. Tate down the path to the front door, which wound in front of the bay window. The light from the living room illuminated Mr. Tate's smiling face as he stopped to waggle his fingers at someone inside before continuing down the walkway. Frowning, Lyon turned to look at what had made Mr. Tate smile.

A moment later, Lyon was trampling through the flowers in his haste to get a better look and pressing his face right up against the glass.

He blinked.

There had to be some mistake. Where was clinical? When had it been replaced by comfortable sofas and colorful cushions and throw rugs and…and paintings that were actually recognizable?

Dazed, he returned to the pathway and followed in Tate's footsteps, but he couldn't resist taking a quick peek at the numbers above the garage doors first.

Just to make sure.

The porch light came on and Lyon heard Mr. Tate say, "Ah, Olivia and Sam."

"Welcome to our home, Mr. Tate. Please, come in."

"I seem to have lost your husband," said Mr. Tate.

"I'm sure he's on his way."

Lyon walked up the steps to the porch, trying to stamp the dirt off his shoes. "I'm here. I was just admiring the fl—" He broke off, his eyes widening at the vision standing in the doorway, balancing Sam on her right hip.

She was his every schoolboy fantasy come true: June Cleaver in glorious, living color. Except that Mrs. Cleaver had never looked quite so good in an apron, especially one worn over a clingy black cocktail dress, nor had she possessed a mass of thick, wavy brown hair that fell past her shoulders. And she *definitely* hadn't worn lipstick in that particular shade of pink.

The warmth that had spread through his body minutes ago suddenly turned into a quick, sizzling heat, making his skin clammy and his clothes feel far too tight.

He watched her delicious pink lips move as she spoke to Mr. Tate, not even realizing that he was in motion until he was standing right in front of her.

Suddenly, the lips turned toward him and said, "Hi, honey." Then they puckered and he watched in fascination as they came closer. Just as they were about to touch his cheek, he turned his head.

The kiss was quick. A little *too* quick for his liking.

He saw the surprised look in her brown eyes as she drew away, and a wicked impulse seized him. Before he knew it, he found himself saying, "No need to be shy, sweetheart. I'm sure Mr. Tate won't mind if you show me how much you missed me today."

Before she could protest or, more likely, kick him in the goolies, Lyon kissed her again.

And kept kissing her.

He savored the feel of her lips, velvety and moist, the touch of her tongue, hot and sweet, and the sound of her pleasure, soft and inviting.

He could have gone on kissing her forever.

If it hadn't been for Sam's tiny fingers fisted in his hair, yanking for all he was worth.

He pulled away from her only when the pain became unbearable, breathing hard, and saw his stunned feelings reflected in her eyes.

"Well done, my boy," said Mr. Tate, chuckling delightedly. "So what's for dinner?"

LIV STUCK the prongs into the well-browned hunk of roast beef and frowned. Somehow, she didn't think it was still supposed to be this hard. She'd tried to follow the directions on all the packages carefully, but the roast hadn't come with written instructions. There was only what the man in the frozen meat shop had told her: brown the meat on high heat, then put it in a 425-degree oven for an hour. She'd memorized everything and followed his directions religiously because she hadn't wanted anything to go wrong with tonight's dinner.

Lyon would kill her if it did.

But the day had been so hectic, with all the people running in and out of the house and with Sam wanting to see, touch and *eat* everything, they had barely finished in time for her to get the roast into the oven and get dressed. She hadn't even had time to get nervous until she'd heard Lyon's car pull into the driveway.

Then he'd kissed her, and the nervousness had miraculously disappeared, along with every scrap of sanity she possessed.

The man could kiss. And kiss. And kiss.

She was pretty sure that if Sam hadn't decided to intervene, they'd still be at it. And that would not have been a good thing. Kissing her boss was bad enough, but she'd done a whole lot more than just kiss him.

She'd *enjoyed* kissing him.

But how could she enjoy kissing him when she wasn't even sure she *liked* him? Mind you, he had behaved much better at the office yesterday; he hadn't yelled so much and he'd been really good with Sam....

No, wait, what was she *thinking?* It didn't matter how polite he was or how good he was with Sam.

She was engaged to Ralph! She shouldn't be kissing anyone else. Especially not Lyon Mackensie.

When she got him alone for a minute, she was going to have to lay down the law. No more kissing. Period.

And while they were at it, no more black bikini briefs and no more dimples.

She nodded to herself and turned her attention back to the beef. She found a carving knife from the cutlery drawer and prepared to slice the roast.

"Mmm, something smells good, honey!"

Liv spun around to face Lyon, who was standing at the kitchen door, grinning at her. She narrowed her eyes at him. Yes, those pesky dimples definitely had to go.

"Tate's busy playing with Sam so I thought I'd come and see how dinner's coming along."

"Forget dinner. What was all that out there about?" She gestured in the vicinity of the kitchen door with the carving knife.

He looked behind him. "All that out where?"

"You know, at the front door."

He frowned.

"The kiss," she said in exasperation.

His brow cleared and the dimples made a miraculous reappearance, damn him. "Oh, that."

That was it? Here she was, agonizing about kissing a man who wasn't her fiancé and all he had to say was, "Oh, that."

"What do you mean, 'oh that'?" she said, outraged.

"I had to do something, didn't I? I mean, a husband has to greet his wife at the door, doesn't he?"

"You could have kissed me on the cheek."

"Yeah, but how convincing would that have been? I mean there you were, all dolled up, standing at the door, waiting eagerly for me to come home—"

Eagerly?

"—from the office, where I'd been slaving away all day—"

Slaving away?

"—trying to earn enough money to put food on the table..."

Oh brother. Liv rolled her eyes and waited.

"Besides," he finished triumphantly a minute later, "Mr. Tate loved it."

And that's what it all boiled down to. Lyon Mackensie was willing to do anything, to go to any lengths to get the birdseed account, including kissing her senseless. But there was only so much she was willing to do to help him. Kissing him went above and beyond the call of duty, no matter how much she enjoyed it.

She gave him a stern look. "No more kissing, understand?"

He stared at the carving knife she was waving in front of him and nodded. "No more kissing."

"And tomorrow morning, you're going to bring an extra suit to work for emergencies."

"Yes, ma'am."

"And for Pete's sake, stop smiling so darn much," she muttered.

"Pardon me?"

"Never mind." She turned back to the roast and tried to cut into it. The knife went about two inches into the meat before it got stuck.

He came up behind her. "Need some help?"

"Here, you try cutting through this and I'll get the platter." She handed the knife to him. A few seconds later, he put it down with a frown.

"Which caterer did you use?"

She smiled at him. "I didn't use a caterer. I thought the best way to get a home-cooked meal was to cook it at home."

Besides, she'd decided that if Ralph wasn't going to let her cook dinner for his mother, she'd just cook it for Mr. Tate instead. After all, if she wanted to be the perfect stay-at-home wife, she'd need to be a good cook. Until now, she hadn't had much practice. Usually, by the time she came home from working late, she just unwrapped a frozen entrée and stuck it in the microwave for dinner. Other times, she just ordered out.

"Have you ever made a roast dinner before?"

"No, but Ralph really likes my meat loaf."

"He actually said that?"

"Well, no...but he ate every bite."

"Hmmph."

Liv saw the way he was glaring at the meat. "Why? What's wrong?"

"How long did you thaw this meat for?"

She looked at him in confusion. "Thaw? But the man at the frozen food shop said it was ready to go into the oven."

"Well, it's still frozen."

"What do you mean, it's still frozen? It's been sitting in the oven for an hour and it looks perfectly cooked."

"Yes, but the core is still rock-hard."

"But...but...it can't be!" she wailed.

What was she going to do now? What were they going to feed Mr. Tate?

"Look, don't worry—"

"How can I not worry?" She threw up her hands and started pacing. "I've ruined dinner! You heard him earlier. He's looking forward to this meal. If we don't serve it to him, he'll...he'll..."

"He'll what?"

"He'll go home hungry!" she said desperately.

Lyon raised a brow. "What happened to 'forget the dinner'?"

"Forget 'forget the dinner'!"

"All right then. I have a plan."

"Well, don't just stand there! Tell me what to do!"

He put his arm around her and led her to a stool at the breakfast bar. "Look, why don't you just sit down and take a little rest and I'll deal with this."

"You don't trust me, do you?" she accused.

"Of course I trust you," he said soothingly.

"Then why aren't you ranting and raving?"

"Because, Miss Hammond, I am a civilized man and what I'm about to do requires a delicate touch. A man can't rant and rave and be civilized and delicate at the same time now, can he?" he reasoned, his blue eyes laughing at her.

Liv groaned. Why was it that she suddenly felt as if she'd fallen down Alice's rabbit hole and ended up in an alternate universe?

THE FIRST THING Lyon noticed when he and Liv came out of the kitchen after salvaging dinner was that their dinner guest had disappeared.

He looked around the living room, where he'd left Mr. Tate and Sam playing on the floor. The only trace that they'd been there were the building blocks and teething rings scattered on the floor.

He turned, panicked, to Liv. "Tell me you've redecorated the rest of the house, too," he whispered.

"Of course I have," she whispered back. "You didn't think I'd take a chance that he'd see the mausoleum you live in, did you?"

He breathed a sigh of relief. "Just checking."

"Where do you think he is?"

"You check the family room, I'll look in the study," he told her.

They hurried away in opposite directions.

When Lyon opened the door to his study, he found to his relief that it was unchanged. It was the only room in the house that he hadn't allowed Lauren to minimalize. Perhaps that's why Liv hadn't touched it, because it actually looked lived-in.

Perhaps a little *too* lived-in.

All right, so it was a mess, and he'd half hoped that Liv would have cleaned up in here a little, just as she cleaned up after him at the office, but maybe that was a little too much to ask. With a sigh, he walked out and closed the door behind him, hoping that she'd had better luck than him in finding Mr. Tate. He walked to the back of the house and entered the family room.

He found both Mr. Tate and Liv standing in front of the fireplace, talking quietly. Sam was fast asleep in his portable playpen. Taking the opportunity to study the room more closely, he saw that, like the other rooms, this one, too, had been significantly redecorated to project a warm cosiness. Although the carpet and the walls were the same monochromatic white as before, Liv had added warmth and color with overstuffed sofas and throw rugs. She'd also added little knickknacks, magazines and books and some of Sam's toys, to give the room a lived-in look.

He shook his head, amazed that this was his house and that she'd been able to accomplish so much in one day. He'd have to remember to ask exactly how she'd done it. He had a feeling that when he'd said, "Do whatever you have to do, I don't care how much it costs," she'd taken him a little too literally.

"Ah, there you are." Mr. Tate turned around and beamed at him. "Come and join us. Olivia was just explaining about the family photographs."

Family photographs?

He walked closer to the fireplace and noticed the assortment of pictures on the mantelpiece. There was a black and white picture of a tall man with his arm around a tiny woman who resembled Liv, both smiling happily at the camera. There was another picture of two little girls, the older one giving the camera a slightly stubborn look that he was beginning to recognize in Liv. Beside it was a picture of the whole family together, obviously on vacation at a beach somewhere, the older couple smiling indulgently at the two laughing teenage girls. There were other pictures of the family, too, and a couple of Sam, but he scanned over them, his attention riveted by the one photograph that had pride of possession in the middle of the mantel.

It was a wedding picture.

Their wedding picture.

In it, Liv was wearing a white gown and veil, looking ethereally lovely, and beside her was…him?

Lyon frowned. The expression on his face, delighted and slightly smug, looked strangely familiar. He was even wearing a tuxedo. But where…

Suddenly, his eyes widened. Of course! This was the picture that had been taken at last year's industry awards ceremony, where Mackensie Marketing had received its first honor. She must have gotten Leroy to scan the two pictures in and then manipulate them on the computer to make it look like one seamless wedding photo.

"When did you two lovebirds get married?" asked Mr. Tate.

"A few months ago," said Lyon.

"Two years ago," said Liv.

Lyon felt an elbow dig into his ribs. "Er, that is, *quite* a few months ago," he corrected.

Liv turned to Mr. Tate with a smile. "I assure you, Mr. Tate, that our son is perfectly legitimate, seeing as I didn't get pregnant with him until we were married for six months. Unfortunately, my husband,'' she began, deliberately throwing Lyon a look of disgust, ''like all men, can't be trusted to remember the single most important day of his life.''

Mr. Tate chuckled. ''My Millie used to say the same thing whenever I forgot our anniversary.''

Lyon put a soothing arm around his ''wife'' and pulled her close to his side. ''Well, you can't blame me, sweetheart. Even though we've been married for two years, it feels like just today that this picture was taken.''

He heard Liv choke against his shoulder, but she disguised it as a cough.

''That's what the ladies like to hear, my boy. Millie always said you can never have too much romance in your life. Isn't that right, my dear?''

''Absolutely. But Lyon is very obliging in that way. He didn't complain at all when I told him he'd have to buy this house, just so we could have our wedding in the little gazebo outside,'' said Liv, nodding meaningfully at the wedding picture.

Lyon realized that she was trying to draw his attention to the background of the picture, which was indeed his own backyard.

''I was just happy she agreed to live here afterward, so it wasn't a wasted investment,'' he said.

Mr. Tate nodded. ''Quite right, quite right. Lovely house. I notice you have some bird feeders outside, Lyon. What kind of birds do you get in these parts?''

Bird feeders? That had to be another one of Liv's ingenious little decorating ideas. What the hell did he know about birds?

He took a deep breath and prepared to lie like a fiend. "Well, sir, I—"

"Oh, you don't want to get him started, Mr. Tate!" interrupted Liv with a laugh. "Why, Lyon can talk about birds till the cows come home. No, it's best to save that conversation for some other time. Now, honey, why don't you get Mr. Tate something to drink, and I'll look in on the dinner."

Lyon was so relieved, he could have kissed her. Then he remembered.

No more kissing.

At least, not until he'd gotten rid of all the knives in the house.

DINNER WENT OFF without a hitch. Well, except for that little fiasco with the roast. Thank God Lyon had been able to salvage the whole thing. It had been a brilliant idea to cut the still-raw meat into slices, lay the slices out on a cookie sheet and stick them into the oven for a while longer. He'd even whipped up a delicious homemade gravy to go on top to disguise the slight toughness of the meat.

Thank heavens Ralph had insisted on going out to a restaurant tomorrow night, thought Liv as she rinsed the last pot and put it in the dishwasher. Imagine if she'd screwed up dinner in front of his mother! Somehow, she didn't think that Ralph would know one end of a partridge from another. For that matter, she doubted she'd be able to figure it out herself. Perhaps cooking lessons would be a good idea. But that would have to wait until next week at the very least.

She turned on the dishwasher, took off her apron and headed for the family room. When Lyon came back from dropping off Mr. Tate, she'd get him to help her with bundling up Sam. The little rascal had a tendency to be cranky if he was woken up accidentally.

She picked up all of Sam's toys from around the room, smiling as she remembered how Lyon had reacted to their "wedding" picture.

It was funny how she'd learned more about him this evening than she'd ever found out in the entire five years she'd worked for him. Perhaps it was because he'd been more relaxed and more human—not to mention less deafening—tonight than ever before. She hadn't once thought of him as beastly. In fact, she'd liked him, liked his easy charm and the way they'd been so perfectly in tune.

Like a real married couple.

She'd even felt sorry for him once, when Mr. Tate had asked at dinner why there weren't any pictures of his family on the mantelpiece. Lyon had answered politely enough and had changed the subject smoothly, but Liv had been shocked. Imagine being abandoned by your mother and growing up in an orphanage! She'd had such an idyllic childhood that the notion seemed almost incomprehensible to her. But it explained so much about him, about his ambition, his drive to succeed. It was almost as if that was the only way he could prove to himself that he was worthy...

Liv stopped in midstride as the truth dawned on her.

Oh Lord, she was a hypocrite of the worst order.

She'd had the nerve to accuse him of not knowing his employees, of treating them like inanimate objects, but they were all guilty of the same thing. No one at the office had ever taken the time or effort to get to know him. They had all been so wary of him, they'd kept their distance. Whenever they'd organized impromptu office lunches or after-hours get-togethers, no one had ever invited him because they'd all taken it for granted that he wouldn't want to come. All his employees ever saw of him was his gruff exterior, but no one had taken the time to get to know the real man underneath.

And she'd been the worst offender because she'd fostered that attitude by acting as a go-between, by being a buffer and keeping him isolated from everyone.

Suddenly, another thought occurred to her. Could it be that Lyon Mackensie was...*lonely?*

It made sense. He didn't have any family and he didn't seem to have very many friends. He had girlfriends, but those didn't usually last very long.

He was almost, she thought whimsically, like a wounded animal that wanted help, but was too proud to ask for it.

Well, she was determined that he wouldn't have to ask for it. Before the week was over, she was going to make sure that everyone at Mackensie Marketing knew the *real* Lyon Mackensie, not the beast who inhabited his body during working hours.

7

LYON GLANCED at his watch and looked out through the open door into Liv's office. Seven forty-eight a.m. She should be here any minute now, with Sam and all of the usual baby paraphernalia in tow. He frowned as he realized just how many times he'd looked at his watch in the past hour, waiting for Liv to come into the office. He always looked forward to seeing her in the mornings, but usually it was because her arrival ushered in the whirlwind of activity that heralded the beginning of the workday, and he was always anxious to get started.

Today, however, was different.

His eagerness to see Liv this morning had nothing to do with work and everything to do with last night. Last night, he'd seen an entirely different side to her and it intrigued him.

Last night, for the first time in five years, he'd witnessed his robotic personal assistant in a panic. He smiled as he remembered how adorably helpless she'd looked when he'd told her that the roast was still frozen. It was incredible to think that there was a skill his Miss Hammond hadn't yet acquired.

Kissing, however, was one skill she had definitely already mastered. Last night, he'd kissed her and

found her sweetly irresistible. Just the thought of
holding her in his arms and having her soft mouth
moving under his made his body ache with remembered delight.

And then, there were the photographs. Last night,
he'd glimpsed into her past through those photographs, and what he'd seen fascinated him. A happy
family. A carefree childhood. The notion was completely foreign to him, yet it held a strange enchant-
ment as well. It was as if he'd glanced into a dream
of what his life could be, if only…

Lyon brought himself up short.

If only what?

There was no way to change his past, no way to
change the person that he was, and it was ridiculous
to even think about it. He was just letting this crazy
charade get to him. Not only was a life of domestic
bliss impossible for someone like him, but he didn't
want it. He was happy as he was, and he'd be even
happier when they clinched the blasted birdseed account, when Mr. Tate went home, and when his life
was no longer populated by babies and birds and
blackmailing personal assistants.

Minimalist. Clinical. Now *that* was the ticket to
happiness.

LIV RUSHED into the office at eight o'clock that
morning. She had tons to do today and she was already running behind. The first thing on her list was
to set up an impromptu meeting between Lyon and
the staff, and then she had to get in touch with the
agency about finding a replacement for herself. As

if that wasn't enough, Sam was being unusually cranky this morning and she still hadn't gotten around to making reservations for tonight's dinner with Ralph and his mother.

"You're late," growled Lyon from the connecting door as she entered her office.

She walked up to him and handed him Sam. "Here, the two of you obviously woke up on the same side of the bed this morning."

His scowl disappeared as he gently stroked the dried tears on Sam's cheeks. "Is he all right?"

She sighed as she put down all of her bags, then took off her trench coat and hung it up. "He's fine. He probably just misses his parents, the poor little guy. Luckily, he won't have to wait much longer to see them. Tina and Paul will be picking him up this evening."

"This evening? They can't do that!"

"Sure they can. They're his parents."

"But…" He trailed off in confusion and looked at Sam, who stared earnestly back at him.

Liv smiled. "I'm sure he'll miss you, too."

"Yes, well." He cleared his throat and seemed to hold Sam a little tighter. "Speaking of this evening, I was thinking of inviting Mr. Tate out for dinner since he's flying home tomorrow."

She shook her head as she took Sam back to take his coat off. "I'm having dinner with Ralph and his mother tonight."

"Oh."

She gave Sam his rattle to play with and began

to unzip his coat. "It's the first time I'm meeting her, so it's a very important evening."

"I see."

"But there's no reason you can't have dinner with Mr. Tate. Just tell him Sam's not feeling well and I'm staying home to look after him. Then you two can spend all evening talking business without me and Sam there to distract you."

He nodded. "Of course, you're absolutely right."

"And you'll be happy to know that I'll be working on finding you a new personal assistant today."

"Excellent."

She lifted Sam expertly out of his coat and turned around to face Lyon again. "Oh, and by the way, there's going to be a staff get-together at around ten-thirty this morning."

He frowned. "I didn't ask to have a meeting scheduled today."

"It's not a meeting. It's Peter's birthday today, so we're having a little celebration with some cake," she said nonchalantly. "I thought it would be a good opportunity for you to get to know everyone a little better."

"So we're back to that again, are we?"

"You promised."

"All right, all right," he grumbled. "Just don't expect me to promote him to president of the company in honor of the big day."

"Darn!" She snapped her fingers in mock chagrin. "And here I was, hoping to soften you up to the idea with a slice of cake and the threat of actually having to make conversation with your employees.''

''A lesser man, my dear Miss Hammond,'' he said, taking Sam from her again, ''would be quaking in his boots.''

A LESSER MAN, thought Liv later that morning, would have needed lessons from a drill sergeant to carry this off. She shook her head in amazement from her perch at the back of the open area as she watched Lyon in action.

The birthday celebration had started out casually enough, although everyone had been surprised that the Beast had actually come out of his office to join in. They'd been wary of him at first, and he'd seemed a little uncomfortable, too, but Liv had tried to encourage Lyon to ask his staff personal questions. She'd hoped that they would become more comfortable with him if he showed an interest in them.

Her plan had worked, though not exactly as she'd envisioned it. Lyon had gotten carried away with the idea, barking the same question at each staff member individually as everyone stood at attention in a circle around him, awaiting their turn. They had answered uncertainly at first, sending Liv questioning glances, but she'd just nodded encouragingly, until everyone had become more confident and, suddenly, the whole thing turned into a game. Lyon was firing off questions one by one, and everyone was trying to answer as quickly as possible, laughing at each other's responses and bloopers. Incredibly enough, even Lyon laughed at some of the crazy answers.

It was amazing how much of a difference laughter made to his face, making him seem more approachable, less daunting than usual. Of course, it also made him very attractive, bringing out those knee-weakening dimples and emphasizing those incredibly blue eyes. At just that moment, he caught her staring at him and gave her an inquiring glance. She smiled and sent him a thumbs-up signal before turning to go back to her office.

There was still a long way to go in bringing Lyon and his staff to a point where they could communicate with each other without her interference, but the ice had been broken and if everyone kept up the effort, things would be fine when she left at the end of the week.

Now if only tonight's dinner with Ralph and his mother went as smoothly, her life would be perfect.

THAT EVENING, Liv's life was just about as far from perfect as it was possible to get. She'd come home from work later than she'd planned, but she'd rushed around like a madwoman in order to get Sam fed and bathed and dressed smartly for his parents' arrival. His playpen, car seat, high chair, suitcase and diaper bag were sitting by the door, ready to go.

The only things missing were his parents.

Liv paced the living room floor with Sam in her arms. She'd expected Tina and Paul to pick him up at six, which would have given her lots of time to

take a shower, get dressed and be ready when Ralph
and his mother came to pick her up at seven-thirty.

Mrs. Fortescue was a stickler for punctuality.
Ralph had mentioned it at least five times when he'd
called her last night to ask which restaurant she'd
made reservations at. Of course, she'd crossed her
fingers behind her back and lied like crazy, because
if she'd told him that she hadn't had time to make
reservations, he would have had a conniption fit.

Not that she would have blamed him. As it was,
she'd spent a half hour on the phone this morning
trying to get reservations at The Birdcage, one of
the premier fowl-serving restaurants in the city.
Luckily, she'd remembered seeing the ad in the Bird
Society magazine that Ralph had lent her. What she
couldn't figure out was why people who were bird
lovers would actually want to eat the poor little creatures…

"Go figure, Sam," she said as she bent down to
check the time on the telephone display.

It was only then that she noticed the message light
flashing on her answering machine. Frowning, she
pressed the button. The first message was from her
sister, calling from campus to tell Liv about the cool
new guy she'd met yesterday. The second message
was from Tina.

"Liv? Are you there?" There was a pause. "Oh,
heck, I guess not. You know how I hate talking to
these things. I'll try you again at eleven a.m., your
time."

The tape machine beeped and Tina came on
again.

"Hi, Liv. I've missed you again. I guess I have no choice but to talk to this thing, huh? How's Sam? Sammy, are you listening? Mommy loves you, sweetheart—"

"And Daddy, too, champ," Paul chimed in.

Sam bounced excitedly in Liv's arms at the sound of his parents' voices, his legs pumping, his hands reaching for the phone.

"Listen, Liv, I can't thank you enough for looking after Sam. You'll be happy to know that Paul and I have worked everything out. I'm bringing you back something special to thank you—"

"His name's José," interjected Paul.

"Oh, shush. She's engaged to, uh, Randall now," said Tina. "Anyway, we're going to grab a bite to eat and head for the airport, so we'll see you tonight at six. Bye-bye, baby."

Liv breathed a sigh of relief and sat down on the couch with an excited Sam on her lap. Everything was okay with Tina and Paul. They sounded happy and in love, just like they'd been when they'd first been married. She almost wished...

Liv sat up on the couch. Wished what? And why was she suddenly picturing that fake wedding photo of her and Lyon in her mind's eye?

She was engaged to Ralph.

Ralph, Ralph, Ralph, Ralph, Ralph.

Her silent chanting was interrupted by the next message.

"Liv, it's me again." This time, Tina's voice sounded different, urgent and tense, and Liv sat up higher. "Listen, Paul's been really sick and the doctor thinks it might be food poisoning. I'm not sure how long it'll be before we can come home. Can you look after Sam a little longer? I'm really sorry to have to ask you and I hope it isn't going to be a problem. There's no one else we can ask, except for Paul's family, but they live so far. I promise we'll try and get back as soon as we can. I'll call again later tonight. Give Sammy a kiss for me.''

Liv held Sam close and dropped a kiss on his head. Poor Paul! She hoped that he would be all right, and that Sam would be able to see his parents again soon.

But for now, she had a slight problem on her hands.

It was impossible for her to take Sam to dinner with her, but who could she leave him with?

LYON STOOD in front of Liv's apartment door and shook his head at the idea of being her ''lifesaver.'' It was a long way from the loudmouthed, obnoxious bully she'd accused him of being last week. When he'd answered the phone earlier and heard Liv's desperate plea for help, he'd said yes to looking after Sam tonight without even thinking about it. A week ago, the notion of baby-sitting a nine-month-old for his personal assistant would have been unthinkable, not to mention that Liv would never even have thought of calling him. He liked the fact that she'd thought of him first when she'd needed help. It gave him the same strange, warm feeling he'd gotten yesterday when he'd brought Mr. Tate home and found Liv and Sam waiting for him.

He knocked on the door and Liv's voice floated out to him from inside. "I'm coming!" A minute later, the door flew open, and Liv stood in front of him.

His eyeballs nearly fell out of their sockets.

Last night she'd looked beautiful in a wholesome, fifties kind of way, but tonight was different. Tonight, she looked subtly sexy and sophisticated in a simple ruby-red cocktail dress that showed off her curvy figure, sheer black stockings that skimmed over her long, shapely legs, and high heels. Her shiny brown hair was swept up in an elegant knot with wispy tendrils framing her lightly made-up face, a style that was light-years away from her Miss Hammond persona. Gone, too, were the glasses, replaced by contacts that brought out the golden lights in her lovely brown eyes. His gaze dropped instinctively to her mouth, which was stained a deep, inviting berry red.

He had the sudden urge to lock the door, take her in his arms, and spend the rest of the night kissing her senseless, unpinning her hair and running his fingers through its silky length, peeling that amazing dress off her soft, creamy body and making mad, passionate love to her. Ralph, his bird-crazy mother and Mr. Tate be damned.

"What's wrong?" she asked.

He took a deep, fortifying breath and forced his gaze to meet her eyes. "Uh, nothing."

"Are you sure? Do I look all right? My dress isn't too flashy, is it? And my hair—" she lifted a hand to anxiously pat the side of her head "—it's not too messy, is it?"

"No, you look great," he said, his gaze caught by the huge ruby adorning her left ring finger. She noticed what he was looking at and held out her hand so he could see the ring more closely.

"Incredible, isn't it?" she said.

He frowned. "Did you pick it out yourself?"

She laughed. "No, it belonged to Ralph's great-grandmother Bernice. He practically had to pry it off his mother's finger so he could give it to me."

"It's too big for your finger," was all he said before changing the subject abruptly. "Is Sam ready to go?"

"Oh, yes, of course. Come in."

She opened the door wider and stood aside. He walked into her apartment, which looked remarkably like his own house did now: tasteful and comfortable and lived-in.

"Hey, Sam, look who's here," she said.

Sam's baby face lit up and he raised both arms to be picked up.

Lyon walked over and lifted the little rascal out of his high chair with a grin. "Hey, Sammy, looks like it's just us boys tonight." He reached into his pocket, took out the small stuffed lion he'd bought earlier as a little goodbye gift and presented it to Sam.

Sam snatched the toy out of his hand and immediately bit into the lion's head.

"That's a good boy," said Liv, sending Lyon an amused look over Sam's head.

Just then, a buzzer sounded near the door, sending Liv into high gear.

She glanced at her watch. "Of all days for him to be early," she said, as she rushed to the intercom, pressed a button and said, "I'll be right down, Ralph."

She turned around and picked up Sam's diaper bag and thrust it at him. "Everything he needs is in here. You'll have to take his car seat with you, and here's a spare set of keys to my apartment. I'll meet you back here later. Ralph says his mother goes to bed early, so I should be back by ten-thirty at the latest." She slipped the keys into his jacket pocket and ran to pick up her purse and wrap from the sofa.

"Wait, what'll I tell Mr. Tate?" he asked, following her to the door.

"Tell him I felt sick at the last minute and you had to bring Sam with you because you didn't have time to get a sitter."

"Look, I don't know much about taking care of babies," he said, opening the door for her.

"You know the basics and Sam adores you. He'll be good, won't you, sweetheart?" She gave Sam a quick kiss on the side of his head. "See you later, baby, and you, too, hon—"

She broke off, about an inch away from kissing Lyon goodbye before she stopped, wide-eyed, her gaze skittering up to his.

For a brief, hopeful moment, he thought she was going to lean in and kiss him anyway, but she pulled back instead, grabbing his hand and pumping it twice before muttering a quick goodbye and flying out the door.

LIV SPEARED a roast potato with her fork and cut carefully into it. Ever since they'd walked into the mock-jungle interior of the Birdcage's atrium lobby, with its squawking tropical birds flying overhead, the hairs at her nape had been standing on end. The feeling had only intensified when they'd been shown into the restaurant itself and seated at a table surrounded by tropical plants.

She had a premonition that something was going to go terribly wrong tonight, so she'd tried to be extra careful all evening.

She'd skipped the salad just in case she ended up with green stuff stuck between her teeth.

She'd skipped the soup just in case she ended up spilling it down the front of her dress.

She'd ordered the cornish hen instead of some of the more exotic specialties of the house, just to be on the safe side.

Now, she had a horrible vision of one of the potatoes flying out from under her knife, making a beeline for the well-powdered expanse of Mrs. Fortescue's chest, sliding down her ample cleavage and into her corseted, green satin-covered bosom, never to be seen again.

Liv hastily put down her knife and picked up her glass of mineral water instead, taking a healthy gulp.

"Is there something wrong with your hen, dear?" asked Mrs. Fortescue.

"Oh, no, it's delicious. I'm just not very hungry tonight, I'm afraid."

"Nonsense. Young women these days are far too skinny. You must keep up your strength if you want to bear my Ralph a strong, healthy son." She turned to Ralph with an indulgent smile. "Isn't that right, darling?"

Ralph blinked. "What? Oh, yes, of course, Mother."

Liv frowned at him. "You think I'm too skinny?"

"I...I..." A slow flush stained his cheeks as his gaze dropped to her chest, which was considerably less well endowed than his mother's. "Well, no, not skinny, exactly—"

"Don't be absurd, dear. Of course he doesn't think you're too skinny. But you must have some meat on your bones before you become pregnant. All that breast-feeding can be exhausting, you know. Why, I breast-fed Ralph until he was three years old and by the time I was done, I'd nearly wasted away to nothing."

Liv choked on her water.

"Don't drink so quickly, dear. You'll give yourself indigestion. Now—" Mrs. Fortescue cut into her roast partridge with considerable relish "—Ralph tells me you have no people. Is that right?"

"People?" repeated Liv blankly.

"Family, dear."

"I do have a sister."

"Yes, of course, but your parents have both passed away?"

"I'm afraid so."

"You poor dear." Mrs. Fortescue patted Liv's hand in sympathy. "Luckily, you have me now, and you must look to me for the guidance your mother would have given you during your wedding preparations."

"Why, thank you, Mrs. Fortescue."

"Tell me, dear, where were you thinking of having the ceremony?"

"Well, we haven't quite decided yet. I thought maybe in a nice little gazebo with a few close friends and family—"

"Heavens! We couldn't possibly have that. Why, you and Ralph must be married at St. Stephen's Cathedral in Baltimore. That's where generations of Fortescues have been joined in holy matrimony. Mr. Fortescue, God rest his soul, and I were married there, too, of course. It's a Fortescue family tradition."

"But—"

"I absolutely must insist, Olivia. Now, how many people do you think you might be inviting?"

"As I said, Ralph and I thought a small wedding—"

"No less than five hundred people, I hope? After all, there are all of the Fortescues to invite, not to mention the Halliwells. I was a Halliwell before I married Mr. Fortescue, you know. And then all our friends from the Bridge League and the Bird Society, and the neighbors, of course. Oh yes, there could easily be five hundred guests to invite."

Five hundred?

Liv put a hand to her head. What was happening

here? What had happened to the cozy, intimate wedding she'd dreamed of having all of her life? The one she'd discussed with Ralph? *The one he'd agreed to?*

"But I thought we said no more than fifty?" she asked Ralph.

"Well, I—" Ralph cleared his throat. "I think Mother might be right, Olivia. I wasn't thinking when we talked about it before, but the Fortescues alone number nearly two hundred. I'm afraid the family will expect a big wedding."

"But I don't want a big wedding."

"Perhaps not, dear, but you're going to be a Fortescue soon and you must realize that there are many responsibilities that come with the privilege of the title."

"But…" Liv trailed off, looking from Mrs. Fortescue's determined expression to Ralph's guilty, pleading gray eyes and to the way he was rubbing his stomach.

She sighed. Poor Ralph. It seemed that talking about the wedding was giving him indigestion. Well, although Liv was willing to compromise on some of the issues, she had no intention of giving in completely to Mrs. Fortescue's demands. So perhaps it would be best for the moment to change the subject.

She managed to dig up a bright smile. "I had the opportunity to read the article you wrote on the Purple-Bellied Polka-Dotted Cuckoo in the latest issue of *Bird's I View* magazine, Mrs. Fortescue."

"You did?" Mrs. Fortescue put down her fork and beamed at Liv. "How wonderful! I do so enjoy sharing my passion with other bird lovers. Did you like it?''

Liv crossed her fingers and ankles under the table. ''It was very interesting. I was especially fascinated by their mating habits.''

''Oh my, yes. They only mate once every five years so, as you can imagine, the mating ritual is quite a rare sight. Of course, this weekend is peak mating season and this is one of the best places in the country to see it. There are quite a few places north of the city that you can go for an excellent viewing. Viewpoint Villa, Watcher's Paradise and Lookout Lodge are some of the best. That's why I was so excited when Ralph told me about you, Olivia. I thought I might be able to get in some bird-watching while I was here. It's one of the hobbies that Ralph and I share, you know.''

''That's wonderful, Mrs. Fortescue.''

''Indeed. Mr. Fortescue wasn't, I'm afraid to say, very passionate about these things, but I insisted that Ralph take an interest. Why, he came to his first Bird Society meeting when he was only six years old. I remember it like it was yesterday...''

Liv uncrossed her fingers and ankles and breathed a silent sigh of relief. The wedding was now forgotten in favor of the history of Ralph's interest in bird-watching.

Poor Ralph. It had to be difficult to be the object of such determined affection and such overwhelming attention. Although, at the moment, he seemed to be quite enjoying his mother's trip down memory lane.

Liv frowned. He'd been very quiet all evening, except when he'd been pressed for an opinion. Then he'd sided with his mother. It was disconcerting to say the least because Liv was used to having Ralph agree with her. It was one of his best qualities—

No, wait a minute. That wasn't quite right. She didn't love Ralph because he was agreeable. Of course not. She loved him because…because…well, because he loved her and he needed her and he was going to give her the kind of life she'd always dreamed of.

But what about love and excitement and passion?

Tina's words echoed in Liv's brain and her mind immediately conjured up the memory of the night when Lyon had kissed her. Even now, the recollection made her body ache with longing.

Tonight, she'd nearly kissed him again. It had been so natural, so instinctive to lean in and kiss him goodbye at the door, but she'd managed to stop herself in the nick of time. And even then, she'd been tempted to go ahead and do it anyway. Luckily, common sense had kicked in at just the right moment and she'd resisted. She had to remember the rule. No kissing. No matter how much she wanted to.

Oh Lord, she was doing it again. Fantasizing about Lyon when she should be thinking about Ralph.

Ralph, Ralph, Ralph, Ralph, Ralph.

"Ma! Ma! Ma! Ma! Ma!"

Ralph, Ralph, Ral—

"Mamamamama!"

The hairs on the back of Liv's neck stood at attention as the familiar baby cries penetrated into her consciousness.

She froze.

It couldn't be.

It couldn't possibly be.

But with her luck, it probably was.

8

WITHOUT THINKING, Liv turned in her seat and shoved aside some palm fronds so she could see where the cries were coming from. Her gaze collided with a pair of familiar baby blues.

Sam gave her a toothless grin as he pounded on the tray of his high chair with his little fists. "Ma! Mamamamama!" he shouted.

Liv turned back quickly and the branches snapped back into place. She found Ralph and Mrs. Fortescue staring at her peculiarly.

Liv smiled weakly. "I, uh, I thought I heard something. A…a strange bird, I think."

"Olivia, are you sure you're all right?" asked Ralph.

"I'm fine. Great. Hunky-dory," she lied. "Please continue, Mrs. Fortescue. I believe Ralph was thirteen when he spotted his first cuckoo?"

Ralph sent her an odd look before encouraging his mother to proceed. Liv pretended to listen avidly while wondering what Lyon and Sam and Mr. Tate were doing here. Well, she knew what they were *doing* here, but what were they doing *here?* This wasn't the type of place Lyon frequented and she doubted very much if he had even known of its existence before tonight. Mr. Tate must have picked it.

Mr. Tate. Thank God he hadn't seen her!

But she couldn't be certain how long her luck would last. She had to get out of the restaurant as quickly as possible, while Lyon and Mr. Tate were still busy eating.

"So, are we ready to go?" she asked.

Mrs. Fortescue stopped in the middle of her sentence and raised her thinly drawn eyebrows. "Are you in a hurry, Olivia?"

"I didn't want to say anything before, Mrs. Fortescue, because I was enjoying your story about Ralph so much, but I'm afraid I'm not feeling well."

Which wasn't too far from the truth at this particular moment.

"Why, whatever is the matter, dear?"

"Well, I was so excited about meeting you and I had tuna fish for lunch..." Liv trailed off, letting Mrs. Fortescue draw her own conclusions from the two perfectly true yet completely unrelated statements.

"Nervous indigestion," diagnosed Mrs. Fortescue, nodding sagely.

Bingo.

"Ralph, you take care of the bill and get my coat from the coat check and then meet us in the lobby." Mrs. Fortescue was all brisk efficiency as she stood up. "Come, dear, you'll feel better once we get you home."

LIV WAS BUSY hiding behind Mrs. Fortescue's womanly proportions in the lobby of the Birdcage when disaster nearly struck. She turned around to see if Ralph was coming back from the coat check when she saw Mr. Tate, Lyon and Sam coming out of the restaurant, heading right toward her.

Panicked, she turned her back to them and grabbed Mrs. Fortescue's arm. "Mrs. Fortescue, don't you need to go to the ladies' room?"

"Whatever for, dear?"

"Well, it is a long ride home and my mother always said you should go before you get in the car."

"I believe I just might be able to contain myself for the twenty minutes it will take us to get to your apartment, Olivia."

"But..." Liv was getting desperate. Mr. Tate was getting closer. She could hear Sam's baby babble even now. "I hope you don't think me rude, Mrs. Fortescue, but I believe you might want to freshen up a little," said Liv, glancing meaningfully at the older woman's powdered cleavage.

"Oh!" Mrs. Fortescue's hand flew to her chest. "Oh my, yes! Thank you for telling me, dear," she said, before hurrying away to the ladies' room.

Liv plastered a smile on her face and turned around just in time to greet Mr. Tate.

"Olivia!" exclaimed Mr. Tate. "I thought you were ill!"

"Mamama!" shouted Sam and launched himself into Liv's arms. Liv caught him and threw Lyon a helpless look over Sam's head.

"Hello, darling," said Lyon, leaning over to kiss Liv's cheek. "Feeling better?"

"Yes, the medication you picked up worked like a charm and I felt so much better, I decided I couldn't possibly let you men have all the fun."

"I told Mr. Tate you'd feel much better by morning. That's how it is with female trouble," said Lyon with a completely straight face.

Liv stared at him in astonishment before a blush started working its way up her face.

Mr. Tate chuckled. "No need to be embarrassed, my dear. My Millie used to suffer from the same thing. Every month, like clockwork. I used to have to rub her back. Perhaps you should have Lyon try that. Millie always said it made her feel much better."

"Yes, honey, perhaps I should give that a try," murmured Lyon, a wicked glint lighting his eyes.

Liv tossed him a quelling look before trying desperately to change the subject. "Have you finished dinner already?"

"We were just on our way out. Sam here was getting a bit overexcited," said Lyon.

"It is way past his bedtime." Liv didn't know how long before Mrs. Fortescue or Ralph came back, but she wasn't taking a chance on her luck holding out. "Shall we go?" she asked, making a beeline for the revolving doors.

When they got outside, Liv hurriedly handed Sam to Lyon. "I'll see you two at home," she said.

"Aren't you coming with us, Olivia?" asked Mr. Tate.

"Oh no, I brought my own car."

"Yes, of course. What about Sam?"

"Oh, his car seat is in Lyon's car. I, uh, I have to visit the ladies' room and then I'll follow you home. Good night, Mr. Tate."

"I'm sorry you had to miss dinner, my dear."

"So am I, but I'll see you tomorrow." Liv smiled and waved off the trio before running back through the revolving door. She skidded to a breathless halt in front of a wide-eyed Ralph and a startled Mrs. Fortescue.

"I needed some fresh air," she explained before asking brightly, "So, are we ready to go?"

"I CAN'T BELIEVE we pulled that off," said Lyon as he sat down on Liv's sofa and loosened his tie.

"We nearly didn't," she said, flopping down beside him and flipping off her heels. "How is it that you and Mr. Tate ended up at the Birdcage? I had to practically beg over the phone this morning to get a reservation."

"When I invited Mr. Tate for dinner, he already had reservations. Apparently, he'd had his secretary make them when he knew he was coming to town, and he was tickled pink at the idea of having Sam along."

"How did Sam like the birds in the atrium?"

Lyon smiled as he remembered Sam's reaction to the parrot Mr. Tate had tried to show him. "He cried a little at first, but when he realized that the birds were more scared of him than he was of them, he calmed right down. After that, he was too busy trying to catch them to be scared."

"It's a good thing he didn't catch any or you know what he'd have done."

"Tried to bite their heads off, no doubt."

She laughed. "Well, I'm glad someone had a good time."

He looked at her sideways. "I take it that things with what's-his-name's mother didn't go too well?"

"His name is Ralph. And meeting his mother was very...interesting," she said primly.

Lyon snorted.

She turned her head to look at him. "And what, exactly, does that mean?"

"It means that you're just being polite. She's a dragon, isn't she?"

"She's not a dragon," protested Liv, then smiled at his skeptical look. "Well, at least not much of one. Anyway, I've dealt with much worse," she said, giving him a pointed look.

Lyon wasn't so sure about that.

He'd gotten a glimpse of Ralph's mother in the lobby of the restaurant this evening, just before she'd hurried away to the ladies' room, and he had a feeling that Mrs. Fortescue was probably a much more effective—though subtler—bully than he. And from what he'd heard about Ralph, he wasn't the type to stand up to his mother. Just why exactly Liv wanted to give up her job to marry Ralph was beyond Lyon's understanding. He knew she thought marriage to Ralph was going to make her happy, but he wasn't convinced.

On impulse, he asked her. "Liv, why do you want to marry Ralph?"

She looked at him in surprise. "Well, I...I..." She stopped, then smiled. "When I was a child, my sister Jenny and I were the most envied kids on the block because we had the perfect family. My dad was sweet and kind and a little bit helpless. Oh, he went out and earned a living so we'd be comfortable, but he needed my mom to take care of him. We all did. My mom was, well, she was amazing." Liv's face was alight with love and, just like the kids in her neighborhood, at that moment, he envied her. "She baked cookies and sewed and took care of the house and all of us and she was so *happy* doing it." She looked at him, her eyes shining with hope and enthusiasm. "That's what I want. I want to be like her. I want a house and kids and I want to stay home and take care of them. Ralph, he's like my father. He *needs* me."

I need you.

The words came unbidden to his mind and he quickly qualified them. What he meant was that the *company* needed her. When she'd left him and his staff alone this morning after Peter's birthday celebration, he'd quickly taken the opportunity to indulge his curiosity about her, and what he'd found out had astonished him.

Although for the past five years she'd managed him with the robotic efficiency he preferred, her relationship with his employees was very different. She was their rock, a mother hen and a sympathetic but no-nonsense big sister all rolled into one. She kept track of their lives, always showing an interest in their families and their well-being. He suspected that, sometimes, she let people take advantage of her sympathetic nature, but also that she loved being needed. She was a born nurturer and someday she'd make a wonderful mother.

The only problem was that he suspected she needed more out of life. She thrived on the challenge of organizing him and his company, and she was damned good at what she did. His staff had been devastated when they'd learned that she was leaving Mackensie's. Lyon suspected that Liv would be even more devastated when she left and realized what a big mistake she'd made.

Because, if Mrs. Fortescue was the managing busybody he suspected she was and Ralph didn't have the courage to stand up to her, Liv would end up being superfluous in her own life. She'd be miserable and unhappy, and that was the last thing in the world he wanted for her.

But it wasn't his place to say anything. After all, Liv was a grown woman, intelligent and capable, and she could surely make her own decisions about what she wanted to do with her life and who she wanted to marry without him throwing in his two cents' worth. So he kept his mouth shut, even though it nearly killed him to do so.

"Your parents sound like wonderful people," he said instead.

"They were. Unfortunately, they were killed in a car accident five years ago."

He took her hand in his and squeezed gently. "I'm sorry."

"It's all right. They had a good, although short,

life and they went together, which is how they would have wanted it.''

"And your sister? That was her in the pictures on my mantelpiece, right?''

She nodded, smiling. ''Jenny's in her last year at university. She's just received a full scholarship to do her graduate studies next year.''

"You must be really proud of her.''

"I am. She's a great kid, smart and funny and beautiful.''

He instinctively touched his fingers to her soft, flushed cheek. ''So are you.''

There was a short, tense silence as she stared at him, her full red lips parted in surprise. He was tempted to lean in and kiss those lips, but he knew she wouldn't thank him for it. He had to remember that she was only his temporary personal assistant, that she was engaged to another man and that she wanted something out of life that he couldn't possibly give her. Before he was tempted to develop a convenient case of amnesia, he stood up and reached for his jacket. ''I guess I should be going.''

She followed him as he made his way to the door. ''Thanks for taking care of Sam for me tonight.''

"The pleasure was all ours. Mr. Tate really dotes on him.''

"Oh, speaking of Mr. Tate, did he say anything about the account?'' she asked.

Lyon nodded. ''He seemed very positive. He's going to run a final check by his people when he gets home and then he'll sign the papers. Now we've just got to keep him happy until tomorrow. He'll be coming by the office in the afternoon to say goodbye to everyone before he leaves."

"Well, it'll be a relief not to have to continue with this charade anymore."

"Yes," said Lyon and, for some reason, the word didn't come out quite as convincingly as he intended it to. "Have you found a replacement for yourself yet?"

"There's one candidate who might be suitable. The agency found her this afternoon, and she's coming in tomorrow for an interview. If everything goes well, she can start on Monday."

"Great," he said.

It seemed that, come tomorrow, they were both going to get exactly what they wanted. So why was it that, instead of being elated, he felt oddly hollow inside, as if there was a great, gaping hole where his heart should have been?

"WELL, MY BOY, it's been a pleasure meeting you and your charming family. Perhaps you and Liv and little Sam here will come and visit me sometime," said Mr. Tate, as they stood in Lyon's office the next afternoon.

"We'd love to, wouldn't we, honey?" asked Lyon.

"What? Oh, yes, of course."

Liv was distracted. She could barely concentrate on what she was saying. Lyon's arm around her shoulder was sending tingles of awareness through her entire body, and the gleam in his eyes as he looked down at her, soft and tender, was doing funny things to her heart.

Just like last night.

Last night, he'd been wonderful, first by agreeing to take care of Sam, then by being so understanding and sympathetic when she'd told him about her parents. For the first time, she felt as if he was interested in her, not just as an employee who could help him succeed in his business, but as a person.

As a woman.

She'd seen it in his eyes when he'd touched her cheek and, at that moment, she'd wanted so desperately for him to just lean forward and kiss her with all the passion and—

She was pulled out of her fantasy by Lyon squeezing her shoulder. "Liv? Honey?"

"Huh?"

"Mr. Tate was just asking you a question."

Liv made a superhuman effort to pull herself together and put all thoughts of kissing Lyon aside. "I'm sorry, Mr. Tate. What was that?"

"I was wondering if you'd be kind enough to send me some information on the Purple Bellied Polka-Dotted Cuckoo. I'm afraid I didn't get a chance to talk to you about its mating habits."

"Of course! I have a very informative article I can send you. It's just a shame that you won't have a chance to see the Purple-Bellied Polka-Dotted Cuckoo in person while you're here. I understand that this weekend is peak mating season, and that this is one of the best spots in the country to see it.

There's a place called Lookout Lodge, just outside town, where you can go for an excellent viewing.''

"I see. Will you and Lyon be going there this weekend?" asked Mr. Tate thoughtfully.

Liv looked up at Lyon, who was trying to send her some kind of silent message, but with all that twitching coupled with the maniacal grin he had on his face, she couldn't quite figure it out. So she made a quick decision. "Why, yes, we wouldn't miss it for the world.''

"Well, now that you mention it, you're perfectly right. Since I'm here, I might as well extend my trip for a few days. No reason to rush off home. So, thank you very much for extending the invitation, Olivia. It would be a great pleasure for me to go bird-watching with the Mackensie family this weekend,'' said Mr. Tate, beaming at her.

Liv looked at him blankly, trying to figure out exactly where she'd lost the thread of the conversation, and what she could do to change the outcome. She tried frantically to think of an excuse.

"Umm, oh dear, I just remembered,'' she said with a weak smile. "What about Sam? We couldn't possibly leave him with a baby-sitter for the whole weekend, could we, honey?''

"What? Nonsense! Why, you'll just have to bring the little tyke along. I always say, you're never too young to learn about the joys of bird-watching. Isn't that right, my boy?''

"Never too young,'' repeated Lyon in a hearty yet patently false voice.

"Well, that settles it, then. I'll have my secretary

change my flight and I'll look forward to Friday. I have a feeling it will be a splendid weekend!''

LIV WAITED all morning for the other shoe to drop, for Lyon to call her into his office and bawl her out for being such an idiot, but the summons never came.

After Mr. Tate had left, Lyon had just ordered her to make the arrangements for the weekend, and then disappeared inside his office. She hadn't heard a peep out of him since.

It was enough to make her very, very nervous.

Perhaps he was punishing her by making her wait for the deafening dressing-down she was sure was to come.

Not that she needed it. She'd already kicked herself mentally a million times for her stupidity. Not only had her preoccupation with kissing Lyon succeeded in delaying the account from going through, but she'd also upped the chances of something going wrong this weekend.

And most alarming of all, she'd extended the charade of being married to Lyon for a whole weekend.

All the trouble this morning had started because she'd been thinking about him instead of concentrating on what she was saying. What would happen when she was forced to endure his casually affectionate touches and pseudo-tender glances for forty-eight more hours?

She'd turn into a wreck, that's what.

Liv sighed and looked at her watch. It was nearly two o'clock. The candidate to replace her as Lyon's

P.A. would be here any minute for her interview. Liv just prayed that the woman had the skin of a rhinoceros and the constitution of an ox, coupled with nerves of industrial-strength steel.

She had a feeling that was what would be required to deal with the Beast this afternoon.

LYON PACED the length of his office for the umpteenth time. He didn't understand it, damn it. Why wasn't he angry? Why hadn't he called her in here and proceeded to blister her ears and fire her for being incompetent?

A week ago, that was exactly what he would have done. Now, all he could do was pace up and down his office and wonder why he felt so...so *relieved*.

He stopped pacing and frowned. It couldn't be because the approval for the birdseed account had now been delayed. It certainly couldn't be because they now had two more days to screw up and have Mr. Tate stumble on the truth about his phony marriage and faux family. So it had to be because he had two extra days to pretend to be married to Liv.

Now why should *that* make him feel relieved?

Lyon resumed his pacing. It had to be his conscience, the damnable nuisance. He knew that what Liv was planning to do was wrong, but by the time she figured it out, it would be too late. She would be shackled for life to wimpy Ralph and his dominating mother.

No, he couldn't let Liv make the mistake of leaving Mackensie's and marrying Ralph, and he had precisely two days to convince her to rethink her decision.

However, if he said anything to her outright, she would only accuse him of being a selfish swine and wanting her to come back to work for him, which, of course, he did, but that wasn't his main objective right now.

His main objective was to make Liv come to the realization—by herself—that marrying Ralph was a mistake. But how? The only thing he could think of was to play upon the attraction they felt for each other. He knew she was as attracted to him as he was to her, except she was fighting her feelings tooth and nail by dictating ridiculous, impossible-to-follow rules like ''No Kissing.''

Well, he'd just have to break the rules. After all, he was doing it for her own good. Once she realized that she was more attracted to him than to Ralph, she would know that she didn't love Ralph. After that, her innate honesty and forthrightness would ensure that she didn't go through with the wedding.

Then, maybe, just maybe, she'd agree to come back to work for him—permanently.

Lyon smiled as he sat down and leaned back in his chair, pleased with the logic of his plan. Suddenly, he was quite looking forward to this weekend.

A minute later, his intercom buzzed and Liv's voice informed him that Miss Harper was here for her two o'clock interview.

He sat up. It wouldn't do for him to let Liv suspect anything, and she would if he acted as pleased as he felt. No, the only thing to do was for him to act like his usual uncivilized, untamed self. She wouldn't suspect a thing.

And if he managed to scare away her replacement in the process, well, all the better.

LIV AND ANNIE SAT on Annie's desk, cringing at the amount of barking and bellowing coming from the Den.

"At least she hasn't come running out of there yet," said Liv.

"And I haven't heard any crying yet, either, so that's a good sign. He hates women who cry," said Annie. "You know, you're going to think I'm crazy, but I've actually missed the Beast's yelling for the past couple of days."

"It's scary, Annie, but I know exactly what you mean."

"So, how much longer do you think she's going to last?"

Liv looked at her watch. "I give her another five seconds."

Annie nodded. "Yeah, that sounds about right."

Two seconds later, they both looked up as the door flew open and a young woman came running out, sobbing.

"He's a beast!" she cried as she ran past.

"Well, now *there's* a news flash," said Liv dryly as the woman fled into the elevator.

THAT EVENING, Liv was just about to gather the courage to pick up the handset and call Ralph and tell him she'd be unavailable this weekend when the phone rang.

"Olivia, it's me, Ralph."

"Hello, Ralph. I was just about to call you."

"Listen, Olivia, I'm afraid I don't have much time to talk. I have to pack and then I need to see to Mother's medication."

"Medication? Ralph, what's happened? Is your mother all right?"

"Oh yes, she's fine. Only we're planning to go away for the weekend. Mother...well, we haven't seen each other in a while and there's lots of catching up to do. Besides, she wants to do some bird-watching this weekend. You don't mind being left alone for a couple of days, do you? We'll be back by Sunday."

Thank you, God.

"Of course not, Ralph. Believe me, I understand."

"I promise I'll make it up to you, Olivia."

"Please, Ralph, don't worry yourself. You just have a good time and give my best to your mother. And don't forget to take your inhaler."

"I won't. Oh, and Olivia?"

"Yes, Ralph?"

"How are you feeling today?"

"Feeling? Oh, yes, the nervous indigestion. All cleared up."

"I'm very glad to hear that. You were acting a bit...peculiar last night."

"I'm sorry, Ralph. I was just a little bit nervous last night."

"Yes, that's what I told Mother. I'll talk to you on Monday, Olivia. Goodbye."

"Goodbye, Ralph."

Liv hung up the phone, feeling oddly relieved. It was strange, but she was actually looking forward to a weekend of bird-watching. Could it be that she'd developed a sudden, secret passion for the Purple-Bellied Polka-Dotted Cuckoo?

Or was it something—or someone—else she'd developed a secret passion for?

9

"WHO WOULD HAVE THOUGHT that a four-hour drive could be so exhausting?" said Lyon as he dropped two suitcases, a diaper bag, a purse and a folded-up playpen by the door connecting their two rooms. "Even Sam conked out."

"It wasn't that bad," said Liv as she laid Sam carefully in the middle of the king-size bed.

"Easy for you to say. You didn't have to sit in the front with Mr. Tate and answer all of his questions. Don't you think he's just a little *too* curious about our marriage?"

"We don't have a marriage and you're just being paranoid."

"Well, you would be, too. I didn't know what you'd already told him over your friendly little phone chats. I kept thinking I was going to blow our cover every time I opened my mouth."

"Poor baby," she said, smiling at him. "Maybe you'd better turn in early if you're so tired. Tomorrow's going to be a busy day, starting with breakfast at five."

"Five o'clock?" Lyon groaned and flopped down on the overstuffed chair by the bed.

Liv tried unsuccessfully to suppress a smile.

When he was disgruntled, Lyon reminded her uncannily of Sam. "Come on, you're an early riser."

"Yeah, but I never thought I'd be getting up at five to go trekking through the woods looking for birds, for Pete's sake!"

"Think of it as research for the birdseed campaign."

"The only birds I'm interested in for the birdseed account are nice little domestic parakeets and budgies, and those I can see at a *reasonable* hour at any pet store."

Her laughter bubbled over and she automatically reached out to smooth a lock of hair off his forehead. Their gazes met, and her laughter disappeared at the raw desire she saw burning in his eyes. Deliberately, he caught her hand and pulled her down on his lap.

"Lyon," she whispered in protest. "Remember the rule. No kissing."

"Hold out your hands," he instructed.

Puzzled, she held them out.

"Excellent," he said, taking her outstretched arms and winding them around his neck. "No carving knife, no rules."

"Lyon!"

"Come on, sweetheart," he murmured, his lips just a whisper away from hers. "You know you want to."

She stared at his mouth, so tempting and so near, and, without thinking, closed her eyes and lifted her lips those last, scant few millimeters and she was kissing him.

The kiss was everything she dreamed it would be. Hot. Wet. *Passionate.*

It was only when he finally broke it off to touch his lips to her throat that a semblance of coherent thought returned.

"We shouldn't be doing this," she said, then moaned as he eased open the top few buttons on her shirt and cupped her lace-covered breasts in his warm hands.

"Why not?"

"Because…" She closed her eyes at the wave of need that spiraled through her when he brushed his thumbs over her aching nipples. "Because you're… you're not Ralph."

"You don't want Ralph. You want me," he whispered, his thumbs caressing the tips of her breasts rhythmically, his lips pressing wet, erotic kisses down the side of her neck.

"No," she said, even as she pressed herself harder into his hands.

"Yes, Liv. What you want right now, at this moment, you'll never get from Ralph." He stopped to look into her eyes, his blue gaze scorching her with its heated intensity. "Admit it."

"All right, yes, I want you. I'm attracted to you." She closed her eyes to block out his disturbing presence. "But how can I be when I'm going to marry Ralph?" she whispered.

"Because you're not going to marry him. You can't," he said flatly.

"And then what?" She pulled away, hauled herself off his lap and started to button her shirt with shaky fingers. "I break up with Ralph, give up my dreams and for what? So we can have a brief fling until you decide that I'm asking for too much of your time and try to buy me off?"

"Liv—"

"And knowing my luck," she muttered darkly, "I'll probably have to buy my own kiss-off gift."

"I'm sorry, Liv." His voice was gruff with emotion as he came to stand in front of her. "I can't guarantee you this perfect life you want. I've never experienced anything like it. When you talk about it, it's like a fairy tale to me, and as much as I would like to give you what you need, I don't think I can."

"Oh, Lyon," she said, her heart aching for him.

"But I can guarantee one thing," he said, his eyes hardening, his jaw tightening, all traces of vulnerability suddenly disappearing. "Ralph and his mother aren't going to give you what you need, either."

All sympathy for him fled, and she looked at him in exasperation. "You don't know that!"

"Sure I do. I'll prove it to you. Close your eyes."

She closed them reluctantly.

"Now, tell me how many children you want."

Puzzled, she answered, "Four. Why?"

"Because that means you'll have to have sex with Ralph at least four times. Can you picture Ralph naked? Can you picture yourself in bed with him? Can you honestly picture him kissing you and touching you like I just did?"

There was a long silence.

"Well?" he barked impatiently.

She opened her eyes and looked at him in irritation. "Give me a minute, will you? I'm still working on picturing Ralph naked."

Growling in disgust, he picked up his bag and stalked out the connecting door to his own room.

"WOULD ANYONE like a cup of coffee?" asked Liv, lagging behind Mr. Tate and Lyon, who had Sam in a baby carrier on his back, through the densely wooded trail.

"Coffee? You and Lyon go ahead and take a break, my dear," said Mr. Tate. "I'll just see what's ahead on the trail and be back in a few minutes."

She wondered what kind of batteries the man was running on; since the moment they'd started hiking at some ungodly hour this morning, he'd been going and going and going, enthusiastically pointing out various species of birds, giving them demonstrations of bird calls and marching ahead with a gusto that made her tired just watching him.

Already, they'd been hiking on and off for the better part of three hours, equipped with binoculars, bird books and instructions from the woman at the front desk on the best trail to take to get a glimpse of the famed Purple-Bellied Polka-Dotted Cuckoo.

Liv was beginning to wish the blasted bird to extinction.

"All right?" asked Lyon as she stopped beside him and slid the backpack off her shoulders.

She nodded and took out a coffee thermos and two plastic cups from her pack. "How much longer do you reckon it's going to take before we can get back to civilization?"

"According to Mr. Tate, it's another hour into the woods before we hit cuckoo territory."

She groaned and leaned her forehead on his chest.

"Hang in there, sweetheart," he murmured against her ear.

"Why?" she moaned. "Why did I have to open my big mouth?"

He rubbed her back soothingly and said, "There, there now. Think of this as the best training sweat and blood can buy."

"Training?"

"Umm. I believe your mother-in-law-to-be is a big fan of bird-watching. Think of all the many, many happy hours you and Ralph and Ralph's mother will enjoy together as a family doing just this."

She straightened and smacked him on the chest.

He held out his hands in mock innocence. "Hey, I'm just telling it like it is."

She poured the coffee into a cup and gave it to him. "Shut up and drink."

Reaching back into her knapsack, she took out a teething cookie for Sam and offered it to him. He took it eagerly and she lifted him out of the carrier to change his diaper.

"I'll do that," said Lyon, taking the diaper from her. "You sit down and drink your coffee."

Ten minutes later, Sam had been changed and fed and cleaned, and they were ready to go again. However, Mr. Tate still hadn't returned. They decided to forge ahead in the hopes of catching up to him. Fifteen minutes into their walk, they came upon the reason for Mr. Tate's delay. Up ahead was a group of ten or so people, their funny hats and binoculars branding them as fellow bird-watchers, all chatting excitedly in hushed tones.

Liv and Lyon made their way into the group of people, looking for Mr. Tate. They found him in the middle of the throng.

"Ah, there you are, my boy," he said to Lyon when he spotted them. "You'll never guess who I've just come across! One of the foremost experts on the North American cuckoo. It's all quite incredible!"

Mr. Tate was nearly bursting with excitement. Liv looked at Lyon questioningly. He shrugged his shoulders and led her forward to be introduced.

"Gwynneth, I'd like you to meet—"

"Olivia!"

"Mrs. Fortescue?"

"Ah, you two know each other already. I should have realized," said Mr. Tate.

"Yes, of course we know each other," said Mrs. Fortescue. "Olivia is—"

"A very big fan of yours, Mrs. Fortescue," interjected Lyon. "Why, she's been positively raving about that article you wrote on the Purple-Bellied Polka-Dotted Cuckoo."

Mrs. Fortescue preened with delight. "Oh, you're *too* kind, Mr...?"

"Mackensie. Lyon Mackensie at your service, ma'am," he said, taking Mrs. Fortescue's hand and bringing it to his lips.

She twittered girlishly before turning to Liv. "I

didn't realize you were going to be here this weekend, Olivia. Ralph said you weren't coming.''

"A last-minute change of plans," improvised Liv. She looked around with increasing dread. "Uh, where is Ralph?"

Mrs. Fortescue frowned. "He was here a moment ago." She turned to Mr. Tate with a charming smile. "Ralph is my son. He's quite an authority on the cuckoo himself, you know. Why, he's been a member of the Bird Society since he was six years old..."

Knowing exactly how engrossed Mrs. Fortescue could become in the subject of Ralph's bird-watching history, Liv took the opportunity to pull Lyon aside.

"What are we going to do?" she whispered frantically. "If either one of them talks to the other about me, we're both sunk!"

"I have a feeling that you're the last thing either one of them wants to talk about," he said.

"What do you mean?"

"I mean, I think they're more interested in talking about birds than people."

"Yes, but what if—"

"Look, all we have to do is go with the story that you're my personal assistant and that you're doing me a favor by helping me out with a client this weekend. Mr. Tate already knows that we don't like to advertise the fact that we're supposedly married. If necessary, I'll take him aside and tell him we'd prefer that he not mention it to anyone."

"Yes, but what will I tell Ralph?"

He grinned. "That I, your boss, begged and pleaded with you to help me out this weekend, and that you just couldn't resist my manly charms, so you agreed."

"He'll never believe it, especially the manly charms bit."

"Liv…"

"Okay, okay, I suppose you're right. We'll worry about the consequences if and when we get caught."

"All right, everyone, we're going to leave the trail now and follow Mrs. Fortescue as she leads us into the mating grounds. Stay together and try not to make too much noise," announced one of the men.

The group began to move, Mrs. Fortescue and Mr. Tate leading the pack; Lyon motioned Liv to stay at the rear of the group. She breathed a sigh of relief. Hopefully, Mr. Tate and Mrs. Fortescue would be too engrossed in bird-watching to talk or to pay any attention to them.

She was just beginning to relax when someone else joined the group.

"Ralph!" she exclaimed.

"Shh," came a whisper from ahead.

"Olivia!" he whispered. "How did you find us?"

"Uh, I guess it was just luck."

Rotten luck.

"Well, it certainly is a surprise."

"Yes, I didn't know that you and your mother were going to be at Lookout Lodge. I thought you'd go to one of the other places your mother mentioned."

"Mother decided that this was the best place. One

of the Bird Society members is the owner. What are *you* doing here?''

''I'm here with my boss. He asked me to help him with a client this weekend, so I agreed.''

Ralph frowned. ''But I thought you quit your job. I thought you said your boss was an obnox—''

She quickly cut him off. ''Ralph, meet Lyon Mackensie, my boss.''

The two men shook hands and, by the grimace on Ralph's face, Lyon used far more force than necessary.

She sent him a narrow-eyed stare. It was bad enough that, thanks to his idiotic blithering last night, she couldn't look at Ralph this morning without having a sudden compulsion to mentally undress him. It was worse that she couldn't seem to get past the buttons on Ralph's shirt, and worse still that Lyon was standing beside her, making his opinion of her fiancé crystal-clear.

''And this must be your son,'' said Ralph, spying Sam, who had been rocked to sleep in his carrier by the motion of Lyon walking. ''Don't you think that perhaps he might be a little too young for this?''

Lyon gave him a belligerent look. ''I always say you're never too young to learn about the joys of bird-watching.''

''That's not his son! Don't you remember? That's Sam,'' said Liv.

Ralph looked at Liv in shock. ''Olivia, do you mean to tell me that *you're* responsible for bringing him here?''

"Well, yes. I didn't have anyone else to look after him."

"Where are his parents? Haven't you been looking after him for far too long already?"

"But I *like* looking after him, Ralph," explained Liv patiently. "Besides, Tina and Paul are still out of town."

They were expected back home tomorrow. Luckily, Paul was feeling much better now. She'd left a message for them telling them where she and Sam were going to be this weekend so they wouldn't worry when they got home tomorrow. If everything went according to plan, Sam would be reunited with his parents tomorrow night.

"I don't know how Mother would feel about that, Olivia," said Ralph doubtfully.

Lyon rolled his eyes behind Ralph.

Liv deliberately ignored him. "Ralph, I, uh, I think it would be a good idea if you didn't tell your mother about Sam. In fact, maybe it would be best if I tried to keep out of your way this weekend altogether. After all, you and your mother wanted to spend time alone and I'd feel terrible if I intruded."

"I'm sure that won't be necessary."

"I insist, Ralph," said Liv firmly. "In fact, I bet we're holding you back right now. I'm sure you'd rather be leading this expedition with your mother than straggling behind with us."

"Well..."

"Go on, dear. Mr. Mackensie and I will just stay back here, out of everyone's way."

"If you're sure you don't mind..."

"I'm positive."

Ralph kissed her cheek, flushing as he saw Lyon scowling at him, and hurriedly went to join his mother.

Lyon opened his mouth and Liv turned on him with a glare. "Whatever you're going to say, I don't want to hear it."

He raised a brow. "Afraid that what I'm going to say is too close to the truth?"

"Afraid that what you're going to say will make me want to throttle you."

He grinned. "At least if you're in jail, you won't be able to marry Ralph."

"You're not going to change my mind about marrying Ralph, so you might as well keep your nasty remarks to yourself."

"We'll just see about that," he murmured.

LYON WALKED INTO his room through the connecting door, eager to take a hot shower and change. Sam wasn't heavy, but carrying him on that backpack all day was hard work and his muscles were beginning to protest.

Nevertheless, he'd enjoyed the day, mostly because he'd spent it with Liv. And now that he'd gotten a closer look at the competition, he was more convinced than ever that she was making a mistake.

He was also more determined than ever to make sure that she didn't end up with Ralph, and tonight was his last chance to change her mind.

"Hello, darling," came a sultry whisper from the middle of his bed.

He nearly got whiplash from the double take he did.

"Melanie?"

The figure in the red silk negligee slipped off the bed and walked toward him. "Surprise," she purred as she twined her arms around his neck and pressed herself against him.

"What are you doing here?" he asked.

"I couldn't wait until the end of the weekend to thank you for the diamond bracelet you sent me. Doesn't it look exquisite?" she asked, holding out her arm for his inspection.

He barely glanced at it. "Yeah, it looks great. How did you find me?"

Melanie smiled enchantingly at him. "I called your office yesterday as soon as I got the bracelet. A very nice girl named Annie told me that you'd left early to go on a business trip this weekend. I persuaded her to tell me exactly where so I could surprise you."

"Remind me to fire Annie," he muttered, then tried to extract Melanie's tentacles from his neck. "Melanie, we need to talk."

She pouted. "Can't we talk later, darling? I've missed you so much all week."

"No, you're not supposed to be he—"

Her red lips zoomed in on his, cutting off his protest.

"WHERE DID YOU SAY his bottle was?" asked Mr. Tate as he opened the door to Liv's room.

"It should be on the coffee table," said Liv as

she followed behind Mr. Tate, a whimpering Sam in her arms. "There, sweetheart, we've almost got it."

Mr. Tate handed her the bottle and she gave it up to Sam's eager fingers. He shoved the nipple straight into his mouth and blessed silence ensued.

Liv laughed. "Now maybe he'll take a nap so I can rest for a minute."

She turned around to sit down on the chair with Sam, and froze.

Through the connecting door, she saw Lyon and a woman in a red negligee locked in a passionate embrace.

"You must be exhausted, my dear. I'm afraid Mrs. Fortescue and I got a bit carried away this afternoon in leading you all so far into the woods." Mr. Tate paused. "Olivia? Are you all right, my dear?"

Liv was startled out of her shock and only then realized that if Mr. Tate turned slightly to the left, he'd be able to see what she was seeing.

She had half a mind to let him.

But sanity quickly reasserted itself and she hurried over to him, turning him away from the connecting door. "I'm fine, MR. TATE. Why don't you freshen up before dinner, MR. TATE, and Lyon and I will meet you at seven-thirty in the dining hall, MR. TATE."

"Yes, all right." Mr. Tate frowned. "What was that noise?"

"What noise?"

"It sounded like it came from the adjoining room."

"I'm sure it's nothing."

"Wait. That sounded like a woman!"

"It must be Lyon singing in the shower again."

"I'll just see what it is. You can never be too careful these days, you know, what with all the kidnappers and murderers on the loose." Mr. Tate brushed past her and headed right for the connecting door.

"No, wait!" Liv ran after him with Sam in her arms.

"Ah, Lyon, my boy. I was just telling Liv you can never be too careful about security these days," said Mr. Tate, beaming at Lyon, who was frozen on the spot, Melanie at his side. "And who is this lovely young woman?"

Lyon swallowed audibly. "It's, uh, it's—"

"It's my cousin Melanie," said Liv quickly. "I called her and asked her to come and help me look after Sam this weekend. Unfortunately, she couldn't drive up till this afternoon. Hello, Melanie." She walked up to Melanie and gave her a light hug, whispering quietly in her ear, "Keep your mouth shut and your clothes on and you won't get hurt."

"What a brilliant idea, my dear," said Mr. Tate.

"Melanie, say hello to my *husband* Lyon's business associate, Mr. Tate."

Melanie's eyes widened as she looked from Lyon to Liv and then took a hasty step away from Lyon. "Hello, Mr. Tate."

"A pleasure to meet you, Melanie. Beauty obviously runs in your wife's family, my boy,'' said Mr. Tate to Lyon, who smiled weakly back at him. ''I'll look forward to seeing you all at dinner.''

Liv watched the door close behind him before turning to Lyon. ''I'll leave you to your happy reunion,'' she said coolly, walking back into her room with Sam and closing the door behind her.

She sat down on the bed and held on to Sam, who was fast asleep, oblivious to the drama that had unfolded in the other room moments before. Liv wished that she could remain as unconcerned about what she had witnessed, but she couldn't. Somewhere in the region of her heart lay a dull, persistent ache that she couldn't quite escape, no matter how much she told herself that what Lyon Mackensie did with Melanie was none of her business.

After all, she was going to marry Ralph, wasn't she?

10

LYON FELT THE CHILL from the cold shoulder Liv was giving him all the way across the room. She'd been strangely quiet all through dinner, letting Melanie and Mr. Tate carry the bulk of the conversation, and she'd avoided looking or talking directly to him for the whole evening.

At first, he'd been pleased at her behavior, gratified that she'd seen fit to react to what she'd seen through the connecting door earlier. That, along with her attitude toward him last night, proved his plan was working. However, as the evening wore on, he'd become more and more irritated, and when she'd made her excuses to go to bed early, he'd followed her.

Now they were in the room she shared with Sam, who was fast asleep in his playpen, and Lyon was determined to make her talk. He leaned against the doorway connecting their rooms, his arms folded in front of him, and waited.

She kissed Sam good-night, then rummaged through her bags for an article of clothing, and went into the bathroom.

He waited.

A few minutes later, the door opened and she

came out, wearing white cotton pajamas with a tightly belted robe on top. She halted at the threshold when she saw that he was still there, then pretended she hadn't seen him and made her way to the dressing table.

He waited.

She picked up a hairbrush and ran it through her hair in a few quick, angry strokes, put it down, turned around and undid the belt on her robe. She took it off, laid it across the chair, walked to the bed and slipped under the covers. She reached out, turned off the light, turned on to her side and was still.

He stared disbelievingly at her. She had the nerve to go to sleep while he was standing here, patiently waiting for her to cave in and talk to him?

"Damn it, Liv!" he growled.

"Be quiet. You'll wake up Sam."

"Good. At least then I'll have someone to talk to."

He heard a sigh from under the covers before she reached out to turn the lights on again and sat up.

"You want to talk? Fine." She trained narrowed brown eyes on him. "You can begin by explaining exactly what you were doing cavorting around with Melanie this afternoon."

"I wasn't cavorting."

She raised a dark brow. "Oh?"

"Melanie showed up this afternoon because she wanted to thank me for the diamond bracelet. She said she couldn't wait and she wanted to surprise me, so she convinced Annie to tell her where we were this weekend.''

''And I suppose you were trying to escape from her thankful clutches,'' she said sarcastically.

''As a matter of fact, I was.''

''Yeah, that's exactly what it looked like from where I was standing. And, except for the fact that your lips were locked together and the fact that I'd have had a hard time slipping a sheet of paper between the two of you, I believe you.'' She lay back down and turned her back to him. ''Good night.''

''All right, you don't have to believe me,'' he said, walking through the connecting door to his own room. ''But you might want to ask yourself why you're so jealous.''

He took off his jacket, unbuttoned his shirt and counted to ten. Just as he finished, he heard the connecting door open behind him.

''I am not jealous!''

He smiled and turned around to face her.

''Don't *do* that,'' she said.

''Don't do what?''

''Smile, damn it. I can't think when you do that,'' she muttered. ''And I'm *not* jealous.''

''Then why have you been giving me the cold shoulder all night?''

''Because I'm disappointed in you.''

''Because I kissed another woman?''

''Because you could have ruined everything.''

''But I didn't.''

''Only because I saved your butt!''

Her cheeks were flushed with indignation and her brown eyes flashed at him.

Lord, she was beautiful.

He reached out and gently caressed her face, and her eyes filled with confusion.

"Lyon?" she asked uncertainly.

"I didn't kiss Melanie, Liv. She kissed me. I was trying to break out of her grasp when you saw us."

"I...I believe you," she whispered.

"Good," he said, cupping the soft curve of her cheek in his hand, "because the only woman I want to kiss right now is you."

"But you shouldn't want to."

"I know."

"And I shouldn't want you to."

"I know."

"But I do."

"I—"

She cut him off by leaning up and kissing him. Her lips were soft and tentative on his, her tongue warm and inviting as she explored his mouth. He put his arms around her and pulled her close, deepening the kiss. She responded with a feverish passion, moaning as he swiftly unbuttoned her pajama top and slid his hands inside to cup her unfettered breasts. Her skin was soft and creamy, her nipples already hard with arousal, even before he flicked his thumbs over them. He leaned down to capture one perfect pink tip in his mouth, sucking hungrily. She arched back, eyes closed, lips parted, and offered more of herself to him.

"Please, Lyon," she whispered. "Make love to me."

Her words sent a thrill of desire rushing through him, and he took her mouth again, kissing her with all the hunger, the urgency, the *satisfaction* that he felt.

This was just what he'd been hoping for since yesterday, that she would finally overcome the notion that wanting him was somehow wrong. Now if he could only convince her once and for all that the last thing she should do was marry Ralph.

Why? asked a little voice in his head. *So Ralph can't have her?*

Yes.

So you can have her for yourself?

Yes.

So you can take away everything she's ever wanted her whole life and replace it with nothing?

As much as he wanted her, as much as he craved the incredible, wonderful life she'd shown him over the past week, filled with love and laughter and light, he knew it could never be his.

With Ralph, at least she'd have a chance of making her dreams come true. With him, she'd have nothing.

That was what she'd been trying to tell him last night. But he'd been too cocky to listen and too stupid to understand, and tonight he'd deliberately lured her in here with the intention of seducing her.

He deserved every lousy name she'd ever called him.

It nearly killed him, but he broke off the kiss and stepped away from her.

Her eyes were cloudy with desire, her lips pink and swollen from his kisses, and his resolve faltered.

"Lyon?"

"Liv, I don't want you to do anything you'll regret in the morning. You..." he stopped, then forced himself to say what he had to say. "You're engaged to Ralph, and you don't want to do anything that might jeopardize your relationship."

"I don't?"

"No, you don't," he said firmly, pulling together the edges of her pajama top, leading her to the connecting door and giving her a gentle push into her own room. "Good night, Liv."

"Good night," she said in a puzzled voice.

He closed the door after her, closed his eyes, leaned back on it and raised his face to the ceiling. Then, on impulse, he tilted his head and opened one eye, fully expecting to catch a glimpse of a faded, slightly tarnished halo above him.

LIV WOKE UP SLOWLY on Sunday morning and stretched languorously. This was the first time in a week that she hadn't been woken up by Sam's cries at the crack of dawn. She smiled, savoring the quiet warmth of the sun flooding in through the window.

Then she jackknifed into a sitting position.

Sam! Where was Sam?

She looked frantically around the room and jumped out of bed. She ran for the connecting door and wrenched it open, only to stop abruptly at the sight that awaited her.

Lyon was stretched out on the floor, surrounded by toys, Sam cuddled on his chest. They were both fast asleep, snoring gently.

Her two guys had obviously worn themselves out playing. She knelt down beside them and quietly picked up the toys and put them aside. Then she turned back to stroke Sam's hair and drop a quick kiss on top of his head. Her gaze slid from Sam to Lyon and she stared at him, marveling at how vulnerable he looked in sleep.

Last night, she'd nearly ruined her entire future by giving in to the temptation of letting him make love to her, but he'd saved her from herself. He'd been the strong one, bringing her back to her senses, even though she knew he didn't believe that marrying Ralph was the right thing for her to do. She'd known from the look in his eyes that he'd wanted her as much as she'd wanted him, but he'd denied himself because he'd had her best interests at heart.

It was incredible to think that, just one short week ago, she'd thought of him as a beast—obnoxious, uncaring and insensitive. Now that she knew him better, she understood that beneath the grumpy, beastly exterior, there beat the heart of a generous, loving, sometimes lonely man.

A man she'd fallen completely, hopelessly, irrevocably in love with.

No, wait, what was she thinking? She couldn't possibly be in love with Lyon!

She loved Ralph, and to prove it, she closed her

eyes and tried to picture him naked, and when that didn't work, she tried to picture kissing him.

But she couldn't. The only man she wanted to kiss, the only man she wanted to touch, the only man she wanted to make love with was Lyon.

She opened her eyes and stared down at him in wonder, cataloguing his craggy features, the bushy black brows, the slightly crooked nose, the firmly sculpted lips and the grooves in his cheeks that could make her weak-kneed with lust.

This was the man she wanted, the man she loved. It was *his* children she wanted to have, *his* house she wanted to keep and *his* life she wanted to share.

He wasn't perfect by any stretch of the imagination, but he was perfect for her.

A deep surge of happiness flowed through her at the discovery. On impulse, she brushed his lips tenderly with hers and left the two males sleeping peacefully.

The first thing she had to do was find Ralph and break off their engagement. Then she'd have to figure out a way to convince Lyon to believe in fairy tales.

Liv dressed in record time and hurried downstairs. She found Ralph in the library, reading a book titled *Cuculus Canorus: the Continental Cuckoo*. When he saw her, he jumped to his feet.

"Good morning, Olivia."

"Hello, Ralph. I was hoping we could have a few minutes together."

"Of course." He gestured for her to sit down on

the chair beside his, took off his wire-rimmed glasses and began to polish them.

"Thank you." She sat down, and then frowned. Why was it that she'd never noticed before how *formal* they were with each other? Had they ever laughed together? Joked together? Argued with each other?

She couldn't remember doing any of those things with him. Their relationship had been friendly and extremely civilized, but lacking in the passion Tina had been so vehement about.

She liked Ralph, but marrying him would have been the biggest mistake of her life.

Liv took a deep breath and prepared to tell him exactly that.

"Ralph, I can't marry you," she blurted out.

"I know, Olivia."

Her eyes widened. "You know?"

He nodded. "You're in love with your boss."

"It's that obvious?"

He nodded again.

Was she the only one who hadn't figured it out? Liv sighed. Probably.

She took Ralph's engagement ring off her finger and handed it back to him. "I'm sorry, Ralph."

"That's all right, Olivia. It probably wouldn't have worked out anyway. I'm afraid Mother just didn't take to you as well as I'd hoped."

Liv suppressed a smile. "No, she didn't, did she?"

"I hope you and Mr. Mackensie will be happy together."

"Thank you, Ralph," she said, standing up. "I want to apologize for intruding on your weekend. I know you and your mother wanted to spend time alone together."

"That's all right. Mother and I will be seeing a lot of each other from now on. I've decided to move back to Baltimore."

"That's wonde—"

"Olivia!" They heard the exclamation a moment before Mr. Tate rushed, gasping for breath, into the library.

"Mr. Tate! What's the matter?"

"It's Sam! There's a strange couple upstairs trying to kidnap him!"

"What?"

"We caught them red-handed. I've called the police and Gwynneth has the villainous pair trapped in your room. Hurry!"

Liv ran to the door and followed Mr. Tate up the stairs, Ralph right behind her. She rushed into the room behind Mr. Tate and stopped short, causing Ralph to bump into her.

On the bed were two figures making angry grunting noises, their heads covered by a quilt, their wiggling feet sticking out from under the covers. Straddling them like an Amazon warrior woman was Ralph's mother, holding Sam and grinning from ear to ear.

"Mrs. Fortescue?" exclaimed Liv.

"Mother?" exclaimed Ralph.

"Gwynneth, darling!" exclaimed Mr. Tate.

"Darling?" chorused Liv and Ralph together.

"I did exactly as you said, George," said Mrs. Fortescue.

"That's my girl!"

"Mr. Tate, what's going on here?" asked Liv.

"Gwynneth and I were just coming upstairs when we saw these two would-be kidnappers sneaking into your room, so we decided to follow them. They picked up Sam while he was sleeping and the woman scribbled what was probably a ransom note and then they started to leave, which was when I grabbed Sam and Gwynneth tackled them. She was magnificent," he said proudly, and Mrs. Fortescue giggled like a young girl.

Liv closed her eyes. She had a really, really bad feeling about this.

Ralph and Mr. Tate helped Mrs. Fortescue to her feet as Liv took Sam and quickly unmasked the "villainous pair."

"Tina! Paul!" said Liv.

"Oh, Liv! Thank God!" said Tina.

"Mama!" said Sam.

Pandemonium broke out as everyone started talking at once.

"Quiet!" roared Lyon from the connecting doorway, where he stood with Melanie behind him.

Dead silence ensued.

"Ralph, untie Tina and Paul. Melanie, you hold Sam until his parents are free. You," he took Liv's hand, "come with me."

"His parents?" asked Mr. Tate, bewildered.

"I can explain everything if you'll just come downstairs with us, sir," said Lyon tersely.

THE JIG WAS UP. By tomorrow morning, Lyon knew, his reputation, his career and his dreams of success would be in tatters around him. Strangely enough, the prospect didn't bother him half as much as it would have a mere forty-eight hours ago.

He took a deep breath and faced Mr. Tate, who had insisted on bringing his "darling Gwynneth" to the library with him.

"Mr. Tate, Liv and I aren't married and Sam is not our son. We were only pretending to be married because you caught us in a compromising position."

Mr. Tate looked in confusion from Lyon to Liv. "Not married?"

"Well, I should hope not!" said Mrs. Fortescue, outraged. "Olivia is engaged to my Ralph."

"Engaged to Ralph? Mackensie, what's the meaning of this?" demanded Mr. Tate, putting a protective arm around Mrs. Fortescue.

The expression on that lady's face was ominous and the look of accusation she leveled at Liv spoke volumes.

This was all his fault. If he didn't convince Mrs. Fortescue that this had nothing to do with Liv, she'd never be able to marry Ralph. Everything she'd ever wanted would be lost to her and it would all be because of him and his selfishness. He had to do something.

Instinctively, he stepped in front of Liv and faced Ralph's mother. "Mrs. Fortescue, I know this is all highly irregular, but it really isn't Liv's fault. She works for me and I'm afraid that I told her I'd fire her if she didn't go along with the story. You see, I was so obsessed with getting Mr. Tate's birdseed account, I didn't think about anyone else but myself. You have to believe that Liv had nothing to do with it. She's a wonderful woman, warm and loving and generous, and she'll be just the kind of wife every mother wants for her son."

He'd barely finished when Liv stepped up beside him. "Don't listen to him, Mr. Tate. It wasn't all his fault, it was mine. You see, I was taking care of my godson, Sam, and I had to bring him in to work the day you came to visit Mackensie's. Lyon was playing with him and Sam, well, you know Sam. He peed all over Lyon's suit and we had to send it in to the one-hour dry cleaners downstairs. In the meantime, he borrowed my clothes. When you came into the office, he was trying to change back into his suit, but the zipper on the skirt got stuck and I was trying to undo it gently because I didn't want him to break it, seeing as how I had to wear the skirt on my date with Ralph that night. Anyway, Sam pressed the button on the intercom and you came in thinking something funny was going on and we knew the whole situation was so bizarre that you'd never believe it, so we pretended to be married." She stared pleadingly at Mr. Tate. "Please, you have to believe that Lyon is the best person to handle your account. He really cares about his clients and he's an advertising genius. Oh, sometimes he likes to growl and roar, but," she turned to gaze at Lyon, "in my heart I know that he's a fine man."

Lyon stared into her brown eyes, his heart swelling at what he saw in them. In that moment, he realized that he wanted her more than he'd ever wanted anything in his life, desperately, completely. He wanted everything she was, everything she represented. He wanted the fairy tale and the happily-ever-after and he wanted it with her, and he'd be damned if he was going to let her marry Ralph. She was going to marry him and he was going to do everything in his power to make her dreams come true.

But first he had to get rid of Mr. Tate and Mrs. Fortescue so that he could tell her how he felt. He turned his attention back to them, intent on hustling them out of the library as soon as possible. He opened his mouth, but then realized that something wasn't quite right.

Mr. Tate was looking at Mrs. Fortescue.

Mrs. Fortescue was looking at Mr. Tate.

Their lips began to twitch.

Their faces began to crumple.

A moment later, they were holding on to each other, howling with laughter.

"I've never heard of anything so…h-hilarious in all my life!" gasped Mr. Tate, tears pooling in his eyes.

"Peeing on his suit!" said Mrs. Fortescue, her ample bosom bouncing with mirth. "I w-wish I'd been there to see it!"

Liv and Lyon stared at each other in bemusement.

"Lyon, my boy," said Mr. Tate when he'd recovered from laughing so hard, "I've never had so much fun in my life as I have this week. Why, spending time with you two and with little Sam has been a delight. Besides, how can I hold any of this against you? If I hadn't come here, I never would have had an opportunity to see the Purple-Bellied Polka-Dotted Cuckoo, nor would I have found my very own true love, Gwynneth." He winked at Mrs. Fortescue, who sighed happily.

"I'm happy to hear that, Mr. Tate, and I'll understand if you decide to give the birdseed account to another firm," said Lyon.

"Nonsense! Your firm came up with the best idea I've seen in years. That campaign will make people sit up and take notice of Tate's birdseed and that's what I want. I'll sign the papers as soon as I get home, just before Gwynneth and I go away on our honeymoon."

"You're getting married?" asked Liv, the astonishment plain in her face.

"Oh yes," said Mrs. Fortescue, taking Mr. Tate's arm and squeezing affectionately. "George popped the question this morning."

"But...but what about Ralph?"

"What about him, dear? I'm sure he'll be very happy with you and I'm sure you'll be even happier without an interfering old biddy like me to get in the way of your wedding plans," she said with a smile.

"But..."

Mr. Tate kissed Liv on the cheek, then grabbed Lyon's hand and shook it vigorously. "Goodbye, my boy. We'll look forward to getting an invitation to the real wedding," he said, his eyes twinkling as he led Mrs. Fortescue out of the library.

Liv was still trying to get over the shock of it all when the library door opened and in came Tina, Paul and Sam, looking none the worse for their little escapade.

She ran to hug her friend. "Tina, Paul! Are you two all right? I'm so sorry about all this."

Tina, an ecstatically happy Sam in her arms, laughed. "Well, this week's certainly been an adventure. We're just happy to be back with our little Sammy, aren't we, honey?"

"You bet," said Paul, his arm around his wife. "We can't thank you enough for looking after him, Liv."

"You're very welcome," said Liv, giving Sam a kiss. "Bye, sweetheart. We're going to miss you."

"I believe that if you ever need baby-sitting services, there are about ten people in our office who'd love to have him for the day," offered Lyon, affectionately stroking Sam's hair.

"We might be taking you up on that offer, pal," said Paul with a grin. "Thanks again, Liv."

Tina, Paul and Sam left, just as Melanie, resplendent in a red satin pantsuit and high heels, sauntered in.

"Oh, hell," muttered Lyon behind her.

"Darling, I've had just about all the excitement I can stand, I'm afraid," said Melanie in a bored voice. "I just came to tell you that I'm going back to the city with that dear, sweet Ralph fellow."

"With Ralph? But what about Lyon?" asked Liv, incensed on his behalf.

"Oh, that's over," said Melanie nonchalantly.

"He broke it to me this morning, but he said I could keep the bracelet. Goodbye, darling." She blew Lyon a kiss and strolled out again.

"Thank God," said Lyon feelingly. "I thought they'd never leave."

She watched as he closed the library door, locked it, opened the window, threw the key outside, locked the window and then came back to stand in front of her.

Feeling more than a little shell-shocked, she just stared blankly up at him.

He looked down at her, sighed contentedly, then took her in his arms and kissed her soundly.

Sometime later, she broke off the kiss. "Did you really break it off with her?"

"Who?" he asked, pressing soft little butterfly kisses on the side of her neck.

"Melanie!"

"Uh-huh," he murmured, his lips moving down her throat.

"What did you tell her?"

He leaned his forehead against hers and stared into her eyes. "That I'm in love with you and I want to spend the rest of my life making all your dreams come true."

Liv swallowed, afraid to believe what he was saying. "So it was just a kiss-off lie and you didn't really mean it?"

"You, of all people, Miss Hammond, should know that I mean everything I say," he said before capturing her mouth in a thorough, bone-melting kiss.

"Lyon?" she said breathlessly a few minutes later.

"Hmm?"

"I broke it off with Ralph, too."

"I told you that you weren't going to marry him. What made you finally realize it?"

She sighed. "I tried and I tried, but I just couldn't picture him naked!"

He growled against her lips and she laughed.

"But I'm pretty sure I'll have no trouble picturing *you* naked, Mr. Mackensie," she said, sweeping his body with a seductive look from under her lashes.

"And why is that?"

"Because I love you," she said, her whole heart in her eyes. Then she smiled. "And because, in about thirty seconds, you *are* going to be naked!"

HARLEQUIN
Duets™ presents

Welcome to Heartbreak Ridge! Meet three of the Lone Star state's sexiest men, who are lassoed by love, courtesy of three of the sassiest women in the West.

LONESTAR LAWMAN

Talented Liz Ireland creates a small heartwarming town with crazy characters and fun, fast-paced comedic tales of romance and marriage in:

#33 The Sheriff and the E-mail Bride
(August 2000)

#35 The Deputy's Bride
(September 2000)

#38 The Cash-Strapped Cutie
(October 2000)

HARLEQUIN®
Makes any time special.™

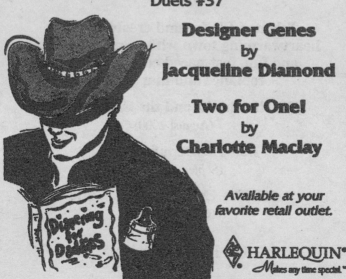

HARLEQUIN
Duets™

**Don't miss
an exciting opportunity
to save on the purchase of
Harlequin and Silhouette books!**

Buy any two Harlequin or
Silhouette books and save
$10.00 off future Harlequin
and Silhouette purchases

OR

buy any three
Harlequin or Silhouette books
and save **$20.00 off** future
Harlequin and Silhouette purchases.

*Watch for details
coming in October 2000!*

PHQ400

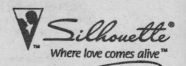

Your Romantic Books—find them at

www.eHarlequin.com

Visit the *Author's Alcove*

➤ Find the most complete information anywhere on your favorite author.

➤ Try your hand in the Writing Round Robin— contribute a chapter to an online book in the making.

Enter the *Reading Room*

➤ Experience an interactive novel—help determine the fate of a story being created now by one of your favorite authors.

➤ Join one of our reading groups and discuss your favorite book.

Drop into *Shop eHarlequin*

➤ Find the latest releases—read an excerpt or write a review for this month's Harlequin top sellers.

➤ Try out our amazing search feature—tell us your favorite theme, setting or time period and we'll find a book that's perfect for you.

All this and more available at

www.eHarlequin.com
on Women.com Networks

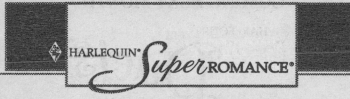
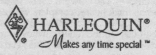

#37

DESIGNER GENES by Jacqueline Diamond
The Bachelor Dads of Nowhere Junction

Carter Murchison still dreams about a mystery lady he met in L.A. who asked him to make a "donation." At the time, he thought she wanted money.... A year and a half later, she shows up in Nowhere Junction, Texas...with a baby! Little does he know that Buffy Armand has a secret to tell him. A secret that will give her daughter a father... and make Carter a bachelor dad!

TWO FOR ONE! by Charlotte Maclay
The Bachelor Dads of Nowhere Junction

Quade Gardiner is shocked when sexy courier Lucy Ballard arrives in Nowhere Junction to deliver...his twin babies? His childhood doctor had told him he'd never have children. Obviously there's been a mistake. Quade tells the sassy brunette to hightail it out of Texas and return the babies to their mother. But Lucy has other plans. She's not leaving until he accepts that the twins—and Lucy, too—are his...!

#38

THE CASH-STRAPPED CUTIE by Liz Ireland
Lone Star Lawmen: Book 3

Down-on-her-luck debutante Natalie Winthrop isn't the rural, home improvement type, especially when sexy, infuriating ex-deputy Cal Tucker gloats over her every misstep! Cal hopes failure—and a lack of plumbing—will send the beautiful, exasperating city woman packing. But when trouble strikes, it's Cal to the rescue. His nearby cabin begins as a temporary shelter for Natalie, but after a steamy embrace, will Cal want to make it a *permanent move?*

KEEPSAKE COWBOY by Carrie Alexander
The Cowgirl Club

Laramie Jones thinks she's inherited a ranch in Wyoming—a dream come true for a member of The Cowgirl Club! To her dismay, she finds a tacky suburban track house, complete with a motley crew of equally shabby animals, plus...Jake Killian. Even though his last encounter with a bull has left the rodeo cowboy in rough shape, Jake's still up for a battle of the sexes. Laramie thinks she can turn the Lazy J into something—anything! Jake would bet his horse she can't, but he's going to enjoy watching her try.

CNM0900